Dead Line

CHRIS EWAN

Minotaur Books
New York

Also by Chris Ewan

Safe House

The Good Thief's Guide to Berlin
The Good Thief's Guide to Venice
The Good Thief's Guide to Vegas
The Good Thief's Guide to Paris
The Good Thief's Guide to Amsterdam

DEAD LINE. Copyright © 2013 by Chris Ewan. All rights reserved. Printed in the United States of America. For information, address St. Martin's Press, 175 Fifth Avenue, New York, N.Y. 10010.

www.minotaurbooks.com

Library of Congress Cataloging-in-Publication Data

Ewan, Chris, 1976–
    Dead Line / Chris Ewan. — First U.S. edition.
        p. cm.
    ISBN 978-1-250-04707-6 (hardcover)
    ISBN 978-1-4668-4744-6 (e-book)
    1. Missing persons—Fiction. 2. Hostage negotiations—Fiction. 3. Marseille (France)—Fiction. 4. Suspense fiction. I. Title.
    PR6105.W36D43 2014
    823'.92—dc23

                                                                        2014010643

Minotaur books may be purchased for educational, business, or promotional use. For information on bulk purchases, please contact Macmillan Corporate and Premium Sales Department at 1-800-221-7945, extension 5442, or write specialmarkets@macmillan.com.

First published in Great Britain by Faber and Faber Limited

First U.S. Edition: August 2014

10 9 8 7 6 5 4 3 2 1

For Jo, as always, and for Jessica,
born during the writing of this book.

Prologue

You're a specialist. This is the most important thing to remember. You have a unique set of skills and abilities. You have exactly the right experience for the task ahead of you. How many people in the world are capable of doing what you do? One hundred? Fifty? And how many of those people are as good as you? None. That's how many. Because you're more than just a specialist. You're *the* specialist. And that's how you're going to succeed.

You're going to begin by compiling a list of everything you'll need. The list will be comprehensive. Some might call it exhaustive but they're the types who'd make mistakes. You know, because their mistakes are what you feed off. They're what you've trained yourself to exploit over the years. You watch their moves and you identify their errors and you turn them to your advantage.

Plus, you're an analytical thinker. It's probably your greatest strength. Other people might buckle under the pressure of the situation. But not you. You always maintain your composure. It's something you pride yourself on, and why shouldn't you? Detachment isn't something that can easily be taught. People either have it or they don't. You have it. There's never been any doubt about that. And right now you need it like never before.

The list.

First, you'll need a vehicle. Not your personal vehicle. You can't afford to be traced, so you'll need something else entirely. An amateur might be tempted to steal something but auto theft poses certain risks you can't possibly indulge. So what you'll do is you'll travel some distance away from Marseilles and you'll buy a vehicle for cash. Crossing a border would be best, but it adds complications you don't need, so you'll head north by bus for several hours. You'll walk to a scruffy dealership on the outskirts of Lyon or St Etienne. An independent place. The kind of outfit where the focus will be on your money and not on your face or your fake ID.

The exact vehicle you buy isn't important but it should be as unremarkable as possible. Instantly forgettable is the effect you're aiming for. The manufacturer will be French, naturally. No bright colours. No memorable decals or custom bodywork. Most crucial of all, it has to be reliable. You can't tolerate a breakdown of any description. So check the tyres. Lift the bonnet. Take it for a spin. Then hand over the necessary cash and drive to Vienne or Valence or Montélimar and find somewhere secluded to switch the plates for a set you've picked up from a supply outlet someplace else.

Next are firearms. You're going to need some. Your handgun is fine. It's untraceable. But you'll need something more. A shotgun is ideal. It packs the necessary visual impact. You have a friend who can help you with that. The fee is one you can easily cover. And really, what does money mean to you right now? It's no more or less irrelevant than everything else. The only thing that matters to you, the only thing worth concerning yourself with, is your assignment.

What else? A ski mask and gloves. Those are for certain. A torch. Pliers and a knife and maybe a hammer. They're distasteful but unavoidable. And plenty of restraints. Nothing complicated. Simple is best. Cuffs and ropes, for sure.

A remote location. That's item number four on your list. Somewhere you won't be disturbed or overheard. Somewhere your vehicle can be concealed. You'll need to scout around but you can't risk drawing attention to yourself. So get a detailed map and study it. Identify possible locations. But remember, you don't want to drive for too long once you have your target inside your vehicle. If something goes wrong – and you're not so arrogant as to think that it can't – then you need to minimise the amount of time you'll spend on the road.

Surveillance. This is the most vital consideration. You'll need some assistance. You can't risk being spotted or remembered, and the more you watch, the more you risk. Your friend can help you with this, too. He's already covered the basics but you need to drill down to the finer details. What are the strengths and weaknesses of your target's security? Where and when are they vulnerable? How can an opportunity best be exploited?

The list is growing. There's more still to come. You're building something dark and mean and intricate here. It needs to be completely squared away. You have to be able to lift it up and inspect every angle of it, every join, without the tiniest sliver of light sneaking through.

And just as your plan is developing, so you're evolving, too. You're changing in ways you never would have thought possible before. But that's acceptable to you. You're prepared to do whatever it takes. Anyone who found themselves in your situation would do what you have in mind if only they could. The sole difference is that you're capable of carrying it through.

Why?

Because you're the specialist. And that's how you're going to succeed.

I

The Abduction

Chapter One

Daniel Trent sensed a tremor in his finger. He was a patient man. It was an attribute he prided himself on. But even he had his limits. His denim shirt was wet at the collar, adhering to his back. His shirtsleeves were rolled past his elbows, exposing forearms slick with sweat. A tendon pulsed beneath his skin. There it was again – the temptation to drum his fingers.

Where were they?

Trent snatched up the tiny china cup in front of him. The residue of his second espresso was tepid and grainy. He swallowed. Grimaced. Set it aside.

The pavement café was jammed with customers. Tourists mostly. The German couple beside him were feasting on cheap bouillabaisse. The husband had spilled tomato and saffron broth on his beard. His wife, lips greasy with shellfish juices, slathered a rouille paste onto meagre croutons.

The waiter hadn't been back to check on Trent in a while but he wasn't offended. Could even understand the guy's reasoning. Not a lot of profit in a man drinking single espressos at this time of night. And Trent was giving off a restless, keyed-up vibe. His self-control was slipping. Patience running low.

Engine noise from the left.

Trent turned his head. Just like he'd turned it every time he'd heard a vehicle approach for the past half-hour. But this time was different. This time he saw exactly what he'd been waiting to see.

A black Mercedes saloon trundled along the street. The windows were tinted, the paint buffed to a liquid sheen. Most vehicles in

Marseilles were covered in a film of sand and dirt and dried salt water, but the Mercedes looked as if it had been cleaned late that afternoon. Probably got cleaned every afternoon, Trent guessed.

The Mercedes slowed until it was idling by the kerb, blocking the single-lane road as if it was parked in its own private driveway.

Sweat trickled down Trent's neck. His throat had closed up, as though unseen hands were choking him. He gulped moist air. Felt it bulge back there, then slide and scrape downwards.

He wedged a crumpled five-euro note beneath the sugar dispenser. Came close to upsetting it. He steadied the tableware, then pushed back his chair. He was tall and long-limbed. Had been gawky as a kid and still could be on occasion. His foot was hooked around the chair leg. The metal scraped and squealed on the concrete and he drew scowls from the German couple as he stumbled sideways and ducked out from beneath the burgundy canopy that overhung the café.

The paved square in front of the Opéra was bathed in a hazy yellow light from a set of ornate streetlamps. Floodlights bounced off the masonry of the theatre house and the red fabric banners promoting to-night's show – a performance by the Ballet National de Marseille.

The production was over and members of the audience were lingering outside. Men in dinner jackets smoked cigarettes and shook hands, speaking in low sardonic voices from the sides of their mouths. Women perspired in gauzy summer dresses, smiling tightly and clutching handbags to their waists as if they feared a violent mugging.

Trent loitered beside an abandoned scooter. Sweat pooled beneath his armpits and swamped his back. His breathing was shallow, the air warm and vaporous. It smelled of dust and heat and cooked seafood laced with boat diesel and brine from the Vieux Port.

The Mercedes didn't move.

Trent blinked wetly and tried to see how many men were inside. Sometimes it was two – a young chauffeur plus a bodyguard. Some-times the bodyguard worked alone.

Amber hazards blinked on. The driver's door opened and a thickset man in a charcoal suit and crisp white shirt stepped out. The body-guard. A lucky break. No chauffeur tonight.

The bodyguard scanned his surroundings, a full 360, his attention snagging on Trent for just an instant before moving on. He took in the seedy bars, the fast food outlets, the rusting dumpsters overflowing with noxious waste, the unlit *epiceries* and *boulangeries* and *tabacs*, the scruffy apartment buildings with faded, crusty render and paint-flaked wooden shutters flung wide.

He was a squat, powerfully built guy. Early-to-mid-thirties with dark hair buzzed close to the scalp. Low forehead. Light stubble. His back was broad, his arms muscular. He had large, square hands, the fingers hooked and curled as if he were wearing boxing gloves.

Trent guessed the guy's suit had been tailored to emphasise his physique. The jacket sleeves were tight around his upper arms, the material bunched as if catching on his biceps.

He had an attentive, serious demeanour. He looked like a guy who lived and breathed his job. He shot his cuff and consulted his watch. Then he paced away through the crowds towards the lighted entrance of the Opéra, his square head swinging from left to right, probing for threats.

And then there they were. The pair of them. Exposed.

They'd stepped out through the glass doors between the stone colonnades before the bodyguard was close. A basic error. The type a guy with hostile intentions might exploit, if he felt so inclined.

Trent pressed his arm against his Beretta. It would be easy to reach under his shirt right now. He could march across the square and barge through the crowds. Fire in a controlled burst. Fifteen rounds, 9 mm calibre. More than ample to kill a man. Enough, probably, to get away from the scene.

He reached out to steady himself. The scooter rocked on its stand.

Jérôme Moreau crossed the square like he owned it. The guy oozed confidence. He radiated ego. Take an average person and show them footage of Moreau right now and what would they think? A movie star emerging from the premiere of his latest film? A city politician on the rise?

He was sharply dressed. Velvet dinner jacket, pressed white shirt, silk bow tie and shoes as dark and lustrous as his waiting Mercedes. His grey hair was oiled and set in waves, his chin clean-shaven. He shielded his eyes with a raised hand, as if rearing back from the blaze of paparazzi bulbs.

Trent clenched his hands into fists and stared at Moreau hard. So hard he felt sure that he would sense it. But Moreau showed no awareness. Maybe he was too wrapped up in himself. Or maybe Trent appeared more composed than he felt. Perhaps he was the only one who could sense the fury coming off him, pulsing outwards, like sound waves from a tuning fork.

He swallowed thickly, then risked a glance at Moreau's wife. Not for the first time, the sight of her punched the air from his lungs.

This was the toughest part. Even thinking about it made his mouth dry as ash.

Stephanie Moreau was young, lithe and beautiful. She was short for a former ballet dancer, coming in somewhere around five foot five even in heels, but she had poise and balance and grace.

Tonight, she wore a silver dress that shimmered as it moved across the slim contours of her body. Her dark hair was swept to one side and loosely curled, exposing her delicate neck and shoulders. Her pale skin appeared almost translucent in the diffuse yellow light. Trent could see the outline of the collarbones beneath her skin, fragile as a bird's.

The bodyguard was alongside them now, ushering them through the parting crowds towards the Mercedes. He guided them into the back of the car, then opened the driver's door and shaped as if to slide in under the wheel.

He froze mid-way. Glanced towards the scooter once more.

But Trent was already gone.

*

A network of one-way streets surrounded the Opéra. Parking was at a premium. Trent returned to his car, a brown Peugeot estate that was wedged into a tight space beneath the green neon glow of a *pharmacie* cross. He fumbled with his key in the ignition. Fired the gurgling engine and swung out into the road.

The interior of the Peugeot was hot and airless. He wound his window low and angled his head into the thermal breeze. A series of turns delivered him to the Quai Rive Neuve. Countless yachts and passenger ferries and fishing vessels were packed into the marina, forming a vast and shifting tangle of masts and rigging. The odour of seawater was strong.

The sleek Mercedes was up ahead, beyond a cream taxi, a motorbike and a grimy delivery truck. Trent pinched the sting of sweat from his eyes and squeezed the accelerator. The dark, shifting waters of the marina flickered by, alive with quivering reflections from streetlamps and headlamps and bar signs and apartment windows.

Half a kilometre more and Trent peeled off to the right, following the Mercedes round a sweeping bend into a tunnel. The swirling yammer of engines and tyres and trapped air was loud and urgent in his ears. He sealed his window and set the fans to MAX. No air conditioning. Detritus blitzed his face. The Peugeot had been parked beneath a sycamore tree for close to a week and fallen seedpods had worked their way inside the vents.

Fluorescent lights zipped by above Trent's head. Industrial fans twirled in hypnotic circles. His mind started to drift, lured by memories of driving through this tunnel before. Memories where he was not alone. Memories where he was laughing, even.

He thought of Aimée. How she'd insisted on playing a dumb game whenever they'd entered the tunnel together. The aim was to hold your breath until you emerged on the other side. It was impossible to do. Physically beyond them. Maybe a free diver would be capable of it. But not Trent. And not Aimée. The tunnel was too long, running under the quay, coming up far into Joliette.

Aimée had liked to pretend otherwise. She'd loved making out that she was still holding her breath long after Trent had quit. He'd tell her she was cheating and she'd shake her head and point to her swollen cheeks, her pursed lips. Her big brown eyes would implore him to believe her.

Then he'd reach across and pinch her nostrils and she'd spit air and bat his hand away and laugh her childish, breathless laugh. She'd pretend to be offended. Protest her innocence. Promise him she could really do it.

Until the next time. When she'd cheat all over again.

Except now he found it hard to believe there could be a next time.

Might never be.

His chin jerked upright and he cursed himself, wrenching the jagged visions from his mind. He crouched forwards over the steering wheel. He squinted hard at the back of the Mercedes. He locked onto its red and amber light cluster like a gambler staring at the gaudy drums of a dive-bar slot machine, willing his last desperate chance to come in.

Chapter Two

Trent was no pursuit expert but he'd known a few in his time. One guy in particular considered himself a real tail artist. Much of his advice was foolish or obvious but something he'd said had lodged in Trent's brain. Picture a thread of elastic between yourself and your mark. Imagine the elastic is at its natural resting point six car lengths behind your quarry. Get too close and the elastic becomes slack and tangles around your wheels. Fall more than twelve car lengths back and the elastic snaps.

Trent knew it was just a fancy way of saying don't get too close or too far away, but he had to admit the image was a hard one to forget. He could picture the elastic now. One end looped around Jérôme Moreau's neck, spooling out through the tinted rear window of the Mercedes, flapping and twirling in the humid night air. The other end tied to Trent's left wrist, tugging at him as he dropped back a short way.

Traffic was light and the road familiar to him. He knew the route they would follow. It wasn't long before he fell into a kind of trance, and as he visualised the straining length of elastic that linked him to the man who'd occupied his every waking thought for the past nine days – the individual responsible for the terror that had taken hold of him like a fever for close to two months now – a queer sense of calm washed over him.

Perhaps it was the perfumed breeze through the churning vents – the scent of baked earth and cooling tarmac and auto exhausts. Perhaps it was the lull of the engine, the flat droning of the Peugeot's tyres. Perhaps it was his own gnawing fatigue, barely assuaged by the two espressos he'd sipped back at the café. But he preferred to think of it as the sense of a resolution drawing close. A reckoning of one variety or another.

He recalled other nights, in surer times, when he'd driven away from Marseilles with Aimée beside him, for no other reason than he needed something to occupy his mind and she'd understood and indulged his restlessness. They'd rarely talked or listened to the radio on these spontaneous trips of his. Mostly, it had been enough for them to be simply moving together, to be hurtling through the black together, cocooned in drowsy warmth and easy silence. Until, after an hour, maybe two, Aimée would squeeze his hand and smile in a weary daze, her eyes crinkling just so, and he'd know that it was time to turn and head home again. Back to the city. Back to whatever work stress or emotional funk he'd felt the desire to escape for a spell.

Tonight, though, he was alone, and the road ahead was wide and flat and dusty. It crested and dipped beneath a cloudless night sky, spattered with stars and a waning moon. The tarmac was bleached and austere in the glare of his headlamps. Broken white lines tapped out a furious Morse code he couldn't hope to decipher.

He passed grubby high-rise apartment buildings pocked with satellite dishes, shambling houses with sagging roofs and austere motorist hotels with glowing signs advertising low nightly rates; passed graveyards with raised stone tombs and concrete overpasses blighted with graffiti and outdoor sports pitches laid with dense red clay; passed industrial warehouses and car dealerships and a swimming-pool concession with a giant, empty *piscine* propped up outside; passed floodlit petrol stations and disorderly road maintenance works.

He pursued the Mercedes. Matching its speed. Tracking its movements. Rapt by those cherry-red light clusters and the fluttering elastic snare that bound him to his prey.

*

The Mercedes left the autoroute some distance before Aix-en-Provence. Trent followed it through a collection of junctions and turns, then along a little-travelled back road that climbed steeply up the side of the broad valley, clinging to a buff stone escarpment that looked out over fields of wheat and rapeseed and terraced grape vines, and long ribbons of streaking red and white vehicle lights.

Trent had been up here in the day. He'd seen the barren, gnarly rocks, the tufts of wild grass and weeds, the bow-kneed umbrella pines and the straggly young saplings thirsty for water. He'd listened to the chirrup of cicadas. The scrabble of lizards. The creak and sputter of swinging irrigation booms in the fields down below.

Now the scene had been reduced to monochrome. The vast black sky and the parchment moon. The salt-grain bugs spinning in the whispery light of his headlamps. The faint luminescence of the instrument panel bathing his hands.

His palms were sweating, his knuckles bunched and aching. The lonely road had made it impossible for him to pursue the Mercedes without being spotted. The bodyguard had allowed a slip in security back at the opera house but it was hard to believe he'd forget to look in his mirrors. And Trent's headlamps were strafing the interior of the Mercedes along with the road ahead. He was as good as tapping the guy on the shoulder.

But he'd always known the time would come for him to show his hand. The Moreau family mansion was less than two kilometres away. For the next few hundred metres, the road widened out and Trent downshifted, ready to overtake exactly where he'd planned.

He was just swooping out when everything changed.

First the dazzle of headlamps on full beam. Then the squeal of rubber and the red flare of brake lights.

Then the impact.

It was savage. A deafening smack.

The Mercedes had been struck from the side by a large off-road vehicle fitted with bull bars. The impact shunted it towards the loose gravel at the edge of the precipitous drop. The Mercedes fishtailed, then straightened up, then bucked wildly to the left, back towards safety.

Defensive driving. But too late to alter the outcome. The Mercedes had lost momentum. Lost position. The big jeep lurched forwards and turned and battered into it on a diagonal trajectory. Now the bodyguard had a choice. Keep driving and tumble off the side, down the high slope into trees and rocks and gullies. Or stop.

He braked more suddenly than Trent had anticipated. The tyres bore down into sandy tarmac and loose shale, the rubber growling in complaint. They locked and released, locked and released, the ABS working hard to wrench the Mercedes to a stuttering halt.

It was more efficient than the system on Trent's ageing Peugeot. He felt the steering go light. The front end begin to skate. Too much speed. Fatal momentum. The Peugeot rammed into the back of the Mercedes with a violent jolt. Headlamps popped and shattered, bulbs extinguishing in an instant. The bonnet buckled and creased and Trent was flung forwards. No airbag to cushion the blow. He butted the top of the steering wheel and his ribs embraced the hub, the horn barking in complaint. Knees and elbows whacked plastic. Then his seat belt bit into his shoulder, jerking him back like a tardy friend heaving him away from a drunken bar brawl just as the first blow had slammed into his chest.

A dazed silence. A moment of stillness.

Trent heaved air. He croaked feebly.

His car had stalled. It was steaming.

Doors flew open on the attack vehicle. Trent could see now that it was a green Toyota Land Cruiser. Figures leapt out into the halogen glare and the drifts of tyre smoke. They barked commands. Trent counted three individuals. They were dressed in jeans and green army surplus jackets with black ski masks over their heads.

The men carried assault rifles. Stocks wedged against shoulders. Fingers clutching triggers. The lead guy fired a burst of rounds into the front of the Mercedes, stitching the bonnet, smashing the windscreen. Sparks leapt from the rifle muzzle, accompanied by a tattoo of deafening claps.

A second guy advanced on Trent and tapped hard on his window with his rifle. Trent lifted his hands by his face. He gazed at the eyes behind the mask. They were fidgety and alert. The guy shook his head. Just once. A warning.

The final guy grappled with the rear door on the Mercedes. It wouldn't budge. He braced his foot against the side of the car and yanked hard. Still the door refused to give. He quit trying. He hefted his rifle above his shoulder and battered the glass with the sculpted polymer buttstock. The glass splintered, then gave out. He raked the fragments clear and leaned into the car.

Trent heard a woman's scream, high and fractured. Smoke billowed up from the bonnet of the Peugeot or the exhaust of the Mercedes, tinged red by the vivid brake lights.

Now the guy was heaving at something. He kept pulling until Jérôme Moreau's head and shoulders appeared through the window. Moreau thrashed and scrabbled in his dinner jacket, trying to escape the man's grip. He didn't seem so powerful all of a sudden. He looked about as helpless as it's possible to get.

Trent strained forwards against his seat belt, thinking of the Beretta beneath his shirt. But the guy watching over him saw it. Another tap at the window. Another shake of the head.

Now Moreau's waist was clear. He waved his arms frantically. There was a moment of resistance – Trent pictured Stephanie clinging to his ankles – before Moreau was wrenched free amid desperate shrieks and tinkling glass. His legs failed to support him. He stumbled and was dragged backwards towards the Land Cruiser, gloved hands clasped over his gaping mouth and wild eyes.

Meantime, the lead guy fired across the bonnet of the Mercedes, throwing up spurts of rock and debris at the side of the road. The bodyguard had kicked open the passenger door and was struggling to get out, but he was pinned by the gunfire.

The guy holding the rifle on Trent began to retreat into the blue-white glare of the Land Cruiser's headlamps. His companion did likewise, shooting even after he'd clambered inside a door at the rear.

There was a fourth man inside. The driver.

The jeep backed up fast, then jolted forwards. It turned sharply and slammed against the side of the Mercedes, tearing free the Peugeot's wing mirror as it sped away down the road.

Trent fumbled to release his seat belt. He grappled with the lever on his door and tumbled out onto his knees. He drew his Beretta from his holster and fired two rounds, his shots echoed by a series of percussive booms from somewhere close behind. A trio of yellow flares skittered across the rear of the jeep. Trent heard the dull *clank* of drilled metal.

But it was no use. The Land Cruiser was speeding away into the encroaching darkness. And he couldn't risk hitting Moreau.

Trent slumped forwards. He released his Beretta and braced the heels of his palms against the coarse road surface. Something liquid slammed into his throat from his gut. He bowed his head. Fought the rush of fear and outrage that was whirling inside him.

Then, through the warped and tinny silence, he heard distressed cries from inside the Mercedes. The tread of hesitant footsteps.

The bodyguard was crabbing towards him, knees bent, arms straight, elbows locked, a large revolver – a Ruger Redhawk – clenched in his enormous hands. He was bleeding from a wound at the corner of his eye. His shirt was torn at the collar, his suit crumpled and dirtied and glittering with beads of shattered glass.

'Who the hell are you?' the bodyguard snarled, in savage French.

Trent gulped air and wiped a slick of drool from his chin.

He spoke French, too. Was fluent, in fact.

'The guy you need now,' he replied.

Chapter Three

The bodyguard edged closer. He sighted down his gun at the centre mass of Trent's chest, stretched out his leg and toed Trent's Beretta away. He squatted to pocket the weapon, maintaining his careful aim.

Trent could hear muffled shrieks from the rear of the Mercedes.

'Is she hit?' he asked.

'Put your hands up.'

'Answer my question.'

'Hands on top of your head. Now!'

It felt strange to Trent, coming face to face with this man he'd been observing for more than a week. He seemed somehow hyper-real, like chancing upon a television actor from one of those moody cop dramas Aimée liked to watch on Canal+. Up close, he struck Trent as way more capable and threatening. There was a bearish physicality about him. He was big. He was tough. He was intense and imposing.

Trent supposed some of that had to do with the long-nosed revolver the guy was aiming at him. The Ruger Redhawk had a barrel length approximating eight inches. Stainless-steel finish. Hardwood grips. Capacity for six rounds. The guy had fired three already. But it would only take one .44 slug to bring Trent's curiosity to an end.

The bodyguard stepped close and patted Trent down fast, feeling around his waist and torso, lingering on his empty shoulder holster. He checked Trent's jeans as far as his ankles, then straightened and spun him round by the shoulder. He jammed the Ruger in the hollow behind Trent's ear, delved a hand inside his front trouser pocket and yanked free his wallet.

'You're bleeding,' Trent told him. 'Near your eye.'

The bodyguard smeared the cut with the dirtied cuff of his shirt. 'You were outside the Opéra,' he said. 'You were watching us.'

Trent didn't respond. He studied the guy over the looming muzzle of the Ruger.

'You followed us,' he went on. 'I saw your car as soon as we hit the tunnel.'

Still Trent didn't speak.

'You work with those men?'

Trent shook his head. Slow and steady. 'You saw me shoot at them.'

'So maybe you were firing blank rounds?'

'How about you put my Beretta against your temple? Satisfy your curiosity.'

The guy grunted and flipped open Trent's wallet. He slid out his driver's licence with his thumb. Squinted at the pixelated image and the details in the sketchy dark.

'I'd like to put my hands down,' Trent said.

It was a few degrees cooler up on the rise. A gentle breeze lifted the denim of his shirt. The sweat that had filmed his body was starting to dry and evaporate. Goosebumps were sprouting on the back of his wrists and at the base of his neck.

The Mercedes's engine was still running. The hum and burble of the large diesel unit disturbed the stillness all around.

'My hands?' Trent said again.

The guy backed away and motioned consent with his Ruger. Trent lowered his arms and plucked pellets of grit from his palms. His mind was spinning with a wild centrifugal force.

'Take a look at my business card,' he said.

The guy grunted again but he removed a small ivory card from a sleeve cut into the wallet. He read over the information he found there. Raised an eyebrow.

'I can help you,' Trent told him.

The bodyguard sniffed, then flipped Trent's wallet closed. He stashed it inside his ruined jacket.

He said, 'Maybe you already helped your friends in the ski masks.'

'You don't believe that.'

'No?'

'It would be a really dumb thing to believe.'

The sound of a door opening interrupted them. They looked over towards the Mercedes. It was canted to the right, the front wing crumpled and deformed. The nearside headlamp was out. The remaining lamp probed blindly at the stones and shrubs by the edge of the road.

Stephanie Moreau staggered towards the rear of the luxury car, leaning on the bodywork for support like a drunk teetering along a bar, ephemeral in the fog of exhaust fumes. For just an instant, something about her silhouette or the way she moved reminded Trent of Aimée, and it felt as if a trap door had opened in the ground beneath him. Then the vaporous gases cleared from around her, the apparition faltered, and Stephanie peered at Trent's Peugeot with bleary, tear-stained eyes. Her silver dress was rucked up on one side, exposing a pale, lean thigh and a grazed knee.

'Alain?' Her voice was shrill. 'What happened? Where's Jérôme?'

'He's been taken,' the bodyguard replied, gravel in his throat. His attention remained fixed on Trent. 'This man says he can assist us.'

'Who is he?'

The question hung in the air. Insects buzzed Trent's face. He could smell something leaking from one of the cars. Coolant, maybe.

'Tell her,' Alain said.

'I'm a consultant.' Trent spoke loud enough for them both to hear. 'I advise people in kidnap and ransom situations. A colleague at my firm sold your husband a K & R insurance policy two months ago. He was concerned about a threat. Perhaps he mentioned it to you?'

She shook her head, just barely, the kink in her side-swept hair bouncing a little. Her features looked slackened, smudged. She had a face out of time. Square jaw, high cheekbones, budded lips, like a Hollywood starlet from the 1940s.

'Why are you here now?' she whispered. 'Tonight?'

'Coincidence,' Trent told her, gauging the doubt in Alain's eyes. 'I was due to arrange a follow-up meeting with your husband to go over some anti-kidnap measures he could put in place. I thought I'd assess his security first. It's simple luck I was here tonight.'

'Luck?'

Trent nodded. 'The first days of a kidnap situation set the tone for how the whole thing will play out. It's fortunate that I can be involved here from the start. And I've seen the people you're up against. They're a professional outfit. That's good. Much better than trying to reason with amateurs. More predictable.'

Stephanie tipped her head to one side, intrigued now, a loose spring of hair falling across her face. She moved as if to approach. Alain motioned her back with his free hand, his arm stiff, palm raised, like a traffic cop.

'We don't know this is a kidnapping.'

'*I* know,' Trent said.

'Because you were involved?'

'Because I recognise the signs. This was an aggressive takedown, no question. But those men weren't looking to harm anyone else.'

Trent glanced off to his side. Stephanie had ignored Alain's instructions and was stumbling closer in her heels. She hugged herself with slender arms and Trent had to fight a sudden urge to go to her. There was something hard to fathom about her appeal. She was almost too perfect, brittle in some complex way, as if she might come apart and unravel at any moment.

'They could have shot you both,' Trent said, catching his breath. 'But they didn't. They need you alive so they have someone to negotiate with.'

Stephanie absorbed his words, her swollen lips moving soundlessly. The summer wind ruffled her hair and pressed the material of her dress against her slim body. She was trembling.

It was becoming difficult to understand how this woman had made him think of Aimée. If she were here, if she'd found herself in Stephanie's predicament, she wouldn't be standing by, shaking and waiting to hear more. She'd have clambered behind the wheel of the Mercedes, hauled it around and sped off in dogged pursuit of the Land Cruiser, no matter how doomed her chances of catching Jérôme's abductors might be. Her impulsiveness and her hot-headed streak were qualities that had often frustrated Trent. Strange how much he missed them.

'What's your name?' Stephanie asked.

He told her, then added, 'But most people call me Trent.'

'You're English?'

'My mother was French.'

'How would you help us?'

He swallowed. No sense in rushing things now.

'The policy your husband took out covers you for ransom payments up to a predetermined level. It also entitles you to my advice. Whether you choose to listen to it or not is up to you. I can tell you a lot more about myself and my record if you decide to appoint me. It's how I usually begin work on a case.'

Trent felt Alain's gaze drilling into him but he kept his focus on Stephanie. She'd begun to collect herself and he saw now that she was tougher and more resilient than he'd imagined. Her cautious manner and her slight frame had deceived him and he supposed they shouldn't have. Didn't dancers put themselves through hell so they could appear composed up on stage when their bodies were screaming in pain? Viewed like that, their every performance was an illusion of sorts. Trent was beginning to gain some understanding of how it might feel.

'Good,' she said, and nodded, as if a decision had been made. 'You'll help us.'

'But *madame*.' Alain's Ruger hadn't wavered. He was squinting along the sights, scrutinising Trent. 'Please consider. We have only this man's word for what he says. Did M. Moreau speak to you about such a policy?'

She bit down on her full lip. 'No,' she muttered.

'We must be careful tonight. You see?'

'Then verify what I say.' Trent turned to face Stephanie directly. 'My records show that your husband had a lawyer advise him on the policy. Do you know who that would have been?'

She nodded. Raised her chin, a glossy lock shielding her eye. 'A friend of Jérôme's.'

'And do you trust this friend?'

'He's a good man.'

'Then call him. Your bodyguard has my wallet and my ID. Have your lawyer check the policy against my credentials.'

Stephanie glanced towards Alain. His blunt face was impassive, but he lowered the Ruger a fraction.

'We can telephone from the house,' Stephanie said. 'You may follow us.'

Trent looked over her angular shoulder towards his Peugeot. The bonnet was shunted beneath the rear of the Mercedes. Broken glass and shards of plastic surrounded the wheels. The front tyre was flat.

'My lights are broken.' He shrugged. 'And I have a puncture.'

'Then you may come with us. Alain can drive and—'

'No, *madame*.' The bodyguard shook his head, sighting back along the Ruger. 'Forgive me, but I cannot allow it. Not until we speak to the lawyer.'

She opened her mouth as if to respond, then reconsidered. She nodded in mute comprehension. Gazed meekly at Trent from beneath long, curling lashes.

'You'll walk,' Alain said. 'It's not far. A kilometre, maybe. There's a fence. A gate. If the lawyer confirms what you say, I'll meet you there.'

'Then I'll see you very soon.'

Alain gestured a short distance back along the road with his gun. 'Wait by that rock. Don't move until we drive away. Understand?'

Trent turned and crossed towards the boulder Alain had indicated. He lowered himself and sat with his elbows on his knees and his hands pressed together beneath his chin. If he had been a religious man, he might have prayed. But instead he clenched his jaw and ground his teeth, silently cursing the fates that were tormenting him so.

Chapter Four

They didn't look inside the Peugeot. There was that, at least.

Trent had felt certain that Alain would duck his head in through the open driver's door, but he was in a hurry to get Stephanie home. And though Stephanie had glanced at a window on her way past, the interior of the Peugeot was in darkness and she hadn't reacted in the slightest. Maybe she hadn't spotted anything. Maybe she had, but she wouldn't process the information until much later. She was in shock. She wouldn't be thinking clearly. Trent knew precisely what she was going through. He'd experienced something similar only recently.

So he'd been lucky in a small way.

And he'd suffered unimaginable misfortune in a much bigger, much more destructive way, too.

Trent watched Alain remove his jacket to reveal the webbed shoulder holster he was wearing over his fitted white shirt. He wadded the jacket round his hand and used it to scoop the shattered windscreen glass from the driver's seat and the dashboard of the Mercedes. He told Stephanie to climb into the front alongside him and he started the engine and edged forwards. There was a moment of resistance as the rear bumper freed itself from the embrace of the Peugeot, then a wrench of metal and broken plastic as the Mercedes dropped free and rejoined the road.

Alain drove off at a cautious speed, the single working headlamp pawing at the darkness ahead, the left front wheel snagging against the distorted wing. One of the rear light clusters had been smashed, but a single bulb was still intact, and Trent watched its aimless twinkling until the Mercedes rounded a looping bend and disappeared from view.

He was tempted to remain sitting on the boulder. He was tempted to quit altogether. His limbs felt leaden and he had the nauseating sensation of having been duped. But the stakes were too high. His need too urgent. And how could he possibly live with himself if he gave up now?

The situation had changed, was all. This wasn't the first time he'd had to adapt to new circumstances and he doubted it would be the last. But he was a resourceful, capable guy. He was well trained and experienced. And his motivation was strong. It was all-consuming.

He forced himself to his feet. Marched across to the Peugeot and flipped off the busted lights. Snatched the keys from the ignition and fetched his mobile from the glove box. He unbuttoned his denim shirt, peeled it from his skin and laid it across the roof of the car. Unfastened his holster and tossed it into the cab, then ducked in towards the rear bench and grabbed a rug to cover what he needed to cover. He slammed the door closed. Kicked it, too. The steel toecap of his desert boot left a dint in the side of the car. A mark of his frustration. It wasn't enough. He pictured himself bending down, gripping hold of the chassis and heaving with his back and his knees until he was able to stand upright and flip the car right over the edge in some kind of superhuman expression of his fury.

He took a long breath, chest quivering as he inhaled. Then he grabbed his shirt and fed his arms through the sleeves and fastened the buttons. He locked the Peugeot and stood back to assess its position. It was pointed at a slant, off to the side of the road, and there was a long steady incline leading up to it. It would be safe enough here. And it wasn't as if the road was busy. Not a single vehicle had passed. Gone eleven o'clock at night. Close to full dark.

It was time to start hiking. To start thinking, too.

*

Twenty minutes' walking and Trent came in sight of the perimeter fence that surrounded the Moreau estate. His pace was slower than usual, a consequence of the bruising to his knees and ribs, as well as the extra time he allowed himself to order his thoughts. He was sweating and his breath was shallow and reedy. A fog of midges swirled around his head, drawn by the heat coming off his body. He didn't waft a hand. Didn't slap his skin when they bit him. It felt like a torment he deserved. Self-pity. It was an indulgence he could no longer afford. He shook loose his arms and legs and rotated his head on his shoulders, like an athlete readying himself for an event he'd been training for his entire life.

The fence was high and imposing. It was constructed from some kind of unfinished galvanised steel. The uprights were bevelled and set close together, leaving just enough space to poke an arm through. Sharpened barbs ran along the top and a series of signs had been secured to the uprights at regular intervals. PROPRIÉTÉ SOUS VIDÉO SURVEILLANCE. *Property under video surveillance.*

The first camera picked him up at the corner of the estate. It was fixed to a steel pole ten feet inside the fence, partway up a steep grass slope that concealed the house from view. He heard the whirr and wheeze of servos in the heated stillness as the camera pivoted to track his progress. Thirty paces more and the next camera took over. More whirring. More tracking.

His scalp itched. The sensation of being closely watched. It wasn't an intrusion he'd ever welcomed but tonight it felt threatening.

He passed four cameras before he reached the gate. The light from a pair of low-wattage bulbs stained the ground an acid yellow. The gate was made from the same galvanised steel bars as the fence, measured to the same height. It had the same barbs along the top. Same cameras protecting it, one on either side. The units turned with a slow electric hum and slanted down at him, zeroing in like laser-guided weapons locking onto a target.

He waited.

The cameras watched him.

The gate remained closed.

A dimly lit intercom was fixed to a post at his side. He approached it and ducked. The speaker crackled into life before he could press the button.

'Wait.'

Alain's voice was gruff amid the static hiss.

The system fell silent.

Trent straightened and ground a heel into the dirt. The gravel driveway was visible through the gate, grey-white against the blackness all around. It rose up to the top of the steep bank, then disappeared from view. All that remained to indicate its route were the lines of tall cypress trees that bordered it on either side and a hazy orb of wavering light that seemed to throb in the darkness way over the hump.

Trent turned his back on the cameras and crossed the narrow road. He was on some kind of ledge. Velvety darkness lay beneath his feet, indigo-black and bottomless. He could see the autoroute way ahead in the distance, down in the flat bowl of the valley. Unseen vehicles moved silently along, surrounded by pulsating coronas of yellow and red. Off to his right, a chain of monumental electricity pylons climbed the escarpment and continued into the sparsely forested zones above. He'd hiked under the thrumming wires just moments ago. Had felt the static buzz around his body like a charged aura.

He sniffed the air. Aromas of wild herbs and flowers and arid dirt. He stepped up to the powdery edge. Inched his toes out over the abyss. He closed his eyes and stretched his arms out at his sides and bounced on the balls of his feet like a diver about to launch himself from a springboard.

He pictured Aimée.

He saw her smiling.

As each day passed, it became harder to conjure his favourite image of her. Morning sunlight on freckled skin, Aimée's drowsy brown eyes watering against the glare. Auburn hair fanned out around her head on stark white sheets, hands curled into loose fists by her ears. Teeth clamped down on the corner of her mouth. Lips shaping a mischievous grin.

He squeezed his eyes tight shut and concentrated hard, sharpening the vision. Sculpting it. Refining it.

Guarding it.

The stamp of footsteps on gravel jarred him from his reverie.

'It's OK,' Alain called, from behind him. 'You can come with me now.'

Trent exhaled and relaxed his pose. He heard the *clunk* of the gate latch releasing. The electric hum as the gate began to swing open.

Still he didn't turn.

'She's waiting for you,' Alain said.

Yes, he thought. *Yes, you're right.*

Chapter Five

Alain insisted on patting Trent down again as he approached the gate. He was a lot more thorough the second time around and he located Trent's mobile right away. He flipped it open and held it out to Trent, the screen glowing like a distress flare in the pulsing black. A four-digit pin secured the phone.

'Enter your code,' Alain said.

'Why would I do that?'

'You do it or you don't come in.'

Trent stared at the guy until the loathing brimmed over in his eyes. The bodyguard didn't relent. Finally, Trent sighed and punched in the sequence.

Alain lowered his face to the phone and thumbed the keys. He cycled through Trent's call list. His contacts. His messages.

He looked up. 'It's empty.'

'Like your head, smart guy. It's a drop phone. Prepaid. They can be useful in kidnap situations. I thought it could be useful here, too.'

Alain snapped the phone closed and slipped it into his back pocket without another word. Then he went through the routine of feeling around Trent's torso and arms and legs, squeezing hard with his big hands. He had Trent remove his boots and socks and put them on again. Then he motioned him forwards and secured the gate behind him.

Alain had slipped on a clean charcoal jacket. It was the same style and fit and colour as the soiled garment he'd been wearing earlier. Maybe, Trent thought, he had a whole rack of identical suits hanging in a wardrobe somewhere, like a uniform store. Trent couldn't recall ever seeing him in a different outfit before.

There was a telltale bulge beneath the jacket where his Ruger was holstered on his left side. But there was no sign of where he was keeping Trent's wallet. No sign of Trent's Beretta.

They walked without speaking towards the crest of the driveway and Trent spent the time thinking carefully about the security measures that Jérôme had in place. A high fence. A steel gate. Surveillance cameras and a bodyguard. The Moreaus took their privacy seriously. It made Trent wonder exactly who they were afraid of, and why.

His eyes were alert, scanning his new surroundings, mapping possible routes back to the road in case he needed to leave in a hurry. The bodyguard moved with purpose beside him. Swollen arms swinging like pistons. Powerful legs pounding the ground. He'd stuck a flesh-coloured plaster over the cut beside his eye but a dribble of dried blood had escaped from beneath. It looked like a stray cotton thread. Maybe, Trent thought, if he tugged on it the guy's forehead would unravel.

'When do I get my phone back?' Trent asked.

'When you leave.'

'And my gun?'

'It's safe.'

'Terrific. Can I have it?'

The guy shook his head with all the emotion of an android. 'When you leave.'

'My wallet, then?'

Alain marched on without responding. The darkness that surrounded them was a living thing. It shimmied and stretched and throbbed. It cocooned them, as if they were alone together on an unlit stage, the auditorium abandoned.

'So, why are we walking?' Trent asked. 'Did you decide that I could use more exercise?'

'You saw the Mercedes.' Alain scowled down at his dress shoes, the band-aid wrinkling up beside his eye.

'You expect me to believe you don't have other vehicles to call on?

Come on, I know Jérôme is rich. That's a given for anyone who takes out a policy that includes my services.'

Alain grunted. His large feet scuffed gravel. Dust coiled up around the cuffs of his trousers like the embers of a deadened fire.

'I wanted to talk to you. Alone.'

'So talk. The only things listening to us out here are the trees.'

They tramped on, their footsteps loud in the darkness, the tall cypresses crowding in on them from either side.

'I don't trust you,' Alain said.

'No kidding. You should have mentioned something sooner.'

Alain glanced across. His movements had a twitchy, mechanical quality. A surplus of nervous energy. Trent recognised the symptoms. He was experiencing them himself. The bodyguard's system had been flushed with adrenalin during the abduction. He'd been overloaded with stress and fear and anxiety. And now he had a whole new set of problems to contend with. Starting with Trent.

'Mme Moreau wants you inside,' he said, like it was the worst idea he'd ever heard. 'The lawyer told us that you're the adviser the policy specifies. We kept you waiting because I asked him to make some calls. He telephoned two of the families you've worked for in the past.'

Trent nodded. The pack of documents that accompanied Jérôme's insurance policy contained a select list of former clients who were willing to vouch for him.

'I've worked for a lot of wealthy individuals,' Trent said. 'A few of them are generous enough to discuss my performance with others who find themselves in a similar situation.'

'They speak very highly of you.'

'They should. I got their loved ones back alive.'

'That's what they told us.'

'But . . . ?'

'But I still don't trust you. M. Moreau never mentioned you to me. He never talked about a kidnapping policy.'

'And you believe that as his bodyguard you should have been told?'

Trent made a clucking noise with his tongue – a sudden *pop* in the unlit stillness. 'Listen, these policies have to be kept completely secret. The records are carefully guarded. Otherwise, you risk alerting potential kidnappers.'

Alain twisted sideways from the hip, staring at Trent as he walked. His jacket was unbuttoned. Each time he swung his left arm, Trent could see the butt of his Ruger and the glint of stainless steel in the moonlight. 'But this is what interests me. Who guards these policies? You? Your company? And yet here you are, just as a kidnapping takes place.'

They were close to the house now. It was a large, modern villa with terracotta roof tiles and a pink or peach render on the walls. A lot of the exterior was covered in climbing plants and flowering bougain-villea. There was a triple garage on the side and a circular fountain out front where a tubby stone cherub was pouring water from an urn.

The property was very brightly lit. It was ablaze in the fierce glow of multiple floodlights that had been positioned among shrubs and foliage beds and palm trees. Trent thought back to the haze of light pollution he'd spotted from the gate. It made sense now. But nothing could have prepared him for the blinding glare.

All things considered, the Moreau residence didn't strike him as a relaxed family home. It felt more like a bunker, squatted low into the ground, hidden by the barbed steel fence and the steeply banked grass and the army of cypress trees, lit as starkly and as deliberately as a high-security prison in the middle of a lockdown.

'So you have concerns,' Trent said. 'The only question is, what are you going to do about it? Seems to me your options are pretty limited. Like I said, I'm the guy you need. And your boss's wife agrees. So what are you left with? My guess is this is the part where you make me tremble with some more of your tough-guy posturing – you know, the mean stare and the body searches and the tantalising glimpses of your revolver – and then you warn me that you're going to be watching me closely from now on.'

'Watching *and* listening.' Alain remained serious. Trent was beginning to suspect he never behaved in any other way. 'You can give *madame* your advice. But you give it to me, also. And if I don't like what I hear –' he tapped his Ruger through the material of his jacket – 'you leave, or I make you go. Understand?'

They skirted the fountain. Water splashed into water beneath the sightless, blissful gaze of the cherub. The wrecked Mercedes was parked in front of an arched timber door studded with ironware and bolts.

'No problem,' Trent replied. 'My approach requires a negotiating team. You'll be a strong member. A dissenting voice can be healthy.'

Alain approached the imposing door. He removed a set of keys from his trouser pocket. There looked to be fifteen keys, minimum, fitted to a sturdy metal ring. He sorted through them until he found the one he needed. Moments later, a deadbolt *clunked* sideways. He found another key. Worked the snap-lock. Then he stiff-armed the door open.

'A dissenting voice.' He came close to smiling but it was the kind of smile that concealed something. 'I think I can guarantee you more than one.'

Chapter Six

The entrance hall was silent and spacious and dimly lit. A ceiling fan rotated above Trent's head, slicing shadows out of the sodium glare coming in through the glass on either side of the door. Ahead was a sweeping staircase, flanked by a pair of black prancing horse statuettes. The floor was laid with pristine white marble tiles.

There were multiple doors leading off from the foyer, all of them closed. Alain selected the first door on the right and guided Trent along a glazed corridor that looked out over the gravel yard and the fountain. The light coming in through the glass was as fierce as a search beam.

'Someone buy the wrong bulbs?' Trent asked, shielding his eyes with his hand.

Alain grunted. He grunted a lot.

'Why so bright?'

'M. Moreau prefers to feel secure.'

'Must feel like a lab rat, too.'

Alain knocked on a door at the end of the corridor, then stepped inside without waiting for a response. Trent followed, finding himself inside an octagonal room where most of the walls were lined with shelves of books. The books all had green leather spines with gold detailing. They were lined up precisely, floor to ceiling, without a gap in between. Trent didn't get the impression the volumes were taken down and opened very often. He wouldn't have been surprised to discover that they were all fakes.

Two further doors and several full-height windows were positioned between the walls of books. Luxurious curtains had been drawn across the windows. The curtains were stitched from a rich, dense green fabric, and backed with some kind of additional lining to keep the bright exterior lights at bay. From his angle by the door, Trent could just glimpse the pearly glint from behind the curtain closest to him.

In the centre of the room was a desk. It was about the size of an average city car and fashioned from lush, highly polished cherry wood. The surface was empty apart from a red leather blotter in the exact centre, an ornate brass lamp and a business-style telephone. The office chair behind the desk was large and imposing. It was generously upholstered in cushioned black leather. And it was empty.

There was a brown leather chesterfield off to one side and two straight-backed visitor chairs positioned in front of the desk. Stephanie was perched on one of the chairs, her willowy body twisted around to face Trent. She was wearing a long, black mohair cardigan over the top of the delicate silver dress. She clutched its cuffs in her fists. It gave her the air of somebody suffering from a head cold.

'M. Trent, thank you for coming.' She spoke with a sense of calm reserve, as if Trent was a businessman who'd turned up for a prearranged meeting in the middle of the day. It was past midnight. 'I'm sorry if we inconvenienced you.'

She stood and took a step towards him. She was shorter than Trent remembered and it took a moment for him to notice that she'd removed her shoes. He glanced down at her bare feet. They were petite, the nails painted a modest pink. But the skin was dry and chafed and the little toe on the right foot seemed to be pointing off at a crooked angle. Dancer's feet. A storybook of injuries.

'You were right to be cautious,' he told her. 'You can't be too careful right now.'

She delved a hand into the pocket of her cardigan, wet her lip with her tongue, and held something out to him. His wallet.

He took it from her, his finger brushing fleetingly against her skin. She withdrew her hand sharply. Nerves, he guessed. She was bound to be jumpy.

He had to fight hard to quash the urge to flip open his wallet. There was a snapshot of Aimée in there. The surface was crinkled, the edges soft and frayed. The picture showed her sitting on a beach in a black bikini, wearing dark sunglasses and pouting to the camera. Her body was trim and tan, her wet hair coiled over one shoulder. They'd just been for a swim together. Out in the placid waters beneath the blazing sun, Trent had pulled her close and told her how much he loved her.

It should have been the happiest of mementoes. A symbol of the certain bliss that lay ahead of them. But now Trent sensed a hidden sadness behind the smile. A gloomy foreboding lurking just out of shot.

He supposed Alain and Stephanie had seen the image and he asked himself if it could be a problem. Possibly, he thought, though it was too soon to know for sure. Nothing he could do about it anyhow. He shoved the wallet into his back pocket and sealed the memory away.

'I take it there's been no contact yet,' he said to Stephanie. 'From the men who took your husband?'

She shook her head fast and lowered herself onto her chair. It was a deft, natural folding of her body. Trent was pretty sure it would take a lot of concentration for her to move without grace and precision.

'Do you think they'll call here?' she asked.

'Almost certainly. Some gangs contact an intermediary. Your lawyer, perhaps. But it's most likely they'll want to speak with you directly. They'll want to exploit your emotional ties to Jérôme. They'll make him give them the number. Unless you think he'd be more likely to have them call your mobile?'

'No-o,' she said, her voice hitching, then falling away. She cast a glance towards Alain. Lowered her eyes and contemplated her doll-like hands. She was picking at the skin beside her thumbnail. It was red and sore. Looked like she tore it often. 'I don't have one.'

Trent was silent for a moment.

'How many telephones in the house?'

'There is only this one,' she said, indicating the desk phone with a tilt of her head.

Trent raised an eyebrow. A property this size usually had plenty of handsets dotted around. And in his experience, young women like Stephanie spent a lot of time on their mobiles, calling or texting friends. It had been one of the things he and Aimée had sometimes argued about.

'Why here?' he asked.

'This is my husband's study.'

'But what if somebody calls for you?'

She glanced towards Alain again. Lowered her face once more, hiding behind her curtain of hair.

Silence in the room.

A stupid question, then. And one she obviously didn't feel at liberty to answer with Jérôme's bodyguard near by.

Trent was starting to suspect that the security measures around the villa weren't simply designed to prevent people getting in. Perhaps they were there to stop people getting out, too.

'What about you?' he asked Alain. 'You took my phone. Do you have one of your own?'

The bodyguard nodded once. His jaw was fixed. Face stern.

'So what do you think? Could Jérôme have them call you on it?'

'It's possible.'

'Is it likely?'

He pursed his lips. 'I do not think so.' He patted his jacket. Opposite side to where his Ruger was stashed. 'But it's no problem. I have it with me.'

'Good. Keep it charged at all times.'

'M. Moreau has a mobile, too. I tried calling it already.'

'Let me guess. No answer.'

'We should try again.'

'Be my guest. Dial as many times as you like.' Trent gestured towards the desk phone. 'But your call won't connect. The first thing the gang will have done is to search him. They'll have found his phone and destroyed it. They can't risk being traced.'

Alain considered the point for a moment, mouth twisted in thought, then he moved alongside the desk and raised the telephone receiver to his ear. He punched a fast sequence into the keypad and stared at Trent and waited. Then a muscle in his cheek twitched and his lips thinned. He lowered the receiver.

'It bounced straight to his message service,' he said.

'It'll stay that way, too. I guarantee it.'

Trent was about to say something more, to suggest where they might begin, when he heard the sudden fierce growl of engine noise and the scrabble of tyres on the gravel outside. The bass thump of a stereo was loud and intrusive. Some kind of electro-pop.

Alain crossed to one of the curtains and peered outside against the harsh white light. He squinted, a pained expression on his face, as if he'd smelt something foul.

'You're expecting somebody else?' Trent asked.

Stephanie smiled tightly. She picked at her thumb some more.

'My husband's son,' she muttered.

The noise of the engine and the brash stereo died at the same instant. A door slammed. Trent heard footsteps on the crushed stone, moving at pace.

'Does he know what's happened?'

'I contacted him,' Alain said, allowing the curtain to fall closed. He blinked fast, eyes watering. 'I warned him not to speak to anyone.'

'OK,' Trent said. He didn't like what he was hearing, but it wasn't anything he could change. 'There'll be tough decisions ahead. His input could be useful.'

'You may hope so,' Stephanie replied. 'For me, I am not so sure.'

Chapter Seven

Jérôme Moreau's son didn't approach by stealth. It took him a long time to jiggle his key into the lock on the front door and he was whistling as he came along the corridor. The tune wasn't anything Trent might have expected. It was fast and shrill and carefree.

The skinny young man who burst into the room wasn't anything Trent might have expected, either.

He was drunk or high or possibly both. He swayed as he entered, his stringy arms flailing loosely from a colourful Hawaiian shirt. He wore a dazed grin beneath a mop of sun-bleached hair and he clapped Alain on the shoulder before swerving past Trent and staggering towards a drinks cabinet on the far side of the room.

He grabbed a cut-glass decanter of whisky and poured a generous measure into a tumbler. He lifted the glass to his face and sniffed it, then wrinkled his nose. He experimented with a taste, recoiled dramatically, and slammed the tumbler back down. He added ice cubes to the mix. Took a larger sip. Hummed in satisfaction.

'Philippe?'

He spun around at the sound of Stephanie's voice and covered his heart with his hand, as if he'd been spooked by a ghost.

'*Maman!*' He summoned a dramatic bow.

'Sit down, Philippe.'

'As you wish, *maman*.'

He rotated his hand at the wrist in a flourish and dropped into the tan leather chesterfield. His body jolted with the impact and he spilt alcohol on his lap. He chuckled stupidly, as if delighted by the moist patch that had appeared on his jeans.

'You're *drunk*,' Stephanie said, and her tone suggested it wasn't the first time she'd said those words to him.

He swayed at the waist, spluttering with laughter.

'He's no use to us like this,' Trent said, voice hard.

'You understand that I'm not his mother.' Stephanie gave Philippe a withering look. 'We're almost the same age. Something he resents almost as much as my marriage to his father.'

Philippe raised his glass to Trent. 'And you are . . . ?'

'The negotiator,' he said, and told him his name. 'I'm here to help get your father back alive.'

'An expert.' Philippe's teeth chipped off the edge of his tumbler. 'Just like Alain. He's the expert who keeps my father safe.'

Trent turned to Alain. The bodyguard hadn't moved since Philippe had stepped into the room. His large hands were buried deep inside his trouser pockets, tendons standing out like thick cords on his forearms. His jaw was clenched, his face betraying neither disapproval nor surprise.

'You let him talk to you this way?' Trent asked.

'He's the son of my employer.'

'And if he wasn't?'

Alain relaxed for an instant. Just the idea of it gave him a wistful, faraway look.

Trent returned his attention to Philippe. He folded his arms across his chest. Summoned his full height. He was just over six feet tall. Athletically built and physically fit. He couldn't match Alain for physical presence but he could cut an imposing figure when the situation demanded it. Especially when the guy he was aiming to impose himself on was drunk or stoned. Especially when the guy in question was sitting down and Trent was standing up.

'You need to drink some coffee,' Trent told him. 'You need to pay attention to what I'm about to say.'

He waved a hand. 'I listen better when I'm drunk. Believe me, it's true. Here.' He held out his glass. 'Pour me some more.'

Trent watched him for a beat, unmoving. The guy was a wreck. The Hawaiian shirt he had on was unbuttoned close to his navel, revealing a dense thatch of knotted blond hair. His stonewashed jeans were rolled at the cuffs over tanned shins and a battered pair of canvas espadrilles. His hair was an uncombed mess, he hadn't shaved in days and the fleshy skin around his sunken eyes and blown pupils was discoloured and pouched.

Philippe shrugged and returned his glass to his lips. He slurped the last of his whisky and tipped an ice cube into his mouth. He grinned a stupid grin, the cube clenched between his molars, like he was smiling around a fat cigar.

Trent didn't wait any longer. He shed his composure like a man stepping out of a shower. He surged forwards, drew back his right arm and swung fast, slapping Philippe hard on the side of the face. His hand was open, fingers spread. The impact was loud and percussive. It stung his palm.

Philippe's head snapped to the side. A trickle of drool escaped his lips. He inhaled on instinct, then croaked and gagged and clutched a hand to his throat. The ice cube was lodged there.

Stephanie gasped and stood up, knocking back her chair. There was no response from Alain. Trent hadn't expected one.

He ducked down and seized Philippe by the waistband of his jeans, yanking him roughly off the couch, the tumbler falling from his hand and smashing on the stone floor. Philippe landed on his side, curled into a ball. He convulsed. He heaved drily. Trent didn't waste time checking his airways. He hoisted him up onto his hands and knees and then he thumped him hard between the shoulder blades using the heel of his hand. Thumped him again, jabbing down fast, the sound like a mallet striking a drum.

No good. The ice cube was still stuck. Philippe gaped up at Trent with his eyes bulging and his mouth wide open as if in a silent scream.

Trent got behind him and wrapped his arms around his torso. He balled his right hand into a fist and clenched it with his left and heaved up and in towards Philippe's diaphragm. One thrust. Two. No difference. He thrust extra hard the third time around.

Philippe convulsed and coughed and hacked up the ice cube, spitting it out of his mouth. He sucked air desperately, groaning and wheezing.

Trent hauled him away from the broken glass. He knelt beside him. Watched Philippe rock his head and sigh and splutter. Waited until he gazed up at him, trembling in shock and outrage.

'Lesson One,' Trent said. 'I don't work for your father, so I don't take any attitude from you. If you plan to be part of this situation, you're going to drink some coffee. If you refuse, you're out. Got that?'

*

Philippe opted to drink the coffee and Alain left the room to prepare it. By the time he returned with a solid silver tray in his hand, Philippe had dragged himself back to the chesterfield. His body was tilted over to one side and his breathing was very deliberate. He was inhaling and exhaling like it was a new and slippery skill he'd just acquired.

Alain set the tray down on the corner of the desk. There was a steaming white mug and an aluminium coffee pot on it.

Trent moved across and picked up the mug. Heat leaked through the porcelain against his palm. The coffee was black and hot and strong. Trent smelled its earthy aroma as he shoved the mug towards Philippe and wrapped his hands around it. He could see Philippe's gaunt reflection in the dark liquid as he lowered his face to take a sip.

It occurred to Trent that Philippe was exactly the brattish, spiteful type of guy who might try throwing the scalding liquid in his face. So he was cautious, but he remained close.

Philippe wasn't drinking fast. He was imbibing from the mug much slower than he had from the whisky tumbler. Trent snatched at Philippe's left wrist and tapped the face of his gold wristwatch. Told him to stop wasting time.

Truth was, Trent wasn't a great believer in the power of caffeine to sober anybody up. But he did believe that shock and fear and intimidation could work, and he was more than willing to test the theory.

He waited until Philippe was slurping at the rim again before reaching out and tilting the mug at the base.

Philippe groaned in complaint, his eyes grown wide.

Trent tipped harder.

The muscles in Philippe's throat pulsed. He tried to lower the mug. Trent held it steady.

Philippe whined through his nose.

'Drink,' Trent said.

He whined with more urgency.

'Drink.'

Philippe's gullet opened. He moaned. He gagged. Hot coffee spilled from his mouth, running down his chin and soaking into his shirt.

'Please,' Stephanie said, from behind him. 'It's enough.'

Trent turned and gave her a savage look. She was sitting forwards on her chair, bare knees pressed together, hands clasped tight in her lap.

He was struck again by the contrast with how Aimée would likely behave. If she were here, she'd have elbowed him out of the way so that she could be the one forcing the coffee into Philippe.

'It's not enough,' Trent told Stephanie. 'The men who took your husband could call at any moment.'

Philippe rocked his head back and gasped. He wiped his jaw with the back of his wrist.

The mug was empty.

Trent seized it and snatched up the coffee pot and poured a refill, holding Alain's eye. The bodyguard stared back, steady and unmoving.

'It's OK,' Philippe said, waving his hand. 'I'm fine now.'

Trent set the coffee pot down. He returned to the sofa. Jabbed the mug towards Philippe.

'Again.'

'It's fine, I said.'

'Again.'

'I'm fine, I tell—'

Trent didn't wait to hear more. He snatched a knuckle-full of Philippe's hair, yanked his head back until his jaw fell open and slammed the mug against his teeth.

'Drink,' he said.

Philippe swallowed some of the coffee but the rest sluiced down his neck and chest. Trent didn't back off. He poured until the mug was empty. Philippe groaned and rolled his head to one side. His skin was flushed around his lips and jaw. It matched his reddened cheek.

'One more,' Trent said.

'But that is enough. Believe me.'

'One. More.'

Trent refilled the mug to the brim. He upended the coffee pot, adding a sludge of grinds to the mix. He fitted Philippe's hand around the mug. Clamped his fingers there.

'Need my help?' he asked.

'No,' Philippe muttered. 'I'll drink it.'

And like a kid clearing all his greens from his plate, he went ahead and did exactly that.

Chapter Eight

Trent took up a position in the centre of the octagonal room and began, as he always did, by describing his background and experience. His delivery rarely changed. It was no different tonight.

He started with the usual oblique references to his formative years in the British military and his early work as an analyst for a secretive branch of the UK government, followed by his switch to a London-based corporate security outfit. He explained how his dual Anglo-French nationality had led him to move to the company's Paris office, where he'd specialised in kidnap and ransom negotiation.

He talked of a demanding five-year period handling kidnap cases across France, Italy, the Balkans, Greece and Spain, where he'd honed his skills and developed his own particular techniques and tactics. Then he mentioned how he'd decided to relocate to Marseilles in the wake of a spate of kidnappings throughout the south of France to set up his own niche firm specialising in all varieties of K & R protection. He outlined the scope of services his firm provided, ranging from the insurance policy that Jérôme had acquired from his colleague and business partner, Aimée Paget, to the guidance he'd hoped to provide to Jérôme concerning anti-kidnap security measures, to the sort of assistance he could offer in the case of an actual kidnapping, such as the Moreaus were experiencing right now.

Twenty minutes' fast talking and then he was done. One o'clock in the morning. Silence in the room. His audience had remained mute throughout. Trent had paid close attention to their reactions when he'd mentioned Aimée's name. None of them had betrayed a thing. There was no indication of any concern or recognition.

Stephanie had hung on his every word, shuffling ever nearer to the edge of her chair. She looked pale and tired and just about ready to drop.

Philippe hadn't strayed from the chesterfield, though now he was pivoted forwards from the waist, his bony elbows braced on his spread thighs, his gaze fixed on the fragments of pulverised glass between his feet. Trent was fairly sure he was suffering from a tide of nausea. He was swallowing audibly. Another mouthful of coffee and he'd likely pass out.

Alain was perched on the end of the desk next to the tray of coffee things, one foot touching the floor, his other leg bent at the knee. He'd shed his jacket and draped it over the chair alongside Stephanie, then loosened his tie and unbuttoned his frayed collar. The Ruger was still in its holster. The holster was still fitted around his shoulder and chest. He looked a lot like a squad detective receiving a debrief.

One spot remained conspicuously unoccupied – the office chair behind the desk. It was the most comfortable seat in the room and it would have given one of his listeners the best possible view of what he had to say. But it appeared that nobody was prepared to claim it. Perhaps it was a subconscious decision to keep the spot open for Jérôme. Perhaps it signified something else. Trent was still weighing up the possible explanations when Philippe cleared his throat.

'We should contact the police,' he said, glancing up at Stephanie and Alain. 'Men we trust there. Men my father can rely on.' Beads of sweat had broken out across his forehead. His skin had a waxy texture and he was squinting myopically, as though the light in the room was too bright for him.

'Not a good idea,' Trent replied.

'Why?' His cheek was still livid. Looked like it might bruise. 'They have the manpower and the resources to deal with situations like this.'

'They also have a different agenda from us.'

'*Us?*'

'That's right. Like it or not, we're a team now.'

Philippe curled his lip. He shook his head at the others in the room.

'He's just looking to get paid for something the police will do better. And for free.'

'Not true.' Trent fixed his gaze on each of them in turn. He was very deliberate about it. 'My fee is covered by Jérôme's insurance policy.'

'But you're just one man,' Philippe persisted. 'I bet the police would assign some kind of specialist unit.'

Trent bobbed his head. 'You're right. They would. But tell me, what would be their goal?'

'To get my father back.'

'Possibly. But they'd also want to try and apprehend the gang. They'd want to prevent the gang from doing this to someone else.'

'Are you concerned they'll put you out of business?'

'I'm concerned they might bungle their investigation. I'm concerned they'd show their hand. When the men who snatched your father get in contact, the first thing they'll tell you is not to talk to the police. And they'll mean it, too. If they catch sight of the authorities anywhere near them, do you know what they'll do?'

Philippe didn't reply. He just stared at Trent, a bluish cast to his lips, a simmering loathing in his sleep-hooded eyes.

'They'll kill your father. Make no mistake. They don't want to be caught. They don't want to come close to risking it. And catching them isn't your concern. Your only thought should be getting your father back alive. I can help you to achieve that, but you have to work with me and you have to work with the gang. This is a negotiation now.' He glanced at Stephanie. She was blinking rapidly. 'You'll have to pay. I'm sorry, but that's the reality. Hoping for any other outcome is like putting a loaded gun against your husband's head and pulling the trigger.'

Stephanie winced but Trent didn't back off. It was vital to get his point across. Not just for Jérôme. For other reasons, too. Reasons that had to do with his own concerns. With Aimée and the bigger objective he was working towards.

Trent turned back to Philippe. 'What do you do for a living?' he asked.

'I'm a businessman,' Philippe replied, though he looked far from it in his ridiculous shirt and his sagging jeans.

Alain snorted.

'What kind of business?' Trent asked.

'A nightclub. In the Vieux Port.'

'He has only a share,' Stephanie explained. 'His partners take their profits in cash. Philippe prefers to consume his in other ways.'

'A lot you know,' Philippe snarled back. 'The way you make your living. On your back for my father.'

'Hey!' Trent snapped his fingers. 'Enough.'

Stephanie's head rolled loosely on her shoulders, like she was reeling from a physical blow. Her plump lips were pursed and moist, as if she were sucking on a straw. Great lips. Wonderful features. But right now her wan skin had pulled taut over her angular cheekbones, and she looked lost and alone and utterly abandoned. Trent could see that she was the kind of woman men would trample other men to protect. He could feel the temptation to go to her. It was a hard instinct to resist.

'We don't have time for this.' He jabbed a finger at Philippe. 'Let's get back to your club. You must have all kinds of suppliers, correct? You need drinks. Snacks. A sound system. DJs. That kind of thing.'

Philippe nodded, an amused slant to his mouth, as if Trent was tragically unhip.

'But you have something they need, too, don't you? They survive because of your custom.'

He sniffed and lifted his shoulders. Maybe the club wasn't doing too well. It wouldn't surprise Trent to hear it. Philippe didn't strike him as the dedicated type.

'My point is, it's the same with the men who've taken your father. You have to set your emotions aside and view this as a business transaction. Think of it like this: these men have a commodity you want. They have Jérôme. But the reverse is also true. You have something they need. You have money.'

'My father has money.'

'Same thing. That's why they targeted him.'

'Or because of the insurance policy,' Alain put in, crossing his arms over his chest, squeezing the revolver with his biceps. 'It's possible they know it exists.'

'Unlikely,' Trent replied. 'But either way, Jérôme is worth something to the gang. And to get him back, you need to barter a deal. And that's where I come in.'

Before he continued, Trent finally did what he'd wanted to do since he'd first stepped into the room. He walked around the oversized desk, rolled back the giant leather chair and took a seat.

A simple process. A comfortable one, too. The chair was well sprung, the leather soft and warm. The backrest was supportive in all the right places. It didn't even creak as he adjusted his weight.

But the effect was telling.

Stephanie gazed at him uncertainly. Philippe appeared stunned. Alain tensed and slipped off the side of the desk, as if sensing a threat.

'This is Jérôme's chair?' Trent asked.

Stephanie nodded, mouth agape.

'And nobody sits here except Jérôme?'

'You should respect him,' Alain said.

'You think he'll be mad at me?' Trent leaned backwards. He smoothed his hands along the armrests. 'Listen, I'm just keeping it warm for him until he returns. Believe me, I want him back alive every bit as much as all of you.'

He scanned the faces in front of him. Philippe and Stephanie averted their eyes. Only Alain held his gaze. His stare was unwavering.

Trent asked himself if maybe the bodyguard sensed that he was lying? If he saw clean through his words?

Because the truth was he didn't want Jérôme back as much as any of them.

He wanted it much, much more than that.

Chapter Nine

'Let's talk money,' Trent said, pressing his fingertips together. 'The insurance policy Jérôme took out with my firm covers him for a ransom payout of up to two and a half million euros.'

Philippe whistled.

'Sounds a lot, doesn't it? And I'm not here to try and save our brokers any cash. If that's what it takes to free Jérôme, then that's what we'll pay.'

'Do you really think they will ask for this much?' Stephanie asked, as if she couldn't quite conceive of the sum.

'No,' Trent told her. 'I think they'll ask for more. They'll start with a high demand, hoping you'll pay it. That way they leave themselves room to come down.'

'How much higher?' Alain asked.

'Three million. Maybe even four. It depends if they know about the policy. It also depends how much Jérôme might be worth.'

'Four million?' Stephanie repeated, breathless now.

'It's a request. That's all. We have to talk them down.'

'But you risk aggravating them,' Alain said. 'They could react badly.'

'Kill him, you mean?' Trent shook his head. 'Think about it: returning Jérôme to us safely is the only way they get paid. And trust me, the worst thing you could do would be to agree to their first demand. They don't really expect to be paid three or four million or whatever it is they actually ask for. The going rate for ransoms of this kind in France right now is somewhere below two million. They're a professional gang. They'll know that. But suppose you consent to pay them four million, what do you think will happen?'

Nobody answered. Trent hitched an eyebrow at Philippe. Philippe shuffled restlessly, unwilling to speak up.

'They'll think you're a soft touch, is what,' Trent said. 'They'll collect your four million and then they'll demand another instalment. This entire process is about squeezing you. Pay them early and they might try for two or more ransoms. I've heard of one family who paid as many as four times. And all the while, they keep hold of Jérôme. His ordeal is prolonged. So the best thing you can do is to engage with them. Negotiate a one-time-only fee. You have to pitch it right. You have to pay the smallest amount of money possible and still get Jérôme home safe. Understand?'

'What if they've killed him already?' Philippe asked.

Stephanie shied away, as if bracing for impact.

'It's simple,' Trent replied. 'Every time they call or contact us we demand proof that Jérôme is still alive. They'll anticipate the request and there are various ways they can satisfy it. The easiest way is to put him on the phone. Next easiest is for us to ask a question that only he could answer. But it's important to remember that they won't kill him if we agree to pay a fair amount.'

'Fair.' Stephanie spat the word.

'To them, yes,' Trent insisted. 'You don't have to like it. You don't even have to understand it. You just have to accept it.'

Stephanie shuddered. She clenched her cardigan around herself.

'Remember, everything they do is designed to manipulate you into paying a better price. My job is to help you analyse the gang's communications and expose their tactics for what they are. But you three have to make the decisions. You have to be comfortable with whatever is decided.'

It wasn't entirely true. Trent was confident he could exert his influence on them when it mattered. He was relying on it, in fact. But it was a line he'd used often in the past and it had always tended to put his clients at ease.

'Three is an ideal number,' he continued. 'You'll each have a vote on team decisions and you'll go with what the majority decide. Alain can be chairman. The two of you', he said, indicating Stephanie and Philippe, 'are more emotionally involved. So in the event that you can't agree on a particular course of action, Alain will make the call. But you each need a different role beyond that, too.'

They looked at him, waiting for more. Nobody spoke. Nobody suggested an alternative arrangement. Trent wasn't surprised. He was often confronted by a curious lethargy among the friends and families of kidnap victims. Plus they were exhausted. It was almost two-thirty in the morning. Before the attack, Stephanie, Jérôme and Alain had been on their way home to bed. And though Philippe might not have planned to end his night just yet, there was a reasonable chance he would have flaked out by now if his father's abduction hadn't altered his plans.

'Alain, you'll be in charge of security. That makes sense given your current role. The house here looks very safe.' Trent nodded towards the glow of halogen around the edge of the thickened curtains. 'That's why the gang attacked you before you reached the gate. But you need to be aware of the risk of follow-up kidnappings. You have to be responsible for the movements of Stephanie and Philippe. That'll be much easier if you all stay inside the grounds.'

'Wait.' Philippe wagged a finger. 'I don't live *here*. I have an apartment in the city.'

'Argue with Alain, not me. If he thinks you're safe to leave, it's his call. I'm pretty sure your father would agree.'

'No way,' Philippe muttered.

Stephanie rolled her eyes.

'You can be the group's liaison to the outside world,' Trent told Philippe. 'You say you're a businessman, then act like it. If there comes a time when we need to contact the police, or if the press become involved, you'll be the family's conduit. Agreed?'

He threw up his hands, as if he couldn't care either way.

'And me?' Stephanie asked.

Trent leaned forwards and placed his hands on the surface of the desk, fingers spread, knuckles raised.

'You have the most important role of all,' he told her. 'You're the one who talks to the gang.'

She leaned backwards, eyes like dark pools. A vein throbbed at her temple, a squiggle of blue ink beneath her skin.

'It's OK,' Alain said. He rested a hand on her shoulder. 'They can speak with me instead.'

'No. That won't work.' Trent locked onto Stephanie. 'Listen, we have to give them what they expect. Then we turn it to our advantage. If Alain speaks to them, they'll be on their guard. They may become more aggressive. But if you answer, they'll believe they're applying pressure in just the way they anticipated. It's good if you sound distressed. It's good if you demand to know that your husband is alive. And most importantly, you can tell them that you can't raise the sort of sums they're demanding. You can tell them that only Jérôme has access to his assets and bank accounts. Forgive me, but you're much younger than Jérôme and it's likely they'll believe you. That's a good thing. They'll begin to understand that you can only pay a reasonable sum.'

Stephanie was silent. She was turning over his explanation. Trent was pleased to see it. Even under duress, she was thinking things through. When the gang contacted them, there'd be times when she'd have to react to new information very rapidly. It was important that her responses were as considered as possible.

'Why don't you talk to them?' she asked.

'At this stage, it's best if they don't know that I'm involved. But don't worry. I'll prepare a script for you. Just a few simple points you should try to get across.'

'You forget that they saw you,' Alain said.

'They saw a guy involved in a car crash on a dark road. That's all.'

'You shot at them.'

Trent shook his head. 'They were fleeing at speed. Even supposing they saw that it was me, they might think I was some kind of back-up security.'

Alain's face was knotted up. He wasn't convinced. Neither was Trent. But he wasn't about to dwell on something he couldn't control.

He braced his hands against the edge of the desk and rolled backwards in Jérôme's chair, then grappled with the central drawer just above his knees. It was locked. There were more drawers on the right and some on the left. They were locked, too.

'I need paper and a pen,' he said. 'Is there some in this desk? Do you have a key?'

'Alain has a key,' Stephanie replied.

Trent turned to Alain but the bodyguard didn't reach for the set of keys he'd used earlier. He simply gathered his jacket from the back of the chair, delved a hand into a front pocket and fetched a small notepad and pencil.

He opened the pad to the first page and passed it to Trent. The page wasn't blank. It was half-filled with a rushed, uneven scrawl. Trent read over the information – a physical description of a man, plus a vehicle number plate. He recognised the description as his own. It was brief but accurate. Alain had recorded his height to within a centimetre and his weight to within a few pounds. The summary of his hair colour and his clothes was faultless. The sequence of numbers and letters printed below the description matched the fake plates he'd attached to the Peugeot exactly.

'I noted it down after we left the Opéra,' Alain told him. 'The number plate I added when you followed us into the tunnel.'

Trent was impressed. He supposed that was the point.

He turned to a fresh page, clutched the pencil tight and began to write.

1. Proof of Life

Is my husband alive? Is he safe? Can I speak to him? Can you prove it? (Think of a question only Jérôme could answer.)

2. Money

I don't have any funds. I don't have access to my husband's bank accounts. I can't raise the amount you're asking for.

3. Insurance Policy

I don't know what you're talking about. My husband doesn't tell me anything. Is he safe? Is he alive? Etc.

'Here.' Trent tore the page free and slid it across the surface of the desk towards Stephanie. 'Don't worry, there's a strong likelihood they won't give you much chance to speak. The call won't last long. Thirty, maybe forty-five seconds. They'll be concerned about the possibility of a trace. They'll tell you not to contact the authorities and they'll mention a ransom. They may specify a figure. They may not. If they do, you can't possibly pay it. Understand?'

The paper shook in her hand. She was nervous but he sensed a resolve in her, too. He'd witnessed the reaction many times. Give someone a responsibility. Make them believe they're the right individual to fulfil an important role. Focus their attention on that one particular task. Then sit back and watch them adapt to it. Marvel at the way they're able to concentrate on their mission to the exclusion of whatever emotions might be swirling through their mind.

'But there is a problem,' she said.

'Go on.'

'This.' She'd flattened the piece of paper on the desk, turning it so that it was facing Trent. Her fingernail was resting just beneath point two on his list: *Money.* 'It's true. I don't have access to Jérôme's accounts. He controls all our funds.'

'All of it?'

She flinched. 'I have a small allowance.'

'How small?'

She glanced at Alain. 'Maybe twenty thousand euros?'

Alain nodded. Trent supposed that he oversaw her spending in some way.

'How about you?' Trent asked Philippe.

'The same,' he mumbled. 'An allowance. No bigger.'

Trent vented air through his lips. It was a hitch he hadn't antici-pated.

'But we're insured.' Alain opened his hands. He showed his square palms to the three of them.

'That's right,' Trent replied. 'But normally the policy reimburses a client once a ransom payment has been made.'

'And in a situation like this?'

Trent sighed. 'I should be able to authorise a cash advance. But it's not ideal. It can take as long as a week. And the payment can't exceed the two-point-five million limit.'

There were other problems, too. Problems he wasn't inclined to share. Aimée had always handled the paperwork for any claim. Trent could do it himself – he'd be able to figure out the procedures if he really had to – but both their signatures were necessary to process a payment. He guessed he could forge Aimée's signature. He'd seen it often enough. But there remained the issue of the extra time the process would take.

And Trent had no idea how much time he might have.

He wanted everything resolved as soon as possible. He couldn't af-ford for any more complications to arise.

'What about you?' Trent asked Alain.

He smirked. 'You think I'm a millionaire?'

'Maybe not. But I think you're smart. I think if you applied yourself you could come up with a fast way to get your hands on some cash. You've worked alongside Jérôme for some time. You must have a few ideas.'

Trent watched Alain carefully. He didn't say anything more. Didn't elaborate. But he saw a flicker of light deep inside the bodyguard's eyes. The slightest contraction of his pupils, as if he were reassessing the situation.

Trent swivelled in his chair. Stephanie was reading back over his prompt sheet. She swallowed hard. Looked from the sheet to the tele-phone. Stared at it with a mixture of fear and fascination.

'Look, it has a speaker,' Trent said. He tapped a button towards the bottom of the keypad. 'We'll be able to listen to everything they say. We'll be right here with you.'

She nodded. Wet her lip with her tongue. Pushed the script alongside the telephone.

'But don't keep watching it,' he told her. 'You'll drive yourself crazy. Silence is one of the most powerful weapons the gang have at their disposal. Making you anxious is a key move for them. Be aware of that and see it for what it is. A negotiating tactic. Nothing more.'

She nodded again and summoned a brave smile. It made her appear more scared and more out of her depth than anything he'd seen so far.

'So what happens now?' Philippe asked, fighting a yawn.

'The hardest part,' Trent told him. 'We wait.'

Chapter Ten

Two months ago

Trent waited for his mobile to ring. His phone lay in the middle of a sagging bed in a cramped and miserable hotel room in Naples, Italy.

The room was a corner unit located on the fourth floor of a decrepit building that had seemed, from the outside at least, to be tilting fatally to one side. The fake terrazzo floor was covered in a fine layer of grime and grit. The cast-iron radiator burned hot as a furnace and there seemed no way to adjust it or turn it off. The worm-holed furniture smelled of mothballs, and the en suite bathroom was a weakly lit den of discoloured porcelain, leaking taps and cockroach husks.

But then, what else did he expect from a two-star place on the fringes of the Forcella quarter, home to shabby open-air markets selling contraband goods, foul-smelling passageways, the best back-street pizzerias in the whole of Italy, and a major clan in the Camorra crime organisation?

He stood by an open window, looking out over a tangled intersection of pedestrian alleyways. It was raining hard outside; had been raining for most of the afternoon into early evening. Water thundered down into the crooked fissures between the close-packed buildings, splattering the cracked stone window ledge in front of him, trickling off electricity cables and telephone lines and laundry racks, sluicing down blown-plaster walls layered in decades of overlaid posters and flyers and graffiti, pounding slickened tarmac, running in countless streams and rivulets and channels and tributaries, carrying dirt and filth and litter towards drains that gurgled like desperate men drowning.

His phone didn't ring.

The vertical red neon sign beside his window blinked disconsolately through the letters *H, O, T* and *E*. The *L* at the bottom wasn't working. An omen, he supposed. A warning to stay elsewhere.

He'd had the opportunity to do just that. Somewhere to the north, beyond the knot of crooked rooftops and the rain and the smog of low grey clouds, was the conference centre on the edge of the *autostrada* where the convention was taking place. *Corporate Security in the Modern World*. A four-day affair. Most of the talks had been given by squint-eyed tech guys, focusing on IT infrastructures and anti-hacking software. Trent had already presented his paper on the risk of corporate kidnapping.

He'd left Marseilles three days ago, seeing it as an opportunity to generate new business and a chance to touch base with his contacts in the Naples police force. Information was his greatest ally. The latest abduction trends, the going rate Italian gangs were charging for ransoms, the number of victims who were released safely or killed – he amassed all the data he possibly could, expanding his records so he could make the best judgements when he was faced with the toughest decisions.

His phone still wouldn't ring.

Why hadn't she called? And why wasn't she answering her mobile? He'd tried calling her many times but a recorded message kept telling him the device was switched off. He'd sent her texts. Heard nothing back.

It wasn't like her. She always talked with him at least once a day whenever he was away. In truth, they tended to speak to one another much more often. Usually they'd chat in the evenings. Sometimes late at night or early in the morning, too. She'd last phoned him at 7 a.m. the day before yesterday. A normal phone call. A perfectly ordinary interaction.

And nothing since.

He eyed his mobile. Dared it not to ring. Challenged it to remain silent.

It didn't make a sound.

Something plummeted deep inside him and coiled in his gut. The something was black and slick and greasy. It turned and twisted and writhed its way into his chest, wrapping itself around his heart and lungs, squeezing and contracting. Suffocating him from within.

He slumped onto the edge of the mattress, dust rising in the stale air.

His flight home was booked for early the following afternoon. He had two appointments scheduled for the morning. The first was with a guy he was thinking of training up locally, a native speaker to assist him during lengthy Italian negotiations. The second was with a potential new client from the conference. An anxious middle management type who'd approached him with a sweaty brow and a wet handshake after his talk.

He could cancel both meetings. He could take a cab to the airport right now and book himself onto a late flight home. Or he could hire a car, drive through the night to Marseilles.

And do what? Confirm his worst fears?

Aimée had been taken. He felt sure of it now. Felt it, in fact, with the same conviction with which he knew that the rain would continue late into the evening, keeping him company along with his haunted thoughts as he paced the unwashed floor of his crappy hotel room and peered down over the twilit passageways, watching blurred figures scurry by, listening to the bleat of car horns and the whine of scooter engines.

He'd already contacted someone he could trust. He'd telephoned the man after the first thirty-six hours had elapsed, dispatching him to check his apartment. He couldn't call the police. Couldn't risk their involvement.

His contact had acted right away. He'd reported back within ninety minutes. There was no sign of Aimée at their home. No evidence of a disturbance. But her car wasn't parked where Trent had said it would be. And she wasn't in any of the local places he'd suggested.

Trent had thanked the man, then had him check again this morning and once more in the afternoon. He had him telephone the local hospitals and a few select individuals in the city's police stations. Same result.

She was gone. And he was seven hundred miles away.

If there was one consolation, it was that they'd talked about this many times; had spoken of it, more than once, as if it was simply inevitable, a circumstance they'd long been destined to face.

At first, Trent had been little more than an irritant to some of the European kidnap gangs. And the astute operators, he suspected, had mostly been pleased with his approach. He was a professional they could work with. A guy who was willing to negotiate without any apparent interest in giving the authorities their scent. But as time wore on, as his business expanded and he became involved in more cases, then it was only logical that he might offend someone who held a different view. Or maybe the gangs might begin to feel he was threatening their livelihood. Reducing their payouts. Frustrating them, at the very least.

And these were tough men. Hard men. Revenge was in their nature. It was something they'd been conditioned to pursue. They couldn't show weakness. They couldn't afford for others to identify it in them. He'd always known that somewhere, some time, there'd be someone who wouldn't hesitate to strike back.

But Aimée had known what to expect. That was something, for sure. He'd schooled her on how she was likely to be treated, where she might be taken and how she would be held. She was a determined character. She was steely. It was one of the traits that had first attracted him to her and he knew that it would take a lot for her to begin to panic. She wasn't someone who'd easily break.

And they had their secret codes, prepared responses she'd provide to the proof of life questions he could ask her captors. Her answers would tell him a great deal about what they were up against. How many men. Whether they were violent. If they were experts or amateurs. How they were treating her. If they were likely to accept a lower ransom sum.

They had everything in place.

He was ready for the call.

But still his mobile didn't ring.

And what good was all their preparation, what use a skilled negotiator, without another voice on the end of the line?

Chapter Eleven

The phone was still and silent on the magnificent desk. It was a perfectly ordinary business phone. Unremarkable in every conceivable way. And yet it was preoccupying everyone inside the study. All eyes were fixed on it. Watching it. Waiting for it to do something that it stubbornly refused to do.

The device was toxic. Trent knew that better than anyone. Better than he could ever have cared to know.

'You should get some rest,' he said. 'All of you.'

It was closing in on three in the morning and Trent's eyes burned with fatigue. Sure, he had a comfortable chair, but Jérôme's study wasn't a room to relax in. It had a sterile, unlived-in feel. There was no clutter. No personality. The uniform ranks of green leather-bound books gave no hint of Jérôme's interests or passions. There were no framed photographs on his desk. No paintings on the wall. The room felt like a display in a furniture shop.

'No.' Stephanie shook her head. 'They may call.'

She looked every bit as weary as Trent. Maybe more so. Her face was ashen.

'It could be days until they contact you,' Trent told her. 'We can take it in shifts. Some kind of rota. I'll start.'

She raised her chin on her long neck. Smoothed the fabric of her dress across her lap. 'You said that I should answer the call. That it should be me.'

He was silent. She was right. He had said it. And he'd meant it, too.

But the locked drawers in Jérôme's desk intrigued him. He wanted very much to see if he could access them. And he'd need some time alone to do that.

'You pair, then.' Trent parted his hands, gesturing to Alain and Philippe.

Alain grunted dismissively, as if reacting to some variety of insult. He moved over to the side of the room and dropped to his backside on the floor. He leaned his head against a curtain and rested his forearms on raised knees. The curtain moulded itself around his shoulders, coming away from the edge of the glass and exposing a glint of blazing light.

Philippe followed Alain's cue and reclined lengthways on the leather chesterfield. He placed his hands behind his head.

'Fine,' Trent said. 'If none of you intends to sleep, then we should make use of the time available to us. Tell me about Jérôme.' He fixed on Stephanie. Raised an eyebrow. 'What kind of a man is he? What type of character?'

Philippe scoffed. 'You ask her?'

'I'm asking *all* of you. It's a simple question. Anything you tell me could help. How will he bear up against the gang? How will he cope with their threats and intimidation tactics?'

'You ask the wrong question,' Philippe said.

'Oh?'

'You should ask how long the gang can resist my father. You should ask how they will cope with *his* threats.'

Stephanie muttered something sour.

'It's true.' Philippe wriggled into a hollow on the couch. He seemed relaxed and composed, as if he was settling in to watch a favourite movie. 'My father is a formidable man. He has formidable friends. He will make these men see that they've made a mistake.'

'Forgive me,' Trent said, 'but he didn't seem so formidable when they pulled him from his car. He looked terrified. He was helpless. And you have to understand, this gang may beat your father. They may deprive him of food and water. They could treat him very badly.'

'Then they would be fools. They would be dead men.'

'*Dead men?*' Trent's pulse quickened. He had to stop himself from leaning forwards in his chair. He was edging closer to something. Closer than he'd been so far.

'That's enough,' Stephanie said, with venom.

But Philippe wasn't inclined to stop just yet.

'Do you know how my father makes his money, *monsieur*?'

Trent had a reasonable idea. He knew something about the legitimate sources of Jérôme's income. And he knew something about the illegitimate sources, too.

'Tell me,' he said.

'He brokers yachts,' Stephanie cut in. 'He imports them and he sells them. This is all.'

'It's not all. He imports many things *inside* these yachts, too. Hidden things. From North Africa. The Middle East.'

'Liar.'

'You deceive yourself. You believe what you wish to believe.'

'And you talk too much.' Alain exhaled hard and unbuttoned his shirtsleeves, yanking them up his muscular forearms. He adjusted the strap of his gun holster and eased his neck from side to side, as if freeing a kink. 'Your terrible father,' Alain said flatly, like he'd heard Philippe riff off the theme too many times. 'The monster who pays for your apartment, your business, the fast car that you drive like a fool when you drink.'

Philippe flashed his teeth. 'You defend him? Why?'

Alain didn't respond.

'Perhaps it's because you'd like us to see how loyal you are? Perhaps you wish us to believe that you don't envy him?' Philippe winked salaciously at Stephanie. Twirled a finger in the air. 'That you don't covet all that he has?' He chuckled to himself. 'Maybe you don't want us to start asking ourselves if one day you might decide to take it all from him?'

Alain grunted. 'This is your big idea? That I helped these men to kidnap your father?'

'I do not say it happened. Only that it's possible. Your job was to protect him. And yet now look where he is. And look where *you* are. Sitting
in his home. Making decisions that could set him free. Or not.'

Alain rocked his head back against the curtain behind him. He
gazed up at the ceiling and cursed in frustration.

'Easy,' Trent said. 'We're getting sidetracked.' He cocked his thumb
and pointed his finger at Philippe. 'The important thing is that you're
telling me your father can handle the situation he finds himself in?'

Philippe pursed his lips. He hummed. Then he nodded. He seemed
absolutely convinced of it.

'And you're also telling me he's not the most law-abiding of citizens.'

'My father is a crook. I do not say that he's a gangster, but he keeps
company with dangerous men. He trades with them. Obtains things
for them.'

'Then tell me about his enemies.'

'Enemies?' Stephanie asked, as though appalled.

'If he helps *some* dangerous men, it stands to reason there are others
he creates problems for. The underworld in Marseilles is competitive.
It's brutal. Everyone knows that. Hell, that's why a guy like Jérôme em-
ploys a bodyguard like Alain. It's why he lives his life behind a high steel
fence. Why he has security cameras and vapour lights all around his
home. So tell me who might want to abduct him. And why.'

Stephanie blinked very fast. She seemed unaware that she was shaking her head.

Philippe grinned inanely, as if Trent were a fool.

Alain scowled and rubbed his palm across his close-cropped hair.
His head was tilted over to one side. He met Trent's gaze with a baleful
look.

'None of you?' Trent persisted.

Alain's eyes narrowed. 'Why do you ask?'

'Because it could help us. I'm trying to form an idea of who we might
be up against here.'

'But you told us an investigation could endanger M. Moreau. You said we have to negotiate. This is all.'

'I'm not suggesting that the information leaves this room,' Trent told him. 'I'm not suggesting we try to find the gang.'

He wasn't suggesting it, but he was thinking it. He wanted to know almost more than he could stand.

If Aimée were here, listening to him now, she'd be giving him one of her knowing looks, the kind where she pushed her mouth to one side and arched an eyebrow. She always delighted in reminding him that he was hopeless at leaving anything unresolved. He couldn't walk away from a minor disagreement or a half-finished crossword puzzle. He hated any kind of logic flaw in a movie. So she'd know that this entire situation was killing him, and for a precious second, recognising that made him feel as if she were near.

'No, you advise us when these men call,' Alain told him. 'This is all you do. You don't ask questions about M. Moreau's business. You don't intrude on his life.'

'I'm trying to *save* his life.'

And in that moment, the weight and the absurdity of what he was saying suddenly hit Trent like he'd stepped in front of a freight train. He shook his head. Scrubbed his face with his hands. He needed a break. Needed space to think. And if the others planned to stay inside the study, then maybe this was his opportunity to take a look around the house. He wasn't sure what he might find. But even the slimmest chance was better than nothing.

'I'd like a glass of water.' He nodded at Stephanie. 'Maybe something to eat. Which way is your kitchen?'

'No.' Alain pushed up from the floor. He readjusted the fit of his holster and his gun. 'You don't go alone. I'll show you.'

Chapter Twelve

The kitchen was located at the rear of the property. Alain led Trent towards it via the entrance hall and a door that was set into the wall behind the sweeping staircase and the prancing horse statuettes. It was vast and impressive. The units looked to be handmade and they were fitted with white granite countertops that were conspicuously empty aside from a gleaming toaster and a designer kettle. There was a range cooker, an American-style fridge-freezer and numerous pans hanging on racks from the ceiling. Everything looked well ordered and spotlessly clean.

The only food Trent could see was a bowl of fruit on an island unit in the middle of the room. A stainless-steel sink was located there, along with a stylish tap fitted to an extendable hose.

Alain crossed towards a glass-fronted cupboard, his shoes squeaking on the white marble tiles. He selected a tall drinking glass and passed it to Trent.

Trent filled the glass from the tap. He drank greedily. Wiped his lips with the back of his hand when he was done.

He filled the glass a second time. Drained it. Poured a third.

'What about food?' he asked, smacking his lips.

'What about it?'

'Is there anything we could maybe heat up?'

'Do I look like a chef to you?'

Alain stretched out his thickened neck, tilting his boulder-like head from side to side. He ran his finger around the back of his collar. Then he wet his hand from the tap and smeared water across his face.

Trent motioned towards the fridge-freezer. 'Maybe I could take a look for myself?'

'Maybe you couldn't.'

Alain stood before him, water dripping from his flattened nose and dimpled chin onto his stained shirt. He looked haggard and knocked about. The water had moistened the thread of blood beneath his plaster and a diluted red streak was snaking across his cheek.

Trent reached out and grabbed an apple from the bowl. Squeezed it in his hand. He bit into it. Chewed. The skin was waxy, the flesh ripe and sweet and juicy.

'You're still suspicious,' Trent said, a spray of apple accompanying his words.

'It's my job to be suspicious.'

Trent took another mouthful of apple. 'And what else does your job involve?'

The bodyguard didn't respond. Water gleamed on his face. The faint bloody track was forking its way through the pitted stubble on his cheek towards the corner of his mouth.

'It just occurs to me,' Trent said, 'that you must have some level of involvement in Jérôme's import–export business. Helping to make sure the shipments get in safely, maybe?'

Alain raised his arm and dried himself with the sleeve of his shirt. Trent could hear the *scritch* of his stubble against the cotton fabric.

'Philippe exaggerates. You shouldn't listen to him.'

'Hard not to.' Trent gestured around him with the hand holding the apple. 'He seems like the only one who's willing to open up to me.'

'I thought you were a negotiator, not a therapist.'

Trent tore off another chunk of apple and looked idly round the rest of the kitchen. It really was immaculate. The only sign of any crumbs or spills was a light dusting of coffee grounds near the kettle. Alain must have scattered them when he was preparing the coffee for Philippe. Otherwise, the room was as sterile as an operating theatre.

'So who does the cooking here?' he asked.

'There's a housekeeper.'

'Huh. And can she be trusted not to talk about what's going on? Or do we need to come up with an explanation for Jérôme's absence? A sudden business trip, maybe?'

Alain folded his arms across his chest, the Ruger riding up in his shoulder holster. He pinched his biceps with the fingers of his crossed hands. His eyes were hooded. A sign of fatigue or distrust? Maybe a combination of the two.

'Not necessary,' he said.

'Why so sure?'

'She's worked for M. Moreau longer than anyone I know. She could have retired years ago but she prefers not to. She's completely reliable.'

'All staff gossip sometimes.'

'She's more like family than staff. And she has nobody to talk with. She lives here.'

'Here? In the house?'

He motioned back towards the entrance hall with a jerk of his head. 'She has a small place behind the garage.'

'Does she have a phone? She might call somebody.'

'No phone.'

'You're sure.'

He nodded. He was sure.

'Doesn't she have to go out for supplies?' Trent asked.

'We have deliveries.'

'What if she needs something extra? Something unexpected?'

'This never happens.'

'But if it did?'

'I would take her. She can't drive.'

'You'd take her? Not Jérôme's chauffeur?'

Alain raised an eyebrow. His face framed a question.

'It's like I told you,' Trent said. 'I've been watching Jérôme. I've seen the guy who usually does the driving.'

'For your surveillance,' Alain said. His voice was low. It was measured. 'For Jérôme's protection.'

'That's right. Tell me about him.'

The muscles around Alain's mouth twitched. His lip hitched up and Trent caught a glimpse of his canine tooth. 'He doesn't have a phone, either.'

'He lives here, too?'

'By the pool.'

'And you?'

'I have a room in the house.'

'Seniority.' Trent nodded. 'Good for you. Must be cosy having Stephanie around. When Jérôme's busy, say.'

Alain squeezed his biceps some more. 'I told you already. You shouldn't listen to Philippe.'

Trent stuffed the apple in his mouth and clenched it between his teeth. He made a show of checking his watch. It was 3.20 a.m. He wrenched another bite.

'We should go and wake the chauffeur up,' he said, chewing with his mouth open.

'Why would we do that?'

'To ask him what he knows.'

'Knows?'

'It's Saturday morning,' Trent said. 'Friday night last night. Not many chauffeurs get weekends off.'

'He's ill. It's why I was driving.'

'Maybe that's what he told you.' Trent worked his jaw to clear some apple from his teeth. 'But seriously, aren't you the least bit suspicious that Jérôme's driver happened to be off duty on the night his car was run off the road and he was abducted?'

*

It was cool and still and quiet outside. The sky was dark and distant beyond the halogen glare. Trent followed Alain around the perimeter of the house, their feet crunching along a pea-gravel pathway. The light from the security lamps was harsh and unrelenting. It pinned them against the wall. Two big men, walking one behind the other. Their shadows loomed over them like ogres.

'So what's your story?' Trent asked. 'What was your background before Jérôme hired you? Were you army?'

Alain grunted. He let go of the limb of a tropical plant that he'd cleared from his path. It sprang back and slapped Trent in the face.

'Police?'

'No,' Alain muttered.

'Then what?'

Alain's shoulders slumped. 'The truth? I was a squeegee punk.'

'Seriously?'

Squeegee punks were street kids who swarmed around traffic whenever it got snarled up at busy junctions in Marseilles. They'd wash your windscreen whether you wanted them to or not. Some people tipped them. Some didn't. Some found that they happened to get robbed at knifepoint if they had their windows open or their doors unlocked.

Alain marched on. He didn't turn. Didn't look back.

'Not exactly your standard route into this kind of work,' Trent said.

Still Alain didn't say anything.

'How did it happen? Did you respond to an ad in the paper? Retrain in close protection skills?'

Alain hesitated, then finally answered. 'I pulled a gun on M. Moreau. I told him to give me his watch. It was a Rolex. Very expensive.'

Trent whistled. 'And did he?'

'No. He offered me a job instead.'

'Wait.' Trent listened to the tread of their feet on the path. 'He offered you a job right there and then? By the side of the road?'

Alain nodded, his long shadow dipping and rising on the wall alongside him.

'This is what he does. It's why he's rich. He judges people. He does it very fast. He did it to me. He saw something in me. He told me I could

73

be useful to him. That he could teach me. And I believed him.'

'You've worked for him ever since?'

'Eleven years.'

'And he's been good to you?'

'The best.'

Trent fell silent. The cicadas were loud in the shrubs by their side. Gnats and flies and moths swirled around them, drawn by the ceaseless, blinding light and their body warmth.

So Alain was a contented employee. Eleven years' service. Plucked from a life on the streets. Given a fresh start. A rewarding salary and a place to stay in a luxury home, high in the hills of Provence. Invited to become a trusted member of the Moreau family.

It was the kind of background that built fierce loyalty. And in Trent's experience loyalty could compensate for many things. It could lead people to overlook certain character flaws. It could even, on occasion, cause them to participate in something terrible.

Had Alain been involved, he wondered?

And if so, then was Trent walking behind a guy who knew what had become of Aimée?

Chapter Thirteen

They rounded the corner of the villa and the thin gravel path opened up into a landscaped garden. It was well stocked with palms and other exotics, screened by pines and poplars and olive trees. Immediately to their left was a terraced area shaded by vines.

An oval swimming pool dominated the centre of the space. It was lit, like everything else, by the dazzling security lights embedded in the shrubbery. But it was also illuminated by a series of submerged bulbs that tinged the water a murky green. A cloud of midges skimmed the surface. Trent could almost taste the chlorine tang.

Behind the pool was a timber outbuilding with glass doors. It had a pitched roof with a circular window in the eaves. A blind had been pulled down behind the window.

The hut was unlit on the inside but the blazing floodlights revealed the interior. Trent could see a modest sitting area with a wicker couch and chair arranged around a low coffee table and a television. Kitchen units were fitted along the rear. On the left was a ladder leading up to a mezzanine platform. A corner of the ground floor was boxed off beneath it. The bathroom, Trent guessed.

Alain rapped a knuckle on the glass doors.

No answer.

He knocked again, then turned and looked at Trent, his skin wan in the pitiless glare of the security lights, the dried track of blood glimmering on his face like an old scar.

'How long has he worked as Jérôme's driver?' Trent asked.

'A year, maybe.'

'And before that?'

'He was a deckhand on a yacht that Jérôme chartered.'

Not another street kid, then. But someone Jérôme had judged and assessed and offered a new opportunity to, just like he'd done for Alain. More loyalty. Maybe.

Trent cupped his hands to the glass. He peered inside. There was no sign of the driver. He thumped the frame. Felt the panel shake.

Still no response.

'Heavy sleeper?' Trent asked.

Alain grunted and reached inside his trouser pocket. His hand emerged with his ring of keys. He began sorting through them.

Trent went ahead and tried the door handle. It opened right away. The door swung outwards against his toes.

Silence inside.

Trent stepped in. He listened hard. A fridge burbled and hummed.

He scanned the cramped interior. It was sparse and uninviting. The furniture was functional but dated. There were unwashed dishes in the sink. A kitchen bin in need of emptying. The chemical odour of a toilet.

'Serge?' Alain called.

There was no response. No rumblings or stirrings from upstairs.

Alain moved around the wicker couch towards the ladder. He hauled himself up the treads and climbed onto the mezzanine platform. He hit a wall switch and light flooded the sloping timber ceiling. Alain paced around up there, dust sprinkling down from the boards.

'Come,' he said, his voice gruff.

Trent mounted the ladder until his head cleared the platform. Alain was crouched low, his back pressed against the angled ceiling boards, his legs straddling a mattress down on the floor. Tousled sheets were thrown back. The bed was empty. A series of low cupboards were fitted into the eaves beneath the lowered window blind. The cupboard doors were open. They were completely bare.

Chapter Fourteen

One month ago

The modest apartment that Trent shared with Aimée in the Panier district of Marseilles felt emptier every day. There was plenty of *stuff* lying around. Teetering piles of DVDs and old CDs. Stacks of newspapers and magazines. Dirty clothes strewn across the floor and trash on every available surface.

But there was no conversation. No laughter. No knowing glances. No hurried, clumsy shedding of clothes and fumbling with clasps. No warm, twisted sheets.

She was gone. Had been missing for one month already. Without word. Without contact. And as each day passed, Trent experienced a creeping dread. What if he'd made a mistake? What if she hadn't been kidnapped? What if something else had happened? Something worse?

He couldn't contact the police. What would he say? That his fiancée had vanished more than four weeks ago and he hadn't reported it until now because he'd been sure that it was a kidnapping for ransom?

And what if he'd been right the first time around? Maybe it *was* still an abduction and the people behind it were biding their time, making him sweat, making him doubt himself?

The phone wouldn't ring. It never made a sound. It perched silently on the kitchen counter, wired up to some digital recording equipment that had grown dusty with disuse.

How many times a day did he check the line? Two, maybe three to begin with. Then it got worse. He found himself checking all the time. And that was a problem. Because what if they called when the phone was off the hook? What if they waited a day or more before calling again?

He was losing control. He was losing his capacity to *think*.

He'd witnessed this kind of destructive spiral in his clients many times. Watched people crumble before his eyes. Usually he was the one holding everything together. But right now he needed help. An objective assessment of the facts from someone whose judgement he trusted.

He flipped open his mobile and dialled the same guy he'd contacted from Naples.

*

Luc Girard arrived within two hours. Trent led him inside and watched as Girard scanned the living room like he was the first responder to a crime scene. Girard's head turned slowly. He sniffed the air. His bulbous nose wrinkled and he walked across and pushed open a window looking over the shabby square that Trent's apartment fronted onto. There were threadbare trees out there, and splintered park benches, and an old, neglected fountain that was empty of water. Across from Trent's home was a children's nursery with a fenced-in playground. Trent could hear the giddy shouts and howls of the children, their cries piercing and shrill, like a twisted rebuke.

'You look like hell,' Girard said.

Trent gazed down at himself. He was wearing an old pair of jogging trousers and a sleeveless blue vest. The vest was stained with last night's takeaway. He could smell his own odour. A musty fug of dirt and sweat.

'And your apartment is a dump.'

Trent could have told him that he and Aimée had opted to live somewhere unassuming because they preferred not to flaunt their success and aggravate any of the regional kidnap gangs. But then he realised Girard was talking about the mess.

Girard moved across to the breakfast bar that separated the living room from the kitchen. He prodded an empty fast food container.

'Do you have any real food in your apartment?'

Trent stared back. Healthy eating was the last thing on his mind right now.

Girard shrugged and withdrew a crumpled cigarette packet from his back pocket. He clamped a cigarette between his lips and sparked a lighter. He took a swift draw, then gestured phlegmatically with the lit end. Look at us, he seemed to be saying. Look at where we find ourselves now.

Girard had a craggy, deeply tanned face. His worn skin was bunched heavily beneath his eyes into weary pouches and sagged loosely around his drooping mouth and fatty jaw. He'd tried to camouflage his hang-dog expression by cultivating a neat goatee beard, but his true salvation was a leonine mane of fine grey hair. It was long at the front and curled in towards his eyes, habitually blocking his vision until he smoothed it back with a practised sweep of his hand.

Today he had on a yellow sports shirt over grey chinos. Back when Trent had known him as a police detective, heading up a specialist anti-kidnap unit based in Nice, he'd favoured a blue blazer over a shirt and tie. Always the same blazer, worn shiny at the elbows. Always the same tie, blue with diagonal red stripes.

'How's the investigation?' Trent asked.

These days, there was only one investigation. It was the same case Girard had been running all by himself for close to eighteen months.

Girard's lips crinkled around his cigarette. Smoke drifted up past his pouched eyes.

No response. Trent wasn't surprised. In all probability, he was the last person in France Girard would tell.

'No progress?' Trent pressed.

Girard pinched the cigarette between his finger and thumb and plucked it from his mouth. He stared at the burning embers like a guy contemplating setting light to something explosive.

'You've heard nothing?' he asked, circling close to Trent's telephone and bending down to study the recording equipment. Ash tumbled from his cigarette onto the machine and Trent tried not to let it bother him.

'There's been no contact,' he conceded.

'It's been a month already?'

'Four weeks, two days.'

'And her mobile?'

'I still can't get through.'

Girard nodded, venting smoke through his nostrils. He straightened and smoothed back his hair, then strolled behind the kitchen counter and grimaced at the mound of dirty crockery in the sink.

'You understand, I know,' he said, 'that there is a question I must ask.'

'She didn't leave me,' Trent replied.

And right then – *bam* – that precious image of Aimée filled his mind. Sunlight on white sheets and freckled skin. The impish smile on her lips. In her eyes. The hint of a secret about to be revealed. A good one. Long cherished. The fan of auburn hair on her pillow. Her hands clenched slackly above her head. An object in her right fist. Held back from him but familiar all the same.

He blinked and saw that Girard was staring at him. His sunken eyes were damp, pupils jinking left and right, like he could see inside Trent's mind. Could watch the scene play out for himself.

Trent banished the memory. Buried it deep. He nodded for Girard to continue.

'Forgive me,' Girard said, and the wavering note in his voice was almost more than Trent could bear. 'But you know that I've seen it before. A husband, convinced that it's an abduction . . .' His words floated away with the cigarette fumes.

'That isn't what's happened. All her things are still here. Her clothes. Her passport.' He bit hard on the side of his mouth. 'We were happy.'

Deliriously happy, but scarily happy, too. Because from early on in their relationship, even as Trent had marvelled at how perfectly they seemed to fit and how wonderful their life together could be, he'd been unable to escape the lurking dread of the pain he'd experience if someone ever took her from him. Their love had made him vulnerable. Made him fearful. Transformed him into the muddle-headed dope he'd become today.

Girard let the moment spool out. He stood there, unmoving, in his canary yellow shirt and his dumb pleated trousers, smoke weaving up from the cigarette in his hand.

'You've heard nothing about her car?' he asked, finally.

'I've heard nothing about anything.'

'And her friends?'

'There are none I can trust not to go to the police.'

Girard remained impassive. Maybe his retirement had changed things. Maybe the implied barb didn't sting any more.

He plugged the cigarette into the corner of his mouth. Palmed back his hair.

'Nobody threatened you?'

'Plenty of people have threatened me.'

'Anyone in particular? A specific gang?'

'Not lately.'

Girard nodded, the cigarette jerking up and down in his mouth, threads of ash drifting into his beard.

'Who knew that you were in Italy?'

'Anyone could know. I was listed as a speaker on the website for the convention.'

Trent was growing impatient. He shifted his weight between his feet.

Girard held up a palm. He pulled free his cigarette and extinguished it on one of the plates in the sink.

'You ask my opinion?' He exhaled the last of the fumes. 'OK, my opinion is that your fiancée was not kidnapped. And you say she did not leave you. What, then, could have happened to her?'

Trent gaped at Girard like a man staring cruel death in the face. He'd asked for this. Invited it into his home. A second opinion. Only now that opinion was rushing at him too fast. Was too hard and uncompromising. He could taste something foul in his mouth. Like

81

dirty water. Like decay.

'We need to begin by retracing Aimée's movements in the days before she disappeared,' Girard said. 'Who did she meet? Where did she go? I'm sorry, but this is the best way – maybe the only way – to find out who may have harmed her, and why.'

Chapter Fifteen

Alain fumbled with his keys as he led Trent in through the front door of the villa. He found the one he was looking for, then inserted it into the deadlock on a door immediately to Trent's left. The tumblers tumbled and Alain passed inside and hit a light switch on the wall but Trent didn't follow straight away. He was staring at the ring of keys left hanging from the lock.

Most of them were standard house keys. But one was different. It was small and stubby, fashioned from aged brass. Trent was pretty sure it would fit the locks on Jérôme's desk. And it was right there in front of him.

He reached out a tentative hand but Alain chose that very moment to stick his head back into the foyer.

'What are you waiting for?'

Trent closed his fingers into a fist. 'Nothing,' he said. 'Go ahead.'

The room was very cramped. Little more than a cupboard. It was only just big enough for the two men to squeeze inside. It was windowless. The air was stale and the only light source was a twitching fluorescent tube fitted to the low ceiling above. There was a desk, a stool, a microphone and a bank of security monitors.

Trent counted twelve monitors, laid out in three rows of four screens. The screens were small. A different image was flickering on each one. Most were colour. The rest had the green-grey wash of night-vision technology. They were fewer in number, located in areas where there were no security lights.

After ten seconds or so, the screens blanked out for an instant before new footage appeared. Another ten seconds and the screens cycled back to the images Trent had first seen. That gave a total of twenty-four cameras.

The images were all exterior shots. On a quick glance, Trent could see the lighted perimeter of the villa, the swimming pool, the driveway and the view from the fence. A digital clock located in the bottom right-hand corner of each monitor read 03.40.

There'd been far more security cameras than Trent had realised. Those inside the gate were well hidden and he guessed that made sense. The cameras on the fence were there as a deterrent. The rest were designed to capture the movements of anyone who managed to sneak inside.

He leaned towards the monitors, studying the buildings that came up on screen. He could see the main villa, the pool house, the garage and what he took to be the cottage where the housekeeper lived. They were all in colour. But there was another structure, too. A squat and slanted timber building with a bowed roof. Rendered in the ghoulish green of night vision, it was surrounded by a thin copse of blurred trees.

The view Trent was looking at showed a rickety door with shuttered windows on either side. Then the screen went blank, replaced by another angle of the shack, this time from the rear. Two windows this time. One of them was shuttered. The other was boarded up with planks of wood that had been roughly tacked across it. It looked like a cabin from a fairy tale, or maybe a horror movie.

There was no way of telling where the cabin might be found. The tree cover didn't jibe with anything Trent had seen so far.

Alain tapped the microphone bud. 'This is how I talked to you at the gate. And from here,' he said, passing his hand over a control panel that was positioned beneath the bottom rank of monitors, 'I can review everything from the last seven days.'

The controls looked relatively straightforward. There was a grid of numbered buttons, a digital display, a series of switches and several plastic dials.

'Do you move the cameras by remote?' Trent asked. He was thinking of the way his progress along the perimeter fence had been tracked.

'It's possible.' Alain's skin was bleached in the fluorescence from the ceiling light. Trent could see his scalp through his cropped hair. 'But they're also fitted with sensors that can capture movement. I prefer to have them work automatically. I'm not always in this room.'

Trent gazed up at the corners of the confined space and at the wall that pressed in on him from behind. He didn't blame the guy. If it was up to him, he'd spend as little time in this room as he could.

'OK,' Trent said. 'Let's see what you have.'

Alain leaned towards the control panel and flicked a couple of switches. He reached for a dial and twisted it to the left.

The footage on the screens began to rewind. The digital clocks counted backwards. Alain went slowly to begin with and Trent concentrated on the monitors showing the swimming pool and the pool house. He watched footage of himself and Alain walking backwards around the pool to enter the timber hut. Their movements had a clockwork jerkiness, like stop-motion animation. A few seconds of stillness and the two of them emerged from the pool house and jolted backwards through the garden towards the house. Trent's eyes switched to an adjoining monitor. He watched their arms and legs twitch as they reversed along the gravel pathway.

The screens rewound further, a flurry of static and broken horizontal lines. Alain increased the speed. The clocks whizzed backwards in unison.

03.22.

03.10.

Trent caught movement in a screen on the top row. A vehicle had driven by the external gate, its there-and-gone movement repeated in a further three screens.

02.50.

02.20.

Trent saw the blur of a cat or a fox passing the fountain out front. The sightless dazzle of the creature's eyes as it turned its head. Then the stillness of the swimming pool. The mysterious green-lit shack, unmoving, undisturbed, alone among the tangled pines.

01.30.

01.00.

00.27. A number of monitors displayed Philippe's low-slung sports car appearing to reverse from outside the house and along the driveway in a cloud of dust before sweeping out of the gate.

00.00

23.57

A middle screen showed Trent and Alain circling the fountain and following the same route. They bolted back along the moonlit drive. Trent walked out through the gate.

Alain glanced at him. Trent didn't say a word.

He was focused on the uppermost screens, watching himself marching backwards along the fence, eyes bright and lidless in the night-vision glow, finally disappearing from view at 23.29.

A fast scan through another twenty minutes and Trent saw the battered Mercedes reverse along the driveway and out through the gate, its single headlamp twinkling in the dark.

Then stillness. Calm. A flickering, blurred repeat of shot after shot, camera switch after camera switch. The time counted down. The footage shifted even faster.

'Wait,' Trent said. 'There.'

Alain punched a switch. The monitors froze.

21.47.

Trent pointed at the second screen from the left, top row. It showed a colour still of the lighted entrance gate. The gate was swung back a short way. A young black guy was passing through. He was staring up at the camera lens. Eyes fearful and wide, mouth gaping and jammed full of stark white teeth.

'That's him,' Alain said. 'That's Serge.'

He hit PLAY on the control panel. The screens buzzed, then advanced in real time, the counters clicking upwards, second by second.

The chauffeur had sleek, very dark skin. He was slim and boyish, with long limbs and a compact torso, as if he hadn't fully grown into his body just yet. His head looked too big for his trim shoulders, perched on a lean neck, and his jet-black hair was tightly curled. He had on a chequered shirt over faded jeans. A blue holdall was slung over his shoulder.

Trent watched the gate swing closed behind Serge and then the cameras picked him up on the other side, flattening himself against the bars. The holdall was down by his feet and his face was angled to one side, eyes downcast. He looked nervous. His whole body was tensed. Every muscle. Every tendon.

He held the pose for a long time. It seemed to take a lot out of him. Pretty soon he was trembling.

Two minutes elapsed before Alain started to fast-forward. He scrolled through almost eight minutes in total, then hit PLAY again the moment the cameras picked up something else.

A green Toyota Land Cruiser with a plastic bull bar on the front, its headlamps switched off.

A door was flung open from the back and an interior light blinked on. A gloved hand reached out and took Serge's holdall. The kid climbed inside.

'What do you think?' Trent asked. 'Do you picture him as one of the guys with the rifles?'

Alain considered it. He uttered a low, guttural grunt. 'Maybe.'

Trent closed his eyes and visualised the three masked figures who'd leapt out of the jeep. No way was Serge the one who'd advanced on the Mercedes and fired at the windscreen. That guy had been too bulky. Too assured in his movements.

And Trent didn't see him as the man who'd hauled Jérôme out of the rear window. That job required muscle. It required boldness and composure. Those were two qualities Serge seemed to lack.

He could have been the one holding the rifle on Trent. That was possible, for sure. He'd seen anxiety in the guy's eyes. Jitters.

But it was nothing conclusive. He could tell himself that Serge had been on the other end of that rifle, but he didn't know it for sure.

'Maybe he was the driver,' Alain said.

Trent made a humming noise. It was a definite possibility. Serge was a driver by trade. And he knew the Mercedes well. Perhaps he'd figured out the best way to take it down.

But someone else had been driving the Toyota when they picked Serge up. So maybe that guy had been behind the wheel. Maybe Serge had fulfilled a different role entirely.

'One thing's for sure,' Trent said. 'He is involved.'

Alain nodded, distractedly. He was pressing his face close to the monitors. Peering at the screens.

'What is it?' Trent asked.

'Number plate,' Alain said, placing the pad of his forefinger beside the rear of the Land Cruiser. 'I can't read it.'

'Looks like they smeared it with something. Mud or grease.'

'And the front is no good, either.' Alain let the footage spool out, watching as the Toyota passed silently along the fence before moving out of range of the final camera.

'Irrelevant,' Trent told him. 'It's probably stolen anyway.' Then, realising he'd said more than he should have – he didn't want to plant ideas in Alain's mind – he tapped the monitor screening footage of the shack. 'What's that?' he asked.

'It's nothing.'

'Looks like a summer house.'

'It's a wreck. It's falling down.'

And yet it was under surveillance. Two cameras. First the front view, then the rear.

Alain punched a button, jarring the camera feed back to real time, 03.52. All appeared to be still. All calm.

Trent was fixated on the shack. The discreet location. The loose cluster of trees. Those shutters and planks across the windows.

Abruptly, he became conscious that Alain was watching him again.

Assessing him. Gauging him. The fearsome Ruger holstered at his side.

Silence between them. The surveillance monitors whirred and hummed and twitched. The fluorescent light buzzed and flickered. He could hear Alain's breathing. Feel the heat coming off his body. Waited for him to speak. To accuse him of something. Maybe make reference to the photograph in his wallet.

The silence went on. Eventually, Trent broke it.

'We should speak to the housekeeper,' he said. 'Ask her if she knows anything.'

'She won't. There's no chance of that at all.'

'Maybe Serge confided in her.'

'He wouldn't have.'

'Why so sure? Only a short while ago you were certain that Serge was ill in bed.'

Alain muttered something under his breath. He shook his head, exasperated, as though he couldn't quite understand how he hadn't swung for Trent yet.

Then a telephone started to ring.

The noise was distant and muffled but unmistakable.

It was coming from the far side of the house. From Jérôme's study.

Chapter Sixteen

Trent burst into the room and circled behind the desk. He wheeled Jérôme's chair out of the way and snatched up Alain's pad and pencil. He locked eyes with Stephanie.

The telephone was ringing between them.

'Ready?' he asked.

She swallowed, then nodded. Perspiration had broken out across the bridge of her nose. The skin around her eyes was shaded purple.

The telephone kept ringing.

Trent pointed with the tip of the pencil towards the scrap of paper Stephanie had placed on the desk immediately in front of her.

'Follow the script,' he said.

The telephone rang some more.

Philippe had positioned himself to the right of Stephanie. He'd turned the spare chair round backwards and was resting his knee on it. His hands gripped the wooden backrest where Alain's jacket was draped. Alain stood by the side of the desk next to the phone, his bunched fists propped on his waist just below his holstered revolver, his feet spread shoulder width apart.

Trent held the pencil above the notepad. He reached out with his spare hand and hit the tiny rubber button with the loudspeaker icon on it.

A click. A burr. The fuzz of static on the line.

A long moment of silence. Enough for Trent to begin to wonder if he'd cut the caller off.

He checked on Stephanie. She was frozen. She was speechless.

Then he heard breathing on the end of the line. It was ragged. It was harsh.

Trent rolled his hand at the wrist, like a stagehand prompting an actor.

'*Allo?*' Stephanie managed, a dry catch in her throat.

More silence. She opened her mouth as if to talk again.

Then there was a voice.

'We have your husband.'

The voice was male. It was deep and guttural, almost a growl. It sounded constricted somehow. Sluggish. As if the speaker's jaw had been broken and wired back together again. As if he was drowsy on painkillers.

It was a distinctive voice. It was memorable.

Trent remembered it for sure.

His heart bucked in his chest like he'd just been shocked out of a cardiac arrest. He clutched the pencil so tightly that it flexed between his fingers. The lead pressed down on the pad.

'My name to you is Xavier.'

The pencil tip gave out. It crumbled. The jagged lead bore down into the thin paper, punching a hole through the top sheet.

'You speak only with me. Call the police and we kill your husband. Lie to me or try to trick me and we kill your husband. Understand?'

'Yes,' Stephanie replied, her voice rising in panic, as if she were framing a question.

Trent gritted his teeth and made a slashing motion with his hand. Jabbed a finger towards the script.

Stephanie gasped. She fumbled the paper.

'Is Jérôme alive?' she said. 'Is he safe?'

'If you do not pay what we ask, we kill your husband.'

Trent pointed at the prompt sheet again.

'Is he alive? Please. Is he safe? Can you—'

'Enough! If you do not pay what we ask, we kill your husband. Disobey me and we kill your husband. Understand? We kill him.'

'I don't have any money. I cannot—'

'Do not lie to me. Xavier knows when you lie. Lie to me and your husband dies. We kill him. Five million euros. Five million! I will call again within two days. Have the money. No police. Have the money.'

There was a loud clatter and then the phone went dead. A flat tone hummed through the speaker.

Stephanie raised a hand to cover her mouth. She was shaking her head repeatedly.

The telephone continued to hum. Trent ignored it. He scratched a note on the pad with the broken pencil.

5 mil euros. No police. No lies. No tricks. Do not disobey.

Beneath it, he wrote:

Xavier.

He underlined the name twice. The lines were heavy, determined.

Xavier.

A name he knew only too well. A name he'd hoped never to hear again. Especially tonight.

Alain stepped forwards and slapped his hand down onto the speaker. The droning ceased with a fractured bleat. He lifted the receiver and punched in a four-digit code – 3131. He listened for a moment. Frowned. Shook his head.

'Number withheld,' he said.

Trent nodded, distractedly. 'I told you. They're professionals.'

'We could install some equipment for next time. Something to trace the call.'

'I'll source a digital recorder,' Trent told him. 'It can be a useful tool. But there's no point trying to trace them. These gangs use prepaid mobiles. A new phone for every call. It's cheap. It's safe.'

Alain held his gaze for a long beat. His mouth was twisted up in thought.

'Maybe not this time,' he said. 'Maybe they'll slip up.'

'They won't.'

'But we could try. What does it cost us?'

Trent dropped the pencil. It rolled in a semicircle on the desk.

'It costs you Jérôme's life if you make a mistake. How do you get the equipment? Who do you ask? What if they talk? And what do you do with the information even if it works? I told you, this is a negotiation now.'

'The police would have the equipment,' Philippe put in. His skin had taken on a greyish tone but his eyes were alert. He was rocking forwards on his chair. 'We should call them. We need them.'

'Too dangerous.'

'You say. But you also told us the maximum they would ask for is four million. And now they ask for five. We can't pay it.'

'You won't have to. I told you: we negotiate. We talk them down.'

'How?' Stephanie had lowered her hand. Her mouth was slack, her lips cracked. 'How do we do this? He does not listen.'

'It was a first call.' Trent could feel his composure leaking away, like a breach in a gas main. 'They can be that way. Remember, it's about impact for them. It's about unsettling you. This is what I told you would happen.'

'You also told us four million, maximum,' Philippe said again.

Trent bowed his head. He stifled a groan. 'So they went higher. We can still negotiate a reasonable sum.'

'Only if they want to.'

'No. I told you. It's a business exchange. The money for the commodity. They *need* the money.'

'We should call the police.' Philippe was staring at Stephanie forcefully. 'We should call them right now.'

Stephanie glanced at the telephone. 'What if they kill him?' she whispered.

'If they kill him then they were going to do it anyway,' Philippe told her. 'They were going to kill him even if we paid.'

'You're wrong,' Trent said.

'We should call them,' Philippe insisted. 'We should ask for their help.'

Stephanie moistened her lips. She glanced at the phone again, then up at Alain. She was pale and she was trembling. She looked like she was suffering from exposure and Trent supposed that in some ways she was. Exposure to the brutality of the situation they were facing. To the gruelling hours and days that lay ahead.

'What do you say?' she asked Alain.

The bodyguard was frowning down at the phone, cupping his chin in his hand, stroking his stubble. He was thinking hard. His forehead was creased, one eye half-closed in a squint, the sticking plaster crinkled and beginning to peel away from his sweat-soaked brow. He grunted to himself, then looked over at Trent.

Trent felt his gut go light. His pulse throbbed in his temple. All of his calm, reasoned thoughts seemed to be thrashing against the inside of his skull. The first signs of panic setting in. This was the moment when everything could unravel. Involve the police and he lost control. Lost the last vague chance he was clinging onto.

This stranger who was wary of him, this man who'd voiced his suspicions right from the very beginning, who'd kept his Ruger close at hand in case his distrust proved well founded, was all that stood between him now and the jarring wrench of failure.

Alain lowered his hand with a sigh. Tapped his knuckles loosely on the edge of the desk.

'I trust M. Moreau's judgement,' he said, voice firm. He nodded at Trent. 'And he entrusted his life to this man. So for now, we do what he says. We don't call the police.'

Chapter Seventeen

Two weeks ago

'It's Moreau,' Girard said, speaking around the cigarette in the corner of his mouth. He pushed past Trent with a brown paper grocery bag clutched beneath his arm.

Trent lingered by the open front door to his apartment. He'd been waiting to hear Girard's verdict for close to a fortnight. They'd started by working together to draw up a pool of suspects. The list wasn't long. Trent and Aimée didn't have a large social circle in Marseilles, a consequence of moving from Paris only three years ago, combined with the secretive nature of their business. There was always the possibility that she'd run into someone random, a figure they couldn't account for, but Girard had made it clear that the statistics went against it. If she'd been attacked in some way, the strongest likelihood was that the culprit was an acquaintance or one of the clients Aimée had met with in the weeks running up to her disappearance.

A wedge of sunlight slashed Trent's face. The irregular concrete plaza of Place de Moulins was silent and deserted. It was ringed by dirt-smeared cars parked bumper to bumper, unoccupied benches and crooked pastel townhouses showing no sign of habitation. A laundered sheet draped over the ironwork balcony across from him might have been drying for hours or days. There were bins that needed emptying and wilting palms gasping for water. The entire area could have been evacuated for all Trent knew. He hadn't ventured outside in more than a week.

He closed the door and pressed his forehead against the smooth timber. Hope seeped out of him like blood from a wound. He turned in a strange kind of daze – as if his body was somehow disconnected from his mind, or as if every bone had been secretly removed and replaced in completely the wrong order – and shuffled, slump-shouldered, along a hallway that seemed as dark and airless as a subway tunnel.

He found Girard standing behind the breakfast counter, shifting the scree of litter and dirty crockery to one side with his arm. Today, the polo shirt he had on was pale blue, his trousers tan. He set his grocery bag down in the space he'd cleared, like an explorer planting a flag and claiming new territory.

'Clean plates,' he said, and removed a pack of white paper plates. 'And something to drink from.' He showed Trent a tube of clear plastic cups.

Trent stared at him blankly and collapsed onto his couch. Magazines and newspapers crinkled beneath his weight. He was wearing a white T-shirt that was yellowed with age over a pair of blue cotton boxer shorts. He couldn't remember the last time he'd dressed properly.

Cigarette dangling from his mouth, Girard pulled food from the bag like a magician performing an astounding illusion. A crusty baguette, a rounded cheese wrapped in wax paper, some grapes, some olives, a bottle of freshly squeezed orange juice and a clear plastic tub loaded with steaming paella. He delved inside the bag one final time for a plastic fork and paper napkins.

'Eat,' he said, and prodded the paella across the counter.

Trent let his head fall slackly to one side. He stared at the silent telephone. The inert recording equipment.

'Tell me,' he said.

Girard's pouched eyes were wet, the whites tinged yellow, as though stained by nicotine. Whatever he saw in Trent seemed neither to impress nor surprise him. He plucked the cigarette from his lips and set it to rest on the wrapped cheese, then prised open the plastic tub and scooped a forkful of perfumed yellow rice into his mouth.

'Tell me,' Trent said again. 'Why Moreau?'

'Many reasons,' Girard replied, rice tumbling from his lips.

'Such as?'

Girard lifted the plastic tub to his chin. He shovelled paella into his mouth.

'Aimée's appointment diary shows she met with him three times.'

'That's not so unusual.' Trent's voice was flat and emotionless. To his bemusement, he felt the same way. It was like he was watching the scene unravel before his eyes. He pictured himself sitting alone in a darkened cinema, scooping popcorn into his gormless mouth as the Trent on the big screen said, 'Some clients need reassuring about our policies. They don't like to face up to the idea that a kidnap could happen to them.'

And, he thought to himself, a lot of their male clients liked to spend as much time with Aimée as they could possibly justify, perhaps kidding themselves that she was there for reasons other than business. He'd never had any problem with that. He understood her appeal better than anyone. She was very beautiful. Strikingly so. She was given to flirtation and she was funny and sweet. On a couple of occasions, clients had misread her signals. One time, Trent had been forced to step in and insist that a client cool his advances. But it was a risk they were prepared to run. The market they were in was tough. Much bigger firms were often wooing their prospective clients. If Aimée's allure gave them a competitive edge, it was one they were willing to exploit.

'She met with him for dinner once,' Girard said. 'Another time was drinks, on the terrace of the Intercontinental.'

The Trent in the movie continued the dialogue, even as it rang tinny and untrue in his ears. 'She's never worked set hours. It's the nature of the business. She meets clients when and where they choose. We don't have a separate office. And we don't bring clients here.'

In truth, Trent rarely met their clients at all unless something went wrong for them. He was good at crisis management, bad at small talk. Aimée was different. She excelled at client liaison. She was courteous and patient and charming. She was willing to spend hours going over the small print of an insurance policy. She was prepared to court clients for as long as it took for them to sign on the dotted line. Complementary skills. A strong partnership. Aimée was the public face of their operation, and for most clients – the lucky ones – she was the only representative they'd ever meet. Trent was the guy in the background, in the shadows. His natural habitat.

K & R was an industry they'd found themselves operating in via separate routes and one that had brought them together when Trent had first been assigned to Paris. Aimée was the local insurance specialist, Trent the trained negotiator. They'd been colleagues for almost a year without acknowledging the attraction between them. It was a small office with a close-knit team. The work was highly stressful. Added complications, no matter how tempting, were to be avoided at all costs.

Then Athens happened. The wife of the CEO of a metal trading conglomerate was abducted. The scenario became a long-drawn-out affair. The client was a flake who kept flip-flopping on Trent's advice. Eventually, Trent's boss took the unprecedented step of flying Aimée over to assist. It became her job to encourage the CEO to view Trent's advice with twenty–twenty vision, rather than through the prism of his own fear and paranoia. Aimée's involvement didn't sit comfortably with Trent. He'd never required anyone's help before. But he had to admit that her input turned things around. The client began to listen to him. After a seven-week marathon of high-wire negotiation, Trent and Aimée secured the wife's release. They returned to Paris as lovers.

From the first moment, Trent prepared himself for the worst. He was a guy who'd built his career by doing precisely that. But to his surprise and consternation, their relationship deepened. The foundations were strong. They had a shared bond. A mutual understanding of the darkness that lurked behind everyday life. An awareness of how easily the facade of safety and security could be punctured by a group of people with the means and the motivation to cause devastating harm.

People not unlike the man who Girard claimed had wrenched his fiancée from him.

Girard said, 'Aimée listed the locations for her first two meetings with Moreau in her diary. But for the third, she had only a time and Moreau's name.'

'Then perhaps the name and the time was enough for her. Or perhaps the location hadn't been fixed.'

'Perhaps.' Girard brushed the rice free from his beard. He smoothed his hair back from his eyes with the hand holding the fork. 'The meeting was at four o'clock on the day before you called me from Naples.'

'We've been through this already. She had other appointments that day.'

Girard nodded. 'And it took time for me to clear them. I couldn't just call these people up, you understand.'

'But you did clear them?'

'All except Jérôme Moreau. Tell me, how much do you know about him?'

The Trent in the room lay inert on the couch. He was sinking down into the cushions. His nerves seemed to be growing more numb with every passing second, like he'd been injected with a dose of anaesthetic and now his entire body was shutting down, fibre by fibre, cell by cell.

'Aimée researches all our clients,' he said. 'But some of it we knew already.' Trent summoned all his concentration and managed to roll out his bottom lip. He guessed it'd look good up there on the silver screen. 'He's very wealthy. Operates a yachting concern.'

Girard swallowed more paella, nodding for Trent to go on.

'At least,' Trent said, 'the yacht trading is the public side of his business.'

'So then you do know.' Girard lifted an oily shrimp from the rice. He sucked the juices from it. Slipped it into his mouth and licked his fingers clean.

Trent would have shrugged if he could, but his body felt heavy as lead. 'A lot of our wealthier clients want the protection we can offer them because they have income streams that aren't entirely legitimate. They mix with different levels of society.'

'Criminal levels.' Girard dropped the tub of paella onto the counter and nudged it aside. He mopped his lips with one of the napkins. Picked up his cigarette and plugged it back into his mouth. 'Moreau is a smuggler. Mostly it's drugs from North Africa. Sometimes firearms.' He drew hard on the cigarette. 'Sometimes it's women. Or children.'

'We don't judge our clients. We can't afford to.'

Girard smoked some more. He tapped ash into the paella. His gaze didn't shift from Trent's face.

'So you're an idealist now,' Trent said.

'His operation is sophisticated,' Girard replied, as if there'd been no interruption to his explanation. 'And his approach is sophisticated, too. He never touches the merchandise. He simply puts his yachts at the disposal of others. This is all.'

'So he's a facilitator.'

Girard nodded.

'For bad men,' Trent said.

'Very bad men. Plus, he knows who to pay and he pays very generously.'

'The police?' Trent asked.

Girard inhaled from his cigarette, raising his eyebrows in a lazy fashion, as if it went without saying.

'Who else?'

'Customs officials.' His voice was husky with smoke. 'Port employees. Local government workers. Some judiciary.'

'Quite a list.'

'He makes public donations, too. He's a patron of the Ballet National de Marseille. His wife is a former dancer. Retired early.'

Trent felt his jaw begin to lock. The deadening had reached his neck. His throat. He could barely swallow. 'Get to the point, Girard.'

Girard scratched his eyebrow, cigarette burning close to his looping fringe. 'I have a friend. An old colleague. His niece dances with the Ballet National. He arranged it so I could speak with her.'

Trent's body seemed to pivot and tilt without his say-so. Magazines and newspapers crackled beneath him.

'I met with her at the Gare St Charles. She was nervous. She made me promise that Moreau would never know that she'd talked with me.'

'Go on.'

'She told me that Moreau pays some of the girls to perform for him. In private, at a villa he keeps in Cassis. He has a thing for ballet dancers.' He gestured with his cigarette, rolling his hand at the wrist, tracing circles with the lit end. 'This girl, the niece of my friend, she tells me she will never go.'

'Because he expects the girls to do more than just dance?'

'For sure. Of course.'

'So he's a rich guy who likes to cheat on his wife with young women. That's not so unusual.'

'Perhaps.' Girard bunched his fists on the kitchen counter, smoke rising up from the cigarette wedged between his knuckles. 'There are just a few girls who dance for him often. They joke about it sometimes. About him. They told my friend's niece that she should do it. That she could make good money. They told her flatmate, too. A girl from Grenoble. She was new to Marseilles. New to the dance company.'

'She went along with it?'

Girard leaned forward over the counter, dead-eyed. 'She danced for him. He complimented her. Told her how well she moved and how fine her body was. He asked to see it. Asked her to dance naked.'

'She refused?'

Girard barely shook his head, like he didn't want to break the spell he'd fallen into. 'She's a dancer. Her body is her life. What does she have to be ashamed of? So she agreed. But naturally, he wanted her to do more than just dance.'

'He slept with her.'

'He tried. She said no.' Girard blinked. 'So he hurt her,' he said, with a sigh of regret. 'Very badly. To begin with, she would not talk about it when she returned home. But she was crying, upset. And she was bruised. Her torso. Her waist. She could not dance. For a month, at least. Then, when she healed, she went back to Grenoble. She refused to speak with anyone at the ballet.'

'Because he's a patron. He threatened her in some way.'

'Of course. But she talked just a little to my friend's niece. She warned her never to go. She said he had a terrible temper. Told her that he was dangerous.' He paused. His voice dropped an octave. 'She believed he might have killed her.'

Trent's mouth was dry. His tongue flaccid and limp. He wondered if this was how it felt to suffer a stroke. This drip-drip paralysis. 'But what does this have to do with Aimée?' he whispered, hoarsely.

'Before he was finished attacking her, this girl broke free from him. She locked herself inside a bathroom. She was very scared. He tried to get in. He was in a rage and it terrified her. He made many threats.' Girard's mouth drooped at the corners. 'So she escaped. She climbed out through the window.'

'OK.'

'But as she was running away from his villa, a car turned into the entrance. The driver braked hard but still the car hit her a little. The girl fell onto the bonnet. She stumbled but she didn't stop. She kept running. But she saw the driver. It was a woman. And seeing this is what she cannot forget. Because Moreau had been angry already. And she feared how he would react when he found that she was gone. She was afraid that he would take revenge on this woman in the car.'

Trent's body was stone now. Immobile.

'I asked for the date when this happened. My friend's niece remembered very clearly. It was a Thursday, a little over six weeks ago. It was the day before you first called me from Naples.' Ribbons of smoke coiled up from his cigarette, waving and writhing in front of his sunken eyes. 'The car was a blue Clio,' he said. 'The same as Aimée's.'

Chapter Eighteen

Trent found himself standing alone with Alain, out by the damaged Mercedes and the dusty red Japanese sports car Philippe had beached beside the fountain. The security lights blazed around them but the sky was beginning to lighten from indigo black to shades of grey. Fifteen minutes more and the sun would be up. Maybe the lamps would finally be turned off.

'You backed me in there,' Trent said. He couldn't quite disguise his puzzlement.

Alain shrugged. He was wearing his tailored grey jacket again. 'You were right about Serge.' He exhaled wearily, mouth curled into a tired and sheepish half-smile. 'Should I tell them about him?'

'Maybe later. Let them sleep first.'

'I'm going to check the pool house again. He must have been communicating with them in some way.'

'He'd be a fool to have left anything behind.'

'He is a fool. He betrayed M. Moreau.'

'We should speak with the housekeeper. We should do it now.'

'I'll do it. But not right away. When she wakes up. It's better if I'm alone. She's worked with M. Moreau for too long to talk with a stranger in the room.'

Trent made a low humming noise. He gazed off along the driveway, as if he almost expected the chauffeur to be walking back towards them through the hazy grey.

'I can drive you,' Alain said. 'There are more vehicles inside the garage. You were right about that, too.'

'Better you stay here. Get some rest.'

'And if your car doesn't start?'

'Return my mobile and I'll call you. My Beretta, too.'

Alain cocked his head to one side and held Trent's eye for a beat. Then he grunted and smiled his wan, fatigued smile again, like a guy reluctantly facing up to paying out on a losing bet. He fished inside his trouser pocket for a plastic key fob that he jabbed towards the Mercedes. The car squawked and its shattered indicators blinked. Alain opened the driver's door, the hinge straining and scraping against the distorted front wing. He reached across to the passenger side, released a catch on the glove box and retrieved Trent's pistol.

'Somewhere safe,' Trent muttered.

Alain backed out of the car and weighed the Beretta in his hand. He assessed Trent with one last, lingering look. Then he extended his arm.

Trent took the pistol. He stripped it and counted the rounds. Thirteen left. He palmed the magazine back in, lifted up his shirt and slipped the pistol into the waistband of his jeans.

Alain delved a hand into his rear pocket and lifted Trent's mobile between his finger and thumb. 'You have a number for this? In case we need to talk?'

Trent took the mobile and flipped it open. He entered his numerical security code.

'It has a number but I don't know it. Tell me yours. I'll call you.'

Alain recited the sequence and Trent typed it in, then hit CALL. A few seconds later, Trent heard a muted chirp coming from the chest pocket of Alain's jacket. A faint blue light pulsed through the charcoal fabric.

'I took the card from your wallet, too,' Alain said. 'It lists a number in Marseilles?'

'My home phone,' Trent told him. 'But try this mobile first. And don't call me from the phone in Jérôme's study. The gang could be trying to get through to you at the same time.'

He nodded to the bodyguard, just once, an abrupt and businesslike farewell between two professionals, and then he pocketed his mobile and turned and marched off along the driveway, his feet pounding the gravel. He didn't look back over his shoulder but he could sense Alain's eyes on him. He made a conscious effort to relax his shoulders and swing his arms and glance from side to side as he walked. Like an average guy out for a stroll. Like a typical visitor with a perfectly reasonable degree of curiosity about his surroundings.

But his prying was far from ordinary. He was searching very hard. He hadn't timed it exactly right. A thin band of hazy pink was just visible beyond the hills on the opposite side of the valley. Another ten minutes and it would have been perfect. But for now the light was still a little murky. He could see a tangle of treetops off to his far right, but it was hard to say if it was the location he was looking for. The ramshackle cabin might be somewhere else altogether.

He logged the possibility all the same, then strode on through the cool morning air. Dust drifted up around his ankles and hands. His Beretta tapped a regular percussive beat against the flesh of his back.

He fixed his attention on the neat rows of cypress trees he was passing. The trunks were lean and straight and protected by dry, toughened bark. And somewhere up above, in amongst the greenery, surveillance cameras were recording his every movement.

He listened keenly for the buzz and whirr of servos or the hum of an electric feed. He searched the ground for raised troughs where cables could have been buried. It took a long time for him to spot what he was looking for. He was close to giving up. But finally he glimpsed a grey plastic junction box screwed to a trunk he was approaching, just above the lowest branches. He traced upwards from the box, following some black electrical wiring. But the camera evaded him and finally he averted his eyes.

The fence was up ahead, at the base of the slope. He could see the cameras fitted to the gate. And as he got close, he could hear them swivel in the stillness. They turned and pivoted and zeroed in on his location.

He walked on, not breaking his stride. The gate buzzed and clunked and dropped on its hinges, then began to swing inwards. He veered right and passed through the gap and out into the middle of the road. The gate shuddered to a halt, then jerked backwards and arced smoothly towards him until it closed with a *thunk* and a long droning buzz.

The cameras spun and dipped and focused down at him. He paused and glanced up and stared into a single lens. He didn't wave. Didn't smile. He simply looked up through the little disc of manufactured glass, picturing his image shuttling through apertures and circuit boards and wires, buzzing back along the driveway, back inside the villa to the cramped and airless security room, materialising on the flickering colour monitor that Alain was sure to be studying. *How much do you know, big guy?* he was thinking. *Are you afraid of me now?*

Chapter Nineteen

Nine days ago

Trent stared at the lens of a security camera mounted on the steel post just inside the solid green gate. It was pointing towards him across the wet night-time street.

He was sitting in the front passenger seat of Girard's Saab. Girard was smoking beside him, slumped low in the olive rain mac he had on. Trent had cracked his window to release the drifting fumes.

'You're certain the cameras are disabled?' Trent asked, not for the first time.

Girard said nothing. Trent turned to find him staring, impassive, the collar of his mackintosh high around his neck. The pouches of leathery skin beneath his sunken eyes appeared more swollen than ever. Perhaps he was getting some way towards feeling as weary as Trent.

'I don't like that we're relying on somebody else.'

Girard took a contemplative puff. 'Tell me,' he said, his voice pinched, 'if a pipe burst inside your home, what would you do?'

Trent blinked at him, the smoke getting in his eyes, making them sting.

'Or if your electricity failed? What then?'

'I'd fix it.'

'And if you couldn't?'

'I'd call someone.'

Girard drew on his cigarette some more, allowing the silence to linger.

'No.' He released a plume of smoke from the side of his mouth. 'You'd call an expert.'

'But your expert is a criminal.'

'The best I know.'

'Can we trust him?'

Smoke writhed before Girard's face. Darkness swelled in his moist eyes. 'It's not a profession that offers guarantees.'

'But you believe him?'

'He told me it was done.' He shrugged. 'You paid him very well.'

Trent looked back across the drenched street. Only an hour ago, during their drive along the coast from Marseilles, they'd watched the storm rage over Cassis. They'd seen the flicker and flash of sheet lightning, the low, bundled mass of raging clouds. But as they'd sped closer, it had felt as if they were chasing the storm away. The lightning and the thunder had stalked on along the coast. The rain that had lashed the windscreen in desperate bursts was now little more than a faint, moist haze, like coastal fog.

Trent opened his door and stepped out into a shallow puddle. He smelled soaked tarmac and saturated foliage and damp earth. Water dripped off the chicken-wire fence behind him. Misted wetness clung to his face and hands.

The gate that guarded the entrance to the villa was a single moulded panel of thickened steel. It was as high as his shoulder, topped with metal barbs. The wall alongside it was even taller.

He could see the sloping roof of the villa just beyond, the terracotta tiles slick with rain. The cluster of bushy trees that surrounded the property were weighed down and dripping with moisture.

He felt oddly numb. He'd been sure that he would sense something when he got here. Some kind of cosmic signal. A tightening of his scalp. Perhaps a whispering in his ear – a haunting trace of Aimée's voice that only he could hear.

But there was just the wetness and the stillness and the creepy, muted vacuum of a neglected street in the first moments following a storm.

The surveillance camera stared blindly at him.

He hoped.

Trent dropped from the wall into soft mulch and rain-soaked shrubs. Thorny branches snagged his dark jacket as he pushed his way through onto a dewy lawn shrouded beneath knee-high ribbons of mist. The villa was smaller than Trent had anticipated. Two storeys, perhaps three bedrooms. But it had large arched picture windows on the ground floor to make the most of the view. And the view was staggering.

A rectangular infinity pool, perched at the very edge of high sea cliffs, framed the outlook. Ahead was only ocean. Blue-black and shimmering. Undulating and cresting. Hemmed down by the swirling bank of menacing grey clouds.

Way off to the left, Trent could see the hazy blur of the storm squall passing on. A single light blinked and dipped in the dark. A buoy, or perhaps a lone ship. The tiny fishing harbour of Cassis was just out of sight.

'It makes you wonder, doesn't it?' Girard asked. He stepped onto the squelching grass alongside him, brushing damp leaves from the sleeves of his mackintosh.

Trent jerked his head around.

'Are you living the wrong life?' Girard pointed his chin towards the view. 'Bend some rules and all this could be yours.'

'It's just a house,' Trent mumbled.

He turned to face the villa and ripped free the Velcro fastener on a pocket on his cargo trousers. He removed a heavy Maglite torch. Slapped it against his gloved palm. Girard's specialist had been tasked with disabling the electricity supply as well as the security cameras, so there'd be no lights inside. Later, Girard would contact him and give him the all clear to come back and reconnect everything before dawn.

'Which door?' Trent asked.

'Middle one.'

Trent twisted the torch lens and a powerful white beam pierced the foggy dark. He swung it downwards, fixing a pair of French doors in the centre of the blazing spotlight. He walked towards them, the beam bouncing with his movements and reflecting off the blackened glass until the glow centred in on the glinting brass door furniture. A key was poking out of the lock, just as Girard's contact had said it would be. Trent rotated the key, then removed it and slipped it into his pocket.

He snatched a breath, seized the handle and twisted it in one fluid movement.

The door opened outwards. No resistance whatsoever.

Trent listened very carefully. He could feel a tightening in his thighs – a tensing of the muscles he'd need to call on if the alarm started to wail.

But he heard no piercing squeal. There was only the low, wheezing burble of the swimming-pool pump, the distant crash and shuffle of the surf at the base of the cliffs, and Girard's ragged breath on his neck.

'How do we know your man hasn't disturbed anything?' Trent hissed. 'Or taken something?'

'He's a professional.'

'He's a thief.'

'You're nervous,' Girard said. 'I understand it. But we mustn't delay.'

Girard didn't understand. How could he? Somewhere inside this house, through this very door, Trent might come face to face with his deepest fear. He might find the proof that Aimée was lost to him for good. That she was never coming home. That the source of all the warmth and light in his life had been extinguished for ever.

His hand trembled, the torch beam vibrating as he aimed it through the gap in the door and cast it around. The spotlight jinked left and right and back again. It revealed a living room with a sleek open-plan kitchen at the rear. The furniture was spare but high-end. The pieces looked to have been carefully selected. There was a lot of cream leather and metal and glass. A display case off to the right contained a model of some kind of super-yacht.

'Come.' Girard reached inside his jacket and removed a torch of his own. He clicked it on, pointed the beam at the ground and nudged Trent forwards.

Trent's movements were painfully slow, like he was submerged in water, and it took an age for him to pass through the door. He swallowed drily. Listened to the buzz and click in his ears. Felt the stillness envelop him and numb his senses.

He stood very still, adjusting to the unlit space and the sensation of his heart firing like a machine gun in his chest. Girard glided past him and cast his torchlight around the kitchen. The counters were bare. He opened cupboards and closed them again. He slid drawers out and in.

There was a door on the far right. Girard inclined his head towards it. Trent swallowed a lump the size of his fist and forced himself to step around by the yacht in the display case, his boots leaving damp treads on the pale marble floors.

He clenched the stippled aluminium casing of the torch and followed Girard into a large garage, cool in temperature. Concrete floor, painted breezeblock walls, a pair of up-and-over doors fitted to an electric mechanism. There was space for two vehicles inside but only one was parked there.

Trent felt the floor tilt beneath him. The car ballooned in his vision, then slammed into focus.

A blue Renault Clio. The driver's door was scratched and dented. The silver diamond emblem was missing from the front.

Aimée's car. Unmistakable. No doubt about it.

He staggered forwards. Extended his gloved hand in slow, jerking increments and tentatively spread his fingers on the window glass. A groan escaped his mouth.

He fumbled downwards. Grasped the catch. Wrenched open the door.

The scent of her favourite perfume rushed out at him. Notes of citrus and jasmine. A synthetic embrace.

He grasped the steering wheel. Bent forwards and mashed his cheek into the plastic. A horrible logic was bearing down on him. *Aimée was very beautiful. Strikingly so. She was given to flirtation and she was funny and sweet. On a couple of occasions, clients had misread her signals...* He thought of Jérôme's *terrible temper*. The rage he'd been in with the dancer who'd spurned his advances. Had Aimée done the same thing? Had Jérôme snapped?

The sound of cautious footsteps roused him and he became aware of Girard stepping around the back of the car. A short pause, then Trent heard the *clunk* of the boot mechanism, then nothing more. The silence lingered. Slowly, Trent raised his eyes to the rear window. He could see Girard's gloved hand on the boot lid.

He stumbled round to join him in a daze.

But all the boot contained was Aimée's spare umbrella and the warning triangle Trent had equipped her with in case she broke down.

He tried to speak. Found that he couldn't. He dumbly opened and closed his mouth as a stinging wetness clouded his vision.

'I'm sorry,' Girard said, voice pitched low. 'You can wait outside, if you prefer...'

Trent shook his head roughly and backed away from the car and burst through the door into the kitchen before his thoughts could catch up to his actions. He lurched through into a hallway, torchlight arcing wildly from side to side. The front entrance to the villa was ahead of him. Stained-glass panels on either side of a glossy black door. There was a carpeted staircase to one side. Trent clambered up.

The balcony at the top overlooked the darkened foyer. Girard came pacing along behind him, his torch projecting a fast-moving disc onto the floor.

Four closed doors led off from the balcony. Trent burst through the one immediately facing him. It opened into a luxurious bathroom. Beige tiles lined the floor and walls. There was a walk-in shower cubicle and a sculpted bathtub. The fittings were high-quality, the soft white towels fluffy and dense.

A mirror above the sink jabbed the flare of his torch back at him. He shielded his face with his arm, then lowered the beam and caught sight of his macabre reflection. His face was gaunt against his liquid black clothing, lips peeled back from gums and teeth.

He wheeled away towards a pebble-glass window positioned over the toilet. It hinged open from the top and looked just large enough for a slim person to climb through. A ballet dancer, say.

Trent seized the handle. He twisted it and forced the unit outwards. It opened very wide. He poked his head through the gap, water dripping onto him from the plastic frame. He shone his torch into the vaporous, shimmying black. A wooden trellis was fitted to the wall just below. Scented plants were knotted around it. It was no ladder but it was just possible that it could bear a young woman's weight. Especially one as light and athletic as a ballet dancer.

Trent was poised to withdraw his torch when he felt a hand on his shoulder. He reared upwards and whacked his head on the window.

'My friend,' Girard said. 'Something you should see.'

Trent clutched his hand to the back of his skull. Girard's expression was sombre. His eyes quivered with a sorry pleading.

'Show me,' Trent managed, before following Girard out of the bathroom towards the open door that lay in wait.

Girard led him into a generously proportioned bedroom. Trent's torchlight revealed a low double bed, neatly made, with a plain grey duvet and plenty of cushions. He saw two bedside units and a single armchair that faced one entire wall of mirror-glass panels. A rounded wooden beam was fitted horizontally across the mirrors at approximately waist height. A balance barre.

So this was where Moreau had made dancers perform for him. Perhaps some had been happy to do it. But at least one of the girls had been terrified.

Girard coughed discreetly and squatted next to a circular rug in the middle of the floor. He aimed his torch downwards and rolled the rug back. There was a rusty brown stain shaped like a lopsided figure eight on the cream carpet beneath.

Trent swayed. He reeled.

'Could be the dancer's,' he muttered.

'We can test it,' Girard replied. 'Take a sample. I can speak to some people I trust.'

'Probably the dancer's,' Trent said again.

But even as he spoke, there was more still to come. He'd spotted something. It was glinting at the edge of the pool of light being cast by Girard's torch.

The item was down on the floor, nestled behind the foot of the bed. Swinging his own torch into the space, Trent slumped to his knees and reached out a lifeless hand.

A necklace.

Fine silver chain, as fragile as spider's silk. The chain was threaded through a solid silver locket. It was polished and smooth, a perfect oval. He removed his gloves and held the necklace in his quaking palm. The clasp was broken. It looked like it had been forced apart. He wedged his squared-off thumbnail beneath the locket's delicate catch. The lid flipped open and a wrenching moan funnelled out from him.

Trent was staring at a picture of himself.

And – *bam* – now he was back in his own bedroom, two months before, his sleep-gritted eyes watering against the dazzling sunlight streaming in through the Venetian blind. Aimée was beside him, her lush hair fanned out on her pillow. She'd just elbowed him awake and was biting down on her lip, fighting a grin. It was a fight she was losing. Her eyes danced with delight. With anticipation of a secret about to be revealed.

And he looked up. Up past her twisted lips and arched eyebrows. Up to her clenched fist. To the object she was holding. White plastic. A stick. There was a tiny greyscale display on it. A symbol on the display. It was a perfect circle with a facsimile grin. A smiley face.

'Wake up, *papa*,' Aimée cooed, and then she reached for her phone on the bedside table and snapped this image of Trent – the very one he was holding in his hand inside the locket – looking startled, dazed, a big stupid grin on his face.

'For me,' she whispered, and her smile was as bright as the sunlight streaming into the room. 'A memory to keep. The day our lives changed for ever.'

*

Later, outside on the misted lawn, Girard was saying, 'Let me contact the right people.' He was talking in an urgent rush, his hand on Trent's shoulder, his voice at his ear. 'I'll speak to the best detectives I know. Honest men and women. They'll arrest Moreau. They'll pressure him until he tells us what happened here.'

Trent's head pitched forwards and he spat up more bile onto the rain-swamped grass. He was listing to one side, the torch gripped limply in one hand, the locket held tightly in his other fist.

'You said it yourself.' Trent's voice was trancelike. Weak. 'He pays the right people. He has influence. Protection.'

'He *has* Aimée.'

Girard didn't say that she was likely dead. He didn't need to.

'No police,' Trent told him. He stared mournfully at the tricksy darkness out at sea. The swirling waters and hidden tides. The dark mysteries lurking beneath. 'Promise me. We search this place. The house. The grounds. All of it.'

'And if we can't find her? What then?'

'Then I'll get to him,' Trent said. 'I'll take him. And I'll force him to tell me what I need to know.'

Chapter Twenty

The sky was a barely-there blue by the time Trent reached the Peugeot. The damage wasn't as bad as he'd feared. The front bumper was cracked and hanging down close to the flattened tyre, and the catch on the bonnet had sheared away so that the bent metal lid was raised upwards like a gaping mouth. A few splintered fragments of headlamp remained, but most of the clear plastic was sprinkled on the dusty ground amid the remnants of the fake number plate he'd attached.

Trent had seen many vehicles in a worse state of repair being driven round Marseilles on a daily basis. The French often used the bumpers of other cars to help them park. They thought nothing of scratching a door or denting a panel. So he didn't foresee a problem with driving the Peugeot back into the city, provided he could patch it up.

The car was equipped with a jack and a wheel-nut wrench and a spare wheel, so the puncture wouldn't be a problem. And he had other tools at his disposal. They were mostly stashed in the rear, where he'd folded the seats down, leaving plenty of space for a man to be laid flat and covered over with the tarpaulin and the blankets he'd spread out. There were ropes there. Plus cuffs for ankles and wrists, as well as a roll of high-tensile duct tape that he could use to lash the bonnet shut and the bumper back into position.

He unlocked the car and climbed in behind the wheel, moving aside the ski mask and his new pair of black leather gloves, eyes drifting to the scarred wooden stock of the shotgun that was wedged into the footwell.

All of the equipment he'd diligently assembled was useless for now. He'd acquired it and laid it out so carefully and it looked sort of forlorn, like a buffet for a party guest who'd failed to show up.

He grunted. The same way Alain tended to grunt. Maybe it was catching.

He was hot and sweating copiously. He was very thirsty.

There was a bottle of water in the glove box. Some snack food, too. Potato crisps and a pack of cold pancakes and some chocolate. It was no feast but it would have been enough to sustain him if the abduction and interrogation he'd planned to carry out had gone on for any length of time.

He drank the water, listening to it glug down his throat, wishing he had some fresh coffee. He felt drained and sluggish from lack of sleep. The blunt aroma of dried sweat rose up from his body. It had soaked into his denim shirt. He lowered his window, reached into his pocket and removed his wallet. He flipped it open. Thumbed out the picture of Aimée.

He smoothed his fingers over the worn surface. Over her dazzling smile. He allowed himself, just for a moment, to remember how he'd removed her sunglasses and she'd cried, only an hour or so later, when he'd dropped to one knee on the burning sand and opened the blue felt box with the ring inside. How he'd uttered those fateful words, asking her to spend the rest of her life with him. How they'd embraced and kissed. How she'd leaned back to slip on the ring and he'd rested his palm on her bronzed abdomen and given the smallest, slightest squeeze to the baby she was carrying.

It was too much. He could still remember the feel of her skin, the taste of sun lotion as he bowed his head and kissed her just below her navel. He jammed the photo away, the wallet in his pocket. He tossed the water aside and twisted the key in the ignition, and the engine coughed and spluttered, then fired up no problem at all.

Trent slapped the dash. The chassis vibrated and shook beneath him. The diesel unit rumbled. He slipped the Peugeot into first and edged across the dusty road in a looping arc, the punctured tyre slapping wetly against the tarmac. He stopped at the opposite side, then reversed towards the edge and finally set off in the direction he'd come from the previous night.

He didn't drive fast. Third gear was enough. The Peugeot was slumped down on the left. The flattened rubber pattered limply.

He crouched forwards over the wheel, scanning the ground on his right. It was mostly rock. Some scrub and weeds and isolated pines. He was thinking back in his mind to the night before. He was trying to recollect the exact sequence of events and figure out how far the Mercedes had managed to go on after the Land Cruiser had bashed into it the first time.

Not far. He found what he was looking for within a couple of hundred metres. There was a steep sandy slope on his right. Tyre tracks in the dirt.

Trent eased the Peugeot to a halt and cut the engine, then stepped out and got down on his haunches. The tracks were clear and distinctive. Off-road tyres. The treads had bit hard into the loose earth. The dry night air hadn't disturbed them in the slightest.

He pushed up from his knees and followed the tracks up the slope. The incline was steep and the sandy earth was loose underfoot. It rushed down in tiny avalanches and stony cascades from around his feet. No way could the Peugeot make it up here. Even the Land Cruiser must have struggled. Trent could see deep gouges in the dirt where the wheels had locked and slipped. On the way up or the way down? Impossible to tell. But the gang's choice of vehicle suggested a reasonable amount of planning. It implied they'd chosen this spot deliberately and had selected the Land Cruiser to make good use of it. Maybe Serge had helped with that.

He scrambled his way to a rocky shelf some twenty feet up. The area was broadly circular in shape and there was enough space to turn a vehicle between the sparse collection of pines that ringed the front edge of the plateau and the giant boulders and limestone cliff-face that teetered over it from behind. There were tracks here, too. A series of parallel, curving tyre treads that bisected one another, describing a three-point turn. And there were footprints. More than one set. They were large and very clear. Heavy boots, Trent guessed. Not so dissimilar from the prints his own boots were leaving. They were mostly concentrated around the tyre tracks, although some headed off in other directions.

Trent followed a set that led towards a knot of pines. He palmed aside a branch and stood still for a moment, listening hard and breathing slow. The scent of resin was strong. He could hear the hum of distant traffic and the buzz of summer insects. The broad valley was laid out beneath him. Fields and vineyards and low, flat buildings, colours bland in the early morning light. He could see the autoroute, and much closer still, almost the entire length of the narrow ribbon of cracked asphalt that slanted up the side of the escarpment towards where he was standing. It was a terrific view. An excellent surveillance point.

He glanced down at his feet. The prints he'd followed stopped right where he was standing. In front of him, a patch of damp wild grass and herbs had been flattened, as if pressed down by something long and thin, like a log. Trent dropped to his knees. He laid himself out in the space, face down. His body fitted inside the impression almost perfectly, except it extended a little way beyond his feet. He rested his elbows on the ground and raised his curled hands to his eyes, miming a pair of binoculars. His view along the road was unobstructed. And he was about as well hidden as it was possible to be.

So this was where their lookout had been positioned. He'd lain prone here and he'd watched the road very carefully, very intently, until he'd seen the first blip from the headlamps of the Mercedes, followed by the visual echo of the Peugeot's lights. And then what? He'd pushed himself up and called to the driver to start the Land Cruiser's engine? He'd instructed the gang to jump inside the vehicle? He'd kept watching until the last possible moment, then hauled on his ski mask and jumped inside the jeep with an assault rifle clutched in front of him, waiting for the sudden fast plunge down the loose shingle slope?

It seemed feasible. But it was no concrete lead.

He stood and brushed strands of grass from his shirt and elbows and the knees of his jeans, looking down at the imprint in the grass. It could be the lookout was taller than him by half a foot or so. Or perhaps he'd wriggled a little. No way of knowing.

Turning, he made his way back to the tyre treads and stared at them once more. He pictured the scene. The tense, dark silence. The abrupt acceleration. The flash of headlamps. The weightless, risky slide and the crunching, jolting impact.

He walked a slow, watchful circle around the area until his eyes were snagged by another set of footprints, leading off towards the base of the limestone cliff. A shallow trench was gouged into the earth alongside them. He followed the markings, quickening his pace as they curved gently to the left, then disappeared behind a pile of boulders. He clambered over the rocks. There was a tight channel in behind. Some kind of natural gulley had been formed out of the chunks of limestone that had settled under the lee of the jagged cliff. He could hear a faint droning that reminded him of the static from a set of stereo speakers.

Then he saw the shoes.

Old white trainers, coated with red dirt and dust. They were attached to a long pair of legs in grubby jeans, crossed at the ankles where Trent could see blue cotton socks. He shifted to his left. The rest of the guy came into view. He was lying face down beneath a pulsing haze of flies. His chequered shirt had hitched up from the waist, exposing the silky black skin at the base of his spine. The flannel material was torn and ragged in the middle of his back, stiff with a congealed reddish stain. His head was clamped between two sandy rocks, like they'd grown up around him.

Trent scrambled his way over the craggy ground until he was standing above the body, one leg on either side. He closed his mouth and pinched his nostrils and reached down through the flies to grasp a weedy arm, taut with rigor.

The body twisted stiffly at the shoulders and neck but not at the waist, and the flies rose up in an angry swarm. It was enough for Trent to confirm what he already feared.

Serge, the missing chauffeur.

The whites of his eyes were yellowed, pupils blown, staring dumbly up at the featureless sky. A track of dried blood had adhered to the side of his mouth. His face was alive with ants, his skin covered in dust and debris, his nostrils and lips ringed with sand. His hair was coated in a fine layer of grit.

But it was the sight of his chest that made Trent rear backwards. The crater was very big and very deep, exposing blood and organs and arteries and glistening flesh. Someone had scooped the very life from the poor guy. They'd stood close and fired a shotgun and blown a hole through his heart and lungs.

Trent buried his face in the crook of his arm. He inhaled his own scent and bit down on his flesh. He glanced behind him, then bent low and delved quickly through Serge's trouser pockets. He didn't find anything and there was no shirt pocket left to be searched. It was gone with the rest of his chest cavity.

Trent let go and watched the corpse slump to the ground and the flies spiral up and then settle. He climbed past the body and up onto a much larger boulder. He scanned the immediate area. Nothing. He extended his search, stepping between rocks, clutching tight to the brittle cliff-face. But there was no sign of the blue holdall Serge had been carrying when he'd sneaked out through the security gate. Trent supposed he shouldn't be surprised. The gang were a professional outfit. It wasn't the kind of thing they'd be likely to overlook.

He returned to the narrow, stony crevice and stood looking down over the body and the swirling insect mass. It was no fancy resting place. It was a hard, barren spot.

He mopped the sweat from his face with the tail of his shirt and listened very hard for the sound of an approaching engine. But there was nothing other than the flat insect buzz and the eerie desolation and the humid, awful stench coming up from below.

Trent supposed there was a reasonable chance that the corpse could lie here for weeks or even months before it was discovered. There was the outside possibility the body might never be found. Perhaps it would be picked apart by birds or gnawed beyond recognition by scavenging animals. But it wasn't a risk he was prepared to run. Alain might venture up here to assess the terrain for himself. And Trent couldn't afford more distractions, or worse, risk the chaos of police involvement.

He crouched on trembling knees and set his hands around a boulder by his feet. It was a sturdy, misshapen rock, about the size of a rugby ball. His fingers dug into the sandy exterior. He bared his teeth and heaved it from the ground. Staggered forwards, bent double with the weight. He held it over the narrow chamber. Then he gulped a mouthful of the fetid scent, snatched his head away and let go.

A muffled, wet *thump* came up at him, accompanied by an urgent hum.

He wafted a stray fly away and bit his tongue. Squinted hard. Found another rock. Then some more. He lifted them and he threw them. He nudged them over the edge with the toes of his boots and he levered them into the chamber with his heels. The soggy thumping sound became more hideous with each repeat. But in time, the noise changed. He heard the clatter of stone hitting stone. The dry clack of boulder meeting boulder. The stirring of the flies reduced to a low murmur. He risked a glance. It was almost done. He scooped up handfuls of dirt and stones and flung them into the channel, working in a frenzy until his nails were jammed with soil and his hands were grazed and scratched. He kept at it until the body was fully covered. Until you couldn't see a finger or a foot or a single curl of hair.

He paused and took one last glimpse of the terrible thing that he'd done. Then he licked the sweat from his lips and finally turned his back on the familiar, predictable guy he used to be, and went off in search of a branch that he might use to scrub away the prints and markings that had led him here.

II

The Negotiation

Chapter Twenty-one

Trent faced his front door. He'd grown to dread returning home. It wasn't because of the hollow sound of his key in the lock or the silence of the hallway. It wasn't because of the tide of loneliness that swept over him as he stepped inside. No, what he loathed most of all was the way his mind betrayed him, his breath catching in his throat as he indulged a faint residue of hope. Hope that Aimée would come rushing to greet him, weak and disoriented, her clothes dirty and her hair tangled in knots. Hope that a light would be blinking on his answering machine with a message from the kidnappers he'd once felt so sure had snatched her. Hope, even, that he'd find her curled up on the sofa in her favourite baggy jumper, flicking through music channels on the television as if none of this were really happening.

It was a hateful, traitorous urge, one that was followed by the savage mule-kick of reality. His hallway was empty. His living room, too. There was no flashing light on the recording equipment he'd connected to the telephone.

No Aimée.

Trent approached the phone and lifted the receiver to his ear. A long flat tone. Still connected, then. He set it down, hand lingering on the cool plastic casing.

The apartment was tidy. Sterile, almost. He'd shoved the stinking wash of mess and litter into bin bags in a sudden frenzy more than a week ago, on the night of his return from Jérôme's coastal villa. He'd tied the bags off and slung them outside. And all the while he'd been developing his plan, the first steps towards reclaiming control over his life.

Now the plan had changed. It wasn't a shift he welcomed but he'd been forced to adapt. The odds against him learning exactly what Jérôme had done to Aimée were growing longer all the while. But he felt more determined than ever. Desperation, maybe. Stubbornness, perhaps. Or simply a reluctance to move on to whatever his life might become without her. But he wasn't beaten yet and he didn't intend to quit until he was certain of the outcome, whatever it might be.

There were no days now when he had any sense of equilibrium. His moods swung wildly, hour by hour, minute by minute. Sometimes he was convinced that she must be dead. Felt certain, with a cold twisting in his gut, that Jérôme must have killed her. But then there were the spells of surging optimism when he allowed himself to believe in an alternative scenario. Like perhaps Jérôme was holding her captive somewhere, or maybe Aimée had felt the need to flee and conceal herself for reasons that were presently unclear to him. And so it went on, an erratic spectrum of emotions, veering from the blackest despair to zealous faith and back again, leaving him feeling as if he were teetering on the edge of lunacy.

His hand slid away from the telephone and he moved into the master bedroom. The bed had been made with military precision, the covers tucked in tight. Blades of pearly light streamed through the Venetian blinds.

Hesitantly now, he eased open the door of the closet, then craned his neck to check behind the side of the bed. He couldn't remember when the habit had first formed. Three weeks ago? Four? And he couldn't readily explain what he hoped it might achieve. He didn't seriously believe he might find Aimée here, as if she were engaged in some outlandish game of hide and seek. He was aware that it pointed towards some kind of mental frailty on his part. The beginning of a breakdown. Maybe not even the beginning. And yet the compulsion to hunt for his phantom fiancée was one he found impossible to ignore. Since the first time, he'd started to believe it would be a bad omen if he didn't search. And so it had become part of his routine.

Dropping to his knees, he lifted the cover on the bed and peeked underneath. He saw the same thing as yesterday. The same as the day before that. Dust bunnies and an expanse of beige carpet, a shade darker than the rest of the sunbathed room.

He replaced the cover and backed out to enter the bathroom. He looked behind the door and swished back the shower curtain over the bath. A few shirts and some shrivelled underwear were drying on the retractable laundry line that was fitted over the tub – signs of his attempts to convince himself that he'd return to a life worth living once he'd confronted Jérôme, one where clean clothes would be something worth concerning himself with again.

He shied away from his pitiful reflection in the mirror over the sink, paced back into the lounge and hauled aside the curtains by the window. He scanned behind the armchair where Aimée had always preferred to read her celebrity gossip magazines and then finished up by peering over the kitchen counter.

He found nothing untoward. Saw no disturbance.

Only one place remained. The space he always checked last of all.

It was a small, windowless boxroom that filled a recess in the middle of the apartment. The previous tenants had used it for storage but Aimée had converted it into a home office for their business. She'd also insisted on squeezing a camp bed inside, claiming that their friends might like to stay over from time to time. In truth, the bed had only ever been used on the rare but spectacular occasions when some minor row triggered an eruption of Aimée's fierce temper and Trent found himself in need of a place to sleep.

Now, the flimsy bed and thin mattress were propped up against one wall, leaving a narrow pathway towards a compact desk and a folding chair. A laptop and printer were stationed on the desk, concealed beneath layers of papers. An open road map of the area around Marseilles had been ringed with several locations. Aimée's broken necklace, the one Trent had recovered from Jérôme's bedroom, was draped over an anglepoise lamp, the locket firmly closed. The lamp was pointed up at the far wall. The wall was covered in photographs.

Trent clicked on the bulb and light blazed upwards.

There were prints of Jérôme and Stephanie entering a restaurant; of Alain leaning against the parked Mercedes in a backstreet alley; of Serge with the driver's window down, wearing sunglasses and smiling toothily at a tune on the stereo. There were blurred images taken from a moving vehicle of the imposing gate outside the Moreau family home and the perimeter fence and security cameras that surrounded the estate; telephoto zoom shots of Jérôme standing on a wooden jetty in a cream linen suit, beside a gleaming super-yacht; snatched glimpses of Stephanie walking through the crooked alleyways of the Panier, glancing in the windows of artisan craft shops not far from Trent's home.

The wall to the right featured plans and diagrams and more maps, logging the route the Mercedes tended to follow on its return to the Moreau estate and highlighting potential weaknesses. One of the vulnerable locations was the exact spot where Trent had readied himself to make his move and where the green Land Cruiser had appeared as if from nowhere to beat him to it.

The left-hand wall was filled with notes. Trent hadn't bothered with paper. He'd scrawled with a marker pen straight onto the magnolia paint. Across the top of the wall he'd set out a timeline of the key events since Aimée's disappearance. Below and to the left were the names of the suspects Girard had identified. There was an asterisk alongside Jérôme Moreau's name. The others had been crossed out. Further to the right was the list Trent had compiled of the equipment he'd need to abduct Jérôme and force him to talk, as well as detailed recordings of Jérôme's movements during the past week. Down on the floor was a paint tin and brush. The simplest way of covering his tracks. Useless for now.

Trent snatched up a marker pen from beneath the road map on the desk. He uncapped it, releasing a sweet, gluey aroma, and stooped near a bare patch on the wall. He wrote one word, the nib of the pen shrieking against the gloss paint.

Xavier.

He stared at the name, then added the date and time of the gang's first call. Beneath, he wrote: *Second call: 48 hours? Ransom: €5 million?*

He leaned back and considered the sum until his eyes strained and his sight blurred, and then he shook his head roughly, tossed the pen onto the map and paced back through to the kitchen. He lifted his phone. Punched in a number. Smoothed his fingers over the dust that had collected on the recording equipment as he waited for his call to connect.

There was a click. A pause. Then a tiny red light on the digital recorder was replaced by a bright green diode. The counter on the illuminated display was set to 00.00.00. The digits began to creep upwards.

There was no greeting on the other end of the line. Just the suck and rasp of breathing.

'It's me,' he said, and heard the burr of feedback from the recording equipment.

He clamped his hand around the receiver, skin wet against the smooth plastic.

Finally, he heard a response.

'I told you not to call.'

'I had no choice.'

'Is it done?'

'The situation has changed.'

Trent waited. He watched the digits on the electronic display count upwards.

'We need to talk.'

Another pause. Longer this time. Trent endured it for nine seconds.

'You'll want to hear what I have to say,' he pressed.

'Where?'

Trent's lip twitched. A trapped nerve. He felt the need to clear his throat. He always did when he was nervous.

Trent gave a location. He added a request. He explained exactly what he needed and he interpreted the silence on the other end as a form of consent. 'You can buy me breakfast,' he added. 'I'm hungry.'

'When?'

'An hour. Sooner if you can make it.'

He lowered the receiver into its cradle and watched the recording equipment power down. The counter froze at 00.01.37. Then the green light went out and the red light bloomed.

He moved aside the headphone wires and rested his finger on the button marked ERASE. He waited a beat. Pressed it.

He rapped his knuckle on the counter. Squeezed his hands into fists and tried to fight temptation. But he couldn't resist. He snatched up the receiver one last time. Checked the dial tone was still good. The low droning sounded bleak and off-key. It resonated with something loose and unstable inside his troubled mind as he paced towards his bathroom and wrenched on the taps to heat up the shower.

*

The young man who was located behind a window in a studio apartment on the opposite side of the square, one floor up, one building along, eased back in his wooden chair. The chair was old. It creaked. One of the rear legs was shorter than the others and the chair tipped sideways, then back, in a familiar tilt. The young man had slipped a cushion behind his back for comfort. At night, he took that same pillow and he spread it out on the fold-up card table in front of him and he crouched forward to sleep, arms crooked around him, like a kid who'd dropped off in the middle of class.

And just like a school pupil, he had a notepad and pencil on the table in front of him. Next to the notepad was a digital camera with a zoom lens. Next to the camera was a prepaid mobile phone. The young man had yet to switch the mobile on. Had rarely powered it up. Beside the phone he had a set of car keys and beside the keys a book. It was a vintage detective novel with yellowing pages that he'd picked up from a market stall just a few streets away. Times when he grew tired of watching Trent's apartment, he'd crack the window to make sure he didn't miss any sounds that might alert him to something, and he'd scan a few pages. He'd finished the book once already. He was almost a third of the way through again.

There was bread and cheese if he got hungry. He had bottled water and energy sodas to drink. There was an air mattress down on the floor for those occasions when he got too sleepy to see straight.

He'd watched Trent go in. He'd jotted down the time in his notepad. Now he was waiting for him to come back out. It might be many hours before he appeared. Days, even.

The waiting was no fun. The whole experience was miserable. But he was capable of enduring unpleasant situations. He'd had plenty of practice. And he was prepared to wait as long as necessary. He'd thought about it carefully, weighed up the pros and the cons, and he'd made a decision – he was going to follow Trent the next time he emerged.

Chapter Twenty-two

Trent tore into a chunk of baguette and smeared it with butter and jam. He took a bite. Then another. He was eating fast. Chewing vigorously.

He washed the bread down with strong black coffee. He needed the caffeine to fuel his brain just as he needed the food to fuel his body. He hadn't slept in twenty-four hours but he hadn't rested properly for weeks now. His thinking felt sluggish. It was as though he was somehow distanced from himself, able only to acknowledge the thoughts he was having and hear the things he was saying on some kind of fractionally delayed feedback. Sometimes he was astonished by his own behaviour. Other times, appalled. This new Trent, the one forged by the strain and desperation of his situation, was no longer someone he could easily predict.

'You eat like a pig,' Girard said.

'Told you I was hungry.'

Girard lowered his voice. 'Killing a man makes you this way?'

Trent ripped more bread free with his teeth. He checked over his shoulder. 'There's been no killing,' he said, while chewing.

'You couldn't do it?'

'No.' His throat bulged as he swallowed. 'But not for any of the reasons you have in mind.'

Girard was sitting on the opposite side of the café table, wearing dark sunglasses that made it impossible for Trent to read his expression. He was reminded of an old-fashioned police mug shot, the glasses like a black slash obscuring the eyes of some dough-faced hoodlum. It didn't help that the morning sun was high in a sky marred only by faint streaks of cumulus. The blinding glare shimmered on the marina waters and bounced off the sleek hulls of the yachts behind Girard and the aluminium table between them.

The café occupied the ground-floor terrace outside a magnificent Haussman-style building, one of many similar restaurants that lined the Quai du Port. Mid-morning, they were mostly frequented by Marseillais drinking a quick espresso, a *café crème* or an *orange pressé*. Trent's breakfast – crusty bread, a croissant, three types of jam, some sliced cheese and a small dish of mixed fruit – was an anomaly. He felt like one himself. All these ordinary people around him, living their ordinary lives, unaware of just how easily their worlds could irrevocably change.

'Then why did you fail?' Girard asked. He sounded as if he was quizzing himself as much as Trent. 'It wasn't the planning.'

'The planning was fine. We identified the perfect spot.'

Girard raised his coffee to his lips and Trent leaned forwards over the table until he could smell the fumes rising from the cigarette Girard clutched in his spare hand.

He said, 'Unfortunately, somebody else identified the spot as perfect, too.'

Girard gulped his coffee too fast. He reacted as if scalded, dropping his cup with a clatter.

'Moreau was kidnapped,' Trent explained. 'Right in front of me.'

Girard said nothing and Trent went on to share the rest of his story, chewing his way through the remainder of the bread as he talked. He wasn't concerned about being overheard. The tables and canvas chairs near to them were unoccupied, Girard was careful to signal him whenever their waiter came within earshot, and though pedestrians, dog-walkers and street beggars passed by, there was ample noise to mask what he had to say. Traffic was snarled up on the quayside – the result of the construction work that never seemed to cease in the city – and between the shouts of men in luminous vests and hard hats, the brash pneumatic rattle of a jackhammer, the bass putter of a generator and the revving of engines, Trent found that sometimes even Girard struggled to hear.

He was spooning the last of the fruit into his mouth by the time he was done.

There were only two pieces of information he hadn't shared with Girard. One he never planned to – finding Serge's corpse. Girard had helped him up to this point, it was true, but he was still a former police detective. Who knew where he might draw the line, especially now that Trent had stepped so far beyond it. And besides, Trent was ashamed of burying the chauffeur's body. He had no desire to speak of it.

The second piece of data he'd held back because he wanted to share it at just the right moment. It was absolutely crucial.

'So . . . what do you plan to do now?' Girard asked, taking a lingering hit from his latest cigarette.

'Get Jérôme back.'

Girard nodded, a look of shrewd calculation on his face, as if the process required nothing more than a period of calm reflection and considered thought. 'And afterwards?'

Trent shrugged. 'Nothing has changed.'

'The family have accepted you?'

Trent pushed his fruit dish aside. 'They're listening to me. For now. I'm returning to the house this afternoon. But the bodyguard could be a problem. Tell me: the girl you talked to, the one who knew the dancer Jérôme attacked in Cassis, did she mention if the bodyguard was there at the time?'

'She did not say.'

'Did you ask her?'

'No, I don't think so.'

'Can you contact her again? I need to know if he could have seen Aimée.'

Girard nodded his consent. Drank more coffee.

'Did you bring what I asked for?' Trent asked.

Girard reached inside his jacket. He removed a tan leather case. It was flat and compact, like a pouch for a set of competition darts. He slid it over to Trent. Watched Trent cover it with his palm, then ease it off the table and slip it into his pocket.

Girard sucked on his cigarette, head over to one side, eyes hidden by his dark glasses. Way above him, high on the hilly ridge overlooking the city, sunlight glinted off the gilded statue of the Virgin Mary atop the candy-striped facade of the basilica of Notre-Dame de la Garde. Some locals considered the statue to be the city's guardian. Trent felt like he could use her protection right now.

'You didn't just meet me for this,' Girard said. 'There's something more.'

Trent squinted into the flinty sunshine. He lowered his gaze from the church and the tumbling cascade of rickety buildings on the far side of the quay, to the dun-coloured Fort St Nicolas. The complex rigging on a tall ship tilted in the corner of his vision. A maritime flag snapped and fluttered.

'You mind?' he asked, gesturing toward Girard's cigarettes.

He reached out and freed one, tamping it down on the table to hide the shake in his hand. He fired Girard's lighter. Inhaled the fumes. Plucked a stray thread of tobacco off his tongue.

'There is something,' he said. 'Something important. I didn't tell you who the ransom demand came from.'

'Then tell me now.'

'It stays between us. I need your word.'

'You have it.'

Trent exhaled towards his brow, feeling the snag and sweep of the smoke against his skin.

'Xavier,' he said, finally.

One word. But it was enough.

Girard swiped the sunglasses from his face. His sunken eyes loomed fat and bulbous.

'You're serious?'

'Why would I make up something like that?'

'Was it him?'

'It's been eighteen months, Girard.'

Girard's thick eyebrows bunched. He stared at Trent with feverish intensity.

'But yes,' Trent heard himself say. 'It was him. It was Xavier.'

Girard emitted a strange choked noise, like something inside him was slowly deflating.

'I need to know how close you've got,' Trent said. 'I need to know where they might be holding Jérôme.'

Girard shook his head dazedly.

'You must have found something.'

'Not enough. Little hints. Nothing more.'

'The theory was that they were using a cave system, wasn't it? Perhaps they're doing the same thing again now.'

Girard looked up towards the ranks of fancy apartments above Trent's head, their ironwork balconies shaded by striped sun canopies. His pouched eyes had an unfocused, dreamlike cast to them.

'Do you have any idea how many caves there are in France?'

'But his gang can't be far away. Based on the drop schedule the last time around—'

'*Based on the drop schedule*.' Girard's jaw was fixed. He was straining to keep it that way. 'It gives us nothing. You think I haven't tried? Nobody talks. They're all afraid of this guy.'

'So look harder.'

Girard shook his head ruefully. He laid his sunglasses down on the table and scrubbed a palm across his face. He checked over his shoulder. Turned back again. 'You know what you have to do,' he said, leaning forwards. 'Make the family pay. Make it quick. Do it soon.'

'This could be the best chance you'll ever get of finding him, Girard. He's somewhere right now, watching over Jérôme. His location is fixed. We just need to find it.'

Girard laughed faintly, like the entire scenario was some elaborate trick designed simply to frustrate him. 'You do not want this.'

'I wouldn't ask otherwise.'

'No. You worry. I understand it. The situation is difficult for you.' He covered his heart with his hand. 'For me, I cannot imagine it. But please, I know how you feel. How you *really* feel. We've talked too many times. You hate police investigations. Hate interference. Especially with this guy. After last time . . .' He shook his head in a dispirited way. Reached over and gripped Trent's balled fist. Clenched it hard. 'So now you must trust yourself. Believe in your approach.'

'It's not that simple. There's a problem with the money.'

'But the insurance policy?'

Trent shook his head. 'I *need* you to look, Girard. Regardless of the risks. I know you'll tread as lightly as you can.'

Girard searched Trent's eyes for a long time. He looked deep inside them. And what he saw there seemed to sadden him greatly.

'And if I find him?' he asked, voice husky.

'I'm only interested in Jérôme. All I care about is Aimée.'

Girard pushed back his chair and summoned a strained smile, like a patient leaving a doctor's surgery after receiving a crushing diagnosis. 'You'll be at the Moreau estate?'

'Later,' Trent told him. 'I have a couple of things to arrange first. But don't try to contact me. It's safer if I call you.'

*

The young man lowered the camera from his eye. The zoom function had worked perfectly. He'd fired off a whole series of shots at a distance approaching something like four hundred metres. The sun was blazing behind him. It was shining directly in Trent's eyes. He'd captured Trent squinting in many of the pictures. But that was fine. It was no problem. Trent was clearly identifiable.

It had been trickier with the man sitting opposite. The back of his head had been pointed towards where the young man was standing. Plus he'd been wearing dark sunglasses for most of the meeting. The young man had had to be very patient. But eventually he'd got his reward. There was one short instant, a precious moment, when the man had removed his glasses and turned his head and faced him directly. And the young man had seized his chance and captured it. One fractional compression of his finger. One simulated electronic shutter sound.

One inescapable piece of digital evidence.

Chapter Twenty-three

Trent decided to drive back towards Aix in the battered Peugeot. It was a risk. A sizeable one. Seeing the car might remind Alain to run the plates. He'd discover they were fakes. But he might choose to do it anyway and there were explanations Trent could provide. He could claim that the dummy plates had been part of the original security test he'd devised, or his way of avoiding being tracked by the criminal gangs he'd frustrated in recent months.

Better to be brazen, he reasoned. Act as if he had nothing to conceal. But there were a couple of things he could do to make things easier on himself. First, he secured his Beretta beneath the steering column with a swatch of duct tape and then he stashed the rest of his abduction equipment in the boxroom in his apartment. Second, he beached the Peugeot in the same spot where it had ended up following the attack on Jérôme. He walked the rest of the way to the Moreau estate with a canvas satchel slung over his shoulder, sweating in the relentless noontime sun, breathing in the familiar scents of warm earth and heated tarmac and wild herbs, his skin tightening and burning, his socks damp with perspiration inside his boots.

The cameras swivelled and tracked his progress from the extreme edge of the property. They monitored him closely, one after the other. He didn't bother with the intercom when he reached the gate. He just stood in the exact centre of the road and waited for the cameras to zero in on him. He picked the left one. Lifted his face to it and stared blankly into the lens. He didn't smile. Didn't raise a hand. Just waited, arms loose by his sides in the stillness and the heat, until the camera jerked a fraction. A moment later he heard an electric buzz and the gate dropped on its hinges and swung inwards.

Nobody came to greet him.

Trent walked alone under the watchful gaze of the surveillance equipment. He ascended the steep gravel rise, passing through the narrow fingers of shade being thrown across his path from the double line of cypress trees, scanning the grounds for a glimpse of the rickety cabin.

He was over the crest and in sight of the house when he heard a dull *thump* and caught sight of a streak of white in the corner of his vision. He turned his head. Locked onto the racing object.

A golf ball.

It had bounced on the striped lawn and kicked on and fallen again and then trundled to a halt not far from where he was standing. There were more balls near by, scattered in a loose grouping across the neatly trimmed grass like a constellation of fallen stars.

Trent kept walking. Thirty seconds. A minute. Then another ball looped down from above and struck the ground and pitched up and bounced on before losing momentum and skittering to a halt.

There was no shout of warning. No concern for his safety.

He crossed the driveway to the opposite side. Within a hundred metres more he was able to watch Philippe take aim at another projectile. He swung hard and removed a chunk of turf as he sent the ball zinging wildly by.

Philippe wasn't dressed for golf. He was wearing oversized sunglasses with white plastic frames, a pair of blue swimming shorts and his canvas boat shoes. His body was slim and wiry with the beginnings of a swell around the belly. He glanced up at Trent as he approached but he didn't wave or nod or otherwise acknowledge him. He simply lowered his face and gathered in another ball with his golf club.

The club was a four or five iron, Trent reckoned, but it was obvious Philippe was no golfer. His stance was wrong, face onto the ball, with his right foot in front of the left, like a swordsman about to lunge at an opponent. His grip was low down on the metal shaft, beneath the rubber handle, and his swing was an awkward, truncated affair that snapped up from the hip and ended at the shoulder, then chopped downwards again. But his makeshift technique was matched with plenty of aggression and the ball zipped fast into the air, then hooked wildly to the left.

'Put me off,' Philippe mumbled, once Trent was within earshot.

Trent glanced down at the slashed dirt and grassy divots that littered the area. He didn't say anything.

Philippe rolled a golf ball beneath the matted sole of his espadrille. A chilled beer bottle was propped against a pristine white leather golf bag that had been slung to the ground near by.

'What's your handicap?' Trent asked.

'I don't have one. I don't play.'

Trent raised an eyebrow.

'This is Jérôme's bag.' Philippe tapped the white leather with the end of his club, nearly upsetting his lager.

Jérôme's bag. Odd. Wouldn't it have been more natural for him to say that the clubs belonged to his father?

'I had to get out of that room.' Philippe gazed down at his feet. 'Had to take a break. Understand?'

'Who's in there now?'

'Jérôme's wife.'

Not *maman*, this time. That was something, at least.

'Then I'll leave you to your game,' Trent said. He wasn't looking at Philippe any more. He was staring pointedly at the tall bottle of iced lager. 'Should I have Alain bring you some coffee?'

Trent saw the tendons in Philippe's bronzed arms tighten and pop. His knuckles swelled around the shaft of the golf club. Trent steadied himself, rehearsing the moves he'd need to make to defend himself.

But Philippe didn't lash out. He just gazed up slowly, eyes hooded, a sly smile tugging at the corner of his mouth.

'He's waiting to speak with you,' he said.

'Good.' Trent nodded, businesslike. 'We need to talk.'

*

The front door opened before Trent had passed Philippe's sports car and the wrecked Mercedes and the circular fountain. Alain filled the doorway, his fists on his hips. He wore a white linen short-sleeved shirt over grey trousers. There was no sign of his Ruger or his gun holster, but Alain's brow was low and knotted, his pose aggressive. He folded his big arms across his chest.

'What's in the bag?' he asked.

'Take a look.'

Trent swung the satchel down from his shoulder and held it out to him by the strap. Alain snatched it and hauled back the flap. He lowered his head inside like a horse burrowing into a nosebag.

Trent kept moving. He shoved his way past Alain until he was standing in the entrance hall. The air was many degrees cooler. He felt his clothes settle against his clammy body. Felt the heat leach out from his skin.

'It's the recording equipment I told you about,' Trent said, over his shoulder. 'And the prepaid phone you took from me before. That's all.'

The foyer was empty. It was silent. The door to the security room was ajar on his left. Light was spilling out of it onto the marble tiles and he could glimpse some of the security monitors. To his right, he could see along the glazed and sunlit corridor towards Jérôme's study. The double doors were open.

'Did you speak with the housekeeper?' Trent asked.

'I talked to her.'

'And?'

'It was as I said. She has no involvement in any of this. No knowledge that can help us.'

'How can you be sure?'

Alain grunted. 'Because I am. That's all you need to know.'

He stepped around Trent and pressed the bag into his chest.

'Thought you trusted me now,' Trent said.

'Arms up.'

'You're serious?'

Alain snarled. His nostrils flared. He was serious. No question.

Trent raised his arms until they were parallel with his shoulders, the satchel clenched in his right hand. Alain swooped in and patted along his arms and down his torso.

'Where's your car?' he asked, feeling around Trent's waist.

Trent told him. He said he'd left it out on the road near where they'd been attacked. Said he'd parked there because he'd wanted to take a look around and study the plateau the gang had come at them from. Said he hadn't found anything of interest beyond some tyre treads that weren't capable of telling them more than they already knew about the Land Cruiser.

Alain straightened and turned Trent around by the shoulders. He patted down his legs from behind.

'Why did you walk here from there?' he asked, his voice fast and rough, like his hands.

'I wanted to scan the roadside. See if anything had been left behind. I thought maybe if we were lucky one of the gang might have tossed something out of the Land Cruiser after they collected Serge. Plus I wanted some air. Some exercise. I don't know how long I'm going to be holed up here. Are we done?'

'We're just getting started. I have some questions for you.'

Alain tapped Trent's shin and made him raise his leg. He tugged at his laces, but before he could remove his boot, a door opened behind them. Both men turned.

'What's going on here?'

Stephanie was wearing a black leotard over white tights. The tights were cut to expose her heels and toes. Pink leg warmers were bunched up around her ankles. She held a pair of ivory ballet shoes in one hand, silk ribbons coiling downwards. A light cotton towel was fitted around her neck and she was using one end to mop her damp brow.

Her face was flushed. She was perspiring heavily. Her hair was pulled back into a tight bun but frizzy strands corkscrewed out from her temples. She was breathing heavily. Her chest was rising and falling in an exaggerated way. Trent could see the outline of her ribs against the snug black Lycra as she inhaled.

He knew he should avert his gaze but his eyes wouldn't shift.

No two ways about it – she was stunning. It wasn't often since he'd met Aimée that any woman made this kind of an impression on him. But Stephanie had.

'Alain?' she asked, and mopped her face some more. 'What's the meaning of this?'

Alain pushed up from the floor. Contemplated his knuckles. He didn't respond.

'It's OK,' Trent told her. 'He's watching out for your safety. He's just doing his job.'

Stephanie pressed the towel to her mouth. She glanced between them both. Alain still didn't speak. But the sideways look he gave Trent wasn't hard to interpret. He was furious.

'Who's monitoring the phone?' Trent asked.

'I've been listening for it,' Stephanie told him. 'Alain, too.'

'Have there been any calls?'

Stephanie hitched an eyebrow at Alain.

'None from the gang,' he muttered. 'A few from some men M. Moreau has business with.'

'What are their names?'

'I can't tell you that.'

'They could be involved in Jérôme's abduction.'

'They're not. There's no chance of that at all.'

Trent paused. Swallowed his irritation. 'And what did you tell these men?'

'That M. Moreau was unwell. That he could not speak with them.'

'They believed you?'

He shrugged. He was studying the floor.

'OK,' Trent said. 'That's good. We don't need any more complications.'

His words weren't subtle. They weren't intended to be. Alain snorted and shook his head. Trent didn't care. Things were going just the way he needed them to. He was striking the perfect tone. He was coming across as reasonable. As concerned. He felt sure that Stephanie was viewing him that way.

He lifted the satchel. 'I have some recording equipment to rig up,' he told her. 'I was just checking with Alain before installing it.'

'Of course.' She let go of her towel. Her leotard plunged into a deep V beneath her throat, the material pulled taut across the slight swell of her breasts. Her pale skin was wet and glistening. 'I'm sure Alain doesn't have a problem with that.'

She lifted her chin. There was authority in her voice. A challenge in her eyes. Perhaps there'd been a discussion between them while Trent had been away. Perhaps Stephanie had told Alain that she was in charge now.

Alain clenched and unclenched his hands. Trent could feel the heat coming off him, could smell an odour that was warm and meaty, like he was running a fever.

'Come through to my studio,' Stephanie said. She turned and paced towards the door she'd opened. Her strides were long and measured, arms and hips swinging freely.

Trent didn't follow immediately. He was aware that Alain wanted to talk some more. That he had something to say.

'I'm sure Alain has many things to be getting on with,' Stephanie said. She cocked her hip and glanced over her shoulder. Fixed him with her gaze. 'Come,' she told Trent. 'Follow me.'

Chapter Twenty-four

The studio was large and spare and starkly illuminated by a series of recessed ceiling bulbs. The light was forensic in its intensity. It was inescapable.

The floor was timber and flexed beneath his feet, as if some kind of spring had been engineered into it. Three of the walls were painted white. The remaining wall was one long mirror. It stretched from left to right and from ceiling to floor. A rounded wooden barre was fitted at waist height in front of the mirror. It reminded Trent, dizzyingly, of the set-up in the room where he'd found Aimée's necklace.

He gawped stupidly at his reflection in the glass. Found that he couldn't look away. The guy in the mirror looked many pounds lighter and several shades paler than he should have done, as if he were recuperating from a major surgical procedure.

Stephanie moved across to hang her towel over the barre, then gripped the beam in one hand and stood upright beside it with her shoulders back, chest out. Her legs were pressed together, knees and heels touching, feet parted at an angle. She stretched her free arm above her head, then sprang up onto her toes. She wasn't *en pointe* – he guessed she'd need to be wearing her ballet shoes to achieve that – but she wasn't far off. Her body alignment was precise, her balance absolute. Trent could see the freckled skin on her back, exposed by the low scoop of the leotard. The spurs and nodules of her spine were pronounced, standing out as if she'd been dieting too hard. But there was plenty of muscle there. It was taut. Hard-packed. She glanced across to find him staring and didn't seem surprised.

'You still dance?' he said, and immediately felt like a fool.

She smiled demurely and unfurled her hand with a flourish. Her face became haughty, a self-aware parody of the serious artiste. Her eyelids fluttered.

'I heard that you were good.'

She rolled her eyes and dropped to her heels, shaking her arms loose. She moved her head from side to side, as though weighing his question. 'I used to be. Perhaps.'

'Only used to be?'

'It was my career.' She shrugged. Laughed faintly. 'My life, actually.'

'So what changed?'

'I was injured.'

'Badly?'

'Very. My knee.' She gazed down at her right leg, as if it had tricked her in some way. 'Now, I dance only for myself. And in the beginning for Jérôme, too.' She nodded to a door that was fitted flush into the wall on the opposite side of the room. 'His study is through there,' she said. 'He liked to watch me.'

Trent could taste the coppery tang of blood. He glanced down at the floor – flashing back for an awful moment to the russet-brown stain Girard had found on the carpet in Jérôme's villa – then across to her feet. Two of her toes were bound in sterile tape.

'For support,' she told him. 'My strength isn't what it used to be.'

He nodded mutely and shifted his focus to the mirrored wall. He avoided his own reflection and gazed instead at her ankles and muscular calves, the bunched pink leg warmers and then the graceful contours of her slender hips. She swivelled and he realised that she was staring into the reflective surface, also. Head on an angle. Long neck tipped to one side. Waiting for him to find her eyes. They were large. Expectant. Encouraging. Aimée had looked at him that way sometimes.

He swallowed. Hard.

'Do you miss it?' he managed. 'The performance, I mean.'

She held his gaze. She was standing only a few metres away, but for a moment she looked cast adrift and isolated in the mirror. Utterly alone in the room.

'I apologise for Alain,' she said, simply. 'He should respect you.'

Trent didn't respond. He sensed that she was warming up to something. Something important. He could see it building in her. She was leaning forwards, as if she were about to launch into a sudden dance movement.

'The situation with Jérôme,' she began. 'The kidnapping. It's ... difficult for me.'

'It's always difficult for anyone in your position. You're no exception, believe me.'

'Please.' She bit down on her lip. Shook her head. Then she glanced quickly towards the door that led into the entrance hall. It was closed. Trent had shut it behind him. She took a deep breath, chest swelling. Looked up at him from beneath lidded eyes. 'There's something I have to show you. Something I feel you should see.'

She turned her back to him then. He could still see her face in the mirror, but it was angled down, brow furrowed. She rolled her lip between her teeth and reached up hesitantly to the strap of her leotard on her left shoulder. She plucked at the fabric, fed a finger beneath. Then she rolled the strap down, easing her long arm through. She freed the strap on the other side. Took a moment to collect herself, then peeled the leotard down as far as her trim waist, covering her small, budded breasts with her forearms.

That was when he saw the bruises and the swelling.

The contusions were yellowed and aged, greenish-blue blurs around her kidneys and spine. There were welts, too. Angry red slashes that criss-crossed just above her buttocks. The skin was pimpled and raised.

Trent felt himself sway. He was aware of a fierce tingling in his fingers, a febrile snap and twitch. Anger. Fear. And worse, the desire to reach out to her. To touch her. Soothe her.

'Who did this to you?' The rage was there in the unsteady pitch of his voice.

Her eyes were closed, head bowed like a penitent. They both knew he hadn't needed to ask.

'He's always careful,' she said softly. 'He does it where people can't see.'

'He shouldn't do it at all.'

His anger cowed her. She trembled, the bruises and sores standing out in colourful relief against her bleached skin.

'You could leave,' he told her. 'Why don't you leave?'

Her eyes snapped open. They were wet and vibrating. He watched them climb the glass until she glimpsed his face and flinched at the horror that was etched there.

'He'd find me,' she whispered. 'He does this when I'm here. If I left...' She shuddered, the thought left unspoken. The implication, too. She'd told him the situation with Jérôme was hard for her. Now he understood why. If Jérôme didn't make it back alive from his abduction, she'd have her way out.

'Does Alain know?' he asked.

'Alain's a good man.'

'Does he know?'

'It's not easy for him. To him, Jérôme is a hero.'

Trent fixed his jaw. He couldn't hide the ferocity that crackled and twitched inside him. The heat that flared in his eyes. He was seeing the evidence of Jérôme's behaviour for himself now. It was no longer just hearsay. The man had assaulted his wife. It wouldn't have taken a big step for him to attack Aimée, too. It wasn't hard to believe that he'd lost all control.

Stephanie looked down meekly and eased up her leotard, feeding her arms back through the straps until she was dressed once again.

One of the straps had twisted up. It terrified him how tempted he was to reach out and straighten it. To rest his hand on her skin. Pull her close.

And not only that, but how badly he wanted to push her back and slap her hard across the face.

He tightened his hand into a ball. Dug his nails into the flesh of his palm until his fist shook.

Complexities he didn't need.

'I see it in you, too,' she said, looking up hesitantly. 'The sadness. There was someone you were close to, wasn't there? Is it the girl in the photograph? The one you carry in your wallet? She's very beautiful.'

He opened his mouth to reply, then felt his response catch in his throat. It was no longer the simple question it had used to be. Hidden intricacies lay behind it now. Whole dimensions he was at a loss to know how to negotiate.

She absorbed his silence with an expression of grave solemnity, as if it held a special resonance for her.

'You must miss her very much.'

He couldn't hold her eyes. There seemed to be a level of understanding in them that unnerved him. And something more, perhaps. An invitation he couldn't begin to assimilate.

He snatched his head away and glanced towards the door that led to Jérôme's study. Lowered his satchel from his shoulder and hefted it dumbly.

'I have to go and connect this,' he said. 'The gang could call at any moment.'

'Of course.' She hunched her shoulders. Hugged herself. 'I understand.'

He turned from her and stepped across the room. Groped for the door handle and passed through into the study. The door eased closed behind him and he slumped back against it, releasing a breath that hadn't seemed to contain enough air.

*

Back in Marseilles, the young man was staring at the small colour screen on the reverse of his digital camera. The screen was lit up brightly against the dingy brown interior of his studio apartment. He was focused on it intently and his eyes were wet and stinging against the electronic glare.

The camera had a whole bunch of useful functions. The young man could toggle a little lever with his thumb and manipulate the image in any way he preferred. He could scroll left or right, up or down. He could zoom out. He could zoom in. He could remove red-eye.

The extreme zoom was his favourite function. He was using it on his preferred image. It was the shot of Trent and the guy at the café, the one where the guy had swivelled in his chair and stared directly towards the young man. The guy hadn't spotted him. He was absolutely certain of that. But the young man had captured his features dead on.

The camera had been expensive. The image it produced was excellent. He could zoom right in to the guy's deeply lined face without the quality of the shot degrading. There was no way anybody could dispute what he'd managed to record.

He smiled and looked up from the glowing screen. He stared out the window and across the scrappy square towards the blue front door to Trent's apartment. His eyes burned and watered, then brimmed over. The young man smiled as hot tears streamed down his face.

Chapter Twenty-five

Trent walked stiffly across the room and collapsed into Jérôme's generous desk chair. The supple leather creaked and wheezed as he adjusted his weight. He reached into his satchel and removed the digital recording equipment he'd purchased just that morning from an electrical store in Marseilles. It was the same system he'd installed in his own apartment and it took him no more than a few minutes to wire it up to Jérôme's phone. He lifted the receiver and checked that the green light came on and the machine started to record. Satisfied, he replaced the receiver and reset the equipment.

He spread his hands on the lush timber. Drummed his fingers. Considered what to do next.

Stephanie's presence in the studio next door bothered him a great deal. So did the open door into the glazed corridor. But if he shut it, he might arouse Alain's suspicion. Better to go ahead and act now. Be decisive. Who knew when another chance might present itself?

He rolled back the chair and bent down to study the drawers fitted into the desk. He tried each of the handles in turn. Every one was locked.

He glanced up. The room remained empty, the windows aglow with afternoon sunlight. He delved a hand inside his satchel, lifted up the false base and removed the leather pouch that Girard had passed him back at the restaurant. The pouch contained a set of eight brass keys. They were small and stubby, each with a very basic but slightly different bit on the end.

Trent had described the desk to Girard in considerable detail. He'd explained about its antique characteristics. He'd spoken of the little brass keyhole fitted to each drawer and he'd asked Girard to pass the information on to the guy who'd laid the groundwork for them to access Jérôme's villa in Cassis. Trent had been pretty sure that the drawers were fitted with warded locks. They were about as basic as locks could get. It was likely the same key would open every drawer and Trent had wanted to know if Girard's contact had a set of old-fashioned skeleton pass keys that might fit.

Girard's guy had obliged, for what Trent had been warned would involve an additional fee, and now Trent had the first key in his hand, pinched between his forefinger and thumb, and he was debating where to begin.

He decided on the thin central drawer fitted above his knees. He poked the key in the lock. There was a fair amount of play between the shaft and the keyhole. The key slipped all the way inside until it met some resistance and then he twisted it to the left. It didn't budge. That was disappointing but no great surprise. The chances of this working were slim to begin with, so the likelihood of the first key doing the job was remote.

He looked up and checked both doors again – the one into the studio and the one leading into the corridor. He listened for any sound or disturbance. There was none.

He withdrew the key and tried the next in the collection. This key had two bits with a notch in between whereas key number one had just featured a single brass block.

He eased the key into the lock. Waited for the resistance. Turned it to the left. Nothing. He jiggled it some more. The lock didn't turn.

He tried key number three, then number four.

Not even close.

He moved on to key five, working faster now, aware that the risk he was running was increasing all the while. He wasn't taking quite so much care as before because he didn't expect the key to work and was just about ready to write the whole idea off as bust.

So he didn't react right away when the key confounded him by rotating a half-turn to the left. He heard the snick of the lock retracting and stared at his finger and thumb, pointed downwards at the floor. He released a faint whistle and very carefully slid the drawer open a short way.

There were papers inside. He eased the drawer back further and found that he'd accessed Jérôme's stationery supply. There was a yellow foolscap notepad, a couple of pens and some quality writing stock as well as a collection of envelopes of various sizes.

There was nothing of any interest to Trent, so he slid the drawer closed, turned the key in the lock and transferred his attention to the uppermost drawer on his right. The same key disabled the lock and the drawer opened just as easily. It contained only one item – a blue leather appointment diary.

The diary was large and thick. It related to the current calendar year, two pages to a day. Trent spread it on his knees beneath the desk. He glanced up and checked the corridor, then flicked through to the day of Aimée's disappearance.

There it was. Set down in the gap beside 4 p.m., in bold blue ink. *Meeting with A. Paget.*

Nothing had been added to the note. No explanation of what the meeting might be for nor where it had been scheduled to take place. There'd been no attempt to erase the record or to disguise it at all.

Trent scanned upwards. There was another entry against 2 p.m., this one surrounded by square brackets. *[C.M.??]*

C.M. The initials of the dancer Jérôme had arranged to meet, Trent supposed. He wasn't sure it mattered any more, though it was something he could verify with Girard.

Trent kept his thumb on the page and flicked forwards at speed until he reached the present date. His quick scan revealed no mention of Aimée, or of Trent, nor anything connected to them both. There were no further references to C.M.

Trent paused and worked backwards from his thumb until he located the two previous meetings Aimée had held with Jérôme. One had taken place just over five weeks before her disappearance. The first was some two weeks before that. The delay and the repeat meetings didn't strike Trent as unusual. It often took some time for Aimée to hook a client and even longer for the documentation to come through from the brokerage firm they liaised with once the initial paperwork had been signed. The purpose of Aimée's third meeting with Jérôme would have been to deliver the complete set of policy documents. One of the things that rankled with Trent most of all was that Jérôme had attacked her, possibly killed her, then delivered the insurance papers to his lawyer as if nothing untoward had occurred.

He felt a surge of heat course through him. Anger that made him want to lash out. He fought to control his temper and settled for tearing free the pages connected to Aimée. He folded them several times, until they were wrapped very tight and very small, and then he wedged them inside the ankle opening of the boot on his right foot. He closed the diary and slipped it away and locked the drawer and moved on to the one below.

He was afraid of what he might find now. His hand shook as he inserted the key. His jaw ached and he became aware of how badly he'd been clenching his teeth. Could there be something of Aimée's in this desk? Her mobile, perhaps? Might he find some concrete evidence of what had been done to her? And what if he did? What then?

'What are you doing?'

Trent's head snapped up. Alain was standing in the doorway to the study clutching a buff cardboard wallet in front of his waist. Trent had no idea how long he'd been standing there.

The drawer Trent had been working on was partway open. He palmed the key and allowed it to fall gently inside. The wire that connected the recording equipment to the telephone was hanging in a loop in front of him. It was split in two. One end was plugged into the phone. The remaining lead terminated in a socket jack. Trent nudged the drawer closed with his knee and delved his hand inside his satchel, depositing the pouch of skeleton keys beneath the false bottom and removing a set of headphones in one fluid movement. He made a show of linking the headphones to the jack.

'All done,' he said, and laid the headphones down on top of the recording equipment.

Alain didn't respond. He was staring towards the side of the desk Trent had been working through. He took a step inside the study. Then another. He moved with purpose across the centre of the room and circled the end of the desk just as Trent gave the drawer a final nudge with his knee.

Alain looked down.

Trent's heart thrashed in his chest. He knew that Alain had come from the security room. He knew for a fact that there were surveillance cameras rigged up outside. But what if there were some inside, too? What if there was a device hidden in the study?

Trent twisted in his seat to face Alain. He tried to breathe steadily and slow his pulse but his eyes were straining to scan the ceiling. He glanced behind Alain at some of the shelves of green leather books. He couldn't spot a camera.

'I have a question for you,' Alain said.

Trent's mind blanked. His stomach eddied and he felt the dread chill of failure.

Alain loomed over him. He was standing very close. Would he snatch open the drawer and go for the incriminating key? Would he demand that Trent remove his boot?

'Tell me,' Alain said, withdrawing a limp, glossy sheet from the buff folder and laying it down on the surface of the desk directly in front of Trent, 'who is this man?' He was pointing at a colour photograph of two men sitting at a sunlit café table. One of the men was Trent. The second was Girard. Alain tapped the tacky print with his finger. 'And why were you meeting with him this morning?'

Chapter Twenty-six

'You followed me?' Trent asked.

'Answer the question.'

Trent delayed his response. He was thinking hard. He was asking himself where Alain could have pursued him from.

He couldn't have set off as soon as he'd left the estate. Trent had heard nothing to indicate he was being followed during his trek to the Peugeot and he'd spent a good half-hour, undisturbed, at the point where the gang had attacked from. No vehicle had approached while he'd been investigating the area nor during the time he'd spent burying Serge's body. He'd been juiced on adrenalin. His senses had been heightened. He felt sure that he'd have picked up on Alain's presence. And besides, if Alain had seen the terrible thing he'd done up on that rise, there was no way he would have allowed him back inside the house. There was no way he would have left him alone with Stephanie.

So he must have picked him up later. Trent's best guess was that he'd spent the time after Trent had left the Moreau mansion carrying out a more detailed background check. Perhaps he'd contacted Jérôme's lawyer again. Trent's address would be listed on the insurance policy documents as the location his firm operated from. Alain must have decided to monitor him there. He must have followed him down to the quayside restaurant for his meeting with Girard.

'You still don't trust me,' Trent said.

'I'm paid not to trust people.'

'Did you take this photograph yourself?'

Alain nodded, just barely. Trent was pretty sure it was the truth. Who else could he have called on for help at such short notice? Who else could he risk involving in the kidnap scenario? Not Philippe. Not Stephanie. Alain had told him that the housekeeper was elderly and couldn't drive, which seemed to rule her out. Another employee of Jérôme's that Trent didn't know of yet? He doubted it. Very few people were trusted enough to be permitted inside the Moreau estate, so the chances of Alain tasking someone with the responsibility seemed unlikely. And Jérôme was a smuggler, a facilitator, a go-between. He wasn't a guy with a crew of men at his disposal.

'What if the gang had called while you were checking up on me?' Trent asked.

Alain vented a low grumble of frustration. He tapped the image of Girard again. The sticky surface adhered to his skin. The photograph was fresh from the printer. Trent could smell the heated ink.

'Who is this man?'

Trent sighed heavily. 'His name is Luc Girard,' he said. 'He's a former police detective. He worked out of Nice.'

'And why did you meet with him? What did you discuss?'

Alain's question suggested that he hadn't been close enough to hear what the two men had said to one another. That was good. A definite plus. And the nature of the surveillance photograph supported the theory. It looked like a zoom shot. Judging by the angles, it had been taken from further along the quay, possibly close to the docking point for the municipal ferry that shuttled passengers to the opposite side of the marina throughout the day.

'I didn't tell him anything about Jérôme, if that's what you're concerned about. I told you, I don't favour police involvement in a kidnap scenario.'

'No? Then why meet with him at all?'

'Sit down.' Trent leaned backwards in the desk chair and knitted his hands together. Alain didn't move. 'Relax,' Trent told him. 'I'll tell you everything you want to know. But it'll take some time, so you might as well sit. And close that door, will you? I'd rather we discussed this in private.'

Alain gauged him for a moment longer, then backed off and went and eased the door shut. It gave Trent an opportunity to make sure the drawer was sealed before Alain returned to the area in front of the desk. He lifted one of the visitor chairs from the floor and twirled it around, finally sitting on it with his forearms draped over the backrest and his chin propped on his hands.

'So go ahead,' he said. 'Talk.'

Trent tapped his thumbs together. He contemplated the photograph of his meeting with Girard. Inclined his head towards the image. 'I wanted to speak with him about the man who contacted us on behalf of the gang. The one calling himself Xavier.'

Alain raised his head. 'But you said—'

'I know what I said. And I didn't give him any details of what I'm involved in here. He knows nothing about Jérôme. He knows me too well to ask about an abduction I'm working on. This was strictly a one-way conversation.'

Alain blew air through his lips. He wasn't convinced.

'I wanted to talk to him about Xavier because I've encountered him in the past. We both have. I told you my first impressions were that the gang we're dealing with are a professional outfit. Now I know it for sure. Xavier is a career kidnapper. One of the best.'

Alain bristled. 'You didn't mention this before.'

'I'm telling you now. All of it. This man', Trent said, nodding towards the photograph of Girard, 'worked with me on an abduction carried out by Xavier's gang over two years ago. They kidnapped the teenage son of a wealthy industrialist. I can tell you his name because his father will be one of the men your lawyer called to check up on me.'

Alain stared at him levelly. He waited.

'Viktor Roux,' Trent said.

Alain nodded. 'We consulted his father. He said we should listen to you and do everything you say.'

Trent felt a small jolt of relief. It was a lesson the Roux family had learned the hard way. He wished they hadn't needed to, though he couldn't pretend he wasn't grateful for it now.

'He won't have given you details,' Trent said. 'But I can. Provided they never leave this room.'

'You have my word.'

Trent had no way of gauging the worth of Alain's promise, though his usual concern for client confidentiality seemed of little significance right now.

'Viktor Roux was snatched from outside a retail store in a backstreet of Nice. The store specialised in role-playing games. Viktor was a real enthusiast. He participated in a regular tournament the store owner held for his best customers on a Monday evening. A friend was with him at the time. He had his nose split with the butt of a rifle by one of the gang members. Fortunately, he called Viktor's parents before he contacted the police. I was involved from the start. We were able to persuade Viktor's friend not to speak with the authorities. And he was able to give us some basic details about the men who took Viktor.'

Trent paused. He looked down at his thumbs. He was rotating them, one over the other. He supposed it didn't look good. A sign of nerves, maybe. He parted his hands. Rested a finger on the edge of the desk.

'It won't surprise you to hear the approach the gang used was similar to the way they snatched Jérôme. Viktor was on foot, so that made things simpler, but they arrived at speed in a blue van and three men leapt out. They wore ski masks. One of the men hit Viktor's friend. The other two bundled Viktor inside the van. It was all over in seconds.' Trent exhaled and met Alain's intent stare. 'The gang's first call came inside twenty-four hours. Their spokesman identified himself as Xavier. He demanded a high ransom. Said Viktor would be killed unless his parents paid in full.'

'And? What happened?'

'I told them the same thing I told you. I warned them not to agree to an early payment. I stressed the importance of negotiating a sensible fee.'

'Did it work?'

Trent shrugged. 'They disregarded my advice. They agreed to pay Xavier's gang in full when he made his second telephone call. A ransom drop was arranged. The gang left a package for us in a nearby café with all the details we'd need. We complied with them precisely and they collected the cash.' Trent paused. He smiled faintly. 'But they didn't release Viktor. Three days went by. Then another call came in. The ransom had been doubled. The gang expected payment within two days.'

Alain shifted in his seat. He gripped and re-gripped the backrest of his chair. 'But what does this have to do with this man?' he asked, pointing a finger towards the image of Girard.

'I'm getting to that. The second ransom demand was a lot for the Roux to take in. Viktor's mother had pushed for the full settlement the first time around. She wanted to do the same again. I counselled against it and Viktor's father began to appreciate the logic in what I was saying.'

'Or perhaps he did not wish to pay the fee.'

'He could afford it. That wasn't the issue. His concern was that he didn't want to prolong the situation indefinitely. He didn't want his son or wife to suffer any more than they had to. So he started to listen to me and to act on my advice. They'd ignored me once and it had cost them. It was an unfortunate lesson for them to learn.'

'And did it work? Your advice?'

'Eventually.' Trent glanced down at the image of himself and Girard sitting at the café table. The camera had captured him squinting against the harsh sunlight. His face looked contorted, the skin tightened and crinkled around his eyes, his teeth bared in a strange grimace, as if he were biting down on something against a searing pain. 'In its entirety, the abduction lasted three hundred and twenty-three days.'

Alain's shoulders slumped. 'Almost a year.'

'Almost. You have to understand, it took a long time to recover from that first mistake. Resetting the gang's expectations was difficult. They were anticipating more frailty from the family and when they faced a tougher response, they did everything they could to break them.'

'Such as?'

'Such as threats. They sent recordings of Viktor begging for his parents' mercy. They sent pictures of him looking beaten and tortured. For many months the gang refused to reduce their demands.' Trent smoothed his palm across the polished surface of the desk, like he was clearing steam from a mirror. It was one he was reluctant to stare into. 'It put a great deal of strain on Viktor's family. His mother in particular. I stressed how easily these things could be faked. I told them how often kidnap victims would be given scripts to read from, that they'd be encouraged to sound as distressed as possible.'

'They didn't believe you?'

'Viktor's mother couldn't. She'd been pushed too far. His father was willing to stay with me for a little longer. But then the gang pushed again. And this time there was no way I could convince them the threat was phoney.'

'Because the family cracked?'

Trent closed his eyes for a brief moment. He did his best to shut out the images that were flooding his mind, then fixed his gaze on Alain. 'No, because the threat was real. The gang left a package in a public bin close to the family home. It was about the size of a shoebox, a polystyrene shell wrapped in brown tape and addressed to Viktor's mother. We opened it together. It was mostly ice and bubble-wrap, at least until we got to the bottom.'

Alain raised an eyebrow.

'They'd sent us one of Viktor's fingers,' Trent said, 'with a promise of more to come.'

Chapter Twenty-seven

'So your advice didn't work,' Alain said. 'Xavier won.'

'Some victory.' Trent mashed the heel of his palm into his eye. It was dry and aching. 'There was a note with the finger. A concession. The gang agreed to halve their ransom demand if the Roux family paid them within thirty-six hours.'

'So you had a breakthrough.'

'A costly one. But yes, it was the progress we'd been waiting for. My advice was that we should push once more. Offer only half of the new amount. The gang would be as tired of the situation as we were. I sensed that they were looking for a speedy way out. Perhaps factions had developed among them. I believed we could turn this to our advantage.'

'The family disagreed?'

'They felt it was a risk too far. They'd suffered for eleven months. The prospect of ending their anguish, not to mention the suffering of their son, was too tempting.'

'Understandable.'

'Perhaps.' Trent shrugged. 'But by sending Viktor's finger to his parents, the gang set in motion an unexpected consequence. Viktor's mother lost all perspective. She couldn't believe that the gang would release him without further harm. So she contacted the police without my knowledge. Without speaking to her husband.' Trent reached out and gripped the colour photograph by its bottom edge. He turned it until the image was facing towards Alain. Pointed at Girard. 'This man headed up a specialist anti-kidnap unit in the serious crime squad based in Nice. He came to the house with his team. He met with Viktor's parents and he convinced them that it was possible for him to apprehend the gang during the ransom drop.' Trent rolled his eyes. 'He promised them justice.'

'You didn't believe him?'

'I didn't care. Catching the gang was irrelevant. A sideshow. I explained that the risk was too great. That they were in danger of undoing all our hard work. But Girard is a skilled detective. He's good at offering reassurance. Once he begins to talk, it becomes difficult to doubt anything he says. And he had the Roux's confidence. He was telling them everything they wanted to hear.'

'What did you do?'

'There wasn't much I could do. It was out of my hands. I'm a consultant. An adviser. Like I told you, my clients make their own decisions. The Roux family made theirs. They went with Girard. The following morning, the gang sent instructions for the ransom drop. It was scheduled to take place at a disused warehouse on the outskirts of the city. Viktor's father took a holdall with the necessary cash inside. That was my final victory. Girard had suggested a bag filled with dummy notes. I argued against it. If anything went wrong, the most dangerous thing would be for the gang to find that they'd been betrayed twice. Viktor's father agreed with me.'

'And since the man who called us yesterday was this Xavier character, I'm assuming something *did* go wrong.'

'Very. Viktor's father left the holdall exactly as he'd been instructed to. Ten minutes later, a van sped into the warehouse. There were two masked men inside. They went for the bag and Girard's team moved in. But they bungled the takedown. They underestimated the people they were up against. The gang were heavily armed. Assault rifles. Shotguns. They got away. But not without consequences. Girard's second-in-command was shot. Twice. She died at the scene.'

'They screwed up.'

'Worse than you know. The dead officer was Girard's lover. He was a mess. He blamed himself. A full investigation might have found him culpable, but he had a distinguished career behind him. A lot of good will. He quit within a week. No disciplinary charges.'

'And the Roux kid?'

'We heard nothing for three days. The situation could have gone either way. It was always a possibility that the gang might take revenge and kill him. That was what I feared would happen. But they chose a different outcome. On the third afternoon, Viktor walked in through the front door of the Roux's home. He'd been released a few streets away. He was dishevelled and dehydrated and he'd lost a good deal of weight, but he was alive, at least.'

'Because his father paid the gang. He followed your advice.'

Trent raised his eyebrows. 'I think it helped. Certainly Viktor's father credited me with the success. But the gang took their revenge for the police involvement all the same. Before they released Viktor, they hacked off his thumb. They returned him to his parents with the thumb in his pocket. No ice this time. Just a dirty rag. There was no hope of it being reattached.'

'They left him mutilated.'

'Physically, yes. But the real damage was psychological. His incarceration had been prolonged and the conditions he'd been held in had been vile. Like many victims, he blamed his family for not securing his release sooner. For almost a year, he'd heard only the gang's version of events. They'd told him he would have been released much faster if his parents had complied with their demands.'

'Stockholm Syndrome.'

'Not exactly. He didn't have any attachment to the men in Xavier's gang. He hated them for what they'd done to him. But he struggled to forgive his parents, too. His father arranged for me to meet with him in the days following his return. It was supposed to be a debrief. Useful for me. It's often a difficult time for the victim but usually they're eager to assist. Not Viktor. He blamed me, too. So far as he was concerned, I'd failed him.'

Alain threw up a hand. 'You can understand this, maybe.'

'Of course. I didn't push him. Just that brief exposure had shown me he was badly messed up. In the months that followed, his parents told me that he had nightmares he couldn't shake. Traumas he couldn't forget. He was diagnosed as suffering from acute anxiety disorders and depression. His parents arranged the best treatment money could buy. But if he made any progress, it was slow. He spent each day blaming them, terrified that the gang would come back. It was hard for him to feel he was truly free.'

'It's sad,' Alain said. 'I'm sorry for the boy. But it still doesn't explain why you were talking to this man.'

'I'm getting to that.' Trent's tone was sharp. 'Like I said, Girard is a good detective. And he's a reassuring figure. He impressed Viktor's parents. They didn't blame him for the bungled takedown. In fact, I'm pretty sure they felt that the threat posed to the gang by the police was one reason they let Viktor go.' He shook his head, clearly mystified. 'In the aftermath of his ordeal, Viktor's father began to believe that his son would never truly recover unless the gang were apprehended. He claimed that if they were arrested and convicted, put behind bars, then his son might have a chance of rebuilding his life.'

'It's a little simplistic, I think.'

'I thought so, too. But his parents were prepared to try anything, no matter how slim the chances of success. So they hired Girard, on a private basis. Viktor's father offered him double his police salary, plus a significant bonus if he identified and apprehended Xavier's gang. On the face of it, the idea was to bring the gang to justice. In reality, I think both men were seeking vengeance. M. Roux for his son. And Girard for his dead lover.'

Alain exhaled, long and low. He reached out a hand and claimed the photograph for himself. He held it before him, contemplating the craggy face of Luc Girard. The broken detective. The man who was seeking revenge on the killer of the woman he'd loved.

Trent said, 'The reason I met with him this morning was to ask if he'd made any progress. To see if he had any clue as to where Xavier might be.'

Alain scowled. 'And did he?'

'He said no.'

'He's still looking?'

'Every day. It's not just his only case. It's his life, now.'

'But you didn't tell him about Jérôme?'

Trent kept his voice level. He focused on not glancing away as he responded. 'Not yet. But he's not stupid. He wondered if I was involved in something related to the gang.'

'What did you say?'

'That I wasn't in a position to tell him anything. Yet. But that if the situation changed, I'd be in touch.'

Alain dropped the photograph. He wrinkled his nose in a show of disgust. 'The situation won't change.'

'He could help us. He might offer us an alternative way of releasing Jérôme.'

'You say he's had more than a year, yes?'

'That's right.'

'And he hasn't found this man. Plus, he made a mistake once already. He nearly cost the boy his life.'

'It's an option,' Trent told him. 'It's something to consider.'

'Do not meet with this man again.' Alain stared at him, mouth set, brow furrowed. 'No police.'

'I told you, he's freelance now.'

'He's police. That doesn't change. And neither does my decision. Understand?'

The door to the study opened behind Alain. Stephanie passed through, cocking her head at his words. She was freshly showered and immaculately made up, her hair styled into a glamorous wave. She was wearing a blue silk blouse over beige trousers. The blouse was open at her neck and Trent could see that she had on a looped silver necklace. A solid silver pendant dangled from the chain. It was oval and reminded him of the locket Aimée had worn. Of his picture inside. He'd been a completely different individual when the photograph had been taken. He'd had no idea of the darkness that lay ahead for him. Of the lies he'd tell.

'What decision?' Stephanie asked. She sounded breezy and alert. There was no hint of the damaged individual Trent had been speaking to just half an hour before. 'I thought we were making all our decisions as a group.' She approached the desk, looking between Trent and Alain, assessing their watchful attitudes and their posturing. Gauging the tension in the room. She plucked the photograph from Alain's grip. Studied it briefly. 'What's this? Who is this man?'

'Tell her.' Trent rolled his chair back from the desk and found his feet. He glanced down quickly and saw that the drawer appeared firmly closed. 'I'm going for a walk,' he said. 'I need some air.' He met Stephanie's eyes as he circled the desk. They were wide and filled with light. It was almost possible to believe he hadn't witnessed the dull torpor in them earlier. 'The recording equipment is all set up,' he said. 'It'll click in automatically. But you should stay by the phone. Better you answer it than the machine.'

Chapter Twenty-eight

Trent paced along the glazed corridor. Ahead of him, the door to Alain's security room was closed. He slowed and scanned the ceiling for video cameras. Didn't see any. Plus Alain hadn't challenged him inside the study. He hadn't demanded to know why Trent had been snooping through Jérôme's desk drawers. It didn't mean there was no internal surveillance. It was always possible that Alain was allowing him just enough rope to hang himself. But Trent was willing to take that chance.

He glanced back over his shoulder. Nobody there. He reached out and tried the handle. It rotated a short way but the door was definitely locked. No way through. He'd left his set of skeleton pass keys inside his satchel in the study but they'd be no good on a modern lock anyway.

Trent backed off and exited through the front door onto baking gravel. He could hear the babble of the fountain and smell the boggy odour of the recycled, aerated water. The plump cherub smiled his inane smile and stared blindly ahead. The sun beat down on the paint-work of Philippe's sports car and the ruined Mercedes.

Trent was just debating which direction to try first when his thoughts were interrupted by a sudden thwack. He raised his head to see Philippe's lean body twisted at the hip, golf club whipped forwards. It appeared that he was improving. The ball travelled high and far. Maybe it was the repetition. Maybe it was the booze. Either way, Trent intended to keep his distance.

He set off to his left, passing between the long garage building and the angular study. He didn't glance inside towards Alain and Stephanie. He kept his eyes dead ahead and walked beyond the pathway that led around back to the swimming pool, emerging onto a small patio terrace. A plastic table and chairs were off to his right, a collapsed parasol poking up through the centre of the table. The cottage that had been built onto the back of the garage was modest and compact. There were two windows on either side of a glazed door and a lean-to conservatory on the far end.

A plump, grey-haired woman in a floral frock was pegging laundry to a clothesline outside. The housekeeper, Trent guessed. She was short and having to use a set of steps to reach the line. Her arms were swollen with fat, the skin bunched loosely at her wrists.

She sensed Trent watching her and her head snapped round. She gave him a wary look, her pudgy hands gripping the clothesline, a peg between her puckered lips.

Trent nodded a greeting, shielding his eyes against the sun flaring off the sheet.

The woman didn't respond.

Trent asked himself if now would be a good time to walk over and show her the picture of Aimée from his wallet. He could enquire if Aimée's face looked familiar to her, perhaps ask if she'd spotted anything unusual about Jérôme's behaviour during the past couple of months.

But before he could make up his mind, it was already too late. The woman left the sheet hanging askew, a corner skimming the ground, and stepped down from her stool to waddle across to the cottage. She took one last searching look at Trent, as though mentally logging his features, then hurried around the far wall.

She'd be on her way to the house, Trent supposed. Reporting to Alain. Nothing he could do about it.

He marched on over the patio and across an expanse of neatly trimmed lawn, the grass scratching drily against his boots. It occurred to him that the estate must require some dedicated landscaping and maintenance. It was the kind of role that would be physically beyond the ageing housekeeper. Was it something Serge had been involved in?

Or did somebody come in from outside? Trent made a mental note to raise the point with Alain.

He kept moving and covered something like two hundred metres before the grass became longer and thicker. He could see the perimeter fence up ahead for the first time and a grove of perhaps twenty olive trees just in front of it. The trees were young and green and looked to have been recently planted. The ground beneath them had been scraped back to bare, dusty earth, though it would be many years before the trees offered up any fruit worth cultivating.

Trent swivelled slowly, surveying the fall of the land and the line of the fence from left to right. There was no loose cluster of trees here. No sign of an isolated cabin.

He turned and hurried back the way he'd come, fighting the urge to jog. He circled around via the housekeeper's conservatory, keeping his eyes down as he marched past the fountain and the cars and across the driveway, then on through the line of cypress trees, traversing the lawn to the right of the house, heading towards the treetops he'd spied early that morning.

The grass here was just as precisely cut, the ground every bit as level. He was starting to understand why Philippe had been tempted to occupy himself with Jérôme's golfing equipment. Trent had played on eighteen-hole courses that weren't nearly so manicured.

He walked on, upping his pace and covering some considerable distance before he turned and found that he could only just glimpse the pitch of the terracotta roof of the house behind him. He realised, with some surprise, that there was a gradual curve to the lawn, minor enough to fool the eye, then increasing to a recognisable slant. The grass became longer as it sloped downwards, mimicking the fringed rough on the golf course Trent had pictured in his mind. Long strands knotted round his toes and ankles so that he could feel the snag and tear as he moved. There were weeds here, and thorns and meadow flowers. Insects drifted up from below, dizzily circling his legs and waist, clouding around his clenched fists.

He was breathing hard. His face was flushed, his body filmed with sweat, his heart beating rapidly. Anxiety, he supposed. Adrenalin. He really didn't want to be stopped before he'd found what he was searching for.

A scattering of trees lay ahead and he sensed he was close. He weaved through almond trees and lotus trees. Then the earth became drier and it wasn't long before he found himself in a stand of aged pines, the soles of his feet sinking through drifts of dead needles, his toes punting hollow-sounding cones. The fence was perhaps thirty feet away. The chirrup of the cicadas in the undergrowth on the other side was loud and insistent, like a maddening samba beat.

There was a sort of clearing in front of him. A break in the trees. And in the centre of the space was the dilapidated shack he'd seen on the surveillance footage.

His first instinct was to search for the cameras. He'd come at the cottage from the side but the images he'd seen on the monitors had been taken from the front and rear. The trees were sparse and it didn't take him long to spot the two devices. They were high up in some tall maritime pines. The trunks had been stripped of all possible hand and footholds until well above the height he might jump to. There was no way of reaching the cameras or of avoiding their gaze. And if the house-keeper had alerted Alain already, there was every chance he might be watching.

But Trent wasn't prepared to quit. He wanted to get inside the cabin. There was a pale green stable door at the front and he approached it at speed, visualising himself hurrying through the first camera's field of vision, then yanking down on the handle once he was in the middle of the shot.

The door was locked. He leaned his weight on it. Pulled the other way. There was some give. The frame looked old and wormholed. It was possible he could kick it through, but it would be difficult to ex-plain why he'd felt the need to if he failed to find anything connected to Aimée.

Slatted wooden shutters guarded the low windows on either side of the door. The timber looked to be as warped as the doorframe and some of the boards were split. Trent approached the shutters to the left of the door, unfastened the rusted iron latch and eased them back against squealing hinges. He cleared away the clotted husk of a spider's web and pressed his face to the blackened glass. The interior was concealed in darkness. He could just glimpse the ghostly outline of some furniture hidden beneath a few old dustsheets. Looked like a rickety table and chairs. Possibly a wardrobe or dresser.

The sash fitting was secured with some variety of internal clasp. It would be easier to force open than the door. It was a possibility, for sure.

'There's nothing in there, you know.'

Trent jumped and spun round in the direction of the voice to find Philippe standing in front of him.

He still had on his blue swimming shorts but he'd covered his torso with a white V-neck T-shirt. He was holding a golf club in his fist, the shaft propped on his shoulder. A sand wedge. Plenty of weight in the head. One solid swing would do a lot of damage.

Philippe adjusted his fingers on the rubber handle, setting them down one after the other, like a musician running through a scale on a flute.

'Why are you here?' He lifted his chin and peered down his nose at Trent. 'What are you looking for?'

'There's a possibility the gang might be watching the main house,' Trent replied. 'I thought it best to make sure nobody was inside.'

Philippe didn't appear convinced. 'It's empty, apart from the rats and the spiders. Has been since my father bought this land. Originally it was going to be knocked down for a stable. Then *maman* decided she didn't like horses any more.'

Trent nodded, wet his lips. He glanced at the golf club, then turned and pressed his face to the window once more. Cupped his hands round his eyes.

'Who has the key?' he asked.

'Nobody. It's only fit for knocking down. If you're worried about intruders, you needn't be. The fence is very secure. And besides,' Philippe said, tapping Trent's shoulder with the golf club, then pointing towards one of the cameras in the trees, 'if anyone was out here, Alain would see.'

Trent sensed the double warning in his words. It was difficult to miss.

'You seem very confident about that.'

'My father is paranoid. The cameras see *everything* that happens here.'

Trent stared up into the unblinking lens. Felt himself shrink.

'Why did you follow me?'

'I didn't,' Philippe replied, as though insulted. 'I was sent to fetch you. There's been another call. They're waiting to play you the recording.'

Chapter Twenty-nine

Trent entered the study with Philippe on his heels. He saw Stephanie and Alain standing alongside the desk in a tense silence, looking down at the phone. Stephanie was chewing her thumbnail. Alain had a hand on her shoulder.

'Cosy,' Philippe muttered, from close by Trent's ear.

'When was the call?' Trent asked.

'Ten minutes ago,' Alain said. 'No more.'

Trent advanced on the desk and unplugged the headphones from the recording equipment. He hit a button, then folded his arms across his chest and listened.

A hiss of feedback was followed by the dull *clunk* of the call connecting. After a short pause, Xavier's animal growl swirled out into the room, thrashing against the walls.

'You have the money?' Somehow, he managed to snarl the words.

'N-no, I don't—' Stephanie stammered.

'You pay the money or we kill him. Five million euros. We know you have it.'

'I don't. I can't get it. The accounts are all in Jérôme's name.'

'Don't lie to us. We know about the insurance. Lie again and the cost goes up.'

Trent could sense that Alain was studying his reaction. He kept his face neutral, his attention fixed on the crackling speaker. If Alain was smart, he'd realise that the reference to the insurance policy didn't prove anything. Jérôme could have told the gang about it himself.

But it did pose a problem. If Jérôme had revealed how much the policy could pay out, the gang now had a base-level asking price that it would be almost impossible to reduce. The negotiation would become a question of how much more the Moreaus were prepared to pay.

Scratchy feedback played on the recording. A long pause. It was clear that Stephanie had been thrown by Xavier's apparent knowledge.

'We know about your negotiator, too,' Xavier said, voice buzzing the air like a chainsaw as he pressed home his advantage. 'Tell him to speak.'

'He's not here,' Stephanie blurted out.

A mistake. Xavier might have been taking a gamble on Trent's involvement, or a bigger gamble on the existence of the insurance policy in the first place. Now both had been confirmed.

'Let me speak with Jérôme,' Stephanie said, collecting herself. 'We need to know he's still alive. We need proof.'

This was better. She'd returned to the script. Trent guessed Alain had played a part in that. Perhaps he'd drawn her attention back to what she should be saying.

'Pay the five million and you can talk to him. We'll return him to you.'

'I don't have it.'

'Don't lie to me. Put the negotiator on.'

'I can get you some money, but not five million. Please. We want to help. But first you must show us he's alive. Ask him this: where did he take me on our second date?'

'No. Another question.'

The instant response didn't surprise Trent. Xavier would be concerned that the question might be a plant. He'd know it was possible that Jérôme had rehearsed certain answers to communicate valuable information about his plight.

But Stephanie hadn't been prepared for the reply. She dithered, then mumbled something offline, presumably to Alain.

'OK,' Stephanie said, sounding confused, 'ask him what my favourite meal is.'

'No. Another question.'

Stephanie whined, frustrated. It took her several seconds to collect herself.

'I'm thinking,' she said.

'Think fast.'

She didn't. She couldn't. But eventually, she said, 'OK. Ask him where we were when he first told me that he loved me.'

Xavier snorted. 'There is a package,' he said, as if ignoring Stephanie's request. 'A gift. You will find it in the negotiator's car. Go now and collect it. Then pay us our money. Or we kill your husband.'

Xavier's threat was followed by a thud. He'd cut the connection. A prolonged beep signalled the end of the recording.

Trent looked up at Stephanie. She was shying from his gaze, hiding behind the curtain of hair that had fallen across her face.

'You did OK,' he told her.

'No, I made an error. I let him know you were here.'

Trent shook his head. 'If what he says about the package is true, then he knew already. And you got a proof of life question across. That's good. What's the answer?'

Stephanie faltered. Her mouth hung open, eyes round. Then she shook her head and swallowed so hard that Trent could see her throat bulge. 'You can hear it from Jérôme,' she told him. 'When we speak with them again.'

'I should go and collect the package,' Alain put in. He was looking between Stephanie and the door. 'Right now.'

'No,' Trent told him. 'We both should. But you can drive.'

*

They took one of the spare vehicles from the triple garage, a BMW sedan in midnight blue. Trent seized the opportunity to take a look inside the outbuilding but all he discovered was an expanse of bare concrete and a silver Volkswagen 4 × 4 with tinted windows that was coated in a film of sand and dust.

'Who maintains the grounds?' Trent asked, pointing towards the vibrant green lawn as Alain sped along the driveway.

'Contractor,' Alain mumbled.

'How often do they come?'

'Twice a week. There are two of them. A father and son.'

'Do you trust them?'

Alain turned and looked at him. 'More than I trust you right now.'

His face was stern, eyes clouded. He'd stopped off in the security room on their way out of the building to fit his shoulder holster around his linen shirt. The Ruger was tucked away snugly, muzzle down beneath his left arm, burnished wooden grips and metal casing catching the light of the afternoon sun. It was loaded. No doubt about it. Alain was acting like a guy who felt supremely confident about his choice of weapon. Not hard, Trent guessed, when he was sitting beside him unarmed.

Alain flipped down his sun visor. He fumbled a clicker and compressed it with his thumb. The electric gate swung open. He paused, drumming his fingers on the gearshift, then sped through and waited on the other side until the gate was secure.

He stayed silent for most of the drive. Trent could tell it was an effort. The guy was breathing hard through his nose, lungs inflating, the Ruger moving in tandem with his expanding chest. He was tightening his hands on the steering wheel, squeezing it like he was wringing a towel. Then it got too much for him and he vented his lungs with a gush of air. Smacked the back of his skull against his headrest.

'Let me guess,' Trent said. 'You don't like that they know about the insurance policy.'

Alain stared across at him, eyes reddened with fatigue and fury. The Peugeot loomed up ahead. Alain wasn't watching the road as he stamped hard on the brakes.

The BMW lurched and snaked and Trent was jarred forwards against his seat belt. His ribs smarted. They were still sore from the crash. He waited until the car had slewed to a halt, and said, 'If it makes you feel any better, I don't like it much, either.'

Alain sucked air through his nostrils like a weightlifter about to attempt a mighty clean and jerk. Trent could picture his lungs expanding rapidly, then contracting like a pair of giant bellows. Put a paper bag to his lips right now and he'd blow clean through it.

'The package is in your car,' Alain said, his words freighted with meaning.

'That's the way I heard it, too.'

'*Your* car. And the package just happens to be inside.'

'OK, I get it.' Trent nodded as he unclipped his seat belt. 'So what do you think? You think I drove up here with a parcel already in my car? Or do you think I left my car here for them? You think that's why I didn't park inside the gate?'

Alain grappled with his own seat belt and barged his door open with his shoulder. He paced towards the Peugeot, his muscular arms swinging fast, fingers clawed and ready to snatch for his revolver.

Trent stepped out, too. The BMW's engine was still running. Warm air shimmied above the bonnet.

'Something you might want to consider,' he yelled. Alain kept moving, fingers twitching. 'Something that could maybe save your life.'

Alain slowed. He glanced back over his shoulder.

'I've known some gangs to lay booby traps,' Trent told him. 'The explosive kind.'

It wasn't true. Nothing like it had ever happened to Trent. But he'd wanted to shake Alain's confidence and bring him up short. Pierce his rage.

Alain hesitated. He was perhaps ten feet from the busted wing mirror. Too close if Trent was right.

He cocked his head and scanned the plateau and the forested ridge on the right, as if searching for a lookout or a guy with a detonator.

Trent stepped up to him, his footsteps rhythmic in the sudden hush. The sun was high above them. Mid-afternoon and the temperature had ramped up by several degrees. There was no breeze. No respite.

The heat reflected up off the gravel road, the spiralling thermals dense and glutinous.

Trent could see the package on the front passenger seat. It was a white polystyrene shell about the size of a shoebox. Brown parcel tape had been wound around the middle of it.

'What do we do?' Alain hissed.

'Do you see any wires?'

Alain shook his head.

'Neither do I. How about underneath?'

Alain squatted to his haunches, his leather shoes creaking in the sun, then down onto one knee on the molten tarmac. He craned his neck and peered beneath the chassis.

'I don't think so,' he said.

'Then we should be OK.'

Trent moved past him and flattened his hand against the burning window glass. He wouldn't need his keys. The car was unlocked. He could see that the door had been forced. The side panel had been levered away from the window seal.

He worked the door handle before Alain had an opportunity to get clear. The bodyguard was leaning back on the heel of one palm, his other arm raised, face averted, braced for a blast.

Trent cracked a grin. He whistled faintly, like Alain was a major dope, then wiped his brow in an exaggerated show of relief. He heaved the door right back and stooped to gather the package, hot air wafting out at him like he'd opened an oven.

The package was light. There was almost no weight to it at all. The polystyrene was warm to the touch. The tape warmer still.

Trent glanced around the cabin of the Peugeot. There was nothing to indicate that it had been tampered with in any way. He ducked his head. His Beretta was still taped to the underside of the dash.

'Let me see,' Alain said.

Trent passed the package back, then watched as Alain weighed and turned the box in his hands. He lifted it above his head and considered the base. There was no writing. No markings.

'What do you think is in here?' Alain sounded as if he was afraid that he already knew the answer.

'A message,' Trent replied. 'Could be harmless.'

'Should we open it?'

'Not here. Open it back in the study. With the rest of the team.'

'Is that wise?'

'Together, you're a unit. You shouldn't act alone.'

Trent didn't have any problem with the concept. He'd been looking for a way to engage Stephanie and Philippe as much as possible. He wanted them invested emotionally in the outcome of Jérôme's predicament. So far, they'd been oddly detached. It was an easy guess that they each had issues with Jérôme. Perhaps something shocking might jar them into realising what was at stake.

And not just for them.

Alain nodded. 'Then bring your car. Follow me and park in front of the house, where it's safe.'

Safe. Not for Trent, but he didn't challenge Alain's suggestion. There was no rational excuse for leaving the Peugeot out on the road.

He fumbled in his pockets for his keys, then looked up to see that Alain had turned from him to face across the road, towards the dirt slope that the Land Cruiser had plunged down during the gang's attack. He raised both hands to protect his eyes from the glare. The Ruger hung menacingly in its holster. It seemed to get bigger every time Trent looked at it.

'What is it?' Trent asked.

Alain lifted the package above his shoulder, like it was an American football and he was planning to throw it towards the end zone. 'Somebody came up here to leave this for us,' he said.

'Does that mean I'm no longer a suspect?'

'Perhaps they're still here.' Alain ignored the barb. 'Perhaps they're watching us, like they did before.'

'I doubt it.'

'We should check.'

He drew his Ruger and approached the dun-coloured slope, the package cradled beneath one arm, the revolver raised in his free hand. His shoes sank to his ankles in the sandy earth and he floundered upwards, swinging his body in an exaggerated arc from the hip.

Trent cursed to himself, then followed, digging his fingers into the baking dirt and hauling himself up fast behind. But they didn't find anybody lurking when they reached the top. There were a few tyre tracks. Some harmless footprints. Trent had been careful not to erase everything after his early morning reconnaissance.

'It looked exactly the same this morning,' Trent said. 'There's nothing new.'

Alain didn't respond. Beads of sweat clung to his nose and chin and eyelashes. He did nothing to wipe them away.

'We should get back,' Trent told him, dusting his hands clean. He could feel the grit beneath his fingernails. The same muck that had lodged there when he'd buried the chauffeur. 'The others will be wondering where we are.'

'What about back here?'

Alain was gesturing with the Ruger to the bank of loose rubble and boulders at the base of the rock shelf that loomed above them.

'No.' Trent's voice was sharp and Alain swivelled, confusion twisting his brow.

Trent jerked his thumb back the way they'd come. 'They'd have no view down to the Peugeot. See?'

Alain raised himself up on his toes and peered downwards. He frowned some more, then glanced longingly at the area where Serge's body lay. Could he sense something, Trent wondered? Was some instinct drawing Alain towards the corpse?

'Let's go,' Trent said. He moved closer and snatched the package from Alain's grip. 'Come on. We're wasting time.'

*

Back in the one-room apartment in Marseilles, the young man doodled with his pencil on the notepad in front of him. The hand not doing the doodling was supporting his chin. His elbow was propped on the table-top. To the left of his elbow was the digital camera. Every so often, when the young man couldn't resist any longer, he'd let go of his pencil and power up the camera and stare at the images he'd captured.

His stomach flipped whenever he contemplated the scene of Trent and the guy at the café. But when he toggled to the next shot he felt stabs of confusion and fear.

Until this morning, he'd assumed that he was the only one watching Trent but he'd been wrong. There'd been someone else. He'd been parked a short distance further along the quay, in a silver off-road vehicle with smoked-glass windows.

The young man had paid no attention to the vehicle at first. Then the driver's window had powered down and a man had leaned his thick forearm on the sill and raised a camera with a telephoto lens to his eye. The lens had been pointed towards the café table where Trent was deep in conversation, and before the young man had paused to consider his actions, he'd snatched a hasty shot of the man in the car.

His angle had been bad and the image couldn't tell him a great deal. He could see that the man was wearing a white, short-sleeved linen shirt, and that his hair was clipped very close to his scalp, army-style. The young man had been afraid to take another photograph. He'd been scared the man in the car would notice him. And within seconds, it was too late anyway because the man had ducked his head back into his vehicle, his window had shuffled upwards and he'd pulled out into the stream of traffic.

It was only once he'd started to drive away that the young man thought to take a picture of his number plate. But by then a sightseeing bus had closed up behind him and the plate was obscured.

The young man hated himself for his mistake. It made him feel queasy to dwell on it. And yet staring at the photograph of the man leaning out of the car window was a kind of torture he found it hard to resist.

Finally, though, when the jagged pains in his chest became too much and the walls of his room seemed to shuffle inwards and crowd around his shoulders, he'd flick a button and switch out of feedback mode. Then he'd take a deep breath and prop the camera on the windowsill and move it from side to side, up and down, until he had a perfect shot of the pale blue front door to Trent's apartment. He'd zoom in. He'd zoom back out again. In and out, forwards and backwards, like he was attached to the door handle by some kind of elastic bungee.

But for now the young man simply doodled and stared out the window at the street scene below. Nothing was moving. Nothing was happening. But that didn't mean he would stop watching. He couldn't afford to miss something vital. Not now. Not ever again.

Chapter Thirty

The package lay on the blotter in the middle of the desk beside the telephone and the recording equipment. Alain approached it with a knife he'd fetched from the kitchen. He was wearing a pair of yellow rubber household gloves. His idea. A way of preserving potential evidence. Trent wasn't too concerned with forensics or future investigations. He was focused on the now. On getting Jérôme back alive. He watched closely from the opposite side of the desk. Stephanie and Philippe faced one another at either end.

The parcel seemed to have grown in size and significance now that it was about to be opened. The polystyrene was a brilliant white against the burgundy blotter and the cherry wood. It throbbed with menace, the brown parcel tape wrapped tight as a tourniquet.

Alain placed one hand on top of the box to steady it, looked up at the others, then pierced the brown tape with the tip of the knife. The blade was thin and very sharp. He made quick work of slicing right around the middle of the box, turning it carefully until he returned to where he'd started.

He set the knife down beside the box and took a moment to collect himself. Then, very carefully, he lifted the lid clear.

Trent saw what he'd been anticipating right away. His reaction was contained. It was different for the others. It took them a moment to process what they were looking at. Philippe was the first to respond. He swore and covered his eyes. Alain wheeled away, dropping the lid. Stephanie shrieked and gripped fistfuls of his shirt, burying her face in his chest.

Trent took a moment to absorb their behaviour. The way Stephanie had turned to Alain interested him in particular. The bodyguard had wrapped his big arm around her and was hugging her tight, smoothing his hand up and down the silk sleeve of her blouse. He didn't seem uneasy about it. There was a familiarity to the pose. It didn't strike Trent as the first time Alain had comforted her that way.

Philippe noticed it, too. He lowered his hand from his eyes until his fingers were spread, clawlike, around his open mouth. He wasn't looking at the box. He was staring at his father's bodyguard and his stepmother, lip curled, as if repulsed.

Trent turned his attention to the contents of the parcel. There was a lot of blood inside. It was dark and thick and oily, and it had settled in a pool perhaps half an inch deep at the bottom of a rectangular crevice that had been sculpted out of the base and lined with some kind of plastic film. The blood had spread around in transit. The parcel had been turned this way and that and the blood had swirled with it, coating the interior.

There was something resting in the blood. It was pale and curled and caked in the greasy fluid. Trent bent down to it. He reached out with his index finger and prodded it. No doubt in Trent's mind. It was an ear.

'What are you doing?' Stephanie demanded. She turned her face away, burrowing into Alain. 'Leave it alone.'

Philippe swallowed thickly. 'I'm going to be sick.'

But Trent ignored their complaints. He dipped his finger and thumb in the blood and lifted the ear out of the shallow trough. Bloody juices slid and dripped down.

'Relax,' he told them. 'It's a fake.'

He shook the ear, feeling the flex of the flesh-coloured rubber. He gathered it in both hands and smoothed his thumb over the reverse. Felt something sticking out in relief. A manufacturer's logo. He cleared it some more, then angled it so that Stephanie could see.

She released her grip on Alain's shirt and gradually stepped away from him. She wiped her nose with the back of her hand. She looked appalled but fascinated.

'It was a trick?' Philippe asked.

'An illusion.' Trent raised a bloody finger to his mouth. He sucked on it. 'Tomato ketchup and olive oil.' He smacked his lips. 'That would be my guess.'

'These people are monsters.'

'No,' Trent said. 'They're worse than that.'

He meant it, too. He'd built his career tussling with gangs just like Xavier's. He'd seen all the wicked scams they employed, all the under-hand tactics. He'd witnessed the harrowing effects of kidnappings on victims and families. In Trent's opinion, it was one of the most heinous crimes anybody could commit.

And yet, he'd been willing to stoop just as low, maybe even further. He reminded himself that the difference between what he'd planned to do to Jérôme and the actions of somebody like Xavier was all in the motive. He wasn't interested in money. He wasn't driven by greed. He wanted answers. A resolution. A way, if it came to it, of bidding good-bye to Aimée and the baby she was carrying.

But in moments like this, seeing the shock and bewilderment and utter disgust on Stephanie's face, he found himself wondering if that was really enough.

'I don't understand this.' Stephanie looked from Trent to Philippe and back again. 'It's sick.'

'It's a ploy. Another tactic. That's all.'

Alain moved closer. He poked the fake ear Trent was holding. 'It undermines them,' he said. 'We know it's not real. They didn't hurt Jérôme.'

'Not yet, maybe. But this is a warning. A threat. And believe me, I've seen with my own eyes that they're capable of carrying it through. Don't fall into the trap of thinking they're goofing around. This might look like something you'd find in a joke shop but the message behind it isn't funny.' He paused. His words reminded him of something. 'Check the lid,' he said.

Alain grabbed it and lifted it in his hand, breaking the adhesion between the surface of the desk and the sticky overlap of the sliced parcel tape. A dark red imprint had been left behind on the lacquered desktop.

Alain peered inside the lid, then recoiled and groaned. He paced over to a brushed stainless-steel bin in the corner of the room. Tilting the lid above the bin, he removed a cotton handkerchief from his pocket and used it to scoop out the glutinous ooze.

'There's something here.' He used a corner of the handkerchief for grip. The object resisted for a moment before tearing free. It was a small plastic bag sealed with tape.

'Open it.'

Alain dispensed with the soaked handkerchief and set the lid of the polystyrene box down on the floor.

'Pass me the knife.'

Trent made a fist around the handle and carried it across to him. He could feel his scalp tighten and shrink. He itched all over, like fire ants were scurrying beneath his skin. His pulse throbbed behind his eyes and he watched closely as Alain pierced the plastic bag with the blade and dipped his gloved fingers inside. He removed a square of white paper.

'Spread it on the desk,' Trent told him.

Alain added the remains of the plastic bag to the bin and wiped the worst of the fake blood from his other hand. Then he returned to Stephanie's side and unfolded the paper. A sheet of lightweight card fell out. It fluttered downwards, turning over and over like a tumbling coin. One side was smooth and pale. The reverse was tacky and multi-coloured. A photograph.

It fell onto the desk face down. Alain turned it upright for them all to see. The shot showed Jérôme sitting in a chair in his tuxedo trousers and sweat-stained dress shirt. His hands were behind him, almost certainly bound. There was a red stain on the front of his shirt. He appeared to have a bloody, split lip, and there was a sickly, greenish

188

cast to his skin. His right eye was puffed up and closed almost to a slit, the area around it a puckered, blackened mess.

A man in a green army jacket and a ski mask was standing beside him. The man was gripping a knuckle-full of Jérôme's hair and he was yanking his head back and to one side, exposing his bulging neck. In his other hand, the man clenched a hunting knife with a curved, serrated blade that he pressed against the base of Jérôme's ear, as if he planned to saw it from his skull.

Stephanie gasped and covered her mouth.

'Animals,' Philippe muttered.

But Trent, though breathless, felt relieved. This was what he'd been waiting for. He wanted them scared. He needed them unbalanced. It would make them so much easier to sway.

Alain was busy straightening out the sheet of paper that had accompanied the photograph. It was typical office stock. He smoothed it flat with the back of his fingers, smearing it with a faint pinkish trace of the counterfeit blood.

NEXT TIME IT WILL BE REAL. PAY US THE MONEY. EMAIL XAVIER222@YAHOO.COM WHEN YOU HAVE THE CASH. YOU HAVE 48 HOURS OR WE CUT HIM AND SEND HIM HOME TO YOU IN PIECES.

Chapter Thirty-one

Trent endured the silence in the room. He waited for Stephanie to express sympathy for Jérôme. He glanced at Philippe, anticipating anger or distress. He listened keenly for the first sign that Alain was about to seize control and suggest what their next move might be. But he didn't hear a word. Nobody spoke. The photograph and the threatening note seemed to have sapped them completely. Where was their outrage, Trent wanted to know? Where was their terror?

It got so he couldn't take it any more. He told them all they should leave the study and take some time to collect their thoughts. He explained that they were in charge of the timetable for the next two days. Another call from Xavier was unlikely. The gang wouldn't be in touch again until they received an email to the account Xavier had set up, or the family failed to meet his deadline. He told them missing the deadline wasn't an option. This was their opportunity to take command. The best way of doing that was to come up with a ransom sum they were willing to pay. It had to be sizeable enough to tempt the gang into an exchange, but the gang would need to understand it was a one-time-only payment. Trent's feeling was that they needed to add something to the insurance payout. The question was how much.

Philippe left first. He headed out the door leading into the glazed corridor with a casual, easy stride, as if he was contemplating a late afternoon swim. Stephanie went second. She offered up a meek smile, then exited by the door that connected with her dance studio.

Only Alain remained. He peeled off his rubber gloves. Tossed them in the bin.

'Can we trace this email account?' he asked, rubbing the skin on

190

the back of his hands.

Trent shook his head. 'I don't see how. Not without calling in some major resources. The official kind. And it's not an account Xavier will check regularly. You can be certain our response will be the only email he'll ever read on it. And he can log in whenever and wherever he likes. He can use any number of internet cafés or computer stores. He could break into somebody's house and use their home PC.'

Alain weighed his response. He rested two fingers on the very edge of the photograph. Shunted it towards Trent.

'Do you think this is staged?'

'Almost certainly.'

'And his injuries? Are they real?'

Trent looked up from the photograph. So at least somebody had been thinking straight.

'If it's not real now,' he said, 'it'll be that way soon.'

Alain inclined his head towards one of the doors. 'Don't you think you should have told them?'

'Don't you think you should have?'

The skin around Alain's eyes tightened into crow's feet. He rubbed the stubble on his chin. Trent sensed he was on the verge of telling him something. But the something wouldn't come. He still didn't trust Trent enough.

'How much more would we need to add to the insurance payout?' he asked.

'Another half-million.' Trent shrugged. 'Three million in total. Maybe more.'

Alain lowered his face to the photograph. He stared at it closely. It was hard to tell what he was looking for. Perhaps he was seeking reassurance that Jérôme's injuries were fake. Perhaps he was trying to assess the level of intent behind the eyes of the man in the ski mask. Or maybe he was asking himself if he could stand to see worse. Maybe he was preparing himself for the possibility of never seeing Jérôme again.

'Would you like me to go and collect my thoughts, too?' Alain asked. 'And leave you alone in this room again?'

'No, you can stay. I'm going to be replaying the recording of Xavier. There may be something we missed.'

'You already know there won't be.'

'It's worth trying. What else am I going to do?'

Alain held his gaze a beat too long, then looked around the study, as if he was searching for the answer to the question Trent had posed. Finally, he grunted and made for the door.

'Where are you going?' Trent called after him.

'To think about money. We're going to need to pay, I think, whether I believe you or not.'

*

Trent kept his word. He settled in Jérôme's leather chair and played back the recording. Right from the start, the bass rumble of Xavier's voice seemed to resonate with some kind of primal fear receptor in his nervous system. An icy, numbing chill coursed through him. The guy had a way of reaching deep inside you and planting something cold and dark in your gut. He sounded like a character from a childhood horror story. He sounded like your worst nightmare made flesh. A guy whose threats seemed as real and as tangible as the breath in your lungs.

Trent listened to the recording right the way through. Then he listened a second time. There was nothing there for him except a profound sense of unease. No slip he could spot. No background noise. Xavier could have been talking from a sound booth or an underground bunker. Trent listened for traffic. He listened for voices. He heard nothing except that strangely penetrative growl. The peculiar way it had of clawing at the insides of your brain like something trapped and scrabbling to get out.

But why wasn't it affecting the others in the same way?

He stopped the playback. Sped forwards.

'Don't lie to me. Put the negotiator on.'

He jumped forwards again.

'There is a package. A gift. You will find it in the negotiator's car.'

The negotiator. The owner of *that* voice knew who he was. He knew that he was involved. And he'd beaten him once before. He'd gotten away with the Roux's money. Led a gang that had killed Girard's colleague and lover. Maybe pulled the trigger himself.

And now he was the one who stood between Trent and Jérôme. He was the guy who'd determine if he'd ever lay eyes on Aimée again.

'Pay us our money. Or we kill your husband.'

Liquid fear trickled down his spine. He shuddered. Couldn't help himself. Then he rolled back his chair, flicked his eyes towards the doorway and eased open the drawer he'd left unlocked.

The skeleton key was still there. He grabbed it and worked quickly through the rest of the desk. One of the drawers was empty. The next contained a laptop. Trent flipped up the lid but when the screen bloomed with light he found that it was password protected. He was no computer hacker, so he was forced to put the laptop away. Another drawer contained pamphlets and registration details and insurance dockets for a number of yachts. Trent flicked through them, crouched low behind the desk. Hidden among the leaflets was a sheaf of information about his own company and the services it offered. Aimée had produced the document on headed notepaper. It looked professional. Discreet. But he uncovered nothing that could point towards who might have targeted Jérôme for abduction. There was no way of linking Jérôme to Xavier. And there was no clue as to Aimée's fate.

He closed the final drawer. Locked it securely. Dropped the key into his satchel.

Then he took one last, lingering look at Xavier's note, and a fog of despair closed in around him.

YOU HAVE 48 HOURS OR WE CUT HIM AND SEND HIM HOME TO YOU IN PIECES.

Chapter Thirty-two

Trent retrieved his mobile from his satchel. He weighed it in his hand and looked over at the open door Alain had left by. Placing the call from the study without checking if anybody was eavesdropping was a risk too far, he decided, and since he was feeling hungry anyway, he made his way to the kitchen.

It was empty. The surfaces were just as clean and uncluttered as he remembered. He opened the fridge and his eyes settled on a plate of cold chicken. The meat looked white and flaky and tender, the waxed skin shiny and crisp. He lifted the plate from the fridge and grabbed a container of milk. He poured himself a glass. Drained it in one go. Poured himself a refill.

He started with one of the drumsticks. He ate it greedily, stripping the flesh to the bone, leaving only a knotted thread of cook's string behind. He sucked his fingers clean, then moved across to the windows overlooking the back yard.

The swimming pool was deserted. The sun loungers, too. He'd half expected to spot Philippe out there, working on his tan. But perhaps he was on the front lawn hitting golf balls again. Or maybe he'd retired to whichever bedroom he was using.

There was no sign of Stephanie, either. Trent supposed she was in her dance studio. Perhaps she was running through some exercises, though he couldn't help picturing her sitting on the floor, legs crossed and arms wrapped around her knees, staring blankly at her reflection in the full-length mirror.

He was pretty sure he knew where Alain was holed up. The door to the security room had been closed when he'd passed through the foyer and he'd spotted a bar of light shining beneath.

Trent returned to the plate of chicken and gathered up a slice of breast meat, jamming it in his mouth. He flipped open his mobile, eased the kitchen door closed and dialled Girard's number.

'It's Trent,' he mumbled, when Girard picked up. He eyed the kitchen door. Couldn't sense anyone close. 'What have you found out?'

'It's only been a few hours. I'm talking to people. It takes time.'

'We don't have it.' Trent grabbed another piece of chicken. Took a bite. 'Xavier had a package for the family. He left it in my car.'

'*Your* car?'

Trent swallowed. 'He knows I'm involved, Girard.'

'He threatened you?'

'Not directly. The package contained a photograph of Jérôme. I'm pretty sure it was staged.'

'How sure?'

Trent told him about the rubber ear and the sham blood.

Girard didn't speak for a moment. Then Trent heard the creak and snap of a cigarette lighter followed by a deep inhalation on the other end of the line.

'I don't like that he left the package in your car. It's like he's taunting you. It's as if he knows something.'

Trent glanced back at the door. There was nothing to indicate that anybody was listening in but he still felt the need to cover his mouth with his hand. 'He doesn't know about Aimée,' he whispered. 'He can't.'

'Perhaps Moreau told him. Maybe Xavier plans to use it against you.'

'There's no reason for Jérôme to mention it to him.'

But not even Trent was sure about that any more. Jérôme had already let slip about the insurance policy. Who could guess what else he might spill?

'Did you speak to the girl again? Did her friend mention the bodyguard being in Jérôme's villa when she was attacked?'

'Her friend didn't say anything about a bodyguard. She only talked about Jérôme.'

'But . . . ?'

'But that doesn't mean he wasn't there. A taxi dropped her off and Jérôme took her upstairs right away. She didn't exactly get a guided tour of the villa.'

Trent thought of the pages he'd torn from Jérôme's diary and stashed inside his boot. 'The dancer's name,' he said. 'Does she have the initials C.M.?'

Girard hesitated. 'Yes. But how do you know this?'

'Don't worry about it,' Trent told him. 'Stay focused on Xavier. But be fast.'

'I'll try.'

'Forget trying, Girard. Just find him.'

Trent hung up and slipped his phone into his back pocket. He tugged his lip in thought, then crept across to the door. He listened hard. Snatched it open. There was no one in sight.

He put the chicken back in the fridge, finished his second helping of milk and walked out into the foyer. And paused.

The door to the security room was ajar. Light was spilling out in a bright wedge onto the marble floor. It was glinting and twinkling around the door rim, as if it was the secret gateway to some magical alternative dimension.

The only sound Trent could hear from inside was the electric hum of the surveillance monitors and the background buzz and flicker of the ceiling light. He stepped closer and prodded the door. It swung back and tapped the wall. Alain's seat was empty. The rows of colour screens were unwatched. Nobody there.

If it was some kind of trap, it was a tempting one. Trent slipped inside. He spread his hands on the desk and scanned the monitors. He saw footage from every camera: views of the perimeter fence, the gate, the driveway, the housekeeper's cottage, the garage, the pool, the pool house and more. The seconds ticked by until the monitors fuzzed and the feedback shifted. He looked from screen to screen, absorbing the latest footage. But something wasn't quite right and it took him a few moments to notice what was wrong.

He couldn't see the summer cabin.

The monitor he'd spotted the cabin on previously was right in front of him. It was powered up and working perfectly well. But there was no view of the front of the shack. No view of the rear.

The image that was presently on screen was dark and indistinct and hard to fathom. He leaned closer. Finally he understood. He was looking at a close-up of the crusty brown bark of a tree trunk.

He frowned, and was still frowning when the monitors fizzed and went blank for a moment before blooming again with the original set of images. But the same monitor had the same problem. Still no cabin. The footage this time was of a knot of tree branches and a single pinecone with a wash of pale sky beyond.

Two cameras was no coincidence. It couldn't be an accident. They'd been moved, but for what purpose? To conceal something, Trent supposed. And to prevent whatever might be happening from being recorded.

He considered his next move. He could try shifting the cameras manually until he had sight of the cabin. But if whoever was out there happened to hear or see the cameras move, they might sneak out of shot before he could find out what was going on. He'd lose the element of surprise and the opportunity to confront the person responsible. So he decided to leave the cameras where they were and hurry to the cabin on foot.

He backed out of the security room and darted through the front door, the afternoon heat bathing his face and hands as he broke into a run. He could smell the warmed mulch in the flowerbeds he was passing and the cloying scent of the bougainvillea that smothered the walls. He glanced over his shoulder and the tubby cherub gazed blankly after him.

He ran hard, swinging his arms, pumping his legs, his lungs soon itching with anaerobic burn. He raced through the humid air and across the blurring grass. And as he increased his speed, as he upped his pace, he had the sensation of time slowing around him in equal measure, the journey taking too long, the distance to the ramshackle building seeming so much greater than before.

But he was getting nearer with every stride. He was closing in on his target, barrelling through the almond trees, the air cooler in the shade, the light dimmer. His tread sounded too loud. His breathing too harsh. He circled to the right, clasped a pine trunk in his arms and peered up into the green canopy. He could see the camera high above, pointing skywards through a clutch of branches. He had no way of knowing how long it might stay that way. It could rotate back at any moment.

He hugged the trunk, panting, and stared out through the sweat sheeting down from his brow and across his eyes.

From the outside, at least, the cottage appeared no different. The shutter on the left was still thrown back from when he'd opened it. The stable door remained closed. Looking at it now, it was hard for him to explain the cabin's strange attraction to him. No matter how badly he wanted to find a trace of Aimée, he couldn't pretend that the odds of her being inside were anything other than remote.

And yet, Jérôme was a risk taker. He was a guy who was prepared to flout the law by transporting illegal goods into France. He was willing to do business with arms traders and drug smugglers and people traffickers. He was prepared to bribe the police and government officials. He was arrogant enough to flaunt his ill-gotten wealth, to cheat on his wife, to believe that he couldn't be caught.

So there was a possibility. A slim one, but not something he could afford to ignore.

He stalked through the trees to the side of the shack, stooped low, treading carefully, his boots sinking down through the spongy carpet of pine needles and dirt and leaves. He paced over to a timber wall that was bowed in the middle and greying with age. Some of the boards had split lengthways. Others were dry and flaking. He flattened himself against the decrepit structure and crept towards the rear corner, his shirt snagging on a splinter. Slowly now, he craned his neck around and scanned the tree line. The second camera was right where he'd expected it to be – zeroed in on the trunk it was fixed to.

His breath caught in his throat. His sight spiralled. He felt dizzy and weak, hot and trembling. He squatted and placed his head between his knees. Glanced down at his boots.

He stared harder.

There was something different about the ground beneath his feet. It wasn't as soft or as cushioned as the earth all around. He scuffed it with his toe, moving aside a fine layer of pine needles and twigs. The surface was smooth. It was hard. He rapped on it with his knuckle. A hollow sound.

He smoothed his hands over the surface. It was a dry timber board. His fingers crabbed sideways, feeling for an edge. He found something else. A small hole. There was a second one near by, half filled with dried mud and fallen leaves. He poked at the filling and it gave way and plunged downwards. He hooked his fingers through the openings. Heaved. The board began to move, pivoting up just in front of him. But it wouldn't shift completely. His weight was pinning it down.

He spread his feet very wide and tried again. This time the board came free in a spray of dirt. It was about the size of a loft hatch, fashioned from a solid sheet of hardwood. Trent flipped it over and laid it down a short distance away, dust rising in the air.

He muffled a cough. He spat. He wiped the damp from his face with the back of his hand and stepped forwards to see what he'd discovered.

There was a dingy chamber below. The beginnings of a staircase. The treads were warped and bowed and half rotted through. Trent wasn't sure if they'd support his weight. Part of him didn't want to find out. It was very dark down there. And there was a strong odour of cold and damp.

But he'd found a secret cavity beneath the cabin where anything might be hidden.

Even Aimée.

Chapter Thirty-three

Trent braced his forearms on the ragged edge of the opening and swung his legs down and in. The first stair tread groaned and flexed but held his weight. His fingers clawed into the chilled mud and loose stone at his side. His toe felt for the next step down. He found it, lower than anticipated. Only his head was outside now. He scanned the straggly wooded area and the stretch of manicured lawn leading towards the house. There was nothing to indicate that he'd been spotted. He took a final gulp of clean air and ducked his head into the gloom beneath.

Thin shards of light poked through the floorboards of the shack. Earth tumbled into his hair from above. He lowered his foot for the next step but what he found instead was the ground. It was firm and uneven with just a little give, like dense clay. The space was very low. He had to stoop to move forwards, shoulders brushing against the floorboards overhead.

Cobwebs clung to his face, getting inside his mouth. Something skittered across the back of his neck. He grabbed at it, scratching with his nails. He missed. Felt it burrowing beneath his shirt, mapping his spine.

The space reeked of wet and decay. Trent walked his hands above his head, feeling the outline of the warped boards. The wan light from above illuminated the tips of his fingers, making his flesh glow. He set his eye to a crack and found that he could see a slice of bare ceiling and the top of the rear wall. He tried another crack. The space above seemed to be one big room. There were no dividing walls. Fissures of light leaked in through the wonky shutters. He could just make out what looked like a table shrouded by an old cloth.

Dust sprinkled his eye.

He blinked and rubbed the heel of his hand until his sight cleared. Returned his attention to the space he was in. He spread his arms out wide and turned in a slow semicircle, his back and legs bent, thighs burning, then stumbled over to the end of the chamber, his feet catching on some kind of discarded rag. The wall was as rough and muddy as the floor. He flattened his palms against it and crabbed along to his left, kicking out with his feet to be sure he didn't miss anything. Soon he hit a corner. He worked his way back in the opposite direction. Twelve paces, no more, until he reached the other side. So the space was relatively compact. Smaller than the cabin above.

He swivelled. The square of light from the hatch he'd come in by was as white and translucent as a drying sheet. It illuminated the space below in greyish tones. He could see an old rotted crate by the bottom of the stairs. Trent supposed the space had once been used for storage. Some kind of makeshift cellar.

But there was nobody down here. No obvious link to Aimée. And he was getting nervous about being underground. He'd left the hatch up above, where anyone could use it to seal him in. And the cameras had been moved for a reason. No way would two cameras shift automatically like that. Somebody had wanted something to happen here that wouldn't be recorded.

If it was some kind of trap, it was a tempting one.

Trent was on his way out, moving fast, when he heard a noise that made him pause.

Muffled laughter. A gleeful yelp. The laughter was female. It drilled inside his brain. His head snapped round.

He heard a playful growl. A man this time.

It triggered more giddy laughing.

Then a muffled whump, like a mattress compressing. More giggling. More laughter. The floorboards shook and quivered. More dust fell down through the gaps.

Trent covered his nose and mouth to stop himself from coughing. He wanted to see who was up there. He wanted to confirm his suspicions.

He scrubbed the grit from his eyes, then pressed his face to a crack in the boards. His angle was no good. He was beneath some kind of storage unit. He moved sideways and tried the next board along, then the one after that, grazing his knuckles on the abrasive surface.

He set his eye to the gap. Better. There was a bed above him. He could see the base of an old mattress that was spilling stuffing through the metal springs underneath. The springs were twanging and squeaking with the movements of the couple on the bed. An arm flopped downwards. The hand was petite. The fingernails painted.

Trent backed up slowly, setting down one heel behind the other, making sure of his footing before moving on. The floorboard he was looking up at wasn't straight. It was bowed and gnarled. Sometimes the gap became so thin that he couldn't see a thing. Other times, it was congested with dirt and muck. He took one more step backwards and his heel clunked against the bottom of the stairs. He froze. Held his breath. But there was no reaction from above.

Still his view wasn't what he needed. He tried the next gap along. It was an improvement. He contorted himself, bending at the ankles and knees, leaning his head right back on his shoulders and grinding his forehead against the board. He peered along his nose. It was a long way from perfect but it was the best he could do.

He could see Stephanie's face. She was sitting upright on the bed. Her silk blouse was undone. Her bra exposed. Bruising, too, Trent supposed. Her head was thrown back, mouth open, eyes closed.

It was impossible to see the guy beneath her but Trent felt like he had a pretty good idea who it would be. He'd already seen how close Stephanie and Alain were. He'd witnessed the intimacy between them. And right now, he really didn't want to hear anything more. Stephanie was whining. The guy was grunting. And Trent was no kind of voyeur.

He turned and grasped for the top step, feeling the dry timber crumble beneath his fingers. He climbed as quietly as he could, timing his footfall with the couple's rhythmic groans.

Late afternoon sunlight glittered through the pine needles above. The air felt clean and good. He drank it in, filling his lungs. Then he crouched and lifted the flat timber board from the ground and fitted it back into position over the entrance hole. He scattered leaves and mud over it again, covering his tracks. He lowered himself onto his backside, his spine resting against the bulging wall of the cabin, his elbows on his knees and his palms covering his ears.

He didn't know how long he stayed there. Twenty minutes. Maybe less. But the light had begun to fade to watery shades of green beneath the tree cover when his daze was broken by the thud of the front door being closed. He felt the shack vibrate.

There was some fast, mumbled conversation. Some laughter. The rattle of a key and the snick of a bolt being thrown.

Trent waited. He counted to twenty in his head. Then he pushed up from the ground and crept along the side of the cabin to stare after them.

But what he saw rocked him back onto his heels. He shook his head. Blinked. Looked again. It was just as bad the second time round.

Trent rolled sideways. His shoulders slumped against the scratchy cabin wall. He stared up at the weakening green light through the trees. The looming pines.

Then he heard a rustle of leaves and looked round to see Alain step out from behind a nearby trunk. He walked closer, staring after Stephanie and Philippe, at the way their arms were entwined and they were leaning into one another, Philippe smoothing his hand over the small of her back.

Alain dropped to his haunches alongside Trent. He rested his fists on his thighs.

'So now you know,' Alain said, looking off into the trees.

'They don't want Jérôme back, do they?' Trent asked.

'Not unless he comes home in a box.'

Chapter Thirty-four

'How long have you known about them?' Trent asked.

'Three, four months,' Alain replied.

'And Jérôme?'

'Hard to tell.'

'Has he said anything to you?'

'Not directly.'

'And indirectly?'

Alain sighed. 'I think he knows. He's been different. Distracted. The last couple of months in particular.'

The last couple of months. Aimée had vanished almost nine weeks ago. 'Have you asked him about it?'

Alain shook his head. 'We're talking about his wife and son here. They've betrayed him.'

'And you?' Trent asked.

'What about me?'

'You've known. You haven't spoken to him about it. Maybe he views that as a betrayal, too.'

Alain pushed up to his feet. He dusted the dirt from his hands. 'Maybe I feel sorry for her.'

'Stephanie? How so?'

He ran a finger around his collar. His shirt was crumpled and pasted to his skin where the straps of his holster had pressed the material against his body. His Ruger was close at hand, nestled beneath his arm. 'She has a difficult time. Cooped up in this place. She can't dance professionally any more. She doesn't get to see her friends. She isn't allowed a telephone.'

'So it's OK that she's sleeping with her stepson?'

'No. It's not OK.'

'Is he the only one she sleeps with?'

Alain's eyes flashed with anger. He shook his head, slowly and deliberately, as if warning Trent not to push him further.

Trent shrugged. 'You two are close. Anyone can see that. And Philippe seems to think there's something going on.'

Alain looked down over him, the Ruger at his side, the green light glowing and flaring around his shoulders. His massive hands clenched into fists down by his sides. His feet were spread shoulder width apart, the left just in front of the right. It would be easy for him to come at him now. He could lash out with a kick. Or swing down with a punch. There wasn't a lot Trent could do to defend himself.

'I wouldn't do that to Jérôme.'

'But probably you'd like to?'

'Doesn't come into it.'

Trent took that as a yes. He couldn't exactly blame the guy. It would be hard for anyone to ignore Stephanie's charms. Difficult for Trent, for example. And he wasn't living in the same house as her. Wasn't responsible for her safety twenty-four hours a day.

'Tell me about the cameras,' he said.

Alain didn't reply.

'They're the reason I came out here.' Trent jerked his thumb in the direction of the device attached to the tree in front of the cabin. 'I saw the door to your security room had been left open. Saw the cameras had been diverted.'

Still Alain didn't speak.

Trent said, 'You moved them for her, didn't you?'

'I didn't move them.'

'Then what?'

He opened his hands and spread his fingers, as if letting go of his anger. He toed the ground in front of his feet. 'I leave the door open sometimes. She moves them herself.'

'But how did you know to leave the door open this afternoon?'

'She asked me to do it.'

'When?'

Alain reached into his back pocket. He removed a scrunched-up ball of notepaper. 'She passed me this.' He held it in his bear-paw palm. 'When we were in the study. Opening the package.'

Trent whistled. He shook his head as he found his feet.

He'd already underestimated Stephanie once but now he realised that she was much tougher and more single-minded than he'd even begun to appreciate. He pictured her reaction when they'd opened the parcel and found the fake ear and the counterfeit blood. The way she'd flattened herself against Alain's chest. The way she'd clutched his shirt. Had she passed him the note right then? Or had she waited a few minutes longer? Did it matter either way?

So she wasn't just a good dancer. She was a talented actress, too. That was something Trent should remember.

Despite himself, he couldn't help thinking of Jérôme. There was no way he could feel sympathy for the guy. All Trent was interested in was securing his release so that he could interrogate him about Aimée. But what must it be like to be in his position right now? How must he feel, knowing that two people entrusted with his life had already betrayed him?

'How would you explain the cameras?' Trent asked. 'If Jérôme ever reviewed the footage, I mean?'

'He never looked. It was always just me. That's how I found out about them in the first place.' Alain met Trent's gaze. He conjured a sad smile. 'She begged me not to tell. She was a mess.'

A real one? Or had she just acted that way?

'Why did they come to this cabin today, anyway?' Trent asked. 'Jérôme's not here. They could have used a bedroom in the house.'

Alain pouted. 'Habit, maybe. This is where they always come. Also, Thérèse – the housekeeper – would tell Jérôme if she ever found out. She hates Stephanie.'

'And Philippe?' Trent asked. 'He's aware that you're compromised?'

'He likes watching me squirm. I'm in an awkward position.'

'Is that why he makes all the jibes about you and Stephanie?'

'I'm sure that's part of it.'

'And the rest?'

'I don't know. I don't care. I gave up trying to understand him a long time ago.'

'But you think you understand him enough to know he doesn't want his father back alive?'

'They're not close. Never have been. And Philippe leads an expensive lifestyle. His business is a joke. He needs new funds. And his father has plenty of them.'

Trent rubbed the back of his neck. His skin was hot and sticky, muscles knotted. 'In other words, he won't pay Xavier what he wants. And neither will Stephanie.'

'They won't.' Alain squeezed the ball of paper in his fist. He thrust it deep into his pocket. 'But I will.'

*

Alain claimed he could get hold of three million euros. No more. No less. He didn't explain how. He didn't elaborate. But he was clear. He was confident. And Trent believed him.

'Will it be enough?' Alain asked, walking alongside Trent as they crossed the lawn towards the house.

'Let's hope so.'

'What do we do?'

'We email Xavier. We make him an offer.'

'What about the rest of the team?'

'New team,' Trent said. 'New unit. It's you and me now. We're Jérôme's best chance.'

And not just Jérôme's, Trent thought. *Mine and Aimée's, too.*

They had the study all to themselves when they entered. Trent hung back and watched as Alain moved around behind the desk and fished his set of keys out of his pocket. He worked his way through the collection until he selected a small brass key that looked a lot like the skeleton key Trent had used. He went straight to the middle left-hand drawer and removed the laptop. He placed it in the centre of the desk and flipped it open, then pecked at a series of keys. He hit ENTER and spun the laptop around until it was facing Trent.

'Go ahead,' he said.

'This is Jérôme's computer?'

Alain nodded.

'Isn't it security protected?'

'I know his password. I told you. He trusts me.'

Not with everything, Trent thought. Not with the existence of the K & R insurance policy. And perhaps not with the knowledge of what Jérôme had done to Aimée. Was it possible Alain hadn't been involved? Was he someone Trent might trust, too?

'We should set up our own email account,' Trent told him. 'It protects Jérôme. And it sends a signal. It tells Xavier that we understand his approach. We appreciate the need for secrecy.'

'Go ahead. You do it.'

'OK. But I have a question first.'

Alain pressed his lips together. He waited.

'The housekeeper,' Trent said. 'Is she a good cook?'

Alain relaxed. He almost smiled. 'You'd like something to eat?'

'More than just something. I'm hungry. And we could be in for a long wait.'

Chapter Thirty-five

The meal was simple but excellent. Pan-fried sea bass, a generous salad, plenty of fresh bread and a carafe of chilled white wine. The house-keeper had carried everything into the study on a silver tray and had laid it out on the desk between the two men just as Trent finished composing his email. She hadn't sneaked a glance at the screen. She hadn't spoken a word. She was just as guarded as the last time Trent had seen her, though she managed a tight smile and a nod when he took his first forkful of fish and complimented her on its taste.

She left the study and closed the door. Trent loaded his fork with more fish and handed the laptop to Alain. He gestured for him to read the message he'd typed out.

To: xavier222@yahoo.com
From: nego.tiator@hotmail.com
Subject: Settlement

We have a settlement for you. This is a one-time-only payment.
It is the maximum amount the family can raise.
The sum is €3,000,000 (three million euros) in cash.
Do not try for more.
The three million is the most the family can pay. This is a sign of their good will.
We require proof of life before the exchange.

The Negotiator

Alain looked up from the screen.

'What do you think?' Trent asked, chewing his fish.

'I think maybe we should offer less. Leave ourselves room to add more.'

'We could do that,' Trent said. 'I thought of it myself. Offer a couple of hundred thousand less, perhaps. Or suggest an odd number. Something that works as a kind of psychological trick, implying it's everything that Stephanie and Philippe are able to pull together.' He grabbed a salad leaf that had been dressed, like the fish, in olive oil. Popped it in his mouth and savoured the taste and the texture. 'But why fool around?' he asked, swallowing. 'It's like this meal. It works because it's straightforward. I think we should make the offer straightforward, too. I think we should make it as easy as possible for Xavier to say yes.'

'What if he asks for more?'

Trent mopped his lips with the linen napkin the housekeeper had provided. 'I don't think he will. Three million is already more than he would have expected to receive. It's more than I'd normally sanction. That carries a risk, it's true. He may believe that he's found a soft touch. But that's why I've made it clear the email is from me. Remember, the two of us have negotiated before. The discussions went on for a long time. Close to a year. They were arduous for me. They were probably worse for him. He has a team of men to keep happy. A host of varying opinions to balance. I'm sending him a message that allows him to avoid all that.'

'Maybe he'll think it's too easy? Maybe he'll suspect a trap?'

'I doubt it. He selected Jérôme very carefully. He knows how he got rich and how he stays that way. He picked a target who wouldn't be eager to have the police involved, crawling around his home and poking their noses into his business. And besides, Xavier's proved to me that he's good at avoiding takedowns. He evaded the police the last time I dealt with him. He'll have learned from that experience. He'll be confident he can get away with it this time, too.'

Alain gazed at the laptop screen. He read the message over again, eyes trawling from left to right, mouth constantly moving. He ripped off more bread. Weighed it in his palm.

'OK,' he said. 'Everything you've said makes sense to me.'

'It makes sense to me, too. But that's no guarantee. I can't say for sure how Xavier is going to react.'

'Then it's time we found out.'

Alain palmed the bread into his mouth and laid both hands over the laptop keyboard. He traced a finger over the trackpad. Paused. Hit a key. The machine emitted a cheerful *ding*, followed by the *whoosh* of the message being dispatched. The processor purred. It whirred. It fell silent.

Alain leaned back from the screen. His eyes were bleary, his brow furrowed.

'Go ahead and eat,' Trent told him, reaching for his own plate. 'He won't get back to us right away. He may not see the message for many hours.'

Alain hesitated. He eyed his meal.

'Eat,' Trent repeated. 'Drink some wine. You just took control of the situation. Enjoy it while you can.'

*

Alain didn't enjoy it for long. He'd only managed a few mouthfuls of sea bass when the door to the study was thrown open and Stephanie burst in.

'Thérèse said you were in here.'

Alain looked up from his plate, his fork halfway to his mouth. He lowered the fork slowly. Pushed the plate to one side. Lifted his napkin and dabbed his lips.

'Somebody has to be,' he said.

Stephanie approached the desk, then hesitated. It took her a moment to process the possible meanings of the open laptop. Her skin whitened and pulled tight across her cheekbones. She clutched at her hair, digging her fingers into her scalp.

'What is this?' she asked. 'What's happening?'

'We made the gang an offer.'

She took a step and reached out as if to snatch the laptop, then paused and pulled back as though it was radiating a fierce heat. She straightened her arms by her sides, locking her elbows. Her lean fingers curled like talons.

'But you can't do this,' she said, shoulders quaking. 'I don't have access to Jérôme's money.'

'I arranged something.' Alain stared at her, impassive. 'Enough to send a message to Xavier.'

'You didn't speak with me first.'

'You were otherwise engaged.' His tone was flat. Face expressionless. 'So was Philippe.'

She bared her teeth and pointed a finger at Alain. 'Don't talk to me that way. You can't do this. You can't act without our agreement.'

Alain glanced sideways at Trent. He raised an eyebrow.

'He already did,' Trent told her. 'It's done.'

She turned on him. Her lips were thin and bloodless, her cheeks sucked in, face as sharp as a blade.

'You said that we're a team. A unit.'

'Your judgement is compromised. Philippe's, too. I'm sorry. My firm's contract is with Jérôme. I'm required by law to act in his best interests. And besides, any refund of a ransom payment from the insurance company we work with requires my say-so. There's no way I could sanction a payout from the policy if I allowed you or Philippe to participate in this negotiation any longer.'

'What did he tell you?' she hissed, flinging her thin arm towards Alain.

Trent hated looking at her then. The dark, glossy hair and the fine bone structure and the flawless skin had transformed themselves into something twisted and vile. She wasn't a beautiful young woman any more. She wasn't a dancer struck low by a tragic injury. She was a broken, trapped creature. An exotic bird who had thrashed against the bars that held her until she was left weak and bedraggled, barely worth saving at all.

'He didn't tell me anything,' Trent said. 'I saw it for myself. Saw both of you. And I think it's best if you leave now. Don't embarrass yourself any more.'

He expected a response. An angry denial of some kind. But it never came. She was there one moment. She was gone the next. All that lingered was the sudden hush in the room and the uneasy sensation of one catastrophe averted and, just possibly, another still to come.

*

Trent spent the next hour with Alain in the study. They listened to Stephanie slamming doors upstairs. They saw Philippe saunter out to his sports car and roar away from the house. They pushed food about their plates. They shared small talk about sports – the football season just passed for Olympic Marseilles and the season yet to come.

They glanced at the telephone. Alain refreshed the laptop. There was no call from Xavier's gang. No email.

'You want coffee?' Alain asked, some time after 8 p.m.

'Sounds good,' Trent told him.

Alain stacked their dishes and glasses onto the tray beside the carafe of wine. They hadn't consumed much. Just a glass each. If the circumstances had been different, Trent could have finished the bottle. The wine had knocked the ragged edge off his nerves. It had soothed him. But there was no telling what might happen next or when. There was no knowing how he might need to react.

He waited until Alain had carried the tray of things from the study and passed along the glazed corridor before moving around behind the desk and crouching over the laptop. The internet browser was open. The temporary email account they had set up was the only page loaded on the screen. He minimised the window and accessed the file directory.

Jérôme's documents were arranged alphabetically in a long list of sub-folders that ranged from *Aventure* to *Solaris*. Names of yachts, Trent guessed.

He moved the screen pointer over the first folder: *Aventure*. He clicked on it and a new window ballooned out of the middle of the screen. A password prompt. The folder was protected.

Trent cancelled out of the window and tried to access three more folders. He got the same result every time. He closed the file directory. Restored the browser with the brand new email account. There was one unopened message. A welcome from the account provider.

He turned and faced one of the shelves of green leather books behind the desk. He rested a finger on the top of a spine. Prised it out.

And surprised himself.

The case was a fake. There was no doubt about that. But there was a real book inside. It was about two-thirds the size of the green leather sleeve. The threadbare jacket was a faded red. The binding was shot and the pages were loose. Trent opened it carefully to the first page. It was some kind of dusty historical text. Not something Trent had read before and not anything he felt like reading now.

He replaced it and took his fingers for a walk along the next set of shelves. More history. He moved on, trying the shelves on the other side of an intervening window. He stumbled across a volume of poetry. Getting colder. He kept looking, kept levering the green leather sleeves from the shelves and inspecting the hidden books they contained. Kept putting them back.

He was still searching when Alain returned. Trent recognised the jug of coffee on the circular silver tray he was carrying.

Alain grinned sheepishly. 'Promise you won't force this down my throat?'

Trent smiled back. He promised. Then he fixed himself a mug of coffee, no cream, and spread out on the chesterfield where Philippe had sprawled the previous night. He drank his coffee. He scanned the uniform ranks of green book jackets.

But he wasn't taking anything in. His mind was elsewhere. He was thinking about Xavier. Thinking about Jérôme and what he might be able to tell him about Aimée. And he was watching Alain from the corner of his eye. Alain was drinking some coffee of his own and he was crouched forward over the laptop, his face and hands lit from the screen glow.

The two of them had fallen into a companionable silence. Truth was, Trent liked Alain. He was a capable guy to be working with. He asked sensible questions. He'd challenged and tested Trent's reasoning. He'd shown himself to be reliable. And though he was clearly loyal to Jérôme, willing to do what was necessary to raise the cash to free him and prepared to stand up to Stephanie and Philippe when it mattered, he was also prepared to act independently when he thought it was the right thing to do.

It was obvious that he'd been looking out for Stephanie for some time. Maybe that was because he was attracted to her. Maybe he was aware that Jérôme beat her and he believed that helping her was the right thing to do. Or maybe he just preferred to do whatever he could to avoid the fallout that would come from Jérôme openly acknowledging his wife's affair with his son. Whatever his true motivation, he'd demonstrated to Trent that he was able to think for himself. He'd shown compassion. And Trent was pretty confident that he'd gained his respect, even if he was still a little way short of securing his trust.

So what he was asking himself was whether he should mention Aimée's name to him again. And, if he did, he was debating how far he should go. Should he just refer to her as his colleague and see how Alain responded? Or should he say more?

Would he end up with an ally, or an enemy?

Was it worth the risk?

He sipped his coffee. He ran his eyes over the rows and columns of matching green book covers, every one identical, every one concealing its true contents. After a time, it got dark enough outside for the automatic sensors to click in and the security lights to power up and he watched Alain go around the octagonal room, drawing the luxurious curtains against the startling glare. And all the while he kept asking himself the same questions: What did the man sitting opposite him really know? And what might he be prepared to share?

Chapter Thirty-six

Trent must have fallen asleep because he was roused by the bleat of the telephone. It was shrill and tinny. The plastic casing vibrated against the desk.

He sat upright and cradled his forehead in his palm. He checked his watch. It was gone 4 a.m.

Alain was standing over by the telephone and the recording equipment. He was white-faced, staring at Trent, waiting for him to react.

The telephone pealed again.

'Ready?' Alain asked.

Trent waved a hand. He got to his feet and peered out at the room. His neck ached. He must have crushed it in his sleep.

'Should I answer?' Alain said.

The telephone rang some more.

Trent groaned and stretched his back. His spine popped. He winced. Staggered across the room.

The telephone rang once again.

Trent punched the speaker button.

'We read your email,' Xavier said. His mighty voice rumbled through the speaker. The bass hummed. The unit buzzed. He sounded curt. Aggressive. 'We told you five million.'

Trent bent down towards the phone. Placed his hands on either side of it and bowed his head. 'The family don't have five million,' he replied. 'They've made you a good offer. You should accept. You won't get more. I guarantee it.'

'Where is the wife? I speak with her.'

'You speak with me now,' Trent told him. 'You always did. Why pretend otherwise? That's why you put the package in my car. That's why I sent you the email.'

'We can make you wait.'

'You could. But you won't. Waiting means more risk for you. More danger for your gang. And three million is a fair payment. You know it. I know it. Let's cut the deal.'

There was a pause. A long one. The speaker droned very faintly, some kind of background resonance.

Finally, Xavier spoke again. 'You have the money?'

Trent looked at Alain. He motioned towards the speaker.

Alain cleared his throat. 'We just need to collect it.'

'When?'

'In the next couple of hours.'

'Where from?'

'Not something you need to know,' Trent told him.

There was more silence. More consideration. Trent was done with giving Xavier time.

'We need proof of life. Let us speak with Jérôme.'

'I have the answer to the wife's question. He told her he loved her at a villa he has, a place near Cassis. It was in a bedroom there. A special room. She danced for him. They were alone.'

Trent's arms went weak. He felt his elbows give. His hands blurred in and out of focus, fingers bulging and swaying.

His temples were burning up. His tongue had bloated. It was fat and rubbery in his mouth.

He raised his head. It took a lot of effort. It felt like his head weighed more than it should have done.

Alain stared at him. He pouted and showed him his hands, palms out, like a guy emptying his pockets. He didn't know. But then he leaned his head to one side and he winced a little and he waggled a hand in the air. As if it sounded likely to him. As if he didn't know for sure but he knew enough about Jérôme – enough about his coastal villa and the customised room with the wall of mirrors and his particular sexual peccadilloes and preferences – to believe that Xavier's response had a reasonable likelihood of being accurate.

Trent's palms slipped on the desk, wet flesh squeaking against polished lacquer. He swallowed. Swallowed again.

'That was yesterday,' he mumbled, his tongue sluggish, like he'd taken an injection in his gum for some dental work. 'This is today. For three million we get to hear his voice.' Nothing. No response. Trent gathered himself. He focused hard. 'You know why I ask this. We're both professionals. Stop stalling. Put him on and—'

'*Allo?*'

A puff of air escaped Trent's lips. That voice, the one he'd been waiting to hear for too long now, the one he'd been imagining for so many tortured days and nights, sounded nothing like he'd expected. It wasn't calm, collected or measured. It wasn't formidable or imposing at all. It was high. It was timid. It was shaky.

'*Allo?*' The voice also sounded constricted in some way. As if someone was holding him by the throat. 'Stephanie? Alain?' The breathing was fast and shallow, more like a pant.

Trent raised his eyes to Alain again. They were hot and swollen in his head. The bodyguard nodded.

'Please. Pay them the money.' Jérôme was making a hurried nasal whine, like he was in pain. Maybe they were pulling his hair. Maybe they were holding a knife against his throat. 'These men are serious. They will kill me. They—'

Trent heard a grunt. A moan, like Jérôme had been punched in the gut.

Then breathing on the line. It was measured. Patient.

Trent said, 'Do we have a deal?' There was no response. Just the ragged inhalation and exhalation of air. The pop and hiss of the speaker. 'What do you say?' The quiet persisted. The breathing went on.

'Relax, Negotiator.' Xavier was smirking when he finally responded. Trent could tell. It was there in the amused, sonorous rumble of his voice. 'You have your deal. And we have further instructions for you.' He paused. Not to compose himself but to enjoy his triumph. To relish it. 'You will find them inside your home. Your apartment in Marseilles.'

Chapter Thirty-seven

They left the Moreau estate in the high-powered BMW. Alain drove fast, speeding down the narrow escarpment with the confidence of a guy who knows a road intimately. Trent gripped the sides of his seat and had to fight the urge to stamp his foot on a phantom brake whenever Alain swooped into a looping curve. The BMW's headlamps seemed always to be playing catch-up with his manoeuvres.

It was dark, the air chill and fresh. Not quite five in the morning and Trent could feel a gritty fatigue in his eyes. He freed one hand from his seat and readjusted the fit of his Beretta in his waistband. He'd fetched it from the Peugeot before climbing into the BMW. Alain hadn't been comfortable with the move – he could tell from the disapproving grimace on his face – but he was in no position to argue the point. He was armed with his weighty Ruger, worn in his holster under the familiar grey jacket he had on.

'Nervous, Englishman?' he asked.

Hell, yes, Trent was nervous. Here he was, being driven to an unknown location to collect three million euros from what was likely a criminal source. Trent wasn't aware of many banks that opened before dawn. Fewer still that carried cash for withdrawal in million-euro sums. And assuming he got through the pick-up unscathed, he had Xavier's latest threat to contend with. First the gang had left a package in Trent's car. Now he claimed that they'd accessed his home. If it was true, there was no telling what they may have seen.

So naturally, he was anxious. But more than that, he was preoccupied. He was thinking again about what exactly Alain might know. In particular, he was thinking about Alain's response to the proof of life information Xavier had provided. There was no way Alain had been certain that Xavier's answer was correct – he obviously hadn't been told by Jérôme or Stephanie precisely when or where his employer had proclaimed his love – but he clearly knew enough to think it was plausible. That suggested he understood that Jérôme had a thing for ballerinas. It implied that he was aware that Jérôme liked them to dance for him in private. And it indicated that he was familiar with the room Jérôme had customised inside his villa for personal performances.

Plus, he was Jérôme's bodyguard. His job was to shield his client wherever and whenever his protection might be required. Alain's role was to be a permanent shadow. Discreet, where appropriate – such as when Jérôme was beating his wife – but close by whenever he might conceivably be vulnerable.

Like, for instance, at his place in Cassis. Like, for example, when a new and untested girl was due to dance for him, or when an attractive female exec was scheduled to drop by with some paperwork for signature. The dancer might not have seen Alain, but there was every chance that he'd been on the premises.

All of which suggested the following:

Alain was probably near by when Jérôme had attacked the dancer who refused to sleep with him.

Alain was probably close by when she ran away.

Alain was also probably there when Aimée showed up, just as Jérôme's unsated lust and anger and aggression were bubbling over. Just as he would have been primed to vent his frustration.

Therefore, Alain probably knew what had happened to Aimée and Alain probably also suspected that Trent knew, or suspected, that Jérôme was somehow involved in whatever had been done to her.

So far as Trent was aware, Alain *didn't* know that he was engaged to Aimée, though it wouldn't be inconceivable that he could have found out. They'd always been a relatively private couple. Outside of their business and the dangerous world it required them to confront, they lived comparatively quiet lives. But a resourceful person like Alain could find people to speak to. There was always someone available. An unsuspecting friend. A neighbour. Plus there was the photograph in Trent's wallet. The shot of Aimée in her bikini. True, she was wearing sunglasses in the picture, but Trent didn't think he was the only guy in France likely to find his fiancée memorable, and he doubted the glasses would have been enough to disguise her from Alain.

So assuming Trent's logic wasn't flawed – something, regrettably, he felt increasingly confident about – the only possible conclusion was that Alain had been suspicious of him from the beginning because he knew what Trent was searching for, he knew Trent was a potential threat, and at some time, somewhere, once Trent's present usefulness was outweighed by the latent danger he represented, Alain would probably act. He would seek to neutralise him. One way or another, sooner or later, there'd come a point down the line where the two men would clash.

'Hey, pay attention.' Alain was snapping his fingers in front of Trent's face. 'I said, do you still have your phone? The disposable one?'

Trent blinked. 'In my pocket.'

'Good.' Alain reached into his jacket, same side as his Ruger, and Trent's heartbeat lagged and stuttered. But Alain didn't go for his revolver. He withdrew his black notebook and offered it across. 'You look worried.'

Trent swallowed. He jerked his thumb towards the wing mirror. 'I thought I saw someone following us. I was afraid it could be one of Xavier's gang.'

Alain switched his gaze to the rear-view mirror. He frowned. 'There's no one there. I would have seen.'

'Guess I'm a little jumpy. It might help if I knew where we were going.'

Alain ignored the suggestion. He freed a hand from the steering wheel and tapped the notebook. 'There's a number on the top page. Dial it.'

Trent's palm was damp. The phone squirmed in his grip. He flipped his mobile open and punched in the number. Raised it to his burning ear.

'It's ringing,' he said.

'Pass it to me.'

Terrific. So now his own personal stunt driver was making a call while he slalomed down the asphalt slope.

If there was one consolation, it was that the call didn't last long. Alain spoke only to let the person on the other end know that he was on his way and that he expected to arrive inside the hour. He made no apology for calling so early. He didn't acknowledge the time at all. And he didn't mention the location of their meeting.

'So where are we headed?' Trent tried again.

Alain tossed the phone back into Trent's lap. 'Don't worry. You'll find out soon enough.'

'We're a team, remember?'

Alain grunted. 'That didn't stop you holding information back from me.'

Trent didn't respond. There was no telling for sure what information he was referring to. It might be any number of things. It might be the fact that he'd faced off against Xavier previously or that he'd contacted Girard. Or it might be much more fundamental.

'Open the glove box,' Alain said. 'Pass me what's inside.'

Trent dropped his mobile back into his shirt pocket and tugged on a plastic catch moulded into the dash. The glove box hinged downwards and the interior bloomed with light.

There was only one item inside. A slim, unmarked white cardboard container. Trent lifted it out. It was heavy. Felt like it was lined with lead.

And in a way, it was. Trent loosened a flap on one end and tipped the box up over his palm. He allowed the first cartridge to roll out. A .44 Remington Magnum. It looked like a small missile. It was tapered and contoured and potentially deadly. This was a round that would kill instantly. Kill messily, too.

Trent fitted the cartridge back into the space at the top of the box. Looked like there were twelve or so rounds inside. And he was pretty sure the Ruger Alain was wearing was fully loaded with matching rounds. Was he being warned? Was this something Alain wanted him to see?

Trent resealed the box and handed it over. Alain stuffed it inside his jacket, on the right, opposite side to his Ruger.

'Expecting trouble?' Trent asked.

Alain didn't say anything. He didn't have to.

Instinctively, Trent rested his hand on the grip of his Beretta. He was beginning to wish he hadn't stuffed it down his trousers. He supposed he could take it out now. Make a show of checking it over. Drop the magazine. Palm it back in. But if he was right about Alain, it could be interpreted as a provocative gesture. It would raise the stakes. And Trent had no use for an early confrontation. He needed to question Jérôme. That couldn't happen until after they'd secured the ransom cash.

'You want to listen to the radio?' Trent reached for the dial.

Alain grabbed his wrist. Squeezed it hard. 'No radio.'

'Then what? Should we take it in turns to sing?'

Alain's head swivelled on his thick neck. His stubble was densely shaded, the plaster by his eye crinkled and dirtied. He stared meaningfully at Trent. Kept staring, even as the BMW ate up the unlit blacktop ahead of them, plunging on into the shimmering darkness.

'No singing.'

'Fine.' Trent jerked his hand free. He rubbed the skin of his wrist through the material of his shirt. 'We'll just stick with the uncomfortable silence then.'

*

The young man stirred and knuckled his eyes. He peered round the grey-lit room, the air mattress bouncing beneath him. He squinted at his watch. Early. But there was a faint vibration outside. A disturbance of the air. The putter and burble of an engine.

He rolled out of bed and stumbled across to the window in his T-shirt and boxer shorts. He pulled back his chair and sat at his desk. There was a green Citroën delivery van parked opposite, rocking gently with the movement of the engine. Fumes pooled out of the exhaust. The driver's door was open into the street. The cab was empty. The van was parked directly in front of Trent's apartment, obscuring the young man's view of the blue front door.

He reached for his pad and pencil. He yawned as he scribbled a note. *5.07 a.m.* There was no sign of Trent but the young man was awake now. He gripped his head in his hands and braced his elbows on the table, and then he settled in to watch and to wait.

*

The awkward silence between Trent and Alain persisted for close to fifty minutes. The autoroute to Marseilles was as quiet and undisturbed as the atmosphere inside the car. The BMW hummed along in the fast lane, rocking and swaying beneath a steadily lightening sky. By the time Alain pulled off the raised flyover that wove between the high-rise office buildings and hotels to the west of the city, and turned towards the dark waters and industrial docks of Joliette, the eastern sky had splintered into pale pinks and misty yellows and warm copper tones. It was just bright enough for him to kill his headlamps.

Alain clearly knew where he was going. The cracked and potholed roads were unsigned and largely unfamiliar to Trent, but Alain negotiated each junction and turn with calm assurance.

They passed metal-sided warehouses and enormous haulage depots and oversized petrol stations with raised, brightly lit canopies fitted out with specialist pumps designed for lorries and trucks. They drove by a fish market teeming with men and women in white jumpsuits and blue plastic boots, carrying trays of fish and ice. They zipped by endless cargo trains and loading cranes, beneath the towering, rust-streaked hulls of dated passenger ferries bound for Sardinia, Corsica and Tunisia. They kept moving, kept weaving, the BMW bumping and thumping over potholes and troughs, until Alain finally pulled off into a gravel parking lot running alongside a derelict storage facility.

He eased the BMW slowly across the yard. Crushed aggregate snapped and popped beneath the tyres. They crawled on and then emerged next to a small harbour inlet. The sluggish water was stained with rainbow streaks of boat diesel. It smelled of fish and salt.

A magnificent yacht was moored right in front of them. It looked to be at least fifty feet in length. It was sleek and white, fitted out with three tiered decks, multiple sun loungers and ample white leather seats, plus a generous amount of smoked glass. Two jet skis were secured to the lowest deck at the rear, close to where a sloping walkway extended from the yacht onto the quay.

The moment Alain brought the BMW to a halt, a thin guy with dusty skin and curly black hair appeared on the middle deck, high above them. He didn't wave. Didn't make any kind of gesture. He just watched.

'Is he Moroccan?' Trent asked.

'Algerian.'

Trent glanced sideways at Alain, who was busy checking his Ruger under cover of his jacket.

'He looks sort of mean,' Trent said.

No response.

'Should I join you?'

'Better you stay here. He knows me.'

Trent wasn't about to argue. *He knows me.* There'd been no suggestion that the man liked or trusted Alain.

Up on the yacht, the Algerian had raised a large black holdall into the air. The holdall was weighted with something. The guy was having trouble lifting it.

Alain unclipped his seat belt and reached towards the ignition.

Trent rested a hand on his arm.

'Why don't we leave the engine running?'

Alain looked between him and the Algerian up on the yacht. He held Trent's eye, then nodded and stepped out of the car, head down, holding his jacket closed in front of his chest with one hand, as if to contend with the limp coastal breeze. His gun hand. Smart guy. He'd be able to reach for his Ruger in a hurry.

The Algerian lowered the holdall and watched Alain mount the ramp at the base of the yacht. The ramp bounced and flexed with his weight. Then the Algerian backed up out of view as Alain climbed the curving staircase to join him on the lofty middle deck.

Trent could no longer see either of them. He was left with just the hum and vibration of the BMW's engine for company. He shuffled down in his seat and gazed up through the top of the windscreen at the towering white yacht. He cracked his window. Loosened his seat belt. Freed his Beretta from his waistband and looped his finger through the trigger guard.

Time passed.

A minute, then two.

Trent tapped his feet in a nervous quick time.

Three minutes.

Four.

He was just turning in his seat to check the yard and the warehouse through the rear window, concerned all of a sudden by his vulnerability to an attack from behind, when Alain came hurrying down the steps towards the bottom deck. He had the holdall in his arms. He was cradling it to his chest, grimacing and leaning back a little to compensate for its mass. He was moving very fast. The ramp compressed and sprang up like a driving board as he bounded across it.

He fumbled open the door behind Trent. Tossed the bag inside with a grunt. Then he circled back round the boot and got in behind the wheel, threw the BMW into reverse and swept backwards in a fast loop.

Trent jerked his thumb towards the bag. 'Is it all there?'

'Three million,' Alain said, breathless. 'Notes are non-sequential.'

Trent whistled again. 'Maybe the Algerian's not such a mean guy. He must really like Jérôme.'

'No, they hate each other.'

Trent stared at Alain. 'Then why'd he give you the money?'

Alain braked hard. He slammed the gearbox into first. Nodded towards where the Algerian was watching them from. 'See the yacht?' he said. 'It belonged to Jérôme. I just handed him the keys.'

Chapter Thirty-eight

Trent was aware that something seemed different on the drive to his apartment. It took him a moment to work out what it was. Then he realised: he was optimistic. Feeling positive, for once.

They had the ransom money. It was a significant sum, but not too large. It felt like it was pitched just right. Enough to tempt Xavier into a genuine exchange. Enough, hopefully, for him to stick to their deal.

And Alain was a strong partner. He'd been proactive. He'd been smart. He'd secured the cash they needed. Sure, there was going to come a time when they'd be on opposite sides again. There was going to be a clash. But right now, the way things stood, Trent was glad to be working alongside him.

'You've done well,' Trent told Alain.

'You sound surprised.'

'Just relieved.'

'It's not over yet.'

'But we're close. We're nearing the end.'

The end of a lot of things, Trent realised. Some good. Some bad. Most unknown.

'But listen,' Trent told him, 'I don't think it would be wise to turn up to my apartment with the money. It could be a trap.'

'I've been thinking the same thing.'

'Then perhaps you could let me out somewhere close? Take a drive with the money until I call you and let you know that it's safe.'

'No.' Alain stared ahead through the windscreen. 'I want to see what they've left for us.'

'I'll bring it to you.'

'No. We go together.'

No sense arguing. Alain was a determined guy. He wouldn't change his mind.

'Well, we can't just leave the cash outside in the car. Too risky.'

'Agreed.' Alain nodded. 'We need somewhere to stash it.'

'There's a guy I trust.'

Alain snatched a look at him. 'A guy.'

'He runs a bakery a few streets from my apartment.'

'A bakery. Terrific.'

Trent shrugged. 'You know a better place you can access at six twenty in the morning?'

Alain grunted. He lifted a hand from the steering wheel.

'Didn't think so.'

Trent pointed ahead through the windscreen and directed Alain along the narrow, winding backstreets of the Panier district until they reached Rue Sainte-Françoise. He had him pull over in the gutter next to a row of low metal bollards. A network of laundry lines criss-crossed the sky above their heads, suspended from thin, shabby townhouses that seemed to be leaning towards one another across the street.

The word BOULANGERIE was stencilled in a semicircle across the plate-glass window of the bakery. The interior was in darkness. Trent reached for the holdall. He started to get out of the car but Alain grabbed his arm.

'This had better not be a mistake.'

'Relax,' Trent told him. 'We'll be back here before you know it.'

'And the money?'

'That'll be here, too. Trust me.'

He stepped out onto the cracked pavement, the holdall tugging down at his arm, the BMW's engine idling and vibrating behind him. The crooked street was silent and deserted in both directions. There was nothing to suggest that they'd been followed.

Trent tried the bakery door. It was locked. He beat his palm on the glass until a light came on in a corridor out back and an overweight guy in a stretched white T-shirt and faded Bermuda shorts appeared. The guy clapped flour from his hands and wiped them clean on his grubby apron, then unlocked the door and hauled it open, releasing the scent of freshly cooked bread.

'Hey, you're back!' the man said, and smiled widely. Then he raised a thick finger. 'One moment. I'll fetch some fresh croissants for you.'

'No, Bernard. Wait.'

Until Aimée had disappeared, it had been Trent's routine to head out for a run or a stroll first thing in the morning, then return home with bread or pastries for breakfast. Bernard was always prepared to open specially for his regular customers.

'I need a favour.' Trent held the holdall out to him. 'Can you look after this for me? I'll be back for it very soon.'

Bernard frowned and leaned his bulk to one side. He peered past Trent at the sleek BMW. Saw Alain crouched forwards over the steering wheel, staring back at him.

Bernard blew air through his lips and studied Trent for a moment. Then he reached out a hand coated in flour to accept the holdall. 'What's in here?' he asked.

'It's no big deal,' Trent told him. 'Just three million euros in cash.'

*

Trent climbed out of the BMW a short distance along from his apartment, brushing flakes of croissant from his clothes. Bernard had insisted on the exchange, as if the baked goods were a fair trade for the cash. If anything went wrong inside his home, he thought, they'd be the most expensive pastries he'd ever bought.

Alain joined him on the pavement and they scanned the street and the square, then the windows above. Two pairs of eyes. Double the protection. The benefits of a team approach.

'I don't see anyone,' Trent said.

'Neither do I.'

'Probably they're gone already. Probably they didn't hang around.'

Which was a good thing, Trent reasoned. He didn't like the idea of being watched. He didn't like the concept of the gang toying with him. But his mood cooled when he saw the front door of his home. It was hanging ajar. The lock had sustained some damage. The metal casing was scratched and mangled. Trent prodded the door with his finger and it swung right open, the lock jangling loosely in its casing, the bolt falling from its housing and bouncing on the floor.

Alain moved alongside him without saying a word. The square around them was quiet. The hallway, too. Six thirty in the morning. Everything still.

Trent drew his Beretta and Alain reached for his Ruger. They exchanged a brief look, then Trent exhaled in a rush and faced up to the empty hallway. He squared his shoulders and straightened his arms, elbows bent a fraction, the Beretta gripped tight in his right fist, his left hand supporting its weight.

'Let's get this over with.'

He stepped across the threshold, legs heavy, as if there were shackles on his ankles. His own home felt alien to him now. It harboured an unknown threat. Violent men had been here. They'd trodden the same path. Eyed the same walls.

They might have done anything at all.

He edged forwards, sighting along the Beretta, his torso swinging in a small, tight arc from the hip. The hallway felt very long. It felt endless. He could hear Alain's breathing behind him. It was nasal. It was laboured. Trent was very aware of the Ruger that was being pointed towards his back.

He stepped cautiously into the living room. Scanned it fast. At first glance, it looked no different from how he'd left it. Nothing had been disturbed. Nothing appeared to have been taken.

But something had been added.

There was a brown business envelope resting on the breakfast bar. It had been set down exactly, squared off against the bottom of the counter.

The envelope was very thin. No bulge in the middle. It was sealed by a thread of string that had been wound between two cardboard discs. Trent supposed that was very deliberate. A gummed flap might carry traces of DNA.

He approached the envelope. Released a halting breath and relaxed his fierce grip on the Beretta. He set the pistol down on the counter. Pushed it aside and shook some of the tension out of his hands.

Behind him, Alain holstered his Ruger and cleared his throat. Trent sensed him taking in the room. Studying it. Adjusting to it. Then he heard his footsteps as he moved closer to him.

'Your place is a dump,' he said.

'So people keep telling me.'

Trent didn't think the envelope could be booby-trapped at all. It looked too slim to contain any kind of explosive charge and there was no sign of any wires or metal tabs or other indicators.

'Why do you have this?'

Trent glanced at Alain, distracted. He was pointing towards the recording equipment connected to the phone.

'It's a precaution,' Trent said.

'From what?'

'From threats. I'm a potential target to these gangs. I have to live with that. Take Xavier. He left this parcel here for a reason. He could have dropped it anywhere for us to collect. But instead he had someone break into my home. It's about intimidation.'

Alain traced a finger through the dust that had collected on the equipment. 'Has he called you here?'

'No. And there's no reason for me not to have told you if he had.'

Trent returned his attention to the envelope. It seemed to fill his vision. He wet his lip. Reached out a hand to the thread of twine. It had been bound in a figure of eight around the cardboard discs. He unwound it carefully. Lifted the flap. He eased up the top half of the envelope and began to slide out what was inside.

He heard a noise from the far side of the room. Turned to see Alain standing half in and half out of the bathroom, his hands on his hips, pushing back the tails of his jacket.

'What are you doing?' Trent asked.

Alain didn't reply straight away. He yanked down the light cord and craned his neck and peered inside the bathroom. Then he hummed, as if unimpressed, switched off the light and pulled the door closed.

Trent let go of the envelope and took a step away from the counter. His pulse had jacked up. It thumped in his temples.

'What is it?'

'These people broke in here.' Alain was facing the sealed door to the boxroom. He extended his arm towards the handle. 'Don't you think we should check the rest of your apartment?'

'No,' Trent blurted. 'Wait.'

Alain circled his fingers round the handle. He peered curiously at Trent. Tipped his head over to one side. He saw something in Trent's reaction. Something he didn't like.

He rotated his wrist. Flung open the door.

Trent advanced quickly. The room seemed to contract and rush towards him, like he was speeding through a collapsing tunnel.

Halfway across, he knew that he'd moved too fast. Been too hasty. His Beretta was back on the counter.

Alain was already inside the room.

Trent veered round the corner and stumbled in behind him.

Alain was facing the end wall, his chin raised, his gaze moving from left to right. Across the photographs. Across the maps. Across all of Trent's notes.

His big hands were by his sides. Fingers loosely curled.

They started to move. His right arm came up and crossed his body. His left hand lifted also and pinched the lapel of his jacket. He twisted at the hip, his arm still moving across his chest towards his armpit. Reaching for his holster. Reaching for the Ruger Trent had seen so many times.

He'd seen it too often.

He reacted very fast.

He surged forwards, closing the space between them. He reached around Alain with his left arm and grabbed his wrist before he could get to the Ruger. His right arm mapped the same trajectory. It slipped inside the jacket that Alain had unwittingly opened, just for him, and his hand grasped the revolver and snatched it free all in one fluid movement.

Alain was still turning. He barged into Trent. Wrenched his right hand free and jabbed him with his elbow, hard in the abdomen.

Trent buckled. His face came down. Alain jabbed again, higher this time, striking his chin. Trent's teeth chipped off one another. His jaw shunted upwards, the blow radiating out through his nose and cheeks and eyes, his sight blurring, skull whipping back.

He felt himself rock. Felt himself teeter.

Now Alain was attacking his hand, wrenching back his thumb, digging his toughened fingers into the small bones of Trent's wrist.

Trent was losing his grip. Losing the gun.

He squeezed the trigger.

The report was very loud. It went off like a grenade. A .44 Magnum round, straight to the gut. Close quarters. Alain grunted and spun and fell backwards like he'd been rugby-tackled. He crashed into the desk. Flung his arms out to steady himself, knocking the lamp and Aimée's necklace to the floor. He flailed for a grip against the wash of papers. Stamped a foot and moved as if to lurch forwards, then wheezed and looked down at his side.

He exhaled in a fast hiss. Clasped his hands to the torn flesh and rushing blood. Gazed up at Trent, his face greenish and drooping, a look of despair and betrayal and incredulity in his eyes.

He slumped back against the desk. Tipped over onto his elbow. Grasped at a sheaf of papers and wedged them clumsily into the gushing, bloody mess.

Trent took a step closer and fumbled his wallet from his jeans. He tugged Aimée's photograph free and held it in his unsteady palm and shoved it towards Alain like he was a cop showing him his ID, the revolver up alongside it, his hands shaking crazily.

'Where is she?' he asked. 'What happened to her?'

Alain squinted but he wasn't focusing on the image. He was grimacing against the pain.

'Her name's Aimée.' Trent tapped the photograph with the muzzle of the Ruger. 'Jérôme hurt her in some way, didn't he? You must know what happened to her. You must have seen. Tell me where I can find her and I'll call an ambulance for you. I'll get it here fast.'

Alain was clenching his teeth, spittle foaming round his lips. He hugged his hands against his gut. His nostrils flared.

'She's my fiancée,' Trent told him. 'Tell me where I can find her. Tell me.'

Alain eyed the photograph. He considered the giant revolver in Trent's hand. He glanced down at his stomach, at the blood pooling round his fingers, coating his wrists, leaking onto the floor. He looked up again. Bared his teeth. Nodded once, sweat drenching his brow.

Alain parted his lips. But not to say the words Trent longed to hear. He tilted back his head and he opened his throat and he unleashed a yell that was as loud and as ferocious as anything Trent had ever heard.

He didn't hear it for long. He pulled the trigger a second time. Another Magnum round, straight to the head.

III

The Drop

Chapter Thirty-nine

Trent watched through the windscreen of the BMW as Girard paced across the square. It was just over twenty minutes since he'd fished the car keys out of Alain's pocket. He'd retrieved the holdall of cash from Bernard and dumped it on the seat behind him. The open brown envelope rested on his lap. He had Alain's Ruger nestled beneath his thigh, the box of spare cartridges in his pocket.

Trent was sitting in the car as a precaution. Alain's scream and the gunshots had been loud. His ears were still ringing, his hearing fuzzed and swirling. He was afraid that his neighbours would have heard the commotion and might come to investigate. Or worse, call the police.

He couldn't afford to be trapped now. He'd come too far. Got too close. So he'd decided to sit in the car with everything he needed, ready to speed away if he was threatened at all.

But now it seemed that he'd been lucky. Maybe the cramped box-room had smothered the noise of the gun. Maybe his neighbours had been shocked awake by Alain's cry but had been left disoriented, uncertain of what they'd heard. Or possibly they were reluctant to become involved in a situation that didn't directly concern them.

Trent wasn't sure what to make of it. He wasn't thinking straight. The whistling and the swooshing in his ears were distracting him – like trying to concentrate while someone vacuumed the inside of his skull. Even now, he wasn't sure if summoning Girard had been the right thing to do. Part of him was tempted to twist the key in the ignition, drive away and press on by himself. But he'd called Girard for a reason. He needed his input. More than anything else, he needed someone to convince him he wasn't losing his mind.

Girard had entered the far corner of the square on foot. Must have parked in a street near the Cathédrale de la Major. He was wearing a blue windbreaker zipped up to his goatee, his hands stuffed inside the front pockets, tenting the lightweight material so it looked as if he was wearing some kind of pouch around his midriff. His head was down, grey locks dangling over his sunken eyes, and it wasn't until he was crossing the road towards Trent's apartment that he glanced in through the fly-spattered glass of the BMW. He did a double take. Hesitated. Trent raised a hand and signalled to him. Girard lingered a moment more, then shuffled closer.

Trent could see that one of the pockets at the front of Girard's windbreaker was lower than the other, as if weighed down by something. The waxy nylon had moulded itself around the object. The outline was thick at one end, elongated at the other. The material had puckered up at the point farthest away from his hand, closest to his zipper.

Girard opened the passenger door and craned his neck, assessing Trent and the tensed way he was sitting, as if he might spring sideways at Girard like a jack-in-the-box. He looked at the envelope on Trent's lap and the black holdall on the bench seat behind him.

Trent noticed that Girard had opened the door with his left hand, which had looked a little awkward. A little unnatural. His right hand was still tucked inside the bulging pocket.

'You're armed,' Trent said.

He saw the twitch in Girard's cheek, the squint of his eye, as if he were embarrassed. He sized up the passenger seat with a momentary frown, like it was a minor puzzle of some kind, then folded himself down and in, the nylon jacket swishing with his movements. He gauged the street outside once more, then eased out the gun. It was a semi-automatic pistol. A Glock. Matte black finish. He balanced it in his open palm like it was a curiosity he'd found on his way across the square.

'It's just a precaution. You weren't making much sense when you called. You were talking very fast.' He slipped the gun back inside his pocket. Rubbed his hands together as if for warmth. 'What's in the envelope?'

Trent parted the seal and slid out the map he'd found. It was neatly folded with a blue-on-green cover that featured a photograph of a glistening Mediterranean cove. The map was a popular acquisition for visitors to the region. Trent had a creased and battered copy somewhere in his apartment. You could buy duplicates from the city's main tourist office or any number of souvenir shops. It was a 1:15,000 scale guide to Les Calanques.

The Calanques were a spectacular twenty-kilometre stretch of barren, rocky inlets, secluded beaches and high limestone cliffs running along the coast between Marseilles and Cassis. The zone had been designated a French national park only recently and it was criss-crossed with treacherous hiking trails. There was a winding D-road running behind the *massif*, but most of the rugged coastline was inaccessible by car. It was a haven for walkers and climbers and nature lovers.

It was a nightmare for Trent.

The map was folded concertina-style. Trent spread it between them, across the steering wheel and the dash. There was a lot of green parkland and a lot of blue ocean. The topography was daunting. There was barely any flat. There were concentric lines everywhere, describing multiple hills and slopes and crevices, the lines becoming dense around the vertiginous sea cliffs.

Trent reached across and stabbed his finger at an area towards the right-hand side of the map. A specific point on the D559 had been circled in black ink, beside a blue symbol that denoted a parking spot. It was the beginning of hiking trail number 7, a demanding and circuitous pathway marked in vibrant red, like a thread of blood twisting and unspooling in a glass of tap water. The trail terminated at the most famous and picturesque of all the beach inlets, the Calanque d'En Vau. The cove had been circled, too.

An arrow had been drawn from the first circle to a few lines of printed text in an uninterrupted patch of green just above.

Negotiator

Park here by 10 a.m. Put the money in the waste bin. Leave your car. Do not look back. Walk to En Vau. You will find more instructions there.

Come alone.

WE KNOW WHY YOU WANT HIM ALIVE.

Trent waited for Girard to process the message. His lips parted. He vented air in a strangled groan, like someone was sitting on his chest.

'Maybe it's not what you think.' There was a reedy tremor in Girard's voice. He sounded as dazed as Trent felt. 'Perhaps you're reading too much into this. Of course you'd want them to release him alive. This is your job.'

'But the message is addressed to me specifically, Girard. I think it's a threat. A statement. They're targeting me. That's why they left the first package in my car. It's why they left this envelope in my home. They know about Aimée.'

'But how could they know?'

'Jérôme.'

'No, we discussed this already. It's too dangerous for him.'

Trent supposed that was right. Jérôme would have to be out of his mind to tell Xavier's gang what he'd done to Aimée. Even under duress or torture? That could alter things, sure. But why would Xavier's gang try to elicit information like that? Why would they even suspect it?

'Wait.' Trent stared across at Girard. 'They must have been watching Jérôme. Before the abduction, I mean. That would make sense, wouldn't it? Look at us. We had him under surveillance. It took us more than a week to identify where he was vulnerable. And we were in a hurry. A rush. But perhaps Xavier has been preparing for longer. Maybe his gang have been monitoring Jérôme for months.'

'You think they saw what he did to Aimée?'

'Not directly.' He glimpsed his reflection in the mirror. His jaw was white and rigid, the skin wet across his brow and deep purple around his eyes. His pupils were dark whorls. 'But maybe they saw the aftermath. Jérôme had to clear up after himself. He probably made his bodyguard help him. They would have been acting suspiciously. Maybe it was enough to make Xavier's gang want to find out more. Maybe they were good at concealing themselves. And watching.'

Girard fell silent. He ducked down and gazed out through the windows at the tall, crooked buildings that teetered all around them. 'If they like watching, they could be looking at us now.'

'Then let them look,' Trent said bitterly. 'They can watch until I find every last one of them and end this thing for good.'

*

The young man eased back in his chair, hiding in the greyscale dimness. Strange that the dark should be his ally now, when for so long it had been his tormentor.

He took his camera away from the window ledge and lowered it beneath the table. Shielded the screen with his cupped hand and glanced down at what was displayed there. His most recent shot featured the blue roof of the BMW and the blur of two figures inside.

He scrolled backwards through the images, the display jerking and tilting as each new shot bloomed. The zoom had worked very well. It had captured everything he could have hoped for. He had the former police detective. He had Trent.

And way before that, back through the shuttling, jolting feedback, he had the other guy, too – the man he'd spotted the previous morning taking a photo of Trent from his car.

The young man had seen him arrive in the BMW with Trent, close to an hour after the delivery van had driven away. He was a squat and muscular type. He moved with the bearing of a guy who could be dangerous when he needed to be and threatening the rest of the time. He was wearing a smart grey suit over a white shirt.

The young man had seen plenty of guys just like him. Guys who

245

expected trouble and were capable of dealing with it. Take, for example, his composed response when they saw that the apartment door wasn't secure and Trent had drawn a gun. The way he'd pulled his own gun and followed Trent inside very calmly and very confidently, pushing the door closed behind him.

Four fast minutes had gone by. The young man had stared at the blue front door, swaying in the gentle breeze, tapping against its frame. He'd kept his finger poised on the camera shutter, knuckle bent, finger aching with the constant light pressure he was maintaining.

Then he'd heard a sudden muffled crack from inside the apartment. There'd been a second muted bang, around a minute later. Something that could have been a shout.

Two men had gone in. Only Trent had come back out.

He was carrying a brown envelope and fumbling with a set of car keys, and he set off at a rushed jog across the square. He returned inside ten minutes, switching a bulky black holdall between his hands. He tossed the holdall into the rear of the BMW and dropped into the driver's seat. The suspension compressed and rocked and then he thumped his palm against the steering wheel before fitting the key in the ignition and staring out at the street.

The young man had pivoted gently forwards on his chair. He'd adjusted his camera lens, angling it down at the car. He'd zoomed in and steadied his focus and compressed the shutter. He'd reached for his pad and pencil and made a careful note of the time.

Chapter Forty

'Suppose you're right,' Girard said. He was smoothing his hand over the map like he was casting runes, the paper crinkling and deflecting under his touch. 'Say they do know about Aimée. Why tell you now?'

'To compromise me,' Trent replied. 'To motivate me to ensure the drop goes through.'

'But why not before?'

Trent's lips tightened. 'They didn't know how I was going to react once I became involved. So they waited until I sanctioned a generous payout. Way more than I'd normally have approved at this stage. They were happy with it. Very content. Otherwise, they'd have used their knowledge to force the price higher.' He sucked air through his teeth. Forced his mouth wider still, muscles quivering in his cheeks, lips taut as cat gut. 'They must believe it's as good as they can get. Now they just want to be certain that I don't try anything at the drop. They want to guarantee that I comply with their instructions.'

'It's a risk.'

'More than a risk.' Trent released the tension in his mouth. Worked his jaw until it clicked, then circled his hand around the area of the map where the gang wanted him to abandon his car and leave the money. 'It's a mistake.'

Girard gazed sideways at him. Waited for more.

'They've pushed too hard.' Trent stabbed his index finger into the map. Almost punched a hole clean through it. 'I don't like this set-up. Not one bit. They're luring me out. Isolating me by insisting I come alone. Why make me walk so far after I drop the ransom? It has to be an hour-long trek to the beach from this point. And now they've told me they know about Aimée, the exchange *has* to work for me.'

'So?'

'So I need a guarantee. I can't afford for them not to release Jérôme. So I can't go by myself. I need back-up, Girard. I need you.'

Girard slumped in his seat. He raised a limp hand and unzipped his jacket with a weak, listless movement, eyes glazed and sightless, and he removed a cigarette from a packet and let it dangle from his lip without lighting it. He blinked. He shook his head. He removed the cigarette, then put it back and moved it around in his mouth some more.

'But we tried this before,' he mumbled, with the glassy, unfocused look of a drunk talking to himself in a mirror running behind a bar.

'They won't spot you this time.' Trent tilted the map towards Girard and nudged his arm. 'Look at this terrain. You don't have to get close. There's plenty of high ground. Plenty of viewpoints. There are rocks and trees all over this area. You can drive the fast road to Cassis, then double back along this route. Park a few kilometres away. Find a location to watch from. You don't need to intervene. You just need to be able to follow whoever comes for the cash. ID them. Whatever.'

'It's dangerous.'

'It's dangerous either way.'

'You have to be sure. No doubts. You have to be absolutely certain.'

'I am.'

'If this goes wrong . . .'

'It won't. Why would it? This time is different, Girard. Everything has changed. You don't have a team of people trying to conceal themselves. You're just one man.' Trent smoothed his hand over the map. He shifted closer in his seat. 'One guy in all of this. And remember, they don't know about you.'

Girard's pouched eyes were fixed on the dusty rear window of the car parked in front of them. His gaze was as stony and blind as that of the naked cherub outside the Moreaus' mansion.

'I trust you, Girard. I do. And this is the chance you've been waiting for. This is the best opportunity you'll get to find Xavier.

To find his gang.'

Girard's head swivelled towards him, fast and frictionless.

'You have to be able to live with this. If they see me . . .'

'They won't.' Trent clenched his arm. 'And it's the right decision. I can live with that.'

*

The young man watched the former police detective step out of the BMW, smooth his hair back from his eyes and quickly scan the cars and buildings close to him. He didn't look up at the apartment the young man was in. He didn't scope his side of the square at all.

Whatever he was searching for, he didn't see it. He didn't linger. He stuffed both hands inside his shiny blue windbreaker, lowered his chin against his chest and walked away in a diagonal trajectory across the square.

The young man made a note in his pad. He recorded the time and the relevant information. Then he angled his camera on the window ledge and captured an image of the man's back as he hurried off the way he'd come.

A minute went by. Two.

Nothing moved. Nothing altered.

Then the BMW's lights came on, front and rear. They dimmed momentarily as the engine fired up. The chassis shook. The exhaust vibrated. The car edged out into the street and glided away at a perfectly normal, perfectly respectable rate of acceleration.

The young man made another note. Then he raised his pencil to his mouth. There was an eraser on the end. He sucked on it. Knocked it against his teeth.

He was looking at the blue front door to Trent's apartment. He was contemplating the way it was hanging slightly open. Not by much, perhaps, but by enough to be noticeable, at least to a guy who'd spent countless long hours staring at the fit and finish of the very same door for several gruelling consecutive weeks.

He was asking himself a simple question but one that was potentially complex. It was a conundrum that could be loaded with rewards or laid with traps. A riddle that might give him all the answers he craved or destroy everything he'd achieved so far.

He was trying to decide if he should go and take a look inside.

Chapter Forty-one

It was around a forty-minute journey to the drop point, out through the city and the suburbs and along the winding *corniches*, the coastal roads. Trent stopped halfway. He pulled into a petrol station linked to a hypermarket on the fringes of the trading estates that sprawled out from east Marseilles. He didn't need fuel but he was curious to see if he was being followed. He waited inside the BMW, its interior artificially chilled by the raging air conditioning he was using to stay alert, and he studied his mirrors. Two minutes went by. Three. He couldn't spot anyone on his tail, so he entered the filling station for a bottle of water and a takeaway coffee, and then he drove slowly the rest of the way, sipping the scalding, bitter brew, stringing the trip out for an extra quarter of an hour.

He had plenty of time. Xavier's instructions had told him to leave the money by 10 a.m. and it wasn't half past nine yet. Besides, he wanted to allow Girard to get into position. To give him the opportunity to find the perfect viewing spot.

From the city outskirts, the road snaked upwards into a barren, hilly terrain, part desert, part forested moonscape. There was a lot of jagged, exposed limestone rock. A lot of sparsely wooded areas, stunted Aleppo pines and arid shrubland.

The road climbed a steep gradient, the BMW sweeping around looping curves that teetered above sheer drops. The sun was a piercing white disc in a vast blue sky. Azure waters glimmered way below. Trent could see the chain of tiny offshore islands, flecked with colonies of grey seabirds. He could see sailing boats and fishing vessels and a bulbous passenger ferry. Nearer still were the sprawling concrete grounds of the university campus.

The holdall of cash bulged on the bench seat behind him. Three million euros. A staggering amount of money. Enough to buy a luxury yacht. Enough to change someone's life for ever. Enough, certainly, to kidnap and kill for.

He chewed the side of his cheek. There was a painful twisting in his guts that had nothing to do with the terrible coffee. Truth was, he'd never functioned as a bagman before. It wasn't his role. He was the negotiator. The schemer. Usually, a family member dropped the ransom money. Sometimes a co-worker or a trusted friend handled it.

It was a dangerous job. It took a great deal of composure. Plenty of courage. And normally, Trent couldn't afford to get involved in case something went wrong and his advice was required urgently.

Not today.

Today he was at the centre of things. He was exposed. The gang had addressed him directly. They'd insisted that he handle the cash. They'd drawn him out to a desolate, barren place, where he was expected to set out on the loneliest, scariest walk of his life.

It was a daunting prospect. Enough to make anyone sweat. And Trent had gone and added to the danger. He'd involved Girard. If it was an error, then it was likely to be costly. The gang had killed before. They wouldn't hesitate to do so again.

After the curves and coils of the climb, the road straightened out, slicing through the rear of the *massif* towards Cassis. Trent consulted the map. He passed a series of rest stops before he neared the lay-by the gang had selected.

He waited for a gap in the string of cars hurtling towards him before pulling over and trundling to a halt beside a lone waste bin with a pitted concrete exterior. He engaged the handbrake. Left the engine idling. Gripped and re-gripped the steering wheel.

A dozen pine trees shaded the pull-in, all of them rangy, limbs sparse. The sandy ground was coated in a bed of dried needles and fallen cones and a wash of sun-bleached litter.

A swollen hillock loomed above him, bare rock poking through straggly undergrowth and stiff wild grass. Off to his right, the land fell away into a shallow bowl before sloping up towards a gnarly ridge. On the other side of the ridge would be the steep descent to the sea.

An emergency breakdown telephone lay dead ahead. It was bright orange in colour, the letters *SOS* branded on the side. Beyond it Trent could see the neat terraced vineyards that overlooked Cassis.

He drummed the steering wheel some more. Scanned the terrain. Felt the BMW rock on its suspension as cars and trucks and coaches thundered by at his side.

He couldn't see anyone. Not a guy in a ski mask. Not a glimpse of Girard.

He cut the engine and gathered Alain's Ruger from the passenger seat. Preferable to his Beretta, he'd decided. More powerful, certainly. And accuracy was no big concern out here. If he was shooting from a distance, no handgun in the world would be much use to him. But if someone came close, he knew for a fact that the Ruger was more than capable of stopping a man.

His palms were wet against the stainless-steel finish as he released the cylinder and plugged the spaces he found there with two .44 cartridges from the cardboard box filled with spare rounds that he'd retrieved from Alain's jacket. He shifted forwards, peeled his shirt away from his back and eased the long barrel down into the waistband of his jeans. The hard outline of the gun pressed into his damp skin as if it were branding him.

The dry morning heat wafted in at him when he kicked open his door and stepped out into the glare. Pale, cracked boulders lined the side of the pull-in. They looked like they'd split in the sun. Trent could feel lazy thermals wafting up from the ground towards his hands. He could sense many thousands of bugs and insects scrambling through the drifts of pine needles under his feet.

He felt more than just the gun against his back now. Felt more than the tug of the spare Magnum rounds that were weighing down his jeans and the mobile that was nestled in his shirt pocket.

There were unseen eyes on him. Some friendly. Others not.

He had no idea where they lurked.

Slowly, methodically, he shut the driver's door and cracked the door at the rear. He lifted out the holdall using both hands, grunting, and nudged the door closed with his knee. He turned once, a complete 360, his boots kicking up a haze of dust and debris, eyes squinted against the dazzling glare, teeth clenched in anticipation of the rifle round that might come from anywhere, at any moment.

He licked his salty lips and paced stiffly towards the waste bin.

The holdall was very heavy. He had to thrust with his legs and heave with his back to get it up and inside the bin. There were flies there. And wasps. They buzzed madly as he disturbed the hot, putrid waste.

The holdall fitted snugly but it poked out at the top. It was easy to see. Noticeable enough to intrigue a passing motorist, certainly.

The gang wouldn't leave it here long, Trent thought. They'd have to make their move soon. They had to be close.

And he had to leave. He had to step away from the wasps and wipe his hands on the back of his jeans and lock the BMW and wait for a gap in the traffic. Then he had to cross the softly melting tarmac, the Ruger gnawing at the base of his spine, his jeans sagging low around his hips, all the while fighting the desperate urge to glance behind him and see who might emerge from among the hot white rocks.

*

The young man edged out from the foul-smelling vestibule at the front of the building where his apartment was located and blinked in the hard morning light.

He'd waited a long time before making his move. Long enough for the square to spring to life around him. Long enough for lights to come on behind windows and for people to stumble out of buildings and shuffle along pavements on their way to work. Long enough for parents to drop their children at the nursery amid raucous yelps and pounding feet; for two old men in cloth caps to gather on an iron-work bench beside the empty fountain in companionable silence; for housewives to drape laundry over the pulley lines set up outside their balconies.

Long enough for the young man to curse himself for his cowardice and the opportunity he'd surely missed.

Long enough for the man in the grey jacket to leave Trent's apartment.

Long enough for Trent to return.

Except neither of them had.

And none of the hundreds of people who'd passed by or lingered in the square had seemed to notice that Trent's door was hanging very slightly open. Their curiosity hadn't been aroused at all. Not by the lapse in security. Nor by the dull claps or the fractured shout of a few hours before.

Now, life on the square had fallen into a familiar morning lull. There was nobody about. The young man couldn't be certain how long it might last but he'd finally made up his mind. He was going to act. He was going to take a chance.

He staggered out into the square, leaning forwards from the hip, like he was battling against a gale-force wind. His face was down and his right hand shielded his eyes, as if from the sun's glare. His left hand was stuffed in the pocket of the hooded sweatshirt he had on.

Thirty fast paces and he was at the other side of the square. Two more and he was outside the blue door. The locking unit was loose. Looked like it might topple out at any moment.

The young man clenched his hand in his pocket. He muttered a few words of encouragement to himself. Then he jabbed the door with the heel of his palm and tried to ignore the watery sensation in his stomach as he took the hardest, heaviest step of his life.

Chapter Forty-two

There was a drainage trough on the other side of the road. Trent stumbled down it, then stepped over a low log barrier and set off across the dusty scrubland that lay ahead. There was no defined path. He would come to one eventually – could see it running diagonally towards the far ridge like a scar in the chalky white rock – but for now he had to walk through untamed land.

The ground fell away at an acute angle, forming a giant, shallow depression that jacked up towards the ridge. The going was rough and uneven. There was a lot of sandy earth and loose rock underfoot. It would be easy to turn an ankle. Low bushes and parched Mediterranean brush snagged the cuffs of his jeans and tangled with his bootlaces. He stomped through rosemary, thyme and myrtle. He trampled wild flowers, laurel and juniper. He moved on relentlessly, his skin crawling with the sensation of being watched. He pounded the ground and swung his arms, and all the while the droning traffic faded gradually from behind until the low hum started to blend with the throb of the blood in his ears.

There was no shade. The tallest trees came only as high as his shoulders. He passed contorted pines and miniature green oaks, a weedy ash or two, and olive trees with knotted trunks. He squinted hard against the blinding light coming up off the baked white rock. He searched for movement. For the glint of a rifle scope. His eyes streamed in the glare.

Not even mid-morning and his brow and neck and back were filmed with sweat. He clasped a palm to his skull and felt a warmth like he'd picked up a noontime boulder.

The brush was dry as tinder. This time of summer, the Calanques were closed to the public because of the risk of wild fires. There'd be warning signs up on the official trails. There'd be red metal chains slung across them to deter hikers from coming through. So it was easy enough to believe he was alone out here. Just him and the hostile men who were watching. And as he got further away, beyond the ridge, he'd be out of sight of the road. He'd be even more vulnerable.

Strange to think that he'd often been here before, and how different the barren environment had felt then. There'd been times when he'd set out on his own for a challenging hike to cleanse his mind of a tortuous negotiation. And there'd been other times, too. Occasions when he'd strolled along these trails with Aimée. When they'd marvelled at the stark beauty of this place, squeezing one another's hands, the straps of a rucksack loaded with picnic things biting into Trent's shoulders. Times when they'd spent whole days on the lonely beaches of Port Pin or Sormiou or, yes, En Vau. Afternoons when they'd lounged in the sun and bathed in the cooling green waters and he'd talked about one day teaching her to sail.

Like the day she'd told him she was expecting his baby. He'd hired a small yacht and they'd sailed into the Calanque de Sugiton, laying anchor a short distance from the beach. They'd lazed in the sun. Swum just a little, canoodling in the tides. Then Trent had returned to the boat for his mask and snorkel and underwater camera, and Aimée had stumbled out of the shallows in her black bikini onto the scalding hot sand. She'd wrung the sea from her hair. Waved to him and settled cross-legged on the beach.

And that was when he'd surged up from the cool waters, planted his feet in the clinging, liquid seabed, and taken her picture. The one he kept in his wallet. The only shot he had of the woman he loved carrying his unborn child.

Trent growled and shook his head. He was getting distracted. Losing focus.

Right now, the terrain ahead of him looked like something out of the Wild West. A lone bird circled the sky way above, its wingspan huge, feathers splayed like probing fingers. It wouldn't be hard to picture a cowboy on a horse traversing the hard rocky slope up ahead. And many hundreds of metres away, in a wide compression near another sheltered parking spot, he saw an old swaybacked pine cabin that might have been a frontier shack or a drinking saloon.

Water would have been good. He should have brought the bottle from the car. He'd have liked nothing more than to pour it over his head. To feel it drain down through his hair, dousing his sizzling scalp.

He checked his watch. He'd been going for just over ten minutes. A long time, considering how exposed he was. He wondered if the hold-all had already been claimed. He wondered what Girard might have seen. He wondered what lay in wait for him beyond the abrupt stone ridge, its jagged summit looming as sharp and unyielding as a blade.

*

The young man hadn't known what to expect. But whatever he'd anticipated, it wasn't this.

The hallway was long and narrow and featureless, like a corridor from an anxious dream, but it led him to a compact living area that was flooded with light. The walls were pale, the furniture modern. There was a kitchen area on his right. A telephone on the counter. Some kind of answering machine wired up to it.

There was no sign of the guy in the grey jacket.

The temperature was neither cool nor hot. The air smelled of nothing perceptible. The only noise was the low murmur of a fridge. He could close his eyes and be anywhere. Nowhere. He could pretend he was in a space entirely his own.

He edged his way to a bathroom. It was basic and clean and tidy. There was a deep tub with a shower curtain drawn across it. A toilet with the seat up.

Next door was a bedroom, brighter still than the lounge. Light streamed in through a set of Venetian blinds, throwing zebra patterns across the duvet. It shone on a silver photo frame on a bedside cabinet – a black-and-white picture of a stunning woman in a floppy summer hat. She was smiling with her mouth and eyes. Her complexion was freckled. Sun-kissed.

The woman was beautiful but the young man felt uncomfortable staring at her. It seemed improper, somehow. He lowered his eyes to the floor, as if in apology, and backed out of the room, swivelling to face a closed door. A closet, maybe?

The young man reached for the handle and a tiny charge buzzed his flesh. Static. His heart tripped and his bladder weakened. Stupid. He shook his head at his foolishness and pushed open the door and right then his stomach dropped and the room began to spin.

Chapter Forty-three

Trent came around the side of the ridge to find the ocean spread out before him. Light winked and shimmered on its undulating surface as if thousands of wine bottles were floating out to sea. Below him, the thin azure slash of En Vau cut into the raking, dun-coloured cliffs on either side. The water was very clear. In the shallows, Trent could see the sandy seabed and patches of dark green algae and weed. The pale golden beach appeared deserted. A single yacht passed the distant mouth of the cove. There was no sign of any of the sightseeing vessels that sometimes journeyed here from Cassis.

Trent picked up his pace. He jogged down the treacherous cliff path, grasping the limbs of wiry green pines that seemed to grow out of the rocks themselves, the resin warm and aromatic on his hands. His face burned and puckered in the gathering heat. The funnels of tan stone he was descending through reflected the sun's rays like a cauldron.

There were craggy rock spurs all along the length of the inlet and two defined peaks marked the entrance to the *calanque*. Trent had seen climbers here in the past. They'd come armed with harnesses and colourful ropes and little bags of chalk dust, and sunbathers would watch them risk their lives as they reclined on the sand. But there appeared to be nobody here today. There was no one to witness the dangers Trent was exposing himself to. There was no sign of Jérôme, nor any indication of what might lead Trent to him.

He was starting to feel sick and dizzy and dehydrated. Was he just chasing the sun out here? Had the gang simply dispatched him to this point while they made off with the bag of cash?

Or was there more down there than he could spy? He couldn't see the rear of the beach from up above. Trees and overhanging rocks shaded it. There was still a chance. One he was prepared to cling to as desperately as he gripped the abrasive limestone cliff face as he skidded and slid his way down.

But when he finally reached the bottom, when his boots sank deep into the fine sand and coarse pebble drifts, the last of his hope seeped away along with his energy. There was nobody waiting for him. There wasn't anything to be found. There was just the beach. Just the scorched sand and the glowing pebbles and the towering, scraped rock on either side of him and the twisted pines and the sea and the relentless, blazing sun.

Trent doubled over, the Ruger nibbling at his spine. He sucked in the dry, cooked air. He thought of the punishing walk back up the cliff and the long, hot tramp to the car that lay ahead.

He straightened and placed his hands on his hips and cursed as he scanned the ridge high above him. Perhaps they were watching him? Perhaps there would be a signal of some kind?

But no, the rocky spurs were unmoving. He closed his eyes against the screaming white glare and panted weakly and fumbled at the pocket of his shirt. He removed his mobile and flipped it open to an inane electronic chime. For a moment, he asked himself if it would be dangerous to call Girard? Perhaps he was in pursuit of a member of the gang? But what good would waiting do?

He shielded the display against the sun with his hand. And right then, just as his thumb hovered above the CALL button, he heard the faint insect whine of an outboard motor.

A rubber dinghy swept into view at the mouth of the inlet, prow raised, white water frothing around the rear. There were two figures on board. One guy was ducked low at the back, holding onto the tiller. Another guy was standing at the front, one foot raised and propped on the grey rubber rim. Both men wore green army surplus jackets, black ski masks and black gloves.

The boat skimmed closer, racing in from the darker, deeper waters towards the spearmint green shallows. It swooped around in a curve, the guy at the back cutting the revs until the craft drifted to rest two hundred metres out from the shore, rocking on its own wash. He let go of the tiller and lifted an assault rifle from his lap. He wedged the stock into his shoulder and propped his elbow on his thigh and sighted through the scope, lens winking in the glare.

Trent dropped his phone to the sand. He reached his hand behind his back, fingers seeking the Ruger. He stood sideways on, the revolver clenched tight. He waited. He didn't want to prompt the man to shoot. He had no cover and his chances of hitting the men on the boat were bad.

The craft tilted and swayed. The guy at the back maintained his steady aim. The guy on the front spread his legs wide, feet planted securely. His back was straight, arms folded across his chest, as if he was carefully and calmly evaluating the situation.

Sunlight flared off the water all around the boat. It glinted off the rifle scope. Trent's eyes watered and blurred. But still he stared on. Watching. Waiting.

In his head, he rehearsed the moves he'd need to make to whip the Ruger out. How he'd drop to one knee on the sand. Squeeze off as many rounds as he could, as fast as he could.

He was still thinking through the mechanics of it all when the guy at the front uncrossed his arms and bent down into the hull. He lifted something for Trent to see, holding it in both hands above his head.

The holdall. Trent recognised it right away. It was no fake. It bulged with the three million in cash. The guy's arms shook under its weight.

He set it back down, then straightened and looked at Trent. He shook his head. He did it slowly, like an exaggerated signal. His shoulders slumped and he showed Trent his gloved palms as if he was disappointed by something. Dismayed, possibly.

Then he swivelled to his left and raised an arm and pointed a gloved finger back towards the entrance of the inlet, high towards a sloping ridge some forty feet above the deep blue waters at the mouth of the cove. There was a patch of greenery there. A few trees. And there were two men emerging from behind a boulder. One of them was wearing a green army jacket and a balaclava. He was holding an assault rifle in gloved hands and he was using it to prod the other man in the back. The second guy was stumbling towards the cliff edge. The nylon of his blue windbreaker gleamed in the sun.

Girard.

Trent started forwards, then stopped. The ridge was perhaps five hundred metres away. There was no easy way to get there from below. Limestone towered above him. He'd have to scramble back up the path, head around the rear of the inlet and find his way out to the spit of rock. It could take him an hour. Maybe more. And the hostile guy was way beyond the range of the revolver.

Trent watched. He couldn't look away.

He saw Girard shoved towards the edge. Saw him windmill his arms. Then the guy with the rifle grabbed him by the shoulder and hauled him round until he was facing up to him, his back to the sea, his heels on the precipice.

There was a curving curtain of rock beneath him. It concealed the drop from Trent's view. He guessed there'd be water down there. Deep water maybe. Or possibly it was just rocks. Which was worse? He didn't know. Didn't have time to consider it any further.

The guy in the ski mask took a step backwards and then his wrist jerked and a clutch of seabirds took flight from the cliffs. Girard crumpled at the waist, his arms grown slack at his sides, and he tipped slightly forwards before tilting back the other way, his head a loose and fatal pendulum, pulling him down and over the cliff as the report from the shot clanked and rebounded around the canyon of chalky rock, accompanied by the panicked squawk and flap and tumble of the fleeing gulls.

Trent listened for a splash. He listened very hard. But the guy at the back of the dinghy had cranked the outboard motor and its churning roar filled his ears. The boat swooped round and blasted out of the inlet, low at the rear, high at the prow, where the lead guy had grabbed a rifle of his own and was aiming it at Trent.

Trent yanked free the Ruger but he didn't fire. A strange kind of inertia took hold of him, as if his heart and his brain had simply stopped. He clenched the revolver numbly at his side and watched the boat race away. Watched the white, foaming suds wash out from the craft towards the porous rocks. Watched the third guy scramble back from the ridge against the blinding sun. Watched the curtain of gnarled limestone. Listened to the zealous keening of the boat's motor fade out into a mournful silence.

Faint waves brushed the shore. The wheeling gulls beat their wings and shrieked and settled on new ledges.

Still Girard didn't appear.

Drowsily, Trent emptied his pockets and unbuttoned his shirt. He yanked free his boots and his socks. He stepped into the tepid shallows and waded out until his jeans were soaked and clinging to his thighs.

He dived forwards and the water whooshed and whirled in his ears, and when he surfaced he kicked with his legs and pulled with his arms and swam hard until he was spitting salt water and gasping for breath and his limbs were heavy.

It took him a long time to reach the rock curtain. Too long, he knew. He kept expecting Girard's corpse to appear floating somewhere ahead of him, tangling in his arms like driftwood. But when he reached the spot where Girard had fallen, there was no trace of him at all. The water was an impenetrable greenish blue. It lapped eerily against the sheer rock. He treaded water and scanned the seesaw surface, feeling the tug of hidden tides against his submerged legs, and then he raised himself up and snatched a fast breath and dived as deep as he could go. But there was only blackness down there. No sense of the bottom. Nothing other than chill water passing through his fingers. Nothing besides the cold and the spiralling vacuum hush and the crushing weight of all the water on his lungs.

The young man felt his head empty of blood. The ground tilted and swayed. It fell away from him and surged back up, as if it was sprung like a trampoline. He slumped and jarred his knees on the floor. Snatched his hand away from something glutinous and milky.

The walls were a dizzying swirl, pinwheeling madly, letters and words jumbled and blurred. Photographs and maps slid around in impossible directions, converging and overlapping and rearranging themselves as if they were being manipulated on the screen of a tablet computer.

The far wall pulsed. It throbbed. The bloody streaks. The pinkish gunk.

And slumped against the toppled desk, limbs slackened, torso crumpled, was the body of the man he'd seen enter the apartment alongside Trent. He could tell by the charcoal jacket he had on. The white linen shirt, stained darkly red. His jaw. The heavy stubble. But not his face. No, not that.

The young man felt reality slide away from him. Felt the floor slide with it. He toppled onto his side, and croaked as his lungs filled with the fetid air. He'd forgotten to breathe. Felt, somehow, that he'd forgotten how.

The rank gush came in fits and starts. Gobbled down, then bubbling up, like he might gag.

But he held on. Held back. Because all around him was the proof of what he'd suspected for so long. The maps. The plans. The ski mask and gloves, the cuffs, the ropes. The shotgun. The dead man. Him most of all.

The young man shook all over. But not with terror. With rage.

He *knew* now. *Knew*, for a fact.

All that had happened. All that had been done and not done.

It was Trent. It was always him.

Chapter Forty-four

Hours later, Trent stumbled in through his unsecured front door. He was weak. Disoriented. When he'd first got back to the BMW, he'd drunk the remainder of the bottle of water he'd left inside, its contents warmed by the sun. But it hadn't been enough to douse the hot coal of fear and frustration that had lodged in his gut or to fight off the twitchy burning sensation in his temples, the first inklings of the headache that was now thumping behind his eyes.

There wasn't much of the drive back that he remembered. It had passed in a hallucinatory blur. A world of warped memories and wild imaginings. Of the flicker of light on water. Of the mirror-bright dazzle of the white sandstone rocks. Of the tumbling, plunging silhouette of the rag-doll friend he'd sent to his death. Girard, buckling, then plummeting; crumpling, then falling; the sequence repeated over and over, making less and less sense.

Trent's hair and skin were crusty with salt and sand. The evaporated seawater had formed a gritty rime around his eyes and nostrils and badly cracked lips. His jeans had dried in the sun during his trek back through the arid landscape, shrink-wrapping his thighs and calves so that he moved with a curious, stiff gait, like his knees were locked in place.

He shed his shirt and dropped it on the floor as he weaved along the hallway towards his living room. There were no new packages left waiting for him but a green light strobed on his answering machine. He hit PLAY. One message. It was from Stephanie, a shrill demand that he call her and tell her what was going on. She must have got his number from Jérôme's lawyer. There was no communication from Xavier.

He wasn't surprised. He didn't expect to hear anything more for quite some time. And even if he did, what could he do? His situation seemed hopeless. Alain was dead, his body splayed on the floor inside the box-room – a problem he couldn't even begin to think of a solution for – and he had no alternative way of raising the cash sums the gang might seek. Yes, he had money. He was comfortably well off. But he didn't have millions of euros at his disposal.

Girard was gone, too, his corpse drawn away by the tides or perhaps sucked down to the seabed. He had an elderly mother, Trent knew. And there was a daughter living somewhere close to Strasbourg. One day soon, if the currents were kind, they would receive a telephone call or a knock at the door that Trent didn't like to imagine.

He yanked the Ruger from the back of his jeans and tossed it onto his coffee table, along with the crushed box of spare rounds. He un-buttoned his fly and showed his back to the closed door of the box-room as he moved into the bathroom. He tussled with his jeans. Peeled them down over his thighs. He had to sit on the toilet to haul them from his calves and feet like he was removing a wetsuit. The denim had left a faint blue stain on the inside of his knee. He shed his underwear, then turned on the shower and stepped into the bath.

He pulled the shower curtain across and edged under the flow. It was icy cold and for a second he thought he might pass out. He braced his hands against the wall tiles and gritted his teeth and bowed his head, letting the cold liquid sluice through his hair and drench his shoulders and chest.

He tasted salt on his lips. Scrubbed his palms around his face and swallowed some of the spray. His skin was slowly loosening, changing from something tight and parched and withered to something that could stretch and move. And though his scalp tingled with a pleasant numbness, his mind was sparking to life. He felt like a man rousing himself from a bewildering dream. And just maybe, he thought, if he could stand to linger beneath the chilly jet, he'd find that he was cap-able of figuring out a new way to get at Jérôme. To find Aimée.

Then the shower curtain swished back and Trent's eyes snapped open and he swivelled to be confronted by a masked figure holding a shotgun.

The guy looked like one of Xavier's gang. He was wearing a balaclava, black leather gloves and a hooded grey sweatshirt. He was holding the shotgun down by his hip. He didn't shoot right away. He hesitated. Flinched, almost. It was a bad mistake. Trent lashed out with his right arm in a spray of water and snatched the shotgun barrel and wrenched it hard to the side but the guy didn't let go. He was short and slight and Trent found that he'd lifted him with the shotgun and heaved him half into the tub.

The guy's shoulder smacked against the white tiles and he rolled onto his back, his lower legs draped over the edge of the bath. He thrashed with his legs and flailed with his hands, trying to swing the shotgun back round and point it towards Trent.

Trent closed the space between them, cold spray hammering off his bare back. He had two hands on the shotgun now and he was forcing it down at the guy like he was trying to crush his throat with a metal bar. He cocked his head. Recognition dawned. The scarred wooden stock, the lengthy barrel, the blued finish. It was *his* shotgun. The one he'd stashed in the boxroom. And there was something odd about one of the guy's hands. Something he didn't have time to process right now.

It had only been a momentary lapse in concentration – mere fractions of a second – but it was enough for the guy to curl a finger around the trigger. Trent lifted his right foot in the air and stamped down hard on his chest. He groaned and slumped backwards. The shotgun had gotten slippery in the spray. It came away from the guy's hands. Trent tossed it out of the bath just as the guy scrambled up to his feet and drove with his shoulder into Trent's gut.

Trent was forced back against the pipework of the shower, spine bending the wrong way. Water danced off the guy's masked head and shoulders as he reached up with a gloved hand and got a grip around Trent's throat and shunted his chin back hard. He braced his knuckles beneath Trent's jaw, crushing his trachea.

Frigid currents cascaded over Trent's face. He blinked up through the spray towards the blurred showerhead and the ceiling beyond. Air wouldn't come. He couldn't breathe. He grasped for a handhold to push his attacker back. Tried finding an eye to gouge or his throat to jab. But his hands seemed to grope only the man's arms or chest or the hood attached to his sweatshirt. He couldn't see what he was doing. The vertebrae in his neck were forced right back by the man's frenzied strength. Trent was half suffocating, half drowning. His system screamed for oxygen. His chest was cramping and aching, lungs itching with a hot acid sting.

His neck slipped back another fraction. He was looking behind himself now. And that was when he saw it. The circular metal fixture on the tiled wall above. The little plastic nipple. He withdrew his hand from the guy and reached up. His fingers were an inch shy.

Dark spots clouded his vision. There was a shrill whistling in his ears.

He strained every muscle. Stretched every ligament. He went up on his toes, water pooling round his feet. If he slipped now it would be over. His neck might break or the guy could bear down on him. But if he didn't breathe soon it would be over anyway.

He squatted a little, then jumped, and his neck overextended with a jolt of hot pain and his airways pinched shut. His fingers grasped at the plastic bud. He seized it and tugged on it hard.

The retractable washing line spooled out from the plug. Trent grasped a fistful of nylon cord in each hand and looped it round the guy's neck. He tightened it like a noose and tugged very hard.

The guy gagged and croaked and his hand fell away from Trent's throat. Trent snapped his face down, feeling his vertebrae snag and pop. The guy was scrabbling and clawing with his gloved fingers at the cord embedded in his skin. His leather gloves were a problem now. He couldn't get a grip. Couldn't slide a nail beneath the thread. And already the string was biting very deep. The guy's mouth was opening and closing, lips smacking hopelessly together. His eyes bulged from behind the ski mask, the whites staining red.

Trent kept the tension high with his right hand and reached up and got a hold of the guy's ski mask with his left. He ripped it away, taking some of his attacker's blond hair with it. He wanted to see who'd come for him. He wanted to stare at the guy Xavier had sent as he squeezed the last of the life from his lungs.

But he wasn't prepared for what he saw. Even with skin flushed and cheeks engorged, even with lips swollen and eyes protruding and a desperate, panicked look of utter terror on his face, Trent recognised the young man buckling to his knees in front of him.

The kid was Viktor Roux.

Chapter Forty-five

Trent placed a glass of cloudy tap water on the coffee table in front of Viktor. The kid was perched on the leather couch in Trent's living room, clutching a towel around his shoulders. He was rocking gently, humming a faint tune. His lank blond hair was dripping wet and he was shivering in his damp clothes. His jaw trembled, teeth clicking off one another.

Trent made a show of picking up the Ruger and the box of cartridges and shutting them away inside a kitchen drawer. He fetched a high wooden stool and sat on it with his back resting against the counter, so that he was facing Viktor and he could keep an eye on the front door to his apartment. The door was hanging open an inch or two. A shaft of sunlight was shining through into the hall.

Trent was wearing jogging trousers and a sleeveless vest. His neck was sore. He guessed he had some kind of kink in his muscles or his ligaments. He could look to the left OK, but he felt a blockage and a hot, searing pain if he tried rotating his head more than a few degrees to his right. His throat hurt, too. There was a cluster of burst blood vessels on his skin where Viktor had tried crushing his windpipe. It looked like a rash or an allergic reaction.

It could have been worse. The shotgun might have gone off before he'd had time to react. There'd have been no surviving it. Not at such close range.

And then there was Viktor. The kid was clearly in shock. His skin was almost as grey as his sodden sweatshirt, the damp hood congealed against his back like a deflated balloon. Trent guessed he was also in pain. His neck was branded with a livid red line from where the laundry cord had bitten into his skin. He'd spat blood onto his towel. He grimaced each time he swallowed and he kept raising his hand to his throat, as if checking it was still intact. It had taken him a long time to regulate his breathing. Even now, there was a soggy rattle when he inhaled.

It was more than eighteen months since Trent had last seen Viktor. Back then, the kid had spent most of their debrief session staring down at the chewed-up nubs of skin on his left hand where his thumb and finger used to be. And when he wasn't contemplating his injuries, he was gazing over Trent's shoulder towards the doors of the sunlit *salon* they were sitting in. The doors were wide open but the kid hadn't seemed capable of accepting it. Trent had guessed that it would be a very long time before he'd feel comfortable in an enclosed space again.

He didn't seem any more composed now. His gaze had a nervy restlessness to it. He was looking all around. Behind him. In front of him. Along the hallway over his shoulder. At the boxroom behind him. But never at Trent.

'What are you doing here, Viktor?'

The kid hummed. He didn't reply. He was no longer wearing the gloves he must have found in the boxroom. Trent had made him take them off and leave them in the bathroom, along with the shotgun.

It was hard for Trent to ignore the damage to Viktor's hand. The cuts weren't clean and surgical. They were rough and uneven. Trent supposed the kid had been offered some kind of cosmetic procedure to neaten things up – he knew for a fact that his parents could afford it – so it seemed likely that he'd chosen to keep his hand that way.

'You broke into my home, Viktor,' Trent said. 'You attacked me. Came close to killing me.'

Still Viktor hummed his inane tune. His thighs and knees were pumping up and down, his lower legs moving like pistons. He gazed once more at the doorway, as if he was contemplating leaving.

'I know you've seen what's in there,' Trent said, gesturing towards the boxroom with his chin. 'I want to know if you're part of this. I need to know if you're working with Xavier.'

The name had a startling effect. Viktor quit humming, mid-note. He blanched, tendrils of wet hair clinging to his face. He appeared to shrink a couple of sizes inside his damp clothes.

'I need to know,' Trent said. 'Are you part of this?'

'Of what?' Viktor's voice was scratchy and pinched. His tongue flicked out, eyes panicked, as though he were trying to take his words back.

'The kidnap,' Trent said.

'I don't know what you're talking about.'

He blinked rapidly. Trent could have pushed harder, but the kid looked like he was about to wet his pants.

'Why are you here?' he asked. 'Last time I spoke with your parents, they told me you were in a special retreat. A place where you could get the support you needed.'

'You talk with my parents?'

'Sometimes. They worry about you, Viktor. You must know that.'

Viktor shuddered and shook his head, as though bewildered. He freed his bad hand from the towel and stroked his throat. Trent found himself drawn to the bunched scars at his knuckles again. Viktor caught him looking and his expression soured.

'I've been watching you,' he said, lip curling, a flash of black in his eyes.

'Watching me?'

'For three weeks already.'

'Why?'

'I've seen the detective come here,' he said, in a breathless rush, as if it proved something important. 'Girard.' Voice sneering. 'You're friends now?'

Trent didn't like how things were shaping up. He knew that Viktor had suffered terribly because of his abduction. But something about the kid didn't feel right at all. There was a curious glimmer in his eyes. A dark lustre, like he was participating in a whole other conversation. Trent remembered that he'd been seventeen years old when he was abducted. Legally, he was now an adult, but he was acting nothing like it.

'Answer my questions, Viktor. Why have you been watching me?'

He smirked, a quick twitch of the muscles in his cheek, hair dangling wetly. 'I always knew you were involved.'

'Involved in what?'

'The bad things that happened to me.'

Trent frowned. 'I was involved as your negotiator.'

'A negotiator who made sure I was held for almost a year. A negotiator who refused to pay the money that could have freed me much sooner. You weren't my negotiator. You were my jailer.'

'I don't know what Xavier told you while you were being held but you can't believe a word of it. You understand that, don't you? He was manipulating you.'

'My parents trusted you,' Viktor said, as though the words tasted bitter in his mouth.

'Do your parents know that you're here? That you're in Marseilles?'

'They do not care.'

'Of course they care. If you'd seen how traumatised they were during your ordeal—'

'*They* were traumatised?' Viktor snatched the towel from his shoulders and hurled it across the room. It slapped wetly against a wall. Sagged to the floor. 'They should have paid. They should have got me out sooner.'

'They did. They tried. You must know that. They must have told you.'

Viktor wasn't listening. He was seething. Eyebrows deeply forked. Skin mottled, smudged blue around his eyes. 'You worked with Girard,' he said. 'I saw him come here. Now I know what you were doing. Both of you, working with Xavier. Using me. Milking my parents. They were weak. They don't see it. But I do. And now you've killed a man. You're a criminal.' His quivering blue lips peeled back over his teeth. They were yellowed, coated with saliva. One of his incisors was brown and decayed. Another consequence of his imprisonment, Trent supposed. Something else he could have had fixed. 'That's why I decided to shoot you. For revenge.'

Viktor's intensity was unnerving. Trent found himself edging forward on his stool. He was afraid Viktor might surge up at him. Lash out in some way. Or maybe he'd attack himself in his frustration. Scratch at his own face. He looked capable of it. Looked capable of anything.

'You're wrong,' Trent told him. 'About everything.'

'Not Girard.'

'Girard is dead,' he growled.

Viktor snorted. His nostril bubbled with mucus. He rubbed his thumb over the scar tissue on his knuckles. It had the look of a habitual gesture, like a religious man fingering prayer beads.

'I don't believe you. I saw him meet with you this morning.'

'It's true. Xavier's gang have abducted someone. We were trying to get to them. But they killed Girard. They shot him just a few hours ago.'

Viktor's eyes narrowed, his hair clinging to his temples like cracks in his skull. 'How do you explain the man in there?' he asked, thrusting his clasped hands in the direction of the boxroom. 'I know you killed him. And you haven't called the police.'

'He was working with the gang, too. He was one of them. It was self-defence.' The lie came easily. How could it not? Trent had spent enough time deceiving people during the past few days. 'There was a ransom drop this morning. I couldn't afford to be delayed. But the drop went bad.'

'And the photos? The maps?' Viktor shook his head. Bared his sickly teeth. 'You've been following someone. Targeting them. You and Girard.'

'*Protecting* them. It's my job. I was trying to stop Xavier. I was working with Girard to track him down.'

Viktor rubbed at his scars. Hard, like he was trying to remove a stain. 'You say he's kidnapped someone? Who?'

'Two people,' Trent told him, and he realised as he said it that in a way it was true. 'One is a wealthy businessman called Jérôme Moreau. The dead man in the room behind you was his bodyguard.' Trent swallowed hard. The rest of what he had to say was lodged in his throat. 'The other victim is my fiancée.'

Chapter Forty-six

'Viktor, I need your help,' Trent said. 'I have to locate Xavier's gang. This situation is out of control. We're past ransoms here. People are getting killed.'

'I can't help you,' Viktor muttered. 'If what you say is true, you'll have to pay him.'

'We did. It didn't work. And there's no more cash. He has my fiancée, Viktor. Think about that. You know what they might do to her.'

Viktor lowered his face. He rubbed the scarring on his knuckles. 'You love her?'

'Very much.'

'Then pay him. Whatever he asks. Find the money.'

Trent growled. He squeezed his skull in both hands. 'You told Girard once that they kept you inside a cave.'

Viktor leaned forwards on the couch, shoulders rounded, hands tucked into his chest like he was trying to protect them. 'I think so,' he muttered. 'A cave, or a cellar, maybe. An old one.'

'Did they ever take you outside?'

Viktor peered at him myopically, as if somehow he'd found himself back in the dingy environment where Xavier's gang had held him prisoner.

'Sometimes,' he whispered. 'They covered my eyes, made me dizzy, so I wouldn't remember the way. Once we were out in the open, they'd remove my blindfold. They took me to a small clearing in some trees. It was always night. Very dark.'

'What about noises? Was there traffic near by? A train? Water?'

'I heard a car one time. They covered my eyes and mouth before it was close.'

'And when you were released? What about then?'

'I told you before.' Viktor shook his head, pulling his hands in towards his belly. 'They drugged me. I didn't come round until just before they dumped me in Nice.'

'Did you see their faces ever?'

'No. They always wore masks.'

'Every day? They didn't forget? Not even once?'

'They never forgot anything. They were very organised. Very disciplined.'

'Disciplined like soldiers?'

Perhaps they had a military background, Trent thought. It would make sense. The operation they'd conducted to abduct Jérôme had been slick. It had been the same story when they'd snatched Viktor. The men Trent had seen had been wearing army surplus jackets and they'd been adept with firearms. He'd come to appreciate how good they were at planning and carrying out their operations. Take the way they'd outmanoeuvred him during the ransom drop that morning. The way they'd outflanked Girard. Twice now.

'I don't know,' Viktor said. 'Maybe.'

'Did they ever talk about themselves? Did they ever mention something that could indicate where they were from or how they knew each other?'

'They never talked like that. They rarely spoke with each other in front of me. Usually, only one of them was with me at a time.'

'Just one? Where were the others?'

'I don't know. They took it in turns to guard me. They switched every couple of hours.'

Like an organised watch, Trent thought. A troop rotation.

'How many men?'

'Four, I think.'

'Four. Not five? Not three? You're sure?'

'I think it was four.'

That would fit, too. There'd been four men involved in the attack on Jérôme. One guy in the car and three guys armed with rifles. It could have been the same in the Calanques. There'd been two men on the rubber dinghy. Another man up on the cliffs with Girard. So where was the fourth guy? Watching Trent maybe. Or more likely he was back at their hideout guarding Jérôme.

'Did Xavier guard you, too?' Trent asked.

Viktor nodded abruptly, like a nervous twitch. 'I hear his voice sometimes. Inside my head. Have you heard it? It sounds like a growl. An animal. It rumbles.'

'I've heard it.'

Viktor swallowed. He raised his hand and twisted it so that the scar tissue was on show, like he was holding a rare artefact up to the light. 'He was the one who did this,' he said, and there was a strange kind of wonder in his voice.

Viktor had a faraway look in his eyes now. Trent got the impression that he'd zoned out of his current surroundings, as if he was back in the cave, or the cellar, or wherever it was that he'd been held. Perhaps he was remembering the flashes of intense pain that had accompanied his injuries. Maybe he was thinking about the moment before he lost his finger, the way it had moved and bent and extended, as any finger naturally would. Or maybe he was thinking about how it had been after his thumb was hacked off. The searing agony. The absence. How a part of him that had always been there was suddenly no longer attached and never would be again.

'I'm sorry,' Trent said.

Viktor blinked. He sniffed. 'If this man has your fiancée . . .' His words trailed away, the thought left incomplete.

Trent slumped. It felt as if something toxic had leaked from inside his brain and was sloshing around in his skull, gumming up his thinking. No, Xavier didn't have Aimée. Not directly. But he could still sever Trent's last potential link to her just as effectively as he'd snipped away Viktor's finger. If he killed Jérôme, then that could be it for ever. Trent might never find her. He'd be haunted by her unknown fate for the rest of his life. The fate of their unborn child, too.

'There's nothing I can tell you,' Viktor said. He picked at the callused skin that covered his knuckle. 'You won't find these men. You won't catch them. Ever. I'm sorry, but it's true. They could have changed their tactics. They could have a new hideout.'

They could, but Trent doubted it. A discreet base would be hard to find. Until it was jeopardised, there was no reason for the gang to try somewhere new.

His gaze slid sideways, towards the inert recording equipment. The silent telephone. He asked himself if Xavier might call again. He wondered if the gang would try to squeeze him for cash now that the Moreaus had paid them a generous fee. They knew that Jérôme had access to information he needed. They'd killed Girard. He was on his own now. He was desperate. Why wouldn't they call? Why wouldn't they contact him again?

Wait.

Contact him *again*.

Trent stared at Viktor. He scrambled down off his stool.

'You've been watching me,' he said.

Viktor ducked and raised his arms in front of his face, as though afraid that Trent might strike him.

'No,' Trent said, and pulled his arms down by the wrists. 'This is good. You told me that you've been watching me. From where?'

Viktor delayed for a moment before answering. 'An apartment,' he said. 'Across the square.'

'How about this morning? Early? Somebody left something here for me. They broke the lock on my door to get inside. Did you see that happen?'

Viktor shook his head earnestly.

'Come on. You must have seen something. Anything at all.'

He swallowed. His lips were moving as if he was rehearsing his words, testing them to see if they might trip him up.

'There was the florist,' he said.

'Go on.'

'It was just after five o'clock. The noise of a vehicle engine woke me. I thought it could be you returning home.'

'And?'

'And there was a florist's van parked in the street outside your apartment. It blocked your front door. I didn't see the driver until he got back inside the van and pulled away.'

'How long was he there?'

'Ten minutes, maybe.'

'Ten minutes to drop off some flowers? I don't think so.'

'Your door was open a little when he left.'

'Because he broke in. You saw that my lock was damaged, right? And what kind of florist makes deliveries at five o'clock in the morning?'

Viktor scanned the room. 'Did you find flowers inside?'

'Not flowers, no,' Trent said. 'He left a package for me.' He paused. Concentrated hard. 'Tell me, was the van branded in any way?'

Viktor nodded. He was confident about it. 'I remember the name. I made a note. *Fleurs de Soleil.*'

Trent was already moving. He was backing away towards the kitchen. He opened a drawer. Cleared some things. Then he removed a telephone directory. He cracked the spine. Riffled the pages with his thumb, ran his finger down through the listings.

'It's on Rue Pavillon.' He looked up from the directory, the wafer-thin pages splayed over his wrist. 'Would you recognise this man again?'

'Perhaps,' Viktor said, more guarded now.

'Think about it. Think about his hairstyle. His clothes. His skin tone. The way he moved his body.'

Viktor gulped. He unzipped a pocket on the front of his hooded top. Reached his good hand inside. 'I don't need to remember. I have pictures.'

Trent dropped the phone book and came around from behind the counter and watched as Viktor wiped the moisture from a compact digital camera. He powered the camera up. It was blue with a zoom lens that slid out and whirred as the aperture opened. A tiny screen on the back blinked to life. Viktor twirled a dial and prodded a couple of buttons, then passed the camera to Trent, an expectant look on his face.

'This is him?'

Viktor nodded.

Trent was looking at an angled shot, taken from above, of a thin, hippyish guy at the side of a small green delivery van. The van had a floral motif on the side and the name *Fleurs de Soleil* in gold lettering in a stylised, cursive script. The guy had long brown hair tied into a ponytail, a rangy beard, and he was wearing a green fleece top.

'This is good, Viktor,' Trent said. 'This is excellent.' He tossed the camera back to Viktor. Ruffled the kid's hair. 'Wait here. I'm going to get some things together.'

Trent didn't take long. He didn't want Viktor to become spooked or try to leave. He got changed very quickly, hauling on a pair of jeans, some socks and his desert boots, then fitting his shoulder holster over the vest he had on before buttoning a khaki shirt. He searched around in the base of the wardrobe for a canvas duffel bag he kept there. Carried the duffel into the bathroom and lifted his gloves out of the pool of water in the base of the tub and stuffed them inside the bag along with the shotgun. He steeled himself to enter the boxroom, doing his best not to look at the blood-spattered walls or Alain's sorry corpse as he added ropes and cuffs, his torch and a serrated hunting knife to his stash. He located his Beretta and lifted up his shirt and slipped the pistol into the holster. He straightened his clothes, then closed the door on the room and inhaled deeply, as if cleaning his lungs. He moved through the living room into the kitchen and opened a drawer and fetched the Ruger and the spare cartridges, tossing them into his bag.

'OK,' he said, tightening the drawstring on the duffel. 'We're ready.'

'For what?' Viktor had been looking sickly already, but right now his skin was pallid and slack.

'To find Xavier's delivery man. To ask him some questions.'

Trent hefted his bag of equipment. He advanced on the sofa. Placed a hand on Viktor's damp shoulder. Partly a reassuring gesture, partly a way of digging his fingers into Viktor's bony frame and lifting him to his feet. The kid's knees almost buckled. Trent spun him round and flattened his hand on his back and steered him along the hallway. He opened the front door. Stopped abruptly.

Stephanie Moreau was standing there, adjusting the fit of the blue polka-dot sundress she had on. Her sunglasses were large and round and dark. She was holding a clutch purse in front of her waist. A familiar red sports car blocked the road behind her, engine running.

She must have got Trent's address from Jérôme's lawyer, too.

'I have to talk to you.' Her lips were pinched and her cheeks hollowed out. She flipped her sunglasses up on top of her head. Her eyes were intent, her gaze piercing.

Trent guided Viktor past her and onto the flagstone pavement. He pulled his front door closed behind him as best he could.

'Do you have a car?' he asked Viktor.

'It's over there,' he said, and pointed off towards the nursery.

'Take this.' Trent handed him the duffel. 'Wait for me. I won't be long.'

Chapter Forty-seven

'Won't you invite me inside?' Stephanie asked. Her fingers were digging into her purse.

'Now's not a good time.'

'We have a right to know what's happening.' She was fighting hard to keep her voice under control. 'We deserve that, at least.'

Trent motioned with his chin towards where Philippe was leaning across the front passenger seat of his sports car, watching them through the side window, like a cab driver waiting on a fare. 'Doesn't look like your ride is planning to stick around for very long.'

Stephanie clenched her purse even tighter.

'Careful,' Trent said. 'You'll break a nail.'

'We've been waiting to hear from you.'

'Oh?'

'I tried calling. I left a message.'

'I heard.'

'Were you going to contact me?'

'Not any time soon. Not if I could help it.'

Now she looked ready to spit. She rammed her purse up beneath her arm, hugging it against her meagre chest. She leaned towards him from the hip, jabbing her finger, her nail like a painted blade.

'You come into my home,' she said, speaking through her teeth. 'You judge me. Exclude me from this process. On what authority?'

'My authority,' Trent told her. 'The authority Jérôme gave to me. He could have given it to you. He could have had it written into the contract he signed with my firm. But he chose not to. Now, why do you think that was?'

Her face morphed into something sharp and sculpted for attack. 'You don't speak to me that way. I won't allow it. I showed you the things he's done to me. How he hurts me.'

'Sure, you showed me. But don't let's kid ourselves. This is no romantic love triangle you're caught up in with Philippe. Take yesterday. Your studio. You showed me more than just your bruises. It was deliberate. A choice. You would have shown me anything to get what you want. Done anything to get away from Jérôme. So go find someone who cares. I'm not paid to.'

Trent began to move away. She snatched at his arm. Dug into his flesh with her nails.

'Who's that boy? Why is he with you?'

Trent shook his head.

'Where's Alain?'

This time, Trent met her glare with one of his own.

'You must know,' she said. She rocked to one side, assessing the front door to his apartment. The broken lock. 'You must tell me.'

He wrenched his arm free, skin tearing. 'Oh, I'll tell you. He was taken.'

'Taken?'

'Snatched. By Xavier's gang. They took the money. Took Alain, also.'

She inhaled sharply. Covered her mouth with her hand.

'What will you do?' she asked.

'Find him. Then find Jérôme.'

'But how? When?'

He shook his head. Smiled a slow, hard smile. 'You must really have looked something up on that stage,' he told her. 'I think you could make an audience believe just about anything you wanted them to.'

Her lips crinkled and tightened. Her face was white, a hard blackness creeping into her eyes. 'What will you do? Tell me. I have to know.'

'Don't worry.' He tossed his chin towards Philippe. 'I wasn't going to ask lover boy for any cash.'

'You said yourself that we should be careful. That we shouldn't provoke them.'

'That was before. This is now.'

She took a step closer. He could feel the vibrations coming off her. The pent-up rage.

'You'll come with us,' she said, and just about resisted the urge to stamp her foot. 'Right now. You'll come and you'll wait for them to call. You'll tell us what to do.'

'No, I'm done with that.' Trent grabbed at her tensed biceps. He hauled her round and steered her towards Philippe's car like a cop man-handling a suspect. He snatched open the low door. Pressed down on her shoulder, then the top of her head, forcing her inside. 'You go home and sit by the phone in your husband's study. Sit and watch the damn thing for as long as it takes. Spend some more of your time hoping they kill him. See what good it does you.'

He slammed the door closed and stepped down off the pavement into the street. Marched away across the sun-bleached square, beneath the plane trees, past the empty fountain.

He found Viktor sitting behind the wheel of a black Volkswagen Golf. The exterior was smeared with dirt and sand and dried salt spray. The duffel bag was on the seat behind him.

Viktor had changed his clothes. He was wearing a plaid shirt over beige cargo trousers. It didn't look like the garments had been lying around in the car. The interior was clean and tidy. Trent guessed he'd called in to whichever apartment he'd been spying on him from to change out of his wet things.

'Drive,' Trent snarled. He clambered inside the Golf. 'And tell me if they try to follow.'

*

Fleurs de Soleil was located at the corner of Rue Pavillon and Rue Paradis, just a short stroll from the Opéra where Trent had loitered, waiting for Jérôme and Stephanie, less than two days before. The shop fronted onto the threadbare grass of the Place du Général de Gaulle. An old fairground carousel was located at the far end of the square and Trent slowed his pace as he walked by.

He didn't know why he did it exactly. He knew it would hurt but it felt like a necessary pain – a way to cement his resolve. A group of young mothers had gathered beside the carousel to watch their children laugh and scream as they twirled round and round on painted horses and in gilded carriages. Each and every delighted yelp was a cruel torment for Trent – a reminder of the child he might never get to meet.

He turned from the scene and walked on, crossing the street to the florist. It was clearly a high-end operation. The name of the store was stencilled in gold onto the windows in the same cursive font that Trent had seen on the side of the delivery van in Viktor's photograph. A vibrant display of blooms pressed up against the glass and a number of extravagant bouquets and plants were fitted into tiered metal stands out front. Trent could smell the flowers and soaked dirt as he approached. The morning was dry and sunny but the pavement was damp. He supposed the plants had recently been topped up with water.

The scent was much more intense when he stepped inside. The temperature was a couple of degrees cooler. He felt the air condense on his skin as he took a moment to adjust to the colourful surroundings.

A trim, middle-aged woman in a green apron was standing behind a service counter. She was busy curling some lengths of white ribbon with a few deft strokes of a scissor blade. The ribbon had been tied around a bouquet of white roses wrapped in translucent pink cellophane. There were a dozen roses. Every stem was the exact same length. The flower heads were pristine.

'Collecting or ordering?' The woman had yet to look up from the ribbon. Trent was surprised that she'd even seen him. 'If you're picking up an order, that's fine,' she said, as if it wasn't remotely fine and Trent should know as much. 'If you want a bespoke bouquet, it's going to have to be tomorrow.'

'It's neither,' Trent replied.

The woman paused. She peered up from behind a heavy fringe. Didn't seem impressed by what she saw.

'Well, speak up.' She set the scissors down and fluffed the cellophane until she was content with its shape. Then she wiped her brow with the inside of her wrist. 'I'm a little rushed today. What is it you want?' Her eyes contracted. 'You're not trying to sell me something, are you? I have all the suppliers I need.'

Trent raised a palm. 'I'm just looking for someone.'

She exhaled in a rush and set the flowers down on a table behind the counter where more bouquets were arranged. The shelves above the table were stocked with a rainbow supply of floral wires, twine and ribbon, a generous collection of green foam spheres and plenty of vases and aluminium tubs.

'She's not here,' the woman said, sharply.

'Excuse me?'

For a moment, Trent's heart stopped beating. Could she mean Aimée?

'Her name's Céline.' She rolled her eyes. 'She's ill today. Or so she claims. And believe me, you're not the first admirer to wander in and ask after her.'

'No.' Trent was beginning to lose patience. 'That's not why I'm here. I'm trying to find the man who delivers your flowers. Is he available? I need to speak to him.'

The woman moved to her side and yanked a length of pale green cellophane out from a wall-mounted roll. She tugged down and sliced the sheet against a metal blade, then draped it carefully over the counter. She lunged behind Trent for a tub of lilies and began sorting through them.

'Arnaud? Why are you looking for him?'

'He delivered some flowers to my grandmother last week. It was a special day for her. The anniversary of her wedding to my late grandfather. Your driver was very kind. He helped her with a vase. I want to thank him.'

The woman squinted at him. 'Arnaud did this? You're sure?'

Trent nodded.

'Doesn't sound like Arnaud.'

'Even so, I'd like to express my gratitude.'

'Well, I can tell him if you like. What's your grandmother's name?'

'I'd prefer to speak with him myself. I have something for him, you see. A small token. From my grandmother.'

'And you don't trust me?' The woman shook her head roughly. Snatched at another stem for her display. 'I should be offended but I don't have the time for it. You'll find him at the Prado market. My husband is covering his deliveries. If you see him, will you tell him that—'

But when the woman glanced up, Trent had already left the shop.

Chapter Forty-eight

The market was busy. Not early-morning busy, but there were plenty of people around. Three o'clock. In another hour the traders would begin packing up for the day.

Trent led Viktor through the crowds, scanning the colourful stalls that faced one another across the grubby strip of concrete. A backbeat of murmured conversation, traders' enticements and scooter horns filled the air. Traffic streamed along Avenue du Prado behind the canopied stalls on Trent's right. Somewhere beneath his feet, subway trains shuttled through blackened *métro* tunnels.

There was a lot of merchandise on offer. Fake watches, plastic sunglasses, cheap jewellery and leather handbags; knock-off DVDs and second-hand console games; fresh ground spices, glistening olives and handmade cheeses. There were blue trays crammed with ice and gaping Mediterranean fish and limp, oily squid and squirming langoustines. There were grocery stalls with pyramid arrangements of sun-ripened fruits and bulbous vegetables.

There were several flower stalls.

Trent counted five before they found the one they were searching for. Most of the tubs and green plastic buckets were empty but the bouquets that remained were thick and generous, stuffed with roses and lilies, sunflowers, gerberas and gladioli. The gold-on-green sign above the stall featured the same flowing script that Trent had seen on the windows of the florist's shop and the side of the delivery van: *Fleurs de Soleil.*

Trent recognised Arnaud, the stringy guy with the long hair and the wispy beard, from the photograph Viktor had shown him. He had on a baggy blue T-shirt with a money belt slung low around his narrow waist, and he was busy wrapping a mixed bouquet in paper for a smiling, well-groomed young man in a business suit. The man was probably taking the bouquet home to his wife or girlfriend, Trent thought. He'd done the same thing for Aimée many times. Perhaps he'd even bought flowers from Arnaud.

Viktor was standing still and staring. Trent grabbed him by the elbow and hauled him away. There was a street café a short distance ahead. Trent guided Viktor into a rubber-strung chair at a circular table with a view of the flower stall from behind the trunk of a pollarded tree. He signalled the waitress and ordered espressos. Then he walked to the newsstand close by and bought a copy of *L'Équipe* that he folded and placed on the table between them.

'You'd make a terrible spy,' Trent told Viktor. 'Relax. Stop staring. He's not going anywhere.'

'But what do we do?' Viktor's face was tight and urgent. He seemed nervous. Flighty.

'We talk to him.'

'When?'

Trent tapped the table. Viktor had been staring again. 'Later,' he said. 'For now, drink your coffee.' The waitress approached their table and set the espressos down in front of them. She slipped the paper bill beneath a glass ashtray, her easy smile faltering as she spotted the scarred mess where Viktor's thumb and finger had once been. She averted her eyes and moved away.

Viktor lowered his hand onto his lap beneath the table, then scowled back across the street, around the tree trunk. 'Do you think he's one of them?' he asked.

'You tell me. He's very thin. Did any of the guys who guarded you strike you that way?'

'I don't think so.'

Trent didn't, either. He'd been comparing Arnaud's build to the masked men who'd abducted Jérôme. It was possible he'd been one of them. Add an army surplus jacket and a ski mask and an assault rifle and it was conceivable that the guy would look a lot more imposing. But still not quite sturdy enough. And if he was involved in taking Jérôme, then it stood to reason that he'd be involved in guarding him, too. He wouldn't be spending his days selling flowers.

'Are you really just going to go over and talk to him?' Viktor asked. 'Right out in the open? With all these people around?'

'Give it a while. It'll quieten down.'

'What if he refuses to tell you anything?'

Trent raised his espresso to his lips. Sipped the bitter coffee. Truth was, he didn't plan on giving the guy a choice. His Beretta was snug against his ribs, inside his shoulder holster. And he had the rest of his equipment in the duffel bag in Viktor's car. It wouldn't be so hard to make the guy come with them. A Beretta could be very persuasive. And once Trent had the guy somewhere remote, he could be very persuasive, too. He could make Arnaud tell him what he wanted to know just like he'd planned to make Jérôme talk.

'So we just sit here?' Viktor asked. 'We just –' he scratched the back of his head – 'wait.'

'That's right,' Trent told him.

He was a patient man. It was an attribute he prided himself on.

He scooped a handful of coins out of his pocket and stacked them on the bill, then flicked open the newspaper. He held it before him with spread arms and started to scan the text.

*

Viktor wasn't good at looking elsewhere. He left his espresso untouched, his attention fixed on the flower stall. His body was hunched up in his chair, one knee raised, hands clutched tightly around his shin, eyes vigilant. He was constantly rocking forwards and backwards, shaking his head, muttering to himself.

Watching Viktor – his restlessness, the indiscreet manner in which he was staring at the guy behind the flower stall – was making Trent only too aware of how consumed he'd been by Aimée's disappearance during the past weeks. The kid must have given himself away a hundred times during the period when he was holed up in the apartment across the square, keeping an obsessive eye on his movements, and yet Trent hadn't noticed him once.

What else had he missed? What other things should he have spotted?

He folded his newspaper and asked Viktor for his camera, then began scrolling through his photos. There were hundreds of images. Some of him. Some of Girard. A few of Alain, including one of him taking a photograph from the window of the silver 4 × 4. Some were of complete strangers who'd just happened to pass by. Trent didn't find anything that might help him, and it was an unsettling feeling, like flicking through a scrapbook of memories he didn't know he had.

Suddenly, Viktor reared up in his chair, breaking Trent's concentration. He'd let go of his leg and was leaning forwards, as if he was about to spring to his feet. His fingers dug into the table, wrists shaking. But it was his expression that intrigued Trent most of all. His face was flushed. His jaw jutted forwards and his eyes seemed to swirl with a strange intensity.

Trent tracked Viktor's gaze. He looked over at the flower stall.

Arnaud was talking to a heavyset man with his back towards them. The man was just an inch or so taller than the flower seller but he seemed to tower over him. The black military-style shirt he had on was stretched taut across his muscular torso, the short sleeves ringed tight around swollen biceps coloured with sleeve tattoos. His stance was wide, the top of a pair of white briefs visible above the waistband of his stonewashed jeans.

'What is it?' Trent asked Viktor.

But Viktor didn't respond. It was as if he couldn't hear, as though he were peering through some kind of soundproofed tunnel that led only to the two men at the flower stall.

The guy in the black shirt was carrying a brown padded envelope that he pressed into Arnaud's chest. He watched as the flower seller lifted the flap and checked its contents.

Arnaud seemed relieved by what he found inside. His shoulders fell and he resealed the flap and nodded and looked around for a safe place to store the envelope. He tucked it somewhere beneath the stall.

When he straightened, the guy with the sleeve tattoos checked the time on his watch. His watch was large and bulky. It had an aluminium wristband that glinted in the afternoon sun.

Viktor's breath caught in his throat. 'Look,' he whispered.

The guy wasn't finished with his watch just yet. He used his thumb to release the metal catch on the strap. The wristband sprang open and hung loosely around his painted arm. He flicked his wrist, rotating it fast. The watch swung around in a complete circuit and ended up exactly where it had started. The guy fastened the clamp. Lowered his arm.

Viktor's body slackened. Trent reached out and grabbed his shoulder. 'What is it?' he asked. 'Do you know that guy?'

Viktor nodded, his eyes misty and roving.

'Tell me.' Trent shook Viktor hard. 'Who is he?'

The guy had turned sideways on. He had a low caveman brow. Eyes that seemed to be set just a fraction too far apart.

'He's one of them,' Viktor managed, in a voice that quavered with amazement and fear.

The guy was walking away now. He was passing through a narrow gap between the flower stall and the butcher's stand next to it. Trent could see that a blue panel van had been double-parked on the street behind, its hazard lights blinking.

'You're certain?' Trent asked.

'I remember the tattoos. And the watch. The gesture.' Viktor gulped air. He jerked his wrist, mimicking the stunt the guy had pulled with his timepiece. 'He was always doing that.'

Trent was out of his chair very fast. He hauled Viktor to his feet by the collar of his shirt. The kid scrabbled at his throat as Trent dragged him away towards where they'd left Viktor's Golf.

Trent didn't pause or look back. He didn't hesitate when the waitress called after them. He'd forgotten his newspaper but he wasn't about to return. He paced through the crowds, Viktor stumbling alongside him, his lungs tight and airless, his heart thumping hard in his chest.

Chapter Forty-nine

Trent handled the driving. He'd taken the keys from Viktor without any discussion. He didn't intend to lose the blue van. He wanted to be in complete control. And besides, Viktor was in no shape to drive. He was curled up in the front passenger seat, his scarred hand tucked protectively under his right arm, his body twisted to one side, as if shying away from the situation. He kept sneaking a look out through the windscreen, then cowering back into his seat.

Trent asked himself if he should pull over and let Viktor out. But he didn't want to stop. Didn't want to delay. Traffic was heavy in central Marseilles. They could get snarled up and lose sight of the van. It wasn't a chance he was willing to take.

'The guy with the tattoos and the watch,' Trent said. 'Is he Xavier?'

Viktor shook his head, quick and wary.

'You're sure? You said they always wore masks.'

'They did. He's not Xavier. But he's definitely one of them.'

'Based on the watch thing?'

'I remember it. And the tattoos. The way he stands. His shape.'

'OK,' Trent said.

'It's him.' There was no faking the terror in Viktor's voice. His words were shaky but his conviction was strong.

Trent nodded. 'I believe you.'

He reached inside his shirt pocket, removed his mobile and flipped it open. He offered it to Viktor. Told him the four-digit security code.

'Type in the number plate,' he said. 'I don't want to forget it.'

Viktor almost dropped the phone. He scrambled to catch it, then prodded at the keypad with clumsy fingers.

The blue van was a Renault Trafic. It was probably no more than three or four years old. It was clean and well maintained. It featured no signwork and no distinguishing marks. Chances were high that the plates were fake but it was about the only thing they'd have to go on if Trent lost the tail.

The van was moving east through the city, heading towards the tunnel that ran under the Vieux Port where Trent had pursued Jérôme, Stephanie and Alain in the Mercedes.

Viktor prodded a final button. 'Should I call the police?' he asked.

Trent didn't respond. The van was preparing to turn left at a junction up ahead. Trent moderated his speed. He didn't want to get too close but he didn't want to get trapped by the lights, either. There were two cars between them.

'I think we should call the police,' Viktor said, like he'd reached a decision for both of them. 'I can do it. I can give them the licence number.'

The lights were green. Trent hung his tongue out of his mouth and made the turn. The van accelerated on. An average speed. Not conspicuously slow. Not unusually fast. Trent didn't believe that they'd been spotted. He guessed it helped that the guy was driving a panel van. There was no glass in the back doors so he was having to use his side mirrors, supposing he used them at all. And none of the gang members would be expecting him to be driving a black Golf.

'Or you can call them,' Viktor said. 'You can tell them what we've learned.'

Trent shook his head. 'No police.'

'But we want them caught, right?'

Trent reached across and snatched his phone. He checked the plate number that Viktor had recorded and then he closed the device and slipped it inside his shirt pocket.

'These men are dangerous,' Viktor told him. 'They could kill us.'

Trent squeezed the steering wheel. Focused on the van. 'Not if I kill them first.'

The van left the city on the A7 autoroute. It passed the docks, then the airport. Its speed stayed just north of legal. It made no erratic manoeuvres. No sudden lane changes. There was nothing to suggest that the guy with the watch knew that Trent was following him.

Trent stayed eight car lengths behind. Three vehicles between them. He squeezed closer whenever an exit approached. Dropped back once they passed a turn-off. He was visualising that straining length of elastic again. Imagining it stretching and relaxing. Pulling tight and slackening off. It was the same piece of elastic that had tied him to Jérôme. It bound them still.

'Do you think he's alone?' Viktor asked.

It was the first time he'd spoken in several minutes. He'd been acting like he'd fallen into a daze. But his sulky tone suggested something else. Maybe he was having second thoughts about teaming up with Trent.

Maybe he was right to be thinking that way.

'I've been asking myself the same thing,' Trent said.

'And?'

'And it's possible there's another guy up front. Maybe even two.'

'You really think so?'

Trent rolled out his bottom lip. 'It's unlikely. The watch guy was delivering something to the flower seller. Probably some kind of payment. A fee for placing the package in my apartment. Why would he need back-up?'

'Maybe the gang don't trust Arnaud?'

'Goes with the territory. But the watch guy wouldn't need back-up to pay him in public. And if they thought that showing up carried any kind of risk of being caught, they wouldn't want a second guy there.'

'So he's on his own?'

'Maybe.'

Viktor glanced across at Trent. 'We could check. We could overtake and look inside the cab.'

'Too risky. If we get alongside, he might spot you. He guarded you for close to a year. And he's seen me before. He could recognise either one of us.'

'Then drive fast. Keep a couple of lanes over.'

Trent shook his head. 'It wouldn't be conclusive. The cab could be empty but there might still be a team of guys in the back of the van. It's better for us to wait and see where he's heading.'

Trent leaned to one side and scanned the instrumentation on the dash. The Golf was running smoothly. It was a well-maintained car with no obvious mechanical tics. It had a powerful engine. But it was low on fuel. The indicator was down below the quarter mark. It was one notch off red. They'd been driving for twenty-five minutes already and there was no telling how far the van might go.

Trent reached out a finger and tapped the fuel dial. 'Do you keep a jerrycan in the boot?'

'Oh,' Viktor said. 'No, I don't have one.'

Trent was silent.

'We can stop for fuel,' Viktor suggested. 'There's a service station coming up.'

'No. We don't stop until he does.'

Trent gritted his teeth. He tucked his chin into his chest and stared hard at the back of the blue van. The elastic was beginning to stretch. He eased down on the accelerator. Burned some more fuel. There was no way this guy was getting away. He wouldn't allow it.

*

Fifteen minutes later the van indicated and peeled off the autoroute at Cavaillon. It picked up a road that skirted the town centre, then continued northwards.

Trent checked the fuel needle. It had dropped into the red. The Golf was a GTI. Built for speed, not economy. Viktor had told him there was a trip computer that could estimate how many kilometres were left in the tank. But Trent didn't want to know. It was likely to be bad news, and why burden himself with that?

The guy driving the van never paused at a junction or hesitated at a roundabout. It was clear that he knew exactly where he was going. And he didn't vary his speed. Didn't turn back on himself or pull over abruptly. Trent was as certain as he could be that they hadn't been spotted. He needed to keep things that way.

It was hot inside the Golf. The late afternoon sun was beating through the windscreen and Trent had turned off the air conditioning to conserve fuel. He'd also closed all the windows to minimise any wind drag. The difference it might make was likely to be fractional but Trent was prepared to do anything he could to protect his opportunity to find out where the guy was going. Even if it meant sitting in an airless glass box, smelling the sweaty funk of two men. Even if it meant putting up with Viktor's complaints about how he was thirsty and feeling nauseous.

Up ahead, the van was indicating again. It slowed and turned into the small village of Le Thor. Trent hit the brakes early and ambled through the junction, allowing the elastic to stretch to its very limit. The village streets were narrow and cobbled. The centre was eerily quiet. The only noise Trent could hear was the judder of the Golf's tyres over the coarse road surface. There were no vehicles coming the other way. None behind them. If the guy in the van was suspicious, this was the perfect place to test Trent.

The road continued on. Plane trees lined the streets. They passed a café that appeared to be closed and approached an independent petrol station with a pair of oil-streaked pumps on a makeshift forecourt. Trent consulted the fuel gauge. He was tempted to pull over and splash in some petrol. But the shop attached to the garage looked shabby and uncared for. There was no telling how quickly he might be able to pay.

The van braked hard up ahead. Trent did likewise. A woman pushing a kid in a buggy crossed the road. The Golf's engine idled. The van trembled and shook. Trent swallowed drily. He loosened another button on his shirt. If the guy jumped out of the van and came at them now, Trent didn't want anything getting in the way of his Beretta.

The woman levered the front of the pushchair up onto the pavement. She smiled and waved her thanks to the van driver and started to walk away.

The van didn't move.

Trent waited.

Carefully now, he eased the Golf into neutral but kept his foot on the clutch. He checked his mirror. The road behind was empty. He could slam the gearbox into reverse if he needed to.

Viktor was looking across at him. He was pale. Seemed to be holding his breath.

Trent didn't speak. He offered no reassurance. Several long seconds tripped by.

Then the van rolled forwards and gathered speed. Trent blew a gust of air towards his damp forehead and pursued the van once more. He followed it to a roundabout and then onto a minor country road.

The road was a problem. It was long and flat and straight, raised up on an embankment running between a series of farm fields. There were cereal crops on their left. Sunflowers on their right. Visibility would be excellent from the van. The Golf would be highly noticeable.

Trent eased off the accelerator. He let the van get ahead of him. He pictured the elastic beginning to shear. He didn't care. It was time to rely on his instincts. They were telling him to back off. He allowed the van to speed away, snapping the elastic cleanly. He fell fifteen car lengths behind. Then twenty. Thirty.

'What are you doing?' Viktor asked.

'Taking a chance.'

'What if he turns?'

'We'll see it.'

The van was growing smaller ahead of them. Sunlight flared off its rear doors. Trent accelerated a little more. He did his best to match the van's speed and maintain the distance between them. Forty car lengths. Maybe a little more. It felt like a reasonable distance. If the road began to curve or the terrain changed, he could adapt and close the gap very quickly. The GTI was designed to be faster than a panel van. It wouldn't be hard to drive it that way.

They passed fields of green agricultural crops. Fields of acid-yellow rapeseed. Fields of hard, ploughed earth. Fields of fruit bushes growing under opaque plastic polytunnels.

They passed isolated houses, looping telephone wires and ranks of cypress trees.

There was a low rocky ridge off to their left. The road was spearing towards it on an acute angle. A few kilometres more and the ridge was much closer.

Then, all of a sudden, the van braked hard without indicating and swept off the road to the left. The tyres spewed dirt and dust. The van bounced and rocked and shook.

Trent shifted forwards in his seat. He increased his speed, eyes fixed on the point where the van had turned. He took his foot off the accelerator as he got close, ready to stamp on the brake and turn sharply if he needed to.

But he continued on. The van had pulled over onto a scruffy gravel yard outside a complex of four or five nondescript concrete buildings with corrugated roofs. They looked like old, disused farm structures.

The guy with the watch and the tattoos was leaping down out of the van's cab, slamming his door behind him.

Trent drove by a neighbouring house with a generous but unruly plot of land. There was a discoloured caravan stationed out front, a mangy Alsatian tethered to a clothesline. Trent kept driving until he found a crossroads half a kilometre further on, then swung the Golf around and headed back.

He slowed again as he passed the yard the van had pulled into. He scanned the sagging chicken-wire boundary fence that separated the complex from the tatty property next door. He saw old wooden picnic tables that were sun-warped and buckled. Saw rusted iron waste bins.

Saw the scramble of austere concrete buildings.

He saw two things that chilled the blood in his veins.

The first was a dark green Toyota Land Cruiser that had been beached beneath some distant fir trees. It was parked nose in, rear out.

The second was an old wooden sign toppled over against the corner of the windowless outbuilding at the front of the lot. The sign was split and the lettering faded. It was obviously no longer in use, but it was still legible. The word *Grottes* was visible in faint white paint, accompanied by an aged drawing of a closed hand with a single finger that pointed towards the rear of the yard.

Trent drove on and sped away down the road.

'See the sign?' he asked.

Viktor nodded without saying a word. His skin was waxy and colourless. His pulse jumped in his throat.

'You thought they held you in a cave,' Trent told him. 'Now we know where.'

Chapter Fifty

Trent drove fast towards the little petrol station in the village. He pumped fuel into the Golf, then purchased some bottles of water from the old man inside. He returned to the roundabout on the outskirts of the settlement and pulled over by the side of the road, on a dirt slope that bordered a sunflower field.

He handed Viktor a bottle of water, then turned in his seat and delved inside the duffel bag, removing his shotgun, his Maglite and a roll of duct tape. He balanced the shotgun across his thighs and set about securing the torch to the blued barrel with the tape.

'What are you doing?' Viktor asked.

Trent didn't suppose he was really that naïve. But maybe he felt the need to act that way.

'Part of their hideout is a cave,' Trent said. 'It must extend inside the limestone ridge that runs behind the outbuildings we saw. If I'm going in there, I have to be able to see what I'm doing.'

'You're going in?'

Trent kept winding the tape round the shaft of the torch and the shotgun barrel. He'd fastened the torch to the right-hand side of the barrel. He supposed the added weight might throw his aim off a degree or two but not enough to be a problem. A shotgun was a very forgiving weapon. Unless you happened to be on the wrong end of it.

'But that's a big risk,' Viktor said.

'What did you think?' Trent asked. 'They were just going to surrender?'

'But we can call the police. They can surround the place. Force the gang to come out. Arrest them.'

Yes, Trent thought, and wreck any chance he had of questioning Jérôme. Maybe bungle the situation altogether. Perhaps mishandle it in a way that would lead to Jérôme being killed before Trent could get to him.

'Like they did at the ransom drop for your release?' Trent shook his head. 'That didn't work out so well. They got away. And one of Girard's officers was shot dead. Besides, if the police surround the place it won't end well. It'll be a siege. There's no predicting how the gang'll react, but the odds won't be in our favour. It's better I go in alone.'

And not only that, it was something he wanted. Something he needed. All the long weeks of waiting, of reacting to the moves and decisions other people had made. He'd had his fill of it. Couldn't take any more. He was going to end things today, his way, on his terms. He was going to punish Xavier's gang for the anguish they'd caused him, for the way they'd disrupted his plans, for what they'd done to Girard, for what they'd caused him to do to Alain, for how they'd delayed him finding his way to Aimée.

He remembered the taunt that had been scrawled on the map of the Calanques: WE KNOW WHY YOU WANT HIM ALIVE. Yes, Trent thought, and it's the same reason why I'm going to leave you all dead. No witnesses. No comeback. Everything had to end with just him and Jérôme. Just the truth, finally, with nothing left to obstruct it.

'But there's four of them,' Viktor said.

'At least.'

'And you don't know what's in there. You don't know the layout.'

'So tell me some more of what you remember. Let me know everything that occurs to you.'

Viktor remembered plenty, but not much that was useful. He told Trent that the chamber he'd been kept in had been just tall enough for him to stand. It had been twelve paces in length. Ten in width. He remembered the dimensions exactly because he'd paced it many times.

He'd had a camp bed set up in there, and a couple of electric arc lights and a portable heater. They'd given him a CD player, but no radio. They'd provided him with a bucket as a toilet and every few days one of the men would bring in a bowl of cold water for him to wash with.

'How deep inside the cave were you?' Trent asked.

'I don't know.'

'But you must have got some idea when they took you outside?'

'I told you before – I was blindfolded. And they led me on different routes. Some nights it seemed to take longer than others.' He shrugged. 'Maybe they walked me in circles.'

Trent had finished securing the torch to the shotgun. He checked the beam was working OK. Then he switched it off and verified that the shotgun was loaded. Tubular magazine, seven rounds.

'This chamber you were in,' he said. 'Think about it some more. What was it like inside? Was it a display cave? Did it have stalactites and stalagmites, maybe?'

'No. It was just rock. It was like I told you. I used to think it could be an old cellar or a bunker.'

That was interesting. If the caves had been open to visitors at some point, then it was likely that they featured mineral formations. Something, anyway, that people would pay to see.

Trent removed his Beretta from his shoulder holster. Inserted a fresh magazine. Fifteen rounds. He stared at Alain's Ruger. Decided against it. It would weigh him down. The shotgun and the Beretta would be enough.

He asked, 'And when they were taking you outside, were you on your hands and knees, or could you walk normally?'

Viktor scrunched his face up in thought. 'They pushed my head down sometimes.'

'How far?'

'Like this.'

Viktor demonstrated by reaching up with his good hand and cupping the back of his neck. He didn't bend at the waist. He just tucked his chin down a short way and hunched his shoulders.

That was interesting, too. If Trent could get as far as the caves, it didn't sound as though he'd need to go scrambling through on his hands and knees. And that fitted with the idea of the caves being open to the public at some point. Sure, some enthusiasts liked to put on hard hats and miners' lamps and go potholing, but the general public would expect to be able to stroll inside generous caverns.

So access shouldn't be a problem. But exposure might be. It could be tough to penetrate the cave system without Xavier's men seeing him coming.

'Get out of the car,' Trent said.

Viktor didn't move. 'You can't leave me here.'

'I don't plan to.' Trent propped the modified shotgun against the gearstick, then grappled with his door lever and stepped out onto the side of the road. 'We're switching places,' he said. 'You're driving.'

*

Trent necked some water while Viktor trundled along the road through the middle of the fields of crops. Their speed was only modest but Viktor was crouching forwards over the dash, clenching the steering wheel, as if the Golf were in danger of careering out of control.

Trent cracked his knuckles, then lifted the shotgun.

'How long will you be?' Viktor asked.

'No way of telling.'

'How will I know if you're OK? How will I know if you're coming back?'

'You'll see me walk out of there and signal you. Once you drop me, drive on ahead and turn where I turned earlier. Then come back and pull over before you get to the yard. Sound the horn if anyone comes at you or tries to escape. Drive away if you feel threatened.'

Viktor stared ahead through the windscreen at the tangle of bland grey outbuildings that were growing in size and menace, speeding towards them. He wet his lip.

'Won't the gunfire be loud?' he asked. 'What if the neighbours call the police?'

'It's all farmland around here. Maybe they'll think it's a bird scarer.'

Viktor glanced across. He hadn't bought it. Trent wasn't surprised.

'Listen,' Trent told him, 'I don't plan to be away any longer than I have to be. This is a lonely spot. It's isolated. It'd take a while for a police unit to get here.' He scanned the terrain by his side. Just crops. Just trees. It was flat and uninhabited. There wasn't a single person to be seen anywhere close. 'These are the bad guys, remember?' he said. 'They deserve what's coming their way.'

Viktor lifted his hand from the steering wheel. He stared at the ugly scar tissue where his thumb and finger had been. There was no light in his eyes. No expression on his face. He just stared at his hand, at the gnarled disfigurement.

'We're close,' Trent said. 'Get ready.'

There was no reaction from Viktor. Mentally, he was in another place entirely.

Trent slapped his hand on the dash. He pointed ahead of them at the complex of concrete buildings. 'Slow down.'

Viktor jerked his foot away from the accelerator. He lowered his hand back to the wheel and steered a course over the crest in the middle of the road, veering towards the left-hand shoulder. He blipped the brakes just as they approached the end wall of the outermost building, slowing the car to a crawl. Trent popped his door and swung sideways in his seat, then stepped out onto the road like he was disembarking from the still-moving carriage of a commuter train. He closed the door behind him with his trailing arm and jumped into the verge. He watched Viktor pull back over to the right-hand side of the road and accelerate on his way.

There were no windows in the wall, so Trent was able to stand upright without any fear of being seen. He waited a beat for the engine noise of the Golf to begin to fade, listening keenly for any disturbance from the yard, then crept through the knee-high grass and thorns. He was holding the shotgun in his right hand, muzzle pointed down at the ground. He took a measured breath but it failed to calm his racing heart. He craned his neck around the corner.

The yard looked exactly as it had done before. The blue van was parked off to the right and the Land Cruiser was tucked away beneath the line of fir trees in the distance. A trio of bare metal craters peppered the Land Cruiser's tailgate. Bullet holes.

The exterior wall alongside Trent continued for fifty feet or more before a second, two-storey building kicked out from it on a horizontal angle. There was a door set into the front elevation of the building. It was old and weathered with a dirty pane of glass at head height. Trent couldn't see anyone through it but that didn't mean they couldn't see him if he stepped out and approached.

Plus there was the Alsatian to think about. It was over in the unkempt garden of the neighbouring property. At the moment it was down on all fours in a patch of long grass, chewing what looked to be the remains of an old vehicle tyre. But if Trent tried circling round and following the line of the fence, under cover of the trees at the edge of the lot, the dog would spot him and it would probably bark.

He snatched his head back and rested his skull and shoulders against the pitted exterior wall. The concrete was hot, warmed by the low evening sun. The air was humid and close. He was sweating copiously. There was birdsong in the trees. Insects circled his face and hands. The road was empty but another vehicle might pass at any moment. And sure, he could drop the shotgun to the ground, but he'd still look suspicious, loitering there.

He moved back the other way. Inched his head around the opposite corner. There was an open field to his side, filled with dry cornhusks grown as high as his chest. There was a gap of a couple of feet between the crops and the side wall of the outbuilding. He could spy three sash windows but the frames were old and paint-flaked and the glass was smeared with dirt. At the end of the wall, the horizontal two-storey building extended out into the field. No door this time. Trent was beginning to think of the structure he was faced with as being shaped like a T. He was at the base of the T. He needed to move around to the top. He gripped his shotgun crossways in front of him, bent at the hip and sprinted into the corn.

Chapter Fifty-one

The corn was tall and dry and stiff. It snagged on his clothes, rustling like a swept broom as he burrowed through. There was a lot of heat trapped down between the stalks. The ground was dusty and hard. His feet kicked up hazy dirt in the heated air and he buried his nose and mouth in the crook of his arm.

His thighs and lower back ached from stooping but his camouflage was good. It was difficult for him to see the side of the building clearly, so it would be next to impossible for any of the gang to spot him. Back in his military days, he'd trained for assaults just like this. Dummy exercises against dummy foes lurking inside dummy structures. But this time it was real. This time it would count.

The horizontal building that formed the top of the T was just ahead. He circled round it, creeping low through the corn, the paper-dry stalks cutting his hands and knuckles where they were bunched around the shotgun. He worked his way towards the edge of the field. Dropped to one knee and scanned the new terrain.

This part of the complex was shaped like a backwards r. The two-storey horizontal building was now on a vertical axis, extending for some thirty feet directly ahead. There were several windows fitted into the grey concrete wall, a half-glazed door in the middle and a pair of French patio doors at the far end. Just beyond the patio doors, a timber structure jutted out to the left. It had a pitched roof and a large display window with sliding glass panels. It looked like an old serving hatch. There was a tattered canvas canopy above the hatch and a faded sign offering ice creams from several seasons ago was secured to one side.

The intervening area was laid out with pink and grey patio stones in a chequerboard style. There were several old picnic tables. A grubby blue sun canopy branded with the Orangina symbol was open above one of them.

Everything looked still. The only movement was the heat wafting up from the patio stones. But the window nearest to Trent was partly open and he could hear the low murmur of a radio.

He edged out from the corn. His face was filmed in sweat and itched all over. There were bugs in his hair and stuck to his clothes. He crept to the side of the building, squatting down on his haunches, his back to the wall. The window was only a few metres away. He could hear the radio more clearly now. It was tuned to a local station. The DJ was yammering away between snatches of Euro-pop.

Trent eased himself upright, his back scraping concrete. His right index finger curled around the shotgun trigger. His left hand gripped the barrel, just below where the torch was secured. He crabbed sideways. One step. Two. He rolled to his right and peeked in through the glass.

He saw a kitchen. There was a Slavic-looking guy seated at a table, his pale face down, hands over his ears, scanning a deck of playing cards. There was a green army surplus jacket draped over a second chair and an assault rifle propped against the wall. There was an open doorway behind the table and a freestanding cooker off to the left. A large pot was boiling on the stove. Steam was mushrooming up from it, tumbling and coiling against the ceiling.

Trent rocked back. He released a breath. At least one guy inside. Possibly more. Maybe as many as three. Somebody had to be guarding Jérôme in the cave. Maybe more than one person.

He asked himself if he really needed to tackle this guy now. He asked himself if he could just creep by and leave him alone. But he didn't know who or what he was going to face inside the cave system. It would be tough enough getting in there and finding his way to the chamber where Jérôme was being held without leaving hostile men to contend with on his way back out.

He slid down the wall and crept along beneath the window, closer to the half-glazed door.

In some ways, the shotgun was perfect for just this scenario. He could burst into the kitchen and fire off a booming round that would cut the guy in half before he was up from his chair. The problem was noise. He guessed the opening to the cave was close by and he didn't want to do anything that might alert whoever was inside. His task would be much easier if he could sneak up on them. But that meant taking a chance with the guy in the kitchen and anyone else inside the house. It meant no gunfire.

Not using the shotgun, or even the Beretta for that matter, was a risk. A big one. Trent had already spotted a rifle and the guy might be sitting there with a pistol in his lap. He wouldn't have any concerns about noise. He'd be perfectly prepared to shoot.

Trent closed his eyes. Told himself to focus. He freed his hand from the trigger of the shotgun and wiped his soggy brow.

Then he heard something. It was distant but unmistakable. A car engine. The scrabble of slowing tyres. It wasn't coming from the yard. It was out on the road.

Viktor.

If Trent had heard it, then the guy inside might have heard it, too. He might be moving.

Trent swept upwards with the shotgun in his left hand, grabbed for the door handle and rolled inside.

The guy *was* moving. He was rising up from behind the table. Pushing back his chair. But he wasn't in a hurry. He was standing with exaggerated reluctance, like checking on the vehicle was a futile but necessary chore. He wasn't expecting Trent. He reared back towards the rifle when he saw him coming. He began to flail. His chair toppled and clattered to the ground.

Trent reached for the pan of boiling water with his right hand. The handle was pointing towards him. There was no lid. He picked it up and felt its weight tug at his forearm and then he flung it towards the guy with a vicious backhand swing.

Boiling water arced out of the pan. Spaghetti came with it. The water hissed as it hit the guy full in the face. Spaghetti clung to his skin and lips. Steam billowed up from him and he yowled and clasped his hands to his eyes as the pan ricocheted off his chest and danced on the floor.

The guy ducked down instinctively, cradling his scalded features, trying to smother the pain. Then his survival instinct clicked in and he roared with fierce outrage and he surged towards Trent blindly, arms outstretched, chin raised, his face flushed and misting with vapour.

But Trent had adjusted. He'd had time to react. He'd raised up his shotgun with his left hand, bringing it crossways over his chest, his right hand fisting around the barrel just above his left as the stock pivoted back over his shoulder.

Then he twisted at the waist and swung with everything he had, whipping his arms forwards, snapping his wrists, the shotgun buzzing the air, stock speeding round, burying itself deep in the middle of the guy's throat. If the shotgun was a baseball bat, then the guy's Adam's apple was a ball on a stick. Trent hit it out of the park. He shunted the guy's trachea somewhere close to his spine. The guy gurgled and went down like his knees had disintegrated. He was dead before he'd hit the ground.

Trent stepped over the guy's red and blistered face, steam eddying round his ankles, and moved towards the doorway at the rear of the kitchen. But he stopped before he got there. He'd heard movement upstairs. Footsteps on ceiling boards. Fast treads on a staircase.

Trent veered sideways and ducked into the space behind the open door, shotgun clutched tight. His shoulder brushed something sharp. He turned and saw a rack of chef's knives fitted to the wall. They were held in place by a magnetic bar. He scanned the blades on offer. Selected a boning knife. It had a sharp point and a narrow blade. Eight inches of uncompromising steel. He held it up by his sweat-drenched brow.

A blurred form rushed into the room, then stopped fast when he saw the guy down on the floor, his feet skidding on spilled water and spaghetti. It was the muscular guy with the watch and the tattoos.

He turned to his right and Trent came around from behind the door and punched the boning knife into his neck.

The knife went down to the hilt, through tissue and muscle and ligaments. It stopped when it hit something solid. Probably the guy's scapula. The guy bared his teeth and yelled and blasted the door with the heel of his hand. The door came fast at Trent. It bounced off his steel-capped boots.

He reached for another knife. It had a wide, tapered blade. Good for prepping raw chicken. Equally good for stabbing a guy in the lung.

Trent thrust the knife into the guy's chest, somewhere just south of where he'd been aiming for, just below where the guy's heart would be. Blood was pooling and bubbling up from the wound in his neck. It was frothing from his lips. One painted arm hung loose and aimless from his shoulder. He pawed weakly at the knife in his chest with the other.

Trent grabbed a third knife. A shorter one this time. He was prepared to slice it across the guy's throat. But there was no need. The guy slumped to the floor, hand slipping from the knife handle. He tipped backwards onto his spaghetti-strewn companion and writhed and twitched and bled out across the grubby linoleum floor.

Chapter Fifty-two

Trent hoisted up the cuff of his jeans and slipped the knife inside his sock. It fitted flush against his shinbone. He rolled his jeans back down, grabbed his shotgun and set about searching the rest of the property.

He moved swiftly but methodically. Doorway by doorway. Room by room.

He started with the ground floor. There was a corridor behind the kitchen leading to some public toilets. One set for women. One for men. There were cobwebs in the corners of the ceiling. The paper-towel dispensers and the toilet-roll holders were empty. Every stall was unoccupied. There was nobody inside.

The corridor opened into a large public dining room. It was filled with laminate tables and plastic chairs. There was litter on the floor. There were fake plants coated in dust and vending machines stocked with dated confectionery and defunct soda brands.

A long L-shaped counter occupied the front of the room, close to the patio doors. A cash register was positioned on it. The drawer was open. There was no money inside. Beneath the cash register was a smudged glass display case, also empty. Behind the counter was a serving hatch that gave access to the kitchen.

There was nothing in the room for Trent. He doubled back into the corridor and mounted the stairs, one tread at a time, scanning the hallway above. He found a bathroom that had been used recently. There were gels and soaps in the shower stall. A damp towel behind the door. Rolls of spare toilet paper stacked up on the floor.

On either side of the bathroom was a bedroom. Each bedroom contained two beds. They had metal frames and thin striped mattresses.

They had stained pillows and expedition-style sleeping bags. Towels were drying on the ends of the frames. A black ski mask had been discarded on one of the mattresses.

Four beds. Four men. Trent had two more to find. And they weren't inside the building.

He moved back downstairs, his shotgun prowling ahead of him, listening hard for any giveaway creaks or squeaks. The two corpses were tangled around one another on the kitchen floor. Trent didn't believe either of the men was Xavier. They'd been too easy to overcome. The guy he'd talked to on the phone was smart and resourceful and cunning.

He stepped around the spilled water and the coagulated spaghetti and the slowly pooling blood, and gathered up the assault rifle that was leaning against the wall. He emptied it of ammo, tossing the box magazine into the corner of the room, and moved out onto the sunlit patio, leaving the stove ring burning a livid red.

He hurried at a stoop towards the cornfield, flung the rifle far out into the middle of the stalks, then ran in a crouch towards the timber building with the serving hatch. He flattened himself against the heated boards that smelt faintly of creosote. He swivelled fast and aimed his shotgun into the interior. But he saw only bare timber.

There was a gravel pathway to his left, leading through some overgrown shrubbery. Black rubber cables ran along the path, connected to a set of electricity sockets fitted to the exterior of the timber outbuilding. Trent remembered what Viktor had said about the chamber where he'd been held. The arc lights and the heater he'd mentioned would need to be connected to an electricity supply somehow. The gang could use a generator, he supposed, but that would be noisy and dangerous inside a cave. This way made more sense. Trent wedged the shotgun stock into his shoulder and set off along the path, tracking the cables.

The shrubs became more overgrown and tangled the further he went. The foliage hadn't been trimmed back in a long time. He had to lever branches aside with the shotgun barrel, as if he was some kind of army grunt stalking through an exotic jungle.

There was an unpredictable jitter in his hands. A fast hum in his ears. He'd killed two men. Killed them brutally. Without hesitation. Without mercy.

He'd done it for Aimée. For himself, too. He had no regrets, felt no guilt, but he couldn't pretend he was unfazed. There was a stale, acid taste in his mouth, a sickly bolus lodged in his throat. He was damp with sweat, short of breath. He had a sense of unreality, as if everything were happening too fast or too slow, his vision too sharp, his hearing too acute. Perhaps it didn't help that he hadn't slept properly in days. Maybe mental exhaustion was setting in, making the world around him appear oddly dreamlike.

He eased aside a waxy, out-of-control fatsia bush with his body-weight and found himself in a small clearing. There was grass here. It was yellow and straggly and trampled underfoot. There was an old wooden noticeboard, completely blank. There was the entrance to a cave.

The opening was wide and high and arched. The rock outside was a reddish tan. It was pocked and fragmented and powdery, fringed with greenery and stunted pines.

The electricity cables weaved inside it.

Trent paced towards the edge of the opening, his legs feeling stiff and ungainly, and squatted low. He rubbed his face on the top of his shirtsleeve. Then he leaned sideways and peered inside.

To his left, beneath the cover of the overhanging rock, the cables snaked towards a pair of plastic extension reels. There were more plugs inserted into the sockets on the reels. More cables running away from them.

Trent could track the cables for no more than ten feet before the darkness swallowed them entirely. He could see nothing else. Hear nobody close.

He took a moment, then stepped into the cave. His fingers felt around the shotgun barrel for the torch, hunting for the recessed switch. He located it under the pad of his middle finger. Made sure his grip didn't stray.

He edged forwards. The cave interior was chill and damp and the air tasted metallic and stale. The silence was mournful, like stepping into an empty cathedral. There was only blackness ahead and above, thick and absolute. It absorbed him completely.

He tightened his finger on the shotgun trigger and risked a pulse of torchlight. It revealed glistening rock folds, pale white, like melted wax, and an iron handrail corroded with rust.

He levered the shotgun upwards and flashed the torch again. A field of stalactites loomed overhead. They were long and thin and slick with mineral deposits. They looked like a rainstorm that had been frozen in time, or like some kind of medieval torture device that was waiting to drop down from above.

Part of the show caves, Trent supposed. And not something Viktor had mentioned.

He turned and walked steadily back towards the pearly sunlight at the entrance to the cave. He moved over to the electricity reels, then followed the cables until just after the darkness consumed them. He pointed his shotgun down at the floor. Flashed his torch. The cables weren't there. He spun to his right. Switched the torch on briefly. No cables. Tried his left and fired the bulb and saw the wires winding away.

He raised the shotgun, snatched a breath of cool air and aimed a brief yellow flare of torchlight into the clotted darkness. It showed a ragged, slanted fissure in the middle of the curving rock wall. The gap was very narrow. Trent had to twist sideways to fit through. Abrasive stone chewed at his arms and back. He worked the torch again. Saw that the way ahead was doglegged, the pinched channel kinking to the right, the cables kinking with it.

Trent ducked his head and led with his shotgun, keeping his back pressed against the rock. The damp stone could be his guide. He didn't want to use the torch too often. Coming through the black, not knowing the route ahead, it would be like painting a target on himself. And if he kept his movements fractional, his footsteps cautious, he could feel his way.

But it wasn't ideal. He had no idea how far he needed to go. And his progress was painfully slow. Too slow. He thought back to the kitchen. To the pan of boiling spaghetti. It had been a big pan. Plenty of pasta. Enough for four or five men. So he guessed that whoever was down here was expecting to be fed pretty soon. Maybe if the food took too long they'd come looking for it. And instead they'd find Trent, wedged inside the knotted passageway, unsure of his bearings.

He stopped moving and held his breath and listened very hard. But all he could hear was the pounding of the blood in his ears.

He jerked into movement again. The cotton of his shirt rasped against the rock. His boots crunched grit and stones.

How far had he come? Ten feet? Fifteen? His body felt cramped. Pinned down. He wanted to straighten up and stretch out but he was afraid of bashing his skull. He wasn't normally claustrophobic but he couldn't help imagining himself getting stuck down here. There could be a steep drop right in front of him. A sheer ledge. He might fall and break a leg. Or maybe, he thought – and this was crazy, which worried him especially – the rock would begin to collapse or swell. Maybe it would envelop him. Crush him. Flatten him like some kind of fossilised insect.

His pulse was up now. His entire body throbbed with it. The air he was inhaling tasted foul and toxic. Maybe there were gases down here. Maybe that's why he was thinking strange thoughts.

He squeezed his eyes tight shut, wringing the sweat from his lids. Then he opened them and blinked and saw something he hadn't been prepared for. The pale yellow of the rock opposite.

He flinched and gazed down at his torch. But it wasn't switched on.

The light was coming from another source.

He could see from the ambient glow that he was in a small opening. The space was tight and confined but just tall enough for him to stand.

The rock behind him curved away to the right, towards where the passage continued on. Towards where the light was originating from.

The glow was arcing and swinging. It was spreading outwards in size, creeping up the slimy rock and sideways around the funnel-like chamber.

And now Trent could hear humming. A carefree male voice, improvising an aimless tune. And behind it the steady *crump* of footsteps.

Trent wedged himself into the rock, pressing his body into all the tiny crevices and knots he could find. His arms felt rigid, fingers slick on the shotgun.

The torchlight spread and bounced, then flared, and a short, tubby guy rounded the corner. He had a torch and a ski mask in one hand. He was flattening his hair with the other.

Trent reacted before the guy had even seen him. He stepped out from his cover and slammed the shotgun muzzle beneath the guy's fatty chin and levered it upwards until his scalp was jammed against the sheer rock behind him.

The guy gurgled. He let go of his ski mask and dropped his torch with a clatter. The bulb was extinguished. Trent compressed the button on his own torch and lit up the guy's face from below. It glowed, pale and spectral, like it was floating in the darkness.

'What the . . . ?' the guy said, then trailed off when Trent pushed his jaw up even harder with the shotgun muzzle.

'Don't,' Trent hissed. 'Don't speak. Don't yell. Don't say a word. Understand?'

The guy tried nodding, but he couldn't move his head. He settled for blinking instead. His eyes were squinted and watering against the torch glare. His skin was flaccid and pasty amid the blackness all around, like an ugly sea creature from the very depths of the ocean. He didn't have the build of any of the guys who'd attacked them from the Land Cruiser. Maybe he'd been the driver.

'Is Moreau down there?' Trent asked. 'Blink once if the answer is yes.'

The guy's eyelids fluttered.

'How many men are—'

But the guy was done listening. Done waiting, too.

He lashed out with his right hand, swinging fast against the shotgun, trying to jab it free from beneath his chin.

It was a mistake. A major one.

The blow wasn't strong enough. The muzzle was wedged good and solid in the cushioned hollow beneath his jaw. Plus Trent was concentrating very hard. He was fiercely alert.

The moment the guy realised that the shotgun hadn't moved, his moist eyes opened right up in the full glare of the torch. Then his lip curled and he whined and trembled and exerted a more urgent pressure on the shotgun, and Trent sensed he couldn't wait any longer and he pulled the trigger.

In hindsight, Trent knew that he couldn't have seen all that he thought he had. For one thing, it must have happened too fast. For another, he'd turned away and snapped his eyes tight closed the moment his finger had ratcheted down. But even so, a part of him believed that he'd watched the guy's face illuminated by the spark in the shotgun barrel. A part of him believed the muzzle flicker had strobed his features, like the flash on a camera lens, only lighting his face from within. The guy's skin had flushed pink. His nostrils and lips had glowed white. Then his head had detonated and erupted outwards into a hail of rock and debris.

The explosion was huge. It boomed and shook and reverberated. It rushed up into the high, thin chamber, then struck uncompromising stone and returned in a percussive wave that howled through the crooked fissure like a raging storm.

Trent had heard nothing like it before. It was angry. It was rabid. It tore at his hair by the roots and thrashed around inside his skull.

His face and hair and arms and parts of his torso were spattered. They were soaked with blood and gunk.

The guy had dropped to the ground. He was slumped backwards under collapsed rock and stone and dust.

Trent clamped a palm to his ear. The madly hurling din was swamping his other senses and it took a few seconds before he realised that he couldn't breathe. His mouth was caked in dust and debris. The powder was on his tongue, filling his throat. He bent down and spat rubble and scooped grit from his nostrils.

When the air finally came it was hot and dusty and singed his lungs.

His every instinct told him to turn and bolt for the exit. But his will told him to go on. It was as hard and uncompromising as the rock that surrounded him.

Stealth was no use to him now. He'd made his presence very clear. All that was left to him was speed and aggression and fury.

So he staggered on down the channel, his shotgun by his hip, his torch lighting the way, a grim rictus of hatred and determination and mania contorting his blood-glazed face.

Chapter Fifty-three

The cavern, when Trent reached it, was lit brightly from within. There was an arc light at the entrance, leading off from the slanted tunnel. The vaulted ceiling was bathed in the startling glow.

Trent lurched round the corner, no hesitation, and took in the rest. The low fold-up bed with the knotted sleeping bag. The second arc light on the far side of the chamber and the portable heater beside it, glowing orange, the air smelling of burning filaments and dust. The pair of camp chairs and the card table and the plastic cooler and the bucket of waste.

There were two men.

They were standing one behind the other.

Trent recognised the guy in front, tottering backwards on his heels. Jérôme Moreau. He was wearing his tuxedo trousers and dress shoes, dirtied and scuffed. His velvet blazer had been replaced with a red fleece jacket, zipped high to his chin. Both hands were clasped together in front of his waist, wrists bound and pinched with cable ties. Stubble grazed his jaw and his grey hair was greasy and unkempt, knotted in the other guy's fist. His face was strained and bloodless, eyes brimming with fear.

The guy standing behind Moreau was wearing a ski mask and a black sweater top with a raised hood. Trent could only see one of his eyes. His teeth were clenched. The hand gripping Moreau's hair was adorned with several silver rings. His other hand drilled an automatic pistol hard into Moreau's ear.

'Stay back,' the guy growled.

Even through the blast distortion in Trent's ears, the voice was recognisable. It was low and rumbling. A bass roar. The straining rasp was there, like his throat was constricted in some way and he was having to force the words out.

Xavier.

'Stay back or I kill him.'

Trent stumbled forwards, head canted to one side, offering up his ear as if it might help him to hear better.

'I said, stay back!'

Xavier pressed the muzzle harder against Jérôme's skull. Jérôme grimaced and tried to snatch his head away but Xavier held him fast.

'Throw your weapon down.'

Trent shook his head. He raised the shotgun to his shoulder. Lifted the barrel beneath his chin.

'You won't shoot,' Xavier said. He sounded confident. Contemptuous. 'You need him alive.'

'Please,' Jérôme muttered.

Xavier yanked on Jérôme's hair and he sucked back a rasping breath.

Trent sighted along the shotgun. His torch was on, the beam centred just south of Xavier's eye, lighting up his mask. He asked himself if he should blind him with the glare, if it might distract him enough, but Xavier was right, he didn't want him to kill Jérôme. Aiming the shotgun was a bluff. A clumsy one. If he had had the Beretta in his hand, maybe he could have risked taking the shot. But the blast radius from the shotgun would be too wide. It would spread out from the muzzle just like the light was coning outwards from his torch. If he hit Xavier, he'd hit Jérôme, too.

'Kill him and you die,' Trent said. He coughed up dirt and grit and spat it onto the ground. 'Like your friend just now. Like your men in the house out there.'

Xavier eased his masked face out from behind Jérôme's head. His lips were pressed flat, mouth pursed. His eye was darting and flickering. He was thinking hard.

'You don't want him dead,' he said again, and his voice sounded like something that belonged inside the cave. It was dark and cold and terrifying. It had a way of penetrating deep inside of you, of setting off a quiver in the base of your spine.

'He dies, you die,' Trent replied.

The guy wet his lip. He slunk back behind Jérôme. Back inside his hood.

He was taller than Jérôme so he was bent back a little, stooped at the knees. But it also looked as though something was weighing him down. Trent adjusted his torch beam and saw the strap over his shoulder. It was black and cushioned.

The holdall of ransom money. He was wearing it like a backpack.

'Reverse out of here,' Xavier said.

Trent didn't respond. He just stared. He could feel the loathing thrashing around inside him, tugging at his lip, hitching up his mouth into a crazed grin.

He couldn't pretend that he wasn't tempted to shoot. He felt sure that Jérôme was responsible for whatever bad things had happened to Aimée. And Xavier deserved to die for the suffering he'd caused Viktor, for the death of Girard's partner and Girard himself, hell, for the terror and distress he'd inflicted on all his victims and their families. Maybe it was easier this way. Kill them both. Leave them down here in the cave, where they might not be found for a long time. Know that he'd avenged Aimée, at least.

But no, he needed to find her. Needed to know for certain if she was alive or dead. If there was any way he might save her or lay her to rest. And he wanted to hear Jérôme's confession. Wanted to force him to beg for his life.

'Walk backwards.' Xavier was raging now. He was wired. 'I can let him go once we're out from here.'

Once they were out of the cave, the scenario would be exactly the same. Xavier couldn't release Jérôme without making himself vulnerable. Trent couldn't lower the shotgun without inviting Xavier to shoot him.

But perhaps the guy would make a mistake. Maybe Trent would have his opportunity.

He tucked the shotgun beneath his chin and edged backwards from the cavern. One foot behind the other, the darkness crowding over his shoulders. After a few steps, he beckoned with his shotgun for the two men to start moving. Xavier nudged Jérôme in the hollow of his knee and he folded backwards at the hip, feet scuffling the ground, his bound hands raised up in front of his face with the gun pressed hard against his temple. Trent led them in a slow, cautious procession out from the lighted cavern and into the blackened channel.

Trent centred the torch on Jérôme's eyes and he flinched and squinted, deep furrows appearing across his brow and the bridge of his nose. Trent moved the torch beam right a fraction until Xavier's dark pupil twinkled from behind his mask and beneath his hood.

'Lower it,' he barked, his voice bounding up the passage.

'I need to see you. To watch you.'

'Blind me and I shoot.'

'I have to see the gun.'

'Lower it.'

Trent relented. He dropped the beam a degree or two. He could still see the pistol and Xavier's glimmering eye. The spittle on his lips. The cable-knit woollen garment that concealed his face.

He edged his way backwards, knees creaking, muscles and tendons pulled tight. The crunching of loose stone beneath his boots told him that he was approaching the spot where the dead guy was slumped. He kicked out until he felt a leg, then stepped over him, being careful not to stumble. He straightened while he could, stretched out his spine, then stooped and kept reversing. Saw Jérôme's grimace as he trod, heavy-limbed, over the corpse. Saw that Xavier never lost focus. Never loosened his grip on Jérôme's hair or the pistol. Never took his eye off Trent.

The channel closed in around Trent's sides. It squeezed and compressed him. He scraped his elbows.

He backed up some more, keeping to his rhythm, his steady pace, making certain Xavier was always in view, until he was finally out from the fissure, back in the cold embrace of the cave entrance, and then outside into the wooded clearing and the light.

'Keep going,' Xavier said. His breath was short. He swayed out from behind Jérôme until both eyes were visible. Shook his head so that his hood fell down, the evening sun beating onto his masked skull. Trent could see the top of the holdall behind his back and the straps on his shoulders. He knew how heavy the bag was. Guessed it must be hurting.

'They're all dead,' Trent told him, and gestured towards the complex of buildings with his chin. 'There's nobody that can help you now.' The torch was still on, even though he didn't need it in the warm dusky light. He could see minor swellings and abrasions on Jérôme's face. Could see his swollen, gummy eyes, blinking and watering. Could see Xavier easing the weight on his back. He was taller and wider than Jérôme. Bigger than Trent. A brute of a man.

'Go to the van,' Xavier said.

For the first time, Trent sensed an opening. Xavier was aiming to get away with the ransom money. He was intending to take Jérôme with him. Probably he'd make him drive. But both men would need to get inside the van. Both men would need to sit in the cab while the engine was started and the van was reversed and turned.

Trent would have his chance.

'OK.' He nodded. 'We'll all go to the van.'

He stepped backwards through the greenery. Back along the path. Onto the patio. Round the timber outbuilding. Always with Xavier in his sights. Always with his finger clenched on the trigger, arms locked and deadened and numb. He longed to flex them. But he couldn't waver. Couldn't betray any weakness.

'Over there,' Xavier said, eyeing a space on Trent's right.

They wheeled around each other. Slowly. Warily. One step at a time. Jérôme stumbled, legs shaking, but Xavier held him up.

'Now you stay there,' he said. 'Don't move.'

Trent shook his head. 'Not a chance.'

Xavier released Jérôme's hair and coiled his arm around his neck. He started to squeeze. To choke him.

Jérôme flailed. He gagged. Xavier ground the pistol into his temple until he stilled, eyes wide, lips peeled back over his gums.

'Stay where you are,' Xavier said again.

He loosened his arm very slightly and began to drag Jérôme backwards across the yard, towards the blue van. Jérôme was sucking air through his teeth, cheeks bulging. His head was tipped back, chin raised, throat pulsing and contracting.

Trent did as he was told. He wanted to move with them. He wanted it more than he could possibly say. His leg twitched with the need for it but he remained still. He watched the gap increase between them. Fifteen feet. Twenty. If the gap grew much more he'd become a tempting target for Xavier. Not a difficult shot with a handgun. But they weren't far from the van now. Another five, ten paces, and they'd be alongside it.

Trent felt the moment slipping away from him. He'd watched Jérôme taken from him once before. Now he was destined to watch a second time round.

There wouldn't be a third. There was no way Xavier could permit it. There'd be evidence all over the hideout. Clues and information to be followed. Xavier's only sensible move was to kill Jérôme as soon as it was safe for him to put a bullet in his brain, then flee as fast and as far as he could. The holdall on his back contained three million reasons why Trent would never see him again.

But there was one reason why none of that might matter.

The Alsatian in the garden next door had started barking. He was yammering and howling and straining at his leash.

Xavier didn't glance towards him.

But he should have done.

The dog was barking at a car. The car belonged to Viktor. Viktor had gunned the Golf's engine and pulled out from the side of the road and was swooping and bouncing into the yard in a cloud of dust and dirt and swirling leaves.

The engine note altered. He'd shifted up a gear. Accelerated harder. The engine squealed. It roared. The tyres spat gravel and the vehicle shimmied, thrashing like a fish's tail. Viktor sawed at the steering wheel. He set course for Xavier and Jérôme. Stamped down on the gas.

Xavier reacted too slowly. He hadn't wanted to turn away from Trent. And when he finally did it was too late. He shoved Jérôme aside, looking to push off from him and jump out of the way.

It worked for Jérôme.

It didn't for Xavier.

Viktor yanked the wheel hard right and clattered into the back of Xavier's knees. Xavier jerked forwards from the waist, head and arms flung out, the holdall swinging wildly to one side. But his legs were pinned and he seemed to zip backwards, like he'd been sucked into a piece of industrial machinery.

The Golf reared up at the front and thumped back down. Viktor braked hard. The wheels locked. They slid. The rear wheels took hold of Xavier's body and clamped him to the ground, dragging him flat against the gravel, compressing his chest, his hooded top wrung tight around his neck. Then the rear wheels jacked up, crunched down, and the Golf came to a skidding halt.

Trent jogged across. He extended the shotgun at the end of his reach and sighted down the long barrel. Xavier's ski mask was torn. It was ripped apart in a diagonal slash from his crushed temple to his ragged throat. His face was frozen and contorted. It was bloodied and smashed. Trent didn't recognise the dead man. Had never seen his face before.

He backed away. Jérôme was slumped to his knees, head bowed. Trent seized his bound arms. He lifted him to his feet. He held him there when his knees buckled, then wrapped an arm around his sweat-drenched back and carried him, like a wounded soldier, across to the Golf.

He opened the back door, pushed his duffel bag into the footwell and shoved Jérôme inside. He went over to Xavier's corpse and rolled him over and freed the holdall of cash from his shattered arms. He clambered into the Golf with the holdall, sitting alongside Jérôme and behind Viktor. Rested a hand on Viktor's shoulder. Squeezed.

'Drive,' he said, into his ear.

'Who did I hit?' Viktor was shaking. Trent could feel the tremors through his hand.

'Xavier.'

'Is he dead?'

'Very. Now drive.'

Viktor looked behind him, eyes widening with alarm as he saw Trent's face. 'What about your fiancée?'

Trent shook his head and lowered his gaze.

'But the police?'

'Forget about the police.' He clenched Viktor's shoulder tighter. 'Trust me. Just get us away from here.'

Viktor snatched at the wheel and turned them in a slow, aimless circle, the car bucking and surging with each nervous twitch of his leg. He joined the road. Accelerated away.

Trent reclined in his seat. He tipped his head back and blinked the moisture from his eyes and stared at the grey felt lining on the roof.

Beside him, Jérôme stirred. He reached stiffly across and tapped Trent's arm with a bound hand.

Trent swallowed. He fixed his jaw and looked down at Jérôme, feeling the sticky tug of the blood that was smeared across his face.

'Thank you,' Jérôme said, with a meek smile. He offered a dirtied palm to shake. 'Thank you, my friend.'

Trent stared at the guy's cushioned skin. At the mud and the cuts and the grazing. At the whorls of dried soil on his fingertips and the filth under his nails. At the bloat around the ties at his wrists.

He exhaled in a weary gust and shook his head, just barely, then turned and gazed out the window at the flat speeding fields and the orange dipping sun.

Chapter Fifty-four

Viktor hesitated at the first major junction they came to after passing through Le Thor. Trent gave him instructions to head to Cassis, then looked at Jérôme, not quite meeting his eyes, and said that he would be reunited with his family at his coastal villa.

Jérôme absorbed the information. He nodded once, then managed a slight, bashful smile and held his bound hands out to Trent.

Trent stared at the looped plastic ties and the way they were digging into his flesh. He considered the guy's short, stubby fingers, the cracked skin of his knuckles and the faint grey hairs that were looped along the backs of his hands. Hands that had harmed Aimée. Caused her pain. Maybe death.

He exhaled in a grunt and shook the visions from his mind, then ducked forwards and rooted around in the duffel bag until he found a pair of snub-nosed pliers and an old towel. The pliers were equipped with wire trimmers. He snipped the plastic ties, then watched as Jérôme rubbed his wrists.

'Who are you?' Jérôme asked.

Trent wiped his face with the towel. 'We'll come to that.'

'I owe you my life.' His voice was dry and straining. 'Both of you.'

Trent couldn't listen to more. He stretched forwards between the front seats and grabbed one of the bottles of water he'd picked up from the garage. He handed it to Jérôme.

The guy smiled his appreciation and raised the bottle to his chalky lips. He drank greedily, noisily, water streaming down his grizzled chin from the corners of his mouth.

'Take it easy,' Trent told him. 'Rest up. We'll talk some more when we get to your villa.'

Jérôme lowered the bottle. 'Will Alain be there?'

Trent caught sight of Viktor's fitful eyes in the rear-view mirror. He held them, then turned and gazed out his window again, contemplating the streaming ribbon of grubby white paint at the edge of the road.

'Don't worry,' he muttered. 'I'll make sure the two of you are re-united.'

*

It was late dusk and a low moon was up by the time Trent directed Viktor to pull over across from the wall that surrounded Jérôme's villa. The street was empty. It was still and silent in the mournful half-light.

Trent motioned for Jérôme to get out of the car. He tossed the hold-all and the duffel onto the pavement, climbed out behind them and approached Viktor's open window. He ducked his head.

They looked at each other for a long moment until Trent reached across and squeezed Viktor's arm.

'Go home to your parents,' Trent told him. 'Make your peace with them and let them know this is over for you now. Move on with your life.'

'But the police?'

Trent shook his head. 'You were never there, Viktor.'

'What if someone saw my car?'

Trent thought about it. 'Dump it somewhere. Toss the keys away. Do it tonight.'

'I'm sorry for your fiancée.'

'Me too, Viktor.'

'But I'm not sorry for killing Xavier,' he said, and looked like he was willing himself to believe it. 'I'm glad that it was me. I won't deny it if people ask.'

'But it wasn't you, Viktor.' Trent shook his head again. 'I should know. I was there.'

Viktor held his gaze, searching for something more in Trent's expression that he couldn't seem to find. Trent bent low and gathered the holdall in one hand and the duffel in the other.

'Go,' he said. 'Get out of here.'

Viktor smiled fleetingly, a hard-to-fathom smile that seemed to communicate everything and nothing at all. Then he slipped the Golf into gear and trundled away down the street.

Trent crossed the twilit road, a bag in each hand, and joined Jérôme by the gate, the blurred tangle of shrubs and trees massed on the other side of the wall like fairytale monsters lying in wait. The surveillance camera was pointed down at them. Trent motioned with his chin towards the security keypad to Jérôme's left.

'The others won't be here for a while,' he said. 'But we should go inside where it's safe.'

Jérôme punched in the code. The gate buzzed and began to swing open, revealing the sloping, tarred driveway, the manicured gardens and the darkened villa.

'I don't have my keys,' Jérôme said. 'They took them from me.'

'Don't worry,' Trent replied. 'I already thought of that.'

He led Jérôme round the side of the villa, past the garage where Aimée's car was hidden, beyond the placid swimming pool and the cliffs and the churning, blue-black ocean, shining darkly in the pale moonlight like liquid metal. He approached the glass patio door, his milky reflection gliding towards him like a ghost. Dropped the weighty holdall to the ground and stooped towards a potted palm. He tilted the terracotta plant pot and felt around for the key he'd stashed underneath. Returning to the villa hadn't been part of his original plan but hiding the key where he could find it had struck Trent as a sensible precaution. He straightened and unlocked the door. Pushed it open. Stepped aside.

Jérôme went in ahead of him. He stood in the middle of the dim, spacious living room, his back to Trent, his hands opening and closing, his head lowered as if in a moment of prayer.

Trent tossed the bags he was carrying onto a white leather chair, reached a hand into the sticky heat beneath his shirt and plucked his

Beretta free from his shoulder holster. He straightened his arm, the Beretta gripped tight.

'Turn around.'

Jérôme swivelled, his frown of confusion morphing into stark surprise. Eyes wide and blurring as he saw the gun.

'My name is Daniel Trent.' It galled him that he couldn't keep the shake out of his voice, no matter how much he tried. 'My fiancée's name is Aimée Paget.'

He stared at Jérôme. Expecting a reaction. But the only reaction he was seeing was shock and fear and bewilderment.

He gestured to a white leather couch across from him, some distance away from the model of the yacht in the display case.

'Sit down, Jérôme. You're going to tell me exactly what you did to her. Where I can find her.' He paused. Composed himself. Fought to control the wobble in his arm. 'Then you're going to beg for your life. Like maybe you made Aimée beg. And then I'm going to kill you and burn down your house.'

Chapter Fifty-five

Jérôme blinked. 'I don't know what you're talking about.'

Trent gestured with his pistol towards the white leather couch.

'Sit down, Jérôme. If you want me to make this hard on you, you should get comfortable first. Could be a long night.' He looked meaningfully at his duffel bag. 'A painful one, too.'

'Please. I'm confused.'

'Then sit down. Allow me to explain.'

There was a fresh purple graze near Jérôme's temple from where Xavier had pressed his gun. There were some minor cuts and contusions across his cheeks and nose and jaw. He'd been roughed up a little, no question, but not as much as the photograph the gang had taken of him had suggested. His injuries had definitely been faked.

Trent didn't plan on being nearly so considerate.

'Sit down,' he said again.

This time, Jérôme walked shakily across to the couch and lowered himself in stages, eyes fixed on the Beretta. He rested his elbows on his knees and scrubbed his face with his palms, then stared out through splayed fingers, tugging down the skin of his cheeks. His eyes were red and bleary. The skin around them puffy and grey. He looked like he hadn't slept properly in weeks.

Trent glanced sideways at his duffel again. It contained all the equipment he'd amassed. The ropes and cuffs. The pliers. The hammer. The blades. But it was all beginning to feel like too much foreplay. He could just squeeze the trigger and be done with it. Could kill the guy and leave. Go without giving him an opportunity to offer up a half-baked excuse.

He felt his finger curl. Watched his knuckle whiten with a curious, detached amazement, like he was staring at the hand of somebody else. He was tired of this. Tired of the whole sorry saga. Tired of clinging to his last frayed threads of hope. Tired of Jérôme Moreau most of all.

'You killed her, didn't you?' he said, through gritted teeth. 'Tell me why you killed her.'

But Jérôme was shaking his head before Trent had even finished speaking.

'Aimée is dead?' he asked, and in his voice was a kind of amazement, a marvelling at the intricate mechanics of a universe he was woefully ill equipped to understand.

Trent felt the hot rage vibrate within him. Tasted bile in his throat. He supported his wrist with his spare hand. He had the shakes. Badly.

'She died here,' he said. 'She must have. In this house. In your bed-room. You killed her two months ago.'

'No, that's not right.'

'Her car is in your garage.'

Jérôme's brow creased in thought. 'That can't be.'

'I found her broken necklace and locket upstairs. Under your bed. There was blood on the carpet.'

Jérôme raised a hand in the air. He pinched the bridge of his nose, like he was wrestling with a complex mathematical theorem.

'I don't know why you believe this,' he said, speaking in a measured tone. 'I know Aimée. Of course I know her. We met several times. I re-spected her. We even shared a meal. But she's never been inside this house. She's never been inside my bedroom. Her car can't be in my garage.'

'You're lying.'

Trent's wrist was jerking and writhing, moving without his say-so, like some alien limb.

Jérôme shook his head, as if mystified. He mouthed the word 'No.'

'Don't lie to me.'

'Who told you this? It sounds to me as if someone has tricked you.'

Trent thought back to what Alain had told him. *He judges people. He does it very fast. He did it to me. He saw something in me.* Was that what was happening now? Had Jérôme made a quick study of Trent? Had he looked at him and seen his weakness – the desperate need burning deep within? The awful longing to know that it had all been necessary, everything justified? The lying, the deception, the five men killed, and Girard, shot because of him?

Trent looked over at the kitchen and the door to the garage. He could grab Jérôme by the throat. Could drag him across the room and kick open the door and bundle him through onto his knees on the cold concrete.

But what if Aimée's car *wasn't* there? What then?

The Beretta was shaking. Two hands weren't enough. His entire body was trembling, like a palsy he couldn't control.

'I can show you,' Trent hissed. 'I can prove it to you.'

To us both.

'I wish you would,' Jérôme told him. 'But put the gun down first. That's a reasonable request, isn't it? That's fair?'

Fair.

Trent was hot and he was sweating. The rabid fever was leaking out of him. It was soaking his scalp and forehead. Trickling down his face. Breaking out across his arms and over his chest and pooling in his groin.

It was worse in his hands. His palms were damp and greased. Fingers slipping. The trigger oscillated wildly. A fraction more and it would be over. All of it done. Concluded.

And what was one more dead body? Jérôme Moreau deserved it. The filthy liar. Trent knew he threatened and assaulted women. He beat them. Stephanie had shown him that. Hadn't she?

Bam.

Moreau bucked suddenly on the couch. His head flew back in a spray of fluids. It pitched to the left and kept on rolling, like whatever complex system of muscles and ligaments had been holding it up had abruptly failed. His neck flexed perversely and his body tumbled after his head, collapsing sideways over the back of the couch, his face pivoted up to the ceiling. There was something amiss with his gaze. It took a moment for Trent to comprehend. Then he saw the gory hole where one of Jérôme's deceitful eyes had been.

Trent groaned. He gaped dumbly at the pistol in his hand. He hadn't felt it discharge. Hadn't experienced the kick.

But Jérôme was dead. Shot down with his secrets. With the precious truth about Aimée.

Trent swayed, slump-shouldered, and a strange animal wail escaped his lips. So he'd given in to the dark instincts swirling inside, to the cheap and gaudy allure of a sudden ending without the resolution he'd set out to find.

He was still moaning when the second shot rang out and tore through the meat of his thigh. He dropped hard and twirled, the Beretta falling from his hand and clattering to the floor. He slammed into the chair with his duffel in it. Knocked the chair over.

There was a man standing in the doorway behind him. A man with a gun in his fist. A man he knew to be dead.

Chapter Fifty-six

Girard paced into the room and kicked Trent's Beretta far away. He contemplated Trent, his head on an angle, then hitched up his trousers and squatted close to him. He was wearing black leather gloves and he motioned with his Glock towards Trent's thigh and the bloody wound he was clutching, inky liquid squirming through his fingers.

'I can see that it hurts.' Girard sniffed. 'And I'm sorry for your pain.' His pouched eyes were wet and baleful. 'But I could have killed you before you turned round. I could have left you without the answers you've been seeking.'

The pain in Trent's leg was a gnawing, animal thing. If he lay still, it hurt. If he moved, claws and fangs ripped through him.

Blood leaked between his fingers with every beat of his racing heart.

'Or I could have shot you in your knee,' Girard said. 'Or maybe your ankle. This would have been worse, too.'

He sighed, as if he found the subject tedious, and pushed up to his feet. He crossed towards the couch and clicked on a tall standing lamp. Light slanted down from beneath the conical shade onto Jérôme's slackened body. Girard pinched Jérôme's chin between his forefinger and thumb, turning his face to the light. He hummed in appreciation when he saw the wound that had killed him, as if he'd sampled a fine wine.

'You're losing a lot of blood,' he said, offhand, and wiped his gloved fingers on his trousers.

Trent writhed on the floor, smearing dark liquid onto the cold marble tiles. He craned his neck and glanced towards where his duffel had been. But it was lost to him somewhere behind the toppled chair.

The tools and weapons it contained were far beyond his reach.

'I sympathise,' Girard said. 'You remember, I think, that I was shot only this morning.'

Trent was breathing rapidly through his nose. He was fighting hard to separate himself from the pain and the panic. Trying to compartmentalise them in his mind.

It wasn't working.

'Of course,' Girard told him, 'I was shot with a blank round. I was wearing a padded vest. But still –' he smoothed a gloved hand over his chest, as if the percussion of the blast still lingered – 'I might have drowned.'

Trent braced himself for the hurt that would come from speaking. 'I swam out to where you fell. I couldn't find you.'

Girard stroked his goatee. He smiled. 'I spent many summer days there as a boy, diving from the cliffs with my friends.' His eyes sparkled darkly. 'We learned to swim deep under water, to surface inside the submerged caves.' He shrugged, as if it was nothing. 'I waited until I was sure you would be gone. And also, I had to recover.' He reached down towards the bottom of the polo shirt he had on and lifted the material to reveal a deep aubergine bruise, dappled around his left nipple. 'It hurt very much.'

Trent snarled. He rasped air through greasy lips. 'You let me think you were dead.'

'I needed you to believe it,' he said, absently tracing his finger over his bruised skin.

'Why?'

He lowered his shirt. 'For the money.' Girard gestured with his gun towards the holdall of cash. 'You'd paid once already. With more pressure, and without my help, we hoped you would pay again.'

'We?'

'Xavier.' He shrugged. 'The men you killed.'

'You were working with them?'

'Always.'

'Throughout the Roux case?'

'And some others that did not involve you.'

Trent lurched to one side. He braced a blood-smeared hand on the tiled floor and slithered backwards until he was propped against the upturned chair.

'You shouldn't have let the boy drive this evening.' Girard tutted and shook his head. 'I followed you from outside Le Thor. If you'd been driving, I guess maybe you would have seen me.'

'But you were working for Viktor's parents. You were hunting Xavier.'

'They were fools. I was happy to take their money.'

'What about your revenge? Your dead colleague? Your lover?'

He rolled out his bottom lip. Contemplated the muzzle of his gun. 'Yes, it was a good story. Romantic. I think you liked it. But she was asking too many questions. She had to go.'

Trent growled. He beat his fist on the floor. His vision was blurring, becoming frayed at the edges. Darkness was slamming in at him, like a series of lights being switched off, one after the other, in a deserted room.

'And Aimée?' he asked, her name a low whisper.

'A coincidence. Convenient to us.'

'What *happened* to her?'

Girard threw up a hand. 'Truthfully, I do not know. I wish that I could tell you. But . . .' he puffed air through his lips and flicked his fingers out from his palm, '*poof.* It's a mystery.'

'*Tell* me.'

'There is not so much to tell.' He spread one gloved hand. Pushed the leather into the webbing between his fingers with the barrel of the pistol. 'I went to your home as you asked, back when you called me from Naples. Your door was open. Aimée was not there. But there were signs of a struggle. Her handbag was upside down on the floor. Her house keys and her car keys, too. Her mobile. Her necklace. It was broken. I guess it was ripped from her throat. And a vase in the hallway had been smashed. I had to sweep the pieces up and throw them away.

I don't think you noticed.'

He smiled flatly. No remorse.

'So you saw some kind of sick opportunity.' Trent grimaced. He clenched his teeth against the searing pain in his leg. 'You took her necklace and you planted it here for me to find. Did you drive her car here, too?'

'Not me.' Girard clicked his tongue. 'Your money paid the burglar to do it. The flower seller. You followed him, yes? It was a mistake, I think, asking him to break into your home, also. I told Xavier this. I warned him. But he wouldn't listen.'

'Why, Girard? Why do this to me?'

'Because we had selected this man,' he said, waving his arm at Jérôme's corpse as if it were explanation enough. 'Xavier and myself. We knew you were his negotiator. And with Aimée gone, with this man appearing to be responsible, we knew you would be desperate. We thought that you would let his family pay more.'

'And I did,' Trent muttered.

Girard nodded, his face carved into a winning grin, like the two of them were sharing a great fortune together. 'We had hoped for more still. Only,' he frowned, 'you were lucky. More resourceful than we anticipated.'

'Aimée was pregnant,' Trent said. 'She was carrying my child.'

Girard sucked air through his lips. He bowed his head. 'Then this is unfortunate, of course. I'm sorry for you both.'

'I'll kill you.' Trent clutched at his thigh. 'Just like I killed Xavier.'

'No,' he said simply. 'Your strength is almost gone. But I can also shoot you again. It's easy for me. No problem. I have a gun. You don't.'

Trent gazed down at his thigh. Blood had soaked through his trouser leg, pasting his jeans to his skin. It had puddled in his groin. It had trickled down his shin, into his sock, wetting the cotton.

'All this time,' he said, and the words rattled inside his lungs. 'Two months, Girard. My fiancée. Our unborn child.'

'Do not think that I'm proud of it.' He opened his mouth to say more, then stopped himself, as if acknowledging that no explanation would ever be good enough. He hummed and smoothed back his hair and hunched his shoulders, smiling sheepishly, as if he'd been powerless to behave otherwise. 'But then, you never did like to involve the police. Always so willing to co-operate with the gangs. To pay them. You colluded, too. Just like me.'

'Not like you. Never that.'

Girard motioned towards Jérôme. 'I had to kill him because of you. Your persistence. He would have convinced you he knew nothing and then what would you have done?'

'I wouldn't have believed him. You made sure of that. I'd have killed him first.'

Girard swayed his head on his shoulders, like a set of weighing scales. 'Then I think maybe you deserve this. Maybe it's right that you die here, also.'

He clicked the lamp off and blackness crowded in. It was dark outside now. Trent's vision flickered and dimmed. He dug his fingers into the flesh of his wound. Roused himself.

He heard Girard make his way to the door. Glimpsed him ducking in a wash of faint moonlight for the holdall. Heard him release a gust of air when he straightened and bore its weight.

He stood in the doorway. Adjusted his grip on the holdall. Looked down at his gun and relaxed his shoulders.

'You know, I think I *will* leave you to bleed. So much blood.' He shook his head. 'See how it clings to you?'

*

Viktor supposed that Trent's advice had been wise. He should abandon his car. Leave it somewhere to be stolen. A suitable area in Marseilles wouldn't be hard to find. Then he could return home to his parents. Try to rebuild his life.

But there was one thing Trent had overlooked. He'd forgotten about the apartment Viktor had been renting.

Standing in it now, with his clothes and his few belongings stuffed in his suitcase, Viktor was amazed by how dismal it looked. Hard to believe he'd been living here. Harder still to know that the man he'd been monitoring so closely, the one he'd been determined to bring down, was the person who'd finally set him free.

He lingered by the window and looked out at the view across the square. It was a scene he'd come to know so intimately. One that he'd watched in the blazing noontime sun, the foggy maritime dawns, the haunted hours of the night.

The streetlamps burned an anaemic yellow. Lights shone in the windows of the houses and apartments. Trent's home was in darkness but the front door was wide open. Must have been caught by a breeze. Viktor felt troubled about leaving it that way. The broken lock was the problem, but perhaps the door could be wedged closed somehow.

He didn't want a stranger becoming curious and wandering inside to find the dead man in the boxroom. If there was any way that Trent could clear up after himself and erase the trail that linked him to Xavier and the mess in Le Thor, then Viktor didn't want him to fail.

Lifting his suitcase from the floor, he walked out of the cramped, mildewed room for the final time, and headed across the deserted square. He paused. Checked all around. Then stepped inside the unlit hallway.

Later, looking back, he couldn't say exactly what drew him all the way in. There was no creeping sensation in his spine. No spectral whisper at his ear. But he did feel a strange compulsion to set down his suitcase and move towards the living room. He did experience some kind of physical pull.

He edged into the darkness ahead, one foot in front of the other, his spread fingers dragging along the wall, and when he entered the lounge, one thing snagged his attention right away.

A blinking green light. A gaudy beacon. It was shining on the electronic equipment wired up to the phone on the kitchen counter.

Viktor flicked on the ceiling light. He glanced back along the hall-way towards his suitcase. He walked forwards. He reached out. Then he withdrew his finger.

He knew it was an intrusion. He had no right to be here. No justi-fication for listening. But for some reason he couldn't begin to explain, he had the sensation that the message was intended for him. Perhaps it was from Trent. Perhaps he was in trouble and he'd somehow guessed that Viktor might come here.

He reached out once again and this time he hit PLAY. A speaker hissed. It crackled. Then a rushed, muffled voice came through:

'*M. Trent, it's been a long time. You must be very worried. We know you miss your fiancée very badly. We have her. She is safe. The baby she carries, too. You will pay us two million euros. There is a package outside in the square, beneath the bench beside the fountain. Take the package, M. Trent. Follow our instructions exactly. Pay us the money and your fiancée will be returned to you. You have forty-eight hours. Pay us, or you will never see your fiancée again.*'

*

Trent marvelled at the blackly spreading liquid that surrounded him. His fingers were clasped tight to his ruined thigh. Release them and the blood would come in a gush. The pain would be intense. But he couldn't just stay there. Wouldn't allow things to end that way.

He freed his gummed hands and bit down against the scorching agony and hunched forwards to reach for his drenched sock. He gripped the handle of the kitchen knife in his slickened fist. Rolled onto his side and pushed up from the chair and launched himself across the room. His bad leg gave out, wouldn't hold him at all, and he clattered into the glass door.

Girard turned, gun swinging.

But he turned too slow.

Trent leapt at him and thrust the knife into the side of his neck. He sawed hard. Feverishly. Kept sawing even as Girard croaked and whirled and shot at him, the lead drilling hot and hard, deep into Trent's lung.

Girard tumbled, clutching at his unstitched throat, his gun abandoned in the spurting horror.

Trent slumped beside him, then teetered onto his side. He was still breathing, wetly, determinedly, long after Girard had moved for the last time.

He lay sprawled on the moon-silvered grass, leaking away into the hard dirt, gazing up at the place where he'd been so sure that Aimée had been lost to him.

Aimée.

His thoughts were with her now. Seeking her out from that cherished space deep inside his mind. His favourite image. Her fine auburn hair fanned on stark white sheets. Fists curled loosely on either side of her head. And her eyes. The hazy smudged brown. The glimmering light deep within.

The light that told him she was waiting, somewhere.

Waiting for him.

Acknowledgements

Prior to writing *Dead Line*, I read many books and articles concerning the kidnap and ransom industry, but in particular, I would like to acknowledge James March's terrific memoir, *The Negotiator*, for its fascinating insights into the methodology and mentality of a professional hostage negotiator.

Huge thanks, as ever, to my agent, Vivien Green, and my editor, Katherine Armstrong.

To the dedicated and talented teams at Sheil Land Associates and Faber and Faber, including Gaia Banks, Lucy Fawcett, Rachel Dench, Hannah Griffiths, Angus Cargill, Alex Holroyd, Alex Kirby, Miles Poynton, Neal Price, Dave Woodhouse, John Grindrod and Eleanor Rees.

To covert operative Katrina Hands.

To Mum and Dad, for a key trip to Marseilles, and to my sister Allie, for all her support.

To Maisie, for long walks and fresh ideas.

To my daughter, Jessica, for her impeccable timing.

And to my darling wife, Jo, for everything that makes any of this possible.